Almost Never

Almost Never

Daniel Sada

Translated from the Spanish by Katherine Silver

Graywolf Press

First published in 2008 as *Casi Nunca* by Editorial Anagrama, Barcelona. This English translation first published in the United States of America by Graywolf Press.

This publication is made possible in part by a grant from the Minnesota State Arts Board, through an appropriation by the Minnesota State Legislature from the Minnesota general fund and its arts and cultural heritage fund with money from the vote of the people of Minnesota on November 4, 2008, and a grant from the Wells Fargo Foundation Minnesota. Significant support has also been provided by the National Endowment for the Arts; Target; the McKnight Foundation; and other generous contributions from foundations, corporations, and individuals. To these organizations and individuals we offer our heartfelt thanks.

ART WORKS.
arts.gov

MINNESOTA
STATE ARTS BOARD

CLEAN
WATER
LAND &
LEGACY
AMENDMENT

WELLS
FARGO

TARGET.

Published by Graywolf Press
250 Third Avenue North, Suite 600
Minneapolis, Minnesota 55401
All rights reserved.

www.graywolfpress.org

Published in the United States of America

ISBN 978-1-55597-609-5

2 4 6 8 9 7 5 3 1
First Graywolf Printing, 2012

Library of Congress Control Number: 2011944859

Cover design: Rodrigo Corral

Translator's Note

Daniel Sada died on November 18, 2011, while this book was in the final stages of production. The translator would like to express her gratitude for his kindness, generosity, and assistance in the preparation of the translation. She would also like to thank Enrique Servín Herrera, Roberto Frías, and Ethan Nosowsky, as well as Ledig House International.

For Gerardo Estrada

Part
In Search of Precious Treasure
One

1

Sex, as an apt pretext for breaking the monotony; motor-sex; anxiety-sex; the habit of sex, as any glut that can well become a burden; colossal, headlong, frenzied, ambiguous sex, as a game that baffles then enlightens then baffles again; pretense-sex, see-through-sex. Pleasure, in the end, as praise that goes against the grain of life lived. Conjectures cut short during a walk on a pale afternoon. Block after block, ascending, then descending. A strain in the step as well as the mind. The subject was one Demetrio Sordo, tall and thin, almost thirty, fond of the countryside where he plied his trade with a modicum of pleasure, but for recreation: what thrills? Nightly games of dominoes in seedy dives, and those strolls—few and quite dull—of a mere mile or two; or a cup of coffee in the evening, always solitary and perfectly pointless; or the penning of letters to known but already ghostly beings. Hence a rut, and—what should he do?: think, already anticipating certainties and doubts: lots of naysaying, and more reshuffling, all of which helped him find the spark he'd been lacking without taxing his brain on that overcast afternoon. Sex was the most obvious option, but the trick would be to do it every twenty-four hours. If only! A worthy disbursement, indeed. So that very night the agronomist went looking for a brothel. He went hesitantly. His mincing steps gave him away. He descended from the taxi and began walking as if on eggshells or as if the soles of his feet were being shredded by shards of glass. He found himself almost smack in the middle of the red-light district, which was not even remotely Edenic and, to make matters worse, was dimly illuminated. This was only the second time he'd visited such an inferno, so he didn't know where to go. Casting about, the first thing he saw was a row of scruffy-looking women in ironwood rocking chairs, each one next to the open door of her own mean hovel. A sordid spectacle stretching along the sidewalk he had started down. Those mincing steps quickly turned into long strides. A sensible sprint motivated by his wish to find a high-class brothel. He stopped and asked a passerby. The man willingly obliged. That one over there or the other farther on. Those are the costliest. Then came an exchange regarding the prostitutes he'd find in each (there were all kinds), though Demetrio preferred not to listen to more descriptions and instead took off apace without so much as a thank-you: and, there they were! one brothel named La Entretenida, and the other, Presunción: two yellow buildings like lumpy quadrangles that lent a touch of luster to the twilight: so—which would it be? A pleasant, somewhat extended quandary. He chose Presunción . . . They charged an entrance fee, as if it were a museum, a bit of a stretch, that: then came a diffident handing over of cash. In exchange, the promise of instant happiness to ward off the gloom, for everything he'd so far fleetingly observed had made an impression, as did the grandeur of the suggestive orange-tinted salon with its many empty armchairs. There was piped-in music but no dance floor: *ranchera* music, exclusively, and ever so loud.

Was this lugubrious vista luxurious? The newcomer, a gawker, took a seat and continued to gawk. The welcome: gracious hospitality: a chubby man kept pointing to a chair: the kindness of a reiterated gesture. The very next instant the same man asked: *What can I get you?* and the still-potential client said: *Wait a minute, wait.* A bashful blush mixed with ardor: Demetrio and his quest in the midst of so much shadowed beauty: overwhelming, but also—

titillating? Fortunately, he began to make distinctions: he saw a swarthy brunette with generous proportions, an eccentric vulgarity who smiled like no other. She, aware of being chosen, deliberately settled sumptuously into her armchair in such a way as to regale the gawker with a full view of her luscious legs. An effective ruse, for Demetrio called her over and, solicitous, velvet voiced—come on over here!—she approached slowly: her wavy mane swayed with added élan. She looked as if she were sashaying down a catwalk. Then, without further ado—have a seat! let's talk! Impatient insinuations necessarily followed by discreet (and somewhat playful) gropings. Modest maneuvers, high tension, a teetering on the edge. In other words, preludes to pleasure: two, yes two, seeking a robust merger, something above and beyond—perhaps—sexual commerce, then devolving into impertinent gawking, come hither and yon, now censorial, now welcoming; to this we'd have to add the shallow delights of the half-light where muteness reigned, making room for a play of features, bonding through lust: almost kissing, but—whack! the waiter's importunity, to which: *Go away! I want sex not drinks.* And Demetrio, turning to the brunette, said: *Hey, listen, you, come on already, let's go to bed.* How abrupt! He must have been really horny. And that was that, no dithering, almost at a run. Let's now summarize their time behind closed doors: it was raining thus imperative for them to seek shelter as soon as possible: a rush to undress and a rush to screw, as well as all the rest, to wit, long kisses with exceedingly motile tongues, as if in time with the cadence of their lower regions; above, an exchange of saliva or prolonged smearing. Hopefully there wouldn't be a sequence of distracting positions. He was spared: and: restrained initiative, hers more than his . . . She offered her ardor, her extra, her unbridled pleasure, which led to almost maudlin caresses, as well as the ever-so-rhythmic hip action that swelled the man's eyes and made his eyebrows rise, peaking, now! at which point Demetrio exploded and as he did so exclaimed: *That's it . . .*

baby . . . yes . . . ! How do you do it . . . Et cetera. And the sudden
gush of sperm and a matchless orgasm with all the corresponding
sensations. Satisfaction. Then hastily and carelessly dressing without even combing one's hair to one's liking in front of the mirror,
not she, not he, not as one should, though the agronomist promised the lusty lass a second visit the following day, and the fee:
as posted, but to the madam rather than the brunette: the madam
being a squat woman with an equatorial waist who occupied a luxurious suite just off the main salon. He entered. A miniature hell.
Danger. Inside, phew, pretentious scents. Shimmering purple armchairs where two bodyguards like reclining patriarchs conversed.
Interruption: and: the bill. Payment. A fortune. One of Madam's
eyes had a cloud in it. What can one say about that mysterious and
imprecise gaze? We might add that nobody betrayed even the hint
of a smile, and she, whose eyes switched back and forth like windshield wipers . . . Madam gave Demetrio his change. Good-bye. An
about-face and . . . Let's see: no reason for him to almost run, even
if he did have the impression that he was fleeing a world in flames.

The foregoing stands as a vast frame around what might appear to be perverse daubs of oily globs that puddle in spots to no
purpose. Herein a riddle: what era are we in? The answer: 1945, the
year the atomic bomb exploded and the Second World War ended.
Modernities. But we are at the other end of the earth, in Oaxaca,
a world cultural center, superior (let us say) to Tokyo. But we are
also with Demetrio Sordo, the sexual agronomist, who one day
among many began to do some bookkeeping. He had been visiting
the Presunción brothel for more than a week. He had been making
love to the brunette every day but Monday. Wonder of wonders:
her name was Mireya, a name in suspended animation because in
the brothel she was known as Bambi. Who knows why this nick-
name, for the wench wasn't delicate, like her namesake. Quite the
contrary. For example, they could have called her Goddess Kali,
because of her exuberance, or Goddess Isis, something like that,

but—Bambi? Let's avoid getting waylaid by a superfluous obsession and focus on the bookkeeping. Demetrio began pouring
numbers onto the pages of a lined notebook. His atomic pen slid
awkwardly across the page. Nerves. In thirteen days a total of 104
pesos, even if they were well spent; counting pleasure by fives,
plus the entrance fee, these by threes, an incomparable boon for
an obsessive. On Monday, Mireya rested. She gave Demetrio fair
warning and the chance to find another to hold in his arms, but
only—as it turned out—that first Monday. The novelty was a slim,
stylish woman, insipid . . . Next: calculate his total income and subtract his expenses. The unexpected extra. Pleasure in the nude.
Shared pleasure gains a firmer and firmer foothold. The dreadful
was undergoing daily transformation: O amour! O silhouettism!
Then, back to the numbers, a bit more than two hundred pesos.
Plus all his other expenses. Also, minus Mondays, for he would no
longer seek a sexual surrogate. He stood firm: no experimentation.
It would be too sad, as it had been with that scrawny thing with a
pretty face. Moreover, he should rest, he must. So, he would, and
that was final: abstinence as relaxation: once a week: yes! otherwise he'd explode. Now comes a description of Demetrio's job:
his workday went from seven in the morning till five in the afternoon, sometimes six, more infrequently seven. Once he'd fulfilled
his obligations, he'd make his way to the lodging house of one
Doña Rolanda, a frail, ultraconservative woman, where he rented
her largest room. The daily routine: his return, his ennui sprinkled
with drops of tolerance. Anyway, until exactly two weeks ago,
automatism—what else!—during the week, for on Saturday and
Sunday he indulged in what could be called "spiritual isolation,"
madness, or an Easter holiday in his rented room, where he had
a radio: turn it on and surrender to the sounds of romantic music
and stupid news broadcasts: countless hours in full-blown reveri-
es. All of which now struck him as loathsome. But at night . . .

2

The rigid hours for breakfast, lunch, and dinner were also loathsome. Key interludes, for in the dining room all sorts of subjects were raised, mostly by Rolanda, a woman who distilled bitterness. Unmarried, virgin, old, on top of a host of other afflictions. We can venture to guess what sorts of ideas made her shudder. Dark and decadent ones. Everything was fair game—the world and its inhabitants—except her far-distant God, the one to which she prayed. Imagine, then, the extent of her solitude, so evident. Abject boredom, even when praying, even when cooking . . . Though she never stopped talking while carrying steaming dishes to the table or fulfilling her lodgers' petty requests. Her monologues brooked no interruptions . . . Breakfast was served almost at dawn, as previously stated. Within the half hour eggs appeared, but sometimes only pastries. Never after that half hour, for the lodgers, four in all, had to leave for work. Moreover, let's figure that three left on the weekends. They returned to their villages in order to—or so they averred a hundred-odd times—enjoy the company of their wives and progeny. Not the agronomist, the obstinate bachelor, not till now. Though it seemed that his nearest of kin resided in the devil's lodgings. And evasive: Monday-through-Friday dinners, that is, conversation, a gathering of working people who often wound up extolling the virtues of their own jobs, Demetrio being the one with the highest salary, perhaps because he was the only semiprofessional among them: oh, the grand implicit advantage. If any of the others had been in business—alas!—they would have walked right out of that house in search of a better life, but they weren't, they were lowly wage earners, all somewhat younger than the agronomist; he, a roaring success! who earned two thousand pesos a month, so for him the pleasure of sex could be a fortuitous indulgence, but something was ruffling him: the aftertaste—how long could it go on? This notion brings us conveniently back to his bookkeeping, carried out during his Sunday-morning seclusion: Demetrio had to include the money he was saving monthly to buy a small house. A measly sum. After so many years of penny-pinching . . . Penny-pinching, indeed, but the investment was growing in the bank: at what percentage? He had it in a fixed-term account, so he saw his totals only once a year. A significant sum. The first time—amazing! when he saw the number, and the second—wow! It really did make sense to save in one of those munificent institutions. He got the information twice. Twice, because Demetrio had spent two years and three months working as the administrator and principal agricultural expert for a ten-thousand-hectare orchard. "Private ranch" would be the more accurate appellation, but the owner refused to call it a ranch, that little word just didn't seem appropriate, for there were no cows, nor chickens nor goats, none of those animals that produce wealth (not even pigs). So, no. Instead: pears, apples, or whatever other ideas for planting and harvesting he had: a clownish contumacy: the agricultural, indeed! In any case, before continuing in this vein, it would do to insert this note: nowadays the subject of ranches is of only peripheral interest, because ranches have no truck with the urban or the violent (our landowner would never have dreamed of planting marijuana or poppies), so we offer this information very much as an aside, only to turn our full attention back to the sexual, for that's what really matters. Let's, however, quickly assert that Demetrio Sordo had nothing to do with marketing the harvest: where it should go: near or far—no, never that! nor the renting of trailers, none of that tedious stuff. On the other hand, he was responsible for the drainage ditches; yes, and for all things related to the purchase of fertilizers and amendments, as well as the best insecticides to prevent plagues and other evils; and the manual work: the making of furrows, ridges, ditches, rows, and even terraces; as well as the rest: breaking clods, hoeing, plowing, grading, mowing, sifting, and threshing, in concert, needless to say, with the peasantry. All of which he carried off with great aplomb, which led the landowner to give Demetrio full jurisdiction over the orchard. Trust. Respect. He visited twice a week. He wanted results and that's what he got. At a serene pace that others might find torturous. But let's leave this for now and turn to the recently sexual. Before, as we said, the agronomist would make his way directly to the lodging house after the day's work; he would arrive beat, to bathe, to rest: seclusion, a clean break, the radio, waiting for dinnertime. Monotony. But ever since he'd met Mireya he made his way straight to the brothel: by taxi: a dirty and desperate dash, only the second time, for by the third, alas, a bath in the orchard, or rather: washing by bucketfuls. As far as that went, we must consider the time it took to heat the water to an optimal temperature. On a stove in a kitchen—of which there were both—though the distance between the bath and the kitchen exceeded 150 feet and counting. Further delays, but that's what Demetrio did the third time and thereafter: quite a chore this coming and going with buckets: four in all: slow considering what preceded and followed: stealing an hour from the workday—indeed! because if the agronomist didn't make it to the brothel on time, Mireya might be occupied with another client, a circumstance he wished to avoid by all means. Those first few days he was, mercifully, spared. Another option was to go to that aforementioned hell and wash there: in her room, before the screw. He asked, fearful of eliciting a negative response . . . No, on the contrary, Mireya said that as long as he did it quickly . . . Well, to clean off the dust of the fields was not a matter of a simple dousing, you had to stand under the water for a long time and thoroughly soap yourself, a privilege for which, Demetrio told her, he would be willing to pay an additional fee. Money for Mireya, secretly—really? and she agreed with a smile.

This mischief, nonetheless, carried a slight risk. Mireya's argument for compliance stressed that the arrangement would end when someone of ill will informed Madam of what they'd chanced to see. An improbable peril, for lovers could always choose to screw under the shower. We mustn't forget that the madam was an odd bird, piling ploy upon ploy: shadows within shadows. True, there'd been no hitches on any of the previous days, no undue attention paid. Though Mireya had a surprise for Demetrio on his tenth visit. She blurted it out with dread, fearing that something so beautiful would end ugly and sad.

One might harbor hopes for good tidings in the wake of that ominous periphrasis "I have something to tell you." Only trembling and silence, however, followed. Mireya looked down at the ground: the rug crisscrossed with arbitrary lines must have given her an idea: a hint of caution: then—what?—and she muttered an utterance and then one more, and a third that barely made sense at all. In the face of such dread, Demetrio turned to his most vulgar memories from their numerous copulations, including a sequence of voluptuous insults that rose spontaneously from the depth of his soul, verbal sputum such as (we will quote but three): *While I'm pounding you with my cock, I want to stick my left index finger up your ass . . . ; Give it to me, baby!;* or: *I want you to be even more of a whore than you were yesterday; I want you to scratch my balls. But what I really want is for you to understand me.* Sexual depravity could go even further: diabolical sex; sexual impudence, a subsequent outburst, but the nature of these statements already indicated the rarefied terror to come.

Such folly deserves a long hiss from decent folk, theoretically and otherwise, though not from Mireya, for whom a string of such phrases must sound perfectly harmless, poor gentleman, dear me, it wasn't as if after his outbursts he'd threatened to kill her with a paring knife, not in a million years, just lust, gushing, and nearly idyllic pleasure. In the end, his behavior was quite original and not wholly beyond the pale, so, returning to "I have something to tell you," let's get right to the words that ensued: she and her calculations: her somewhat fearful *ahems*. At issue was a new command from Madam, one that redounded to her benefit: from now on Demetrio would have to pay an additional fee for each lay, for the simple reason that no prostitute could be reserved for anybody's exclusive use; if he visited the brothel on a daily basis he would be obliged to sleep with others.

Ouch. Capricious, given his steady patronage. Such unhealthy devotion was causing universal unease at the Presunción: this was the first time in its history a client had come to sin as punctually as he went, with intrepid daily devotion, to his job. . . . His needs, oh yes—but why with Mireya, when there were much hotter ones to be had? He'd fallen in love, by an arrow pierced: a catastrophe. This was a business, not a marriage agency: hence the extra fee: let's see: five pesos the first day; the second, five additional pesos; the third, five more, and that makes fifteen; by the fourth, it was already twenty; the fifth, twenty-five; the sixth, thirty, and—enough already! because the seventh: remember he took a rest? The thing was, by letting one day pass, just one! he effected a return to the reasonable price of five pesos. Great idea. Ouch. A whim. He had no choice! Precise disclosure of the facts accompanied by a lowered head and a tied tongue. Demetrio considered it unfair, this madcap lack of proportion, and decided he would face down the madam that very day: *I'll give her a piece of my mind when I go to pay her. I know her bodyguards will be with her, but I don't care.* Then, footfalls; in anger, one could say. The agronomist did not dress or groom himself carefully; he'd dashed out ungirded.

Was he in the right? Then, he entered brusquely and encountered Madam and her bodyguards in slothful indolence, lounging in armchairs with springy backs and plush pillows: and: three (incidental) guffaws: and without further ado:

"Listen, Mireya just told me that you . . ."

"If you want to talk to me, you'll have to make an appointment. Today I can't. Tomorrow either. In a couple of days if you want . . . Do you? Tell me now, because if not . . ."

"Okay . . . The day after tomorrow."

"Come see me at five in the afternoon."

"At five?"

"Yes. That's the only time I have free. I'll see you here."

"Good. We'll be alone?"

"Alone. I promise."

3

He'd made a strategic gain, small but accompanied by the happy thought that an appointment is an appointment. Even so, Demetrio still had to invent a decent pretext for departing from the orchard long before five in the afternoon. Later, when he took stock of the strength of his position, and considered that he had never left work early before, he concluded that any excuse whatsoever would suffice. All he had to do was throw out an "I have to leave," and, how could his subordinates, those lowly hicks, possibly reproach him? Power gave him elbow room: ah! self-sufficiency, daring, a dose of disdain, and other attributes that help us understand that his personality consisted of not offering explanations. The hour had come. Face-to-face, Madam and the agronomist. Tentative preambles. Alone in the aforementioned room. And he, finally, straight to the point:

"With all due respect, I'd like to say that your decision to steadily increase my fee doesn't seem fair."

Faced with such boldness Madam's anger (and amusement) were sure to ensue, and without pausing she fired back:

"Look, all my girls are hot, though I admit, some more so than others. If you want only Mireya, you know how things stand, and if you don't like it, go somewhere else! Otherwise, you won't get Mireya . . ."

"What?"

"You heard right. I won't rent you Mireya. And now I'm going to call my bodyguards."

"No, wait! You win. I agree. I'll pay."

"What do you plan to do?"

"I'll come every day except Mondays, which is when she rests . . ."

"Let's leave it at that. Now, go."

Then and there the idea of requesting a raise popped into the agronomist's mind. A boon in any case. An appointment with the owner of the orchard as soon as possible (God willing, tomorrow!), for only two weeks remained till the Christmas holidays. As he made his way toward the only taxi stand in the vicinity, there on the city outskirts, his mind was abuzz with practical thoughts, in spite of the ruckus around him: treacherous red-light district . . . full of futile screws? And so in counterpoint, to balance things out, came the spark of the healthy idea that he should branch out, for there were as many loveworthy women as fish in the sea. Respectable love, sacred love, love that would last to an advanced age and have endless sexual summits. Or, as the priests put it: "Until death do us part." How easy it was for him to absorb such never-abeyant monumental truths! Yes, but what about Mireya: within reach: amorous, forthputting. The memory of her with legs widespread brought back to his ears those loving words uttered two afternoons ago: *I like you more and more each time. I hope you keep coming.* Phrases spelled carefully out, phrases that might just bore into the agronomist's dreams: his future dreams. In the meantime, today's, perhaps; though he might also dream about the owner of the orchard; that gentleman with a sun-beaten face, tinged with a yellowish hue: so judicious and affable. The salary: an abstraction, gray or brownish in color . . . Let us note that Demetrio didn't go to bed with Mireya that day—her upset, would she cry for love? mentally shaken by the what-ifs—for he'd already gone to the brothel to find a solution for what had none: the only good that came out of his appointment with the madam was that the next day the fee would return to normal: five pesos. Now to make another appointment as soon as he reached his lodgings, where there was a telephone. One of the few in Oaxaca. The temporal stride taken here obeys a desire to avoid obvious foreshadowing, such as the call soon made, the appointment, the agreement on a time and place: all in good course, as it were: without obstacles. Instead, let us make note of the smiles of the grand employee and the grand boss, face-to-face, while—let us say— they both drank punch: nibbled on snacks: mouths chewing as if mumbling. Then Demetrio's preamble: he stammered; he simply couldn't find the words for his request, considering his dedication to his work, only to drift, let us say *gently*, to the great responsibilities the management of . . . No, not that, no! More stammering. Better to endow his request with valor: straight to the issue of a raise, in a whisper, direct, and then: *Yes, that's fine. I'll give you a small raise: fifteen percent—how does that sound? Starting in January.* In the meantime, a Christmas bonus: tomorrow: which would have been his due anyway and which Demetrio had failed to take into account, so, while licking his lips, he scratched his head three times. Not until January, uh-oh, though he didn't say it, he thought it. Nevertheless, there was the other: the Christmas bonus . . . more than enough to pay the madam for the services of she who had surely cried—though not excessively—the previous night.

Mireya may have ended up crying even more that same night, for at the last minute Demetrio again decided not to visit her. Emotional punishment, or indolence, or fortitude, or an attempt to stem the lavish outflow of cash: which turned out to be simple. It seems the boss had been expecting his request. Be that as it may, we must add that during the meeting neither devoted a single sentence to the daily doings of the orchard. The owner was well aware of his employee's efficacy. Therefore the finale, both discreetly

bowing, neither daring to offer a parting handshake, then the return and spiritual excitement of he who found news awaiting him
at the lodging house: a letter. Rolanda handed it to him almost as
if it were a red-hot ember; from whom? his faraway mother, she'd
gleaned from reading the back of the envelope. Bad or wonderful
news? The surprise revealed in total reclusion. Fanciful speculations with each tearing (few) of paper. Then ensued the clumsy
unfolding: three per sheet, but even so it is worth noting the scru-
pulousness of the maneuver. Then he read:

Dear Son,
I know you are coming to spend Christmas with me. But I'd
like you to come sooner and accompany me to a wedding in my
hometown. As you know, because of my age and infirmities, I
couldn't possibly attend such an event alone . . .

To explain, his mother lived in the large house she'd inherited
along with an ample amount of cash. Accompanying her were
servants—a poorly paid woman and man—who did all the usual
chores. She'd been a merry widow for five years. Mother of three:
Demetrio, the eldest; and Filpa and Griselda, both married to
gringos; one from Seattle, a city that is superior, as a world cultural center, to, let us say, Naples; and the other from Reno, a city
that is superior, as a world cultural center, to, let us say, Badajoz;
that is, they were out in the world, prisoners of marriages or perhaps already adapted and trained to live out their monotonous
and well-ordered lives. Of course, they pretended to be strong,
especially as they rarely came to Parras, the nicest town in the
state of Coahuila, a world cultural center superior to, let us say,
Brussels. And, so, things being what they were, Demetrio was the
one left to accompany his mother. The wedding would be held in
Sacramento, Coahuila, a world cultural center superior to, let us
say, Luxembourg. We must consider, by the way, the long stretch

of desert between Parras and Sacramento. A vast expanse without highways, unthinkable for a bus to risk riding on those rugged roads, potholed paths poorly or not at all paved, not even so much as graveled. The marriage would take place on the eighteenth of December; we are now the tenth, so, easy to do the math. The letter continued, though not profusely, not more than a spare sheaf of sententious sentences that softened the initial request: emphasis on the date, the understanding that the mother took for granted her son's yes, this being the norm, she would say "come" and he would: he let himself be led around like a dog by his master, especially because his mother's orders were infrequent, thus all the more compelling, as was this one, for it indicated a change of tack. Demetrio noted the careful calligraphy and even imagined his progenitor by candlelight: a bold image, somewhat diluted, but nonetheless . . . It was inferred that no telegram would follow. Nothing like, "I'll be there, you can count on me. I'll go with you." To leave, yes, and with no thought to the mayhem this might unleash . . . Departure tomorrow, the day after tomorrow at the latest, just before dawn; indeed, he had no choice . . . and feeling his way . . . No, he wouldn't say good-bye to Mireya, but he would inform his boss . . . a brief telephone call: family affairs, circumstances beyond my control, and bye-bye. Christmas vacation would begin, Demetrio knew, on the eighteenth, so, to repeat: it is the tenth, therefore . . .

Oh, yes, of course, the bonus: handy, well-earned, right? This shouldn't cause a problem, so he took care of it himself the following day. He wrote himself a check, for his was an authorized signature. In passing let us make note of the agronomist's absolute integrity: not one peso more nor one penny less, from which we can infer that he already knew the amount he was due, and, alas! The bad part—each time he rang his boss's house to discuss the untimely trip, the wife answered—was turning over to an assistant the task of paying accounts due. This the easiest solution, considering his haste, but the responsibility, the possible blame, all yet to be seen . . . uncertainty: What a concession! How equivocal! But only till his return: in theory: at the beginning of the New Year: oh no! Would everything be okay, God willing!? After perusing the letter the docile son packed his suitcase. Hastily. He packed carelessly and slept briefly. He counted sheep. He didn't put on his pajamas.

And . . .

It took two days (almost three) to get to Parras. The coming rub. Nasty calculus, and, well, what's done is done, as they say, the agronomist spent the night in his Oaxacan room per usual and left at daybreak for the outskirts of the aforementioned cultural city, where there was a runway for small airplanes.

Now, to regress for a moment, it's worth mentioning one of Doña Rolanda's habits: she loved to read the local newspaper. The irregularity of these rustic publications made reading about mundane maladies and natural disasters that much more exciting. One issue a week was the norm, but more normal was for it to fail to appear, though news of great consequence warranted a limited-edition gazette, printed and sold out in a trice: an infrequent occurrence, only in cases of extraordinary events—bad? good? thus it was with the bomb: that perverse achievement that culminated in an explosion and mushroom cloud: though . . . on the other end of the earth: over there in Japan, thousands dead . . . That horror, with a host of details, was mentioned one Thursday by the landlady to her fellow diners, who, wholly unconcerned, continued to scoop up her beans. Then came her final flourish:

"Any moment now another bomb will explode and the world will come to an end."

Guffaws in response, not a single indication of alarm. The news, it seems, had been attended to as if a leaf had fallen from a tree. Full focus on the scrumptious. Beans for dinner . . . this the only dish, though plentiful, accompanied by plump rolls . . . It's also worth mentioning, by the way, that beans made with lard are much tastier, as these were on this occasion.

"The bomb was dropped from an airplane."

Silence or the continued shoveling of food. Words, which ones? Only hers . . . tossed into the air.

"What? Aren't you worried?! The world is about to come to an end!"

Demetrio shook his head, just as smug as can be, made a move to stand up to assert his authority, and did so, but first he wiped his tangled lips and spoke.

"Look, señora, if the world is going to end, let it end already."

"What?!"

"Yes, let it end; after all . . ."

The others chimed in: "Let it end, let it end." Derision for the defeated one; though: how callous this mediocre—somewhat shameful?—merrymaking, enough to make Doña Rolanda feel crushed by the indiscretion (that almost infantile chorus of "Let it end!" continued), my, my! the lady felt intimidated but not before she'd done further damage by uttering one last sentence: *It's just that, can you imagine how many Japanese have died!* In response: not a sigh, not even for the sake of politeness: nope! why second the motion? May she and her facts fade straightaway. Hence, already shrunken and small, she uttered one last word: "Hi-ro-shi-ma," a vague subconscious input Demetrio unwittingly recorded, so effectively that when he was sitting on a bench in a rectangular room, that is, a waiting room, he muttered the word as if trying to spit it out. The small plane that would carry him to Nochistlán had limited capacity: eight passengers. The agronomist was quite familiar with this grasshopper-like flight. And all the while: "Hi-ro-shi-ma, Hi-ro-shi-ma." And, by way of counterpoint, a view of the concrete: the awaiting plane. And then the imagined: the bomb: from what height was it dropped? His guts churned at the mere thought that he would board a plane that might be carrying—a bomb! Terrifying associations growing grimmer and grimmer . . . Moments later the announcement of the plane's departure. There weren't eight passengers, only five, and still his fears: that the contraption would fall or that the bomb would explode in midair. Nevertheless, the boarding and the takeoff and finally the airborne motion: thick clouds angrily shook the plane, enough to make one think the worst. Bah! We needn't dwell on this because nothing terrible happened. Landing put an end to the paranoia after a miserable hour that, by the way, had the landlady not mentioned the bomb or the airplane and even less the thousands of dead Japanese—careful now!—would have been COMPLETELY NORMAL, for this was not the first time Demetrio had taken this flight.

Inevitable regression once his feet touched the ground. Memories of Mireya, a fleeting but always sensual silhouette: "For sure she'll get it on with others and at some point while she's doing it she'll shout out my name." Such miserable thoughts made the agronomist ill, but, what could he do to rid himself of something that had already become abhorrently persistent?: "She'll miss me. My naked body will appear in her dreams." And as he turned away from the Nochistlán airfield, he redoubled his efforts to stroll along the pavement with a graceful air, and we say "air" because the local breeze caressed him: swirled around him, perhaps, to purify the traveler's incantation: "No-chis-tlán," "Hir-ro-shi-ma," "Mi-re-ya," "Pa-rras," verbal scraps, parsimonious swaying that finally touched down on an unreal, deep, shifting surface, whereby the agronomist would soon forget Oaxaca completely. Nor did he wish to cram himself into that future frame called Parras, on which his mother appeared embossed (unblemished), or better said: where decency sparkled in colorful abstraction . . . From Nochistlán, which was not by any measure a world cultural center, he would take the bus to Cuautla, which wasn't either (unless someone would like to claim otherwise). From there he would board a train to Mexico City, which was, of course: that urban area had to be the most important cultural center in the world, wouldn't you say? And now, getting back on track, so to speak, we are now approaching the drudgery of the culminating leg of the journey. Demetrio knew what it meant to spend thirty hours on a train. Standing up, sitting down, eating poorly, getting depressed as he sank into silence, and it was even worse if someone tried to engage him in conversation. He rudely cut short anybody who dared, even raising a fist as if to fight if a stranger insisted. Once he had done just that: mercilessly slapping a quite shameless man who had provoked him: *You think you're man enough to get into a fistfight with me?* He never should have said that, the agronomist's violent outburst had been most improbable, such a quiet, well-behaved gentleman, so much for that! He had been so fierce that the train conductors forced him off at the next station without refunding even one cent of his fare. The conductors' last argument (while shoving him) just as the train pulled away was regarding the expense of healing the wounded man, parting palaver that settled accounts between them . . . On the ground, prone, his suitcase tossed and broken, Demetrio had sworn at the capped men, who could no longer hear the inventiveness of his invectives. The consequences were awful. Sparing many details, suffice it to say that on that occasion the agronomist spent forty-eight hours in that accursed backwater. The tedium of hour upon cheerless hour made him yell at nobody in particular. A madness the locals duly respected. His own private problems had no ramifications, so, why censure him? better he wear himself out shouting his head off, and that's just what he did, trembling, as if someone had poured a bucket of cold water down his back. How fortunate the muffling gloam hid, for better or for worse, his reddened face! Then the good services of the people at the station, where he slept on a pile of empty, scratchy gunnysacks. But first they gave him two soups: one greenish and the other gray. He slept poorly, in large part because his bedding smelled of burro piss. Horrible! Violence turns into disaster and recovery takes time. Demetrio recalled all this when the interruption came this time around, and the rudeness of his retort consisted of: *I'm so sorry, but I don't want to talk to anybody. I've got too many problems.* That's it! and he raised no fist. Precaution. Regret. Good manners.

In any case, he'd reach Saltillo; hmm, Saltillo, who knows what it was . . . Here it is important to contemplate how singular and solitary his tribulations were: Demetrio strained to carry his enormous suitcase. The wreck of a man ascending and descending the train's metal stairs. Still to come was the difficulty of the next embarkation: the noisy train trip to Parras, four additional suffocating hours in pursuit of that pre-Christmas joy, the welcoming embrace between mother and son: this, the annual event . . . irritability upon arrival, for after each had spoken a few kind words he begged to rest: *Please, I want to sleep.* After those last four hours he just had to! now!

His mother understood. In this deflated state he retired to a room full of altars crowded with saints. A host of sacred eyes spying: upon a sinner seeking refuge. Tomorrow more fuss and bother because they would leave early for Sacramento: trains, stairs, his mother's excessive chatter: all quite predictable. For now, let us focus on a single fact: Demetrio slept fourteen hours straight, watched over by porcelain saints who would do nothing at all. As fate would have it, he turned his back on them, so to speak: and: Demetrio—was he cold?—also covered his head, but . . . in sleep's underworld there appeared words suggesting landscapes of great depths; as for the sleeper, he experienced a succinct sashaying of sensations; barely a murmur . . . cloying syllables such as: "Hi-ro-shi-ma": hell? the wedding and God embracing the newlyweds: a photograph with mountains in the background. Another of the devil laughing as enormous tongues of fire licked the newlyweds. Finally: a circuitous flickering: heavy sleep, the road to relief . . .

4

So much to talk about. A random recounting of minor troubles and modest joys. The breakfast conversation was merely a sketch that mother and son would fill in with details and inventions on the train. It was five in the morning, and due to their nerves, or their haste, they decided to finish chewing their toasted *totopos* and bread on the way to the station in their horse-drawn carriage. Among the most important things the mother—her name was Telma—told her offspring was one as portentous as:

"I'm sure you will find the woman of your life in Sacramento, the woman who will be the mother of your children."

For Demetrio, this was a vain prophecy. He'd rather imagine Mireya's marvelous vagina and her breasts like well-hung melons. She was the ideal, even the superlative, *mamacita*, who would bear him a whole legion of children . . .

"Did you hear me? There are lots of good and beautiful women in Sacramento; dutiful, not at all tiresome. What do you think?"

"I'll see. Maybe I'll give it a shot."

This was the main subject of conversation en route. Hour after hour she insisted. Irksome to the son, who had to hold his tongue. Not a chance he'd spill the beans to Doña Telma; what if he told her that he was sleeping with a spectacular whore in Oaxaca, and even that he had screwed her in many different positions? A son should never confess such depraved sins to his mother. What a terrible lack of respect that would be—right? hence it behooves us to set this scene in a precariously balanced rowboat. A touch of anxiety, a hint of fright, perhaps a moment of relief or something of the sort, all anticipated hours beforehand. Apropos, we must relate a geographic detail Doña Telma and her son, Demetrio, discussed on their way to Sacramento in the first-class carriage—"first" implies the presence of ceilings and walls upholstered in green velvet . . . anyway, the point is that the Nadadores River runs parallel to the railroad tracks for two and a half miles. If you think that there's no friction in this kind of kinship, there's no point in mentioning the subject. But the mother thought there was, for she had heard that sometimes the rising waters covered the rails. An anomalous event that created the illusion that the train was floating. Many had witnessed this delightful effect from afar, but to experience it from inside the train: to feel afloat and derailed: which she never . . . maybe this would be the first time? Fear. And, it being December, the river is higher, they say, or the contrary: almost not. Hence, until they passed that stretch . . . just before La Polka station, where mother and son would detrain with their heavy suitcases. A bit more than a mile before said station the river bore east. And the only thing they, as well as the other passengers, saw at any given moment was a sprinkling of the rails: the one on the left: where: unwanted kisses: liquid moderation, which outside observers might have perceived as flotation. Probably not. The river had risen, undoubtedly, but not enough to produce a more or less virtual image . . . And having thus avoided serious difficulties Doña Telma offered her gratitude to God, and Demetrio seconded that, if only to cover his bases. They crossed themselves ostentatiously, though the one, full-fledged; the other, hypocritical. Anyway, they'd almost reached La Polka. Both had stood up, the son carrying the heavy suitcase to the exit: he staggered under its weight. His mother had warned him that they would have to cross the Nadadores River by boat. On the other shore a horse-drawn carriage would take them to Sacramento. Two old-fashioned conveyances that then and perhaps even now remain the same . . . Yes, there was the proof, at that point in the century nobody had yet taken the initiative to build a bridge: how difficult could it be so as to avoid the rowing nuisance? For how long had it been thus? And how about buying an automobile to replace the horse-drawn carriage. No, no modernity here, and hence we have mother and son trembling in the boat. Rowing the whole way. The narrow boat was agile. The current would never hold sway. A gentle pull, ah; a glimmer of danger: yes: as stated, the cloud of dust still to come: a mock or imminent attack? the latter: which is what regrettably occurred: the wheels churning dust off the ground: as if to replicate rusticity they arrived in town like a couple of clowns (dust even in their armpits)— Sacramento was three miles from the river. Before that: a third of a mile from La Polka to the riverbank, but on the other side. The load, for Demetrio. Suffice it to say that the aforementioned crossing was more perturbing than the dusty jaunt: a bath at once, compulsory, with brush, soap, and soap-root plant, as soon as they arrived at the home of Aunt Zulema, Doña Telma's cousin, where they would stay, for the town had no hotels, not even a modest one, not even a hostel. In short, the clouds of dirt were an added touch. A form of welcome . . . aggressive? Constant coughing, starting with the coachman. The important thing is that mother and son conversed between bouts. She repeated that Sacramento had an abundance of . . . et cetera. Demetrio's rude riposte: *You've told me more than ten times, Mama. And what if it turns out not to be true? Better just forget about it.* But the mother, wearisome and defeated, nonetheless hedged her bets: *At least in my day there were lots of beautiful women . . . I don't know about now . . . Hopefully it will be like it once was.* And once it was like this and like that, and as the horse-drawn carriage made its way through the streets of the town: one over here, another over there, wow, such well-groomed beauties—abloom! such bodies! such faces! such tresses! through the dust . . .

The magic dust acting as a filthy screen: do the beauties bathe . . . and how many times a day? If so, as Demetrio imagined, it would be the ultimate consolation, because the gaga gawker was already fully engrossed in painting pictures in his mind. He could imagine them (almost) floating. And above all, how beautiful they must be when even with all this dust . . . was there really that much? Demetrio imagined them naked, like Mireya, sculpted, but, why the comparison when any one of them was ten times as good as . . . ? Walking loveliness: well-nourished. The agronomist probably thought that those he was watching (lecherously) would attend the wedding. A host of invitations—with any luck! At night, visual delerium: many baths in between . . . In the meantime the aftereffects of the strenuous journey: colossal exhaustion. For Demetrio felt as though he'd come from the other end of the earth. Hence there rose from his subconscious the utterance "Hi-ro-shi-ma"— disgusting! so many dead. No! he wasn't in Japan but rather in this small place: where life was flourishing—gorgeous! so healthful, so removed from catastrophes and other degradations . . . To clarify: Sacramento was horrible. A town staked down in the middle of a desert in a broad valley: irredeemable ugliness, except for the local women . . . Divine wisdom, could it possibly compensate? or not? Still to be seen if all were really so angelic . . . and hot! And of foremost importance: capable of whipping up a hearty stew.

An incidental fact. The scene of the dust-laden ones' arrival at their relative's house may seem spurious after the chug-a-chug-chug of the trip: a whole day long. The weather was cool, pleasant: a hoax in the month of December. By the same token, a dust storm at that time of year: why?

A local phenomenon, and on to the next thing: the dirty embrace. Zulema, with her expansive happiness, bubbling profusely about so many things (unstoppable, incorrigible), and the recent arrivals with their timid pleas: *We want to take a bath. May we?* Or: *It's urgent,* and other such phrases sprinkled about. But Zulema: *No! Wait! First let's talk.* How unkind! Or do we need to know that the hostess hadn't seen Telma in more than ten years? She'd met Demetrio when he was about sixteen, and now an agronomist, a bachelor; tall and thin; such a manly impression he made. *I'm so glad you brought him. He'll find beautiful women here*—spot-on!—*I assume you have demanding taste. Well, you'll find a lot to choose from around here, you'll see.* But a bath, please. The deliberate delay was due to the absence of showers in Sacramento, no exceptions, not even for the wealthiest: so: by the bucketful. And putting the water on the woodstove to heat: a delay, even of two or three hours, would still be a delay: and: no way could they attend the wedding filthy. *Don't worry, that won't happen.* A terrible hostess, this Zulema. An old maid, and bitter to boot, a sweet face despite the wrinkles, obvious right away she wasn't used to having guests; at the house, to be precise, because in her grocery store . . . but that's another story altogether . . . Her obstinacy triumphed against the two clamors for cleanliness. The contingency plan: conversation! But mother and son remained silent. Even Telma's eyelids drooped at the onslaught of words hurled their way. Silence as revenge and sleep as revenge. The three of them sat in the salon. The suitcases on the floor. The hostess still had not assigned her guests a bed or beds because she was summarizing her entire life, bringing them up-to-date. Unstoppable, incorrigible. A bother. If the dear lady had not had such a pretty face, Demetrio would have strangled her, in fact he felt quite like doing so, as he looked at his own large, bony hands, which he began to raise above his head as if he were learning flamenco, while the other continued with her verbal grist. Playing the fool, she made an awkward mention of the number of suitors who, shall we say, had sniffed her out: and: all rejected! any excuse would do, the premise being her pride (without adjectives) of feeling herself desired. A bit later it was she who took the initiative and said she had neither beds nor rooms available (liar, two closed doors in plain view, how odd!), that all three of them would sleep in the only bed she had: hers, quite creaky. If the dear lady hadn't had a pretty face, Demetrio would have chosen to sleep on the floor, but the proximity of mature beauty: come on!: she was but a distant aunt. What if he brushed against those hanging breasts. *I'd like to sleep in the middle. May I?* The mother said nothing, she was already nodding off. But Zulema said: *Yes! Of course*, then calmed down, finally.

She didn't even offer them something to eat. Didn't even mention the subject.

Could Demetrio's bony hands with their flamenco flourishes have soothed her?

No!

His aunt then embarked on a second discursive romp. She began talking about the family tree. Recounting those who had died and those whose whereabouts were unknown.

And bathing? It was getting late. Pressure. A brief lapse getting briefer whereby each minute became a stigma with meaning, not to mention the squeezed seconds: ticking: throbbing, a range of rudeness, more than one raised eyebrow between the guests. And the filth? More, then. And the redolence of the threads of their garments. And what about the wedding? A calamity, the only option was to wash in cold water. Alas, mention has already been made of the unseasonably chilly air. A shivering bath . . . The last to wash was the agronomist. Anyway, they were late and wouldn't arrive in time for the service, better, at least. Such a predictable ritual . . . Let's go straight away to the party outdoors, the mother, aunt, and son together . . . He, proudly wearing a fairly wrinkled gray suit, though of high quality . . . There simply hadn't been time to press it. We have to take into account the jammed suitcase, packed with such haste in Oaxaca. The same goes for the mother and her pink dress—flamboyant: due to her haste in Parras: let's proceed, it doesn't matter anyway; the aunt was another story, with her well-pressed deep blue dress . . . The bride was a niece in her twenties, her belly six months gone and showing. The party would be held in the playground of the local primary school.

Dust . . .

As long as there's dancing . . .

A dusty orchestra, and dusty beauties.

A crush of crinoline: encountered upon arrival. For Demetrio the sight of such concealing garments was regrettable. Harshly corseted women. Exasperating uniformity. Only the beauties' waspish waists could be seen. No asses or legs—quite a pity! because, where's the excitement? Busts, yes: though: no striking cleavage. Faces, yes: and what faces they were! Green eyes aplenty, enormous: most of the women were like cats: though a few dogs with brown eyes; a donkey or two, not even worth mentioning; one or another fox . . . let's see . . . plenty of these in most milieus: and: now, yes: delight for the sake of diversity. So many women for so few men. And they kept arriving: in droves, really! and the men?: here and there. All to the advantage of Demetrio, who was recalling the moment he entered the Presunción brothel, yonder, that is to say, at the other end of the earth: in Oaxaca, oh, all those randy asses, who, compared with these Sacramento dolls, were hardly worth remembering. Moreover, one could conjecture that these beauties—so fair and so varied, glimpsed fleetingly and from afar—held the promise of many a hearty stew, each and every feature, but more of that later, hmm . . . Now for the most evident, the many eyes, and their honeyed looks above all . . . Perhaps up close Demetrio would find, if he decided to scrutinize closely, one or another telling detail: this one would make a good *chorizo con huevos;* that one was the queen of any of hundreds of pork dishes, and so on, but then came one: a goddess emergent, oh, and upon her his eyes settled—oh my!, he couldn't stop staring at her, no, not even when the bride and groom arrived. Distractions? Not for him; for the others, perhaps. Unto himself: *She is the most beautiful woman I have ever seen in my life.* He espied the striking green of her eyes from thirty feet away. A vague moan escaped his lips, accompanied by a slight quivering thereof, and the muttering of syllables: and: his aunt and mother caught a glimpse of his hidden indiscretion. They spoke to him.

Some claim that when one person stares at another, the other will finally stare back: thus it came to pass between them; a magnet or—who knows what! (whose plan?)—the green: the setting, and the bodies passing back and forth between them: furtive interruptions, but no real distractions, because of the focus and the commitment between she who had just arrived and Demetrio, wow!: a honing in, to such an extent that her parents, who stood with her, had words for her. Her mother nudged her arm, as did his mother over here. Here, not a word passed, but there, father and mother whispered and wagged index fingers. Now they were both obliged to look elsewhere, although their bond had already postulated a "hence," referent to when the newlyweds initiated the dancing . . . Which didn't take long—thank goodness! anon!, along with all the lauding and applause . . . As a result, it was as if an invisible machine suspended in midair were moving x number of males in pursuit of seated females. In the end there arose a musical dynamic that consisted of holding waists and taking steps. Eighteen couples—giving it their all! The movements were quite corny, waltzing, which would have looked even cornier if viewed from the top of any tree: a changing—and pretentious?—flower, or something of the sort, whatever occurs to you. Couple number nineteen was missing. Let's watch Demetrio ask the aforementioned woman to dance. The parents looked him up and down, from head to toe. His wrinkled suit at night—consider the advantage of the dim lighting—wouldn't matter even when they did notice, perhaps later. Anyway. Couple number nineteen's steps were discreet: he was quite tall (almost six feet) and she rather short (what would you call five foot two?). Be that as it may, they never took their eyes off each other; moreover, and because of their somewhat awkward steps, they were continually bumping into other couples. Sorry here, sorry there, and sorry yonder. Their dancing deteriorated as they sidled over to the edge of the dance floor, which didn't matter because first and foremost they had to introduce themselves: he took the initiative: his name, where he was from, his profession, his reason for being in Sacramento, and the unrivaled privilege of being face-to-face with a *ranchera* goddess . . . No, how could he use such an inaccurate adjective; he must remain cool . . .

And on they went. They danced four rounds.

Vigilant parents. No problems observed. His enormous bony hands made no mischief.

Before leading her back to her seat, he asked for her address so that he could write to her, from Oaxaca! The answer was a cinch: General Delivery, Sacramento, Coahuila. He carried no pen, so consigned it, effortlessly, to memory. Then came her name: Renata Melgarejo. Difficult. What a hodgepodge of a family name! Her given name: a bit odd, though sonorous. True, Mireya's was more vivacious, but it was a whore's name, whereas this one— how could he think of her? Decent: a bit; indecent: no, not that! Re-na-ta as opposed to Mi-re-ya. Purity tending toward impurity . . . Better not to think such filthy thoughts. Better to think about the sanctity therein, in her sweeter than sweet demeanor and her body, oh, like a wildflower . . .

"I will write you twice a month. You are enchanting." He used the familiar "*tú*" form of address.

"We just met and already so familiar?"

"I'm sorry—oh boy! It's just that I'm from the city . . . Please, forgive me."

"When you return, if you return, I'll allow it."

A fleeting association: Mireya never made a fuss about that, in fact, she never made any fuss at all.

"Of course I'll come back. I promise you. You are the most beautiful woman I've ever met in my life and, I presume, the kindest. It would be a great honor for me to see you again soon."

"You have a way with words. I like what you've said, and I must confess, I'd like to hear more."

In the face of such fair rusticity, the agronomist could not possibly use the base language that he used with Mireya, perhaps eventually, but who knows when.

"I will always speak tenderly to you. With words as soft and beautiful as you are."

"And I will always be grateful."

A chivalrous adieu. Obsequious smiles for the parents as he accompanied Renata to her seat. When he turned his back upon all of that—quite decently done, of course—Demetrio took long jaunty strides across the basketball court. His mother and aunt greeted him with smiles. They: eager. He: excited. It was still not time, however, to speak about how things had gone with the girl. Instead, what was worth noticing after the agronomist's abrupt about-face was that Renata and her parents were leaving: we still have to find out why: perhaps these gentlefolk had decided that their daughter should not dance with another: this also to the outlander's advantage, who thought in a flash: *I've got my foot in the door. I'm like a Prince Charming from far away.* He said as much within earshot of his mother and aunt. They: swelling with pride, smiling. It was best he say no more. Every silence is strategic. It might also help him to think ahead, especially because he was pondering the nature of the summary impressions he'd made upon those who had left, impressions that might even be marvelous: the outlander appeared to be a well-educated man, with good social standing and a promising future; moreover, his height—incredible! impressive!— his self-confidence, his good manners, that sort of thing. Correct impressions of Demetrio, but ones that he had foisted upon the departed trio. Now, here come the comments of his own dear aunt! who didn't hold her tongue—nor did she overstate her joy—: *I know that family. One of the most respectable in Sacramento.* That's all, then on to the next subject. Doña Telma wanted to congratulate the newlyweds, especially the parents of the bride: old friends of hers, and most important: the inviters who'd wired to Parras. Anyway, the three of them proceeded: best wishes were proffered. The introduction of the agronomist son. Then followed more praiseworthy observations pertinent to the couple's happiness—a sampling? Naw, enough already! The party's over. Let's be gone! And why even dip our toes into the flood of verbiage provoked by Renata and Demetrio's spin on the dance floor, once they were back at the home of that aunt, who mentioned in passing how bad the food was, how there weren't even enough tables, and, oh—so many unbearable details? Just to make clear, the agronomist ate neither potato salad nor sandwiches made with scrawny bits of chicken soaked in chorizo juice. Would such aloofness be harmful? No, because at least the hungry man had his plate full of love's frenetic beginnings, more than enough to keep him up all night talking. And now for an aside: Renata Melgarejo was the only daughter left to those refreshingly respectable gentlepeople; the other four, all older, had already been carried off by other outlanders, outlanders with great futures! Et cetera. Many weddings. Ugh! An anodyne extension of the conversation. Bitter pills for Demetrio to swallow as he begged for a bed. Please. Agreed. *Go to sleep!* the aunt finally exclaimed. Gossip's full delight to be enjoyed on the morrow. And there he lay in the middle of the mattress, unblanketed. He wore lightweight pajamas. Now for the final frame: the bedded trio—but careful! all wearing pajamas. Dreams and fatigue lasting till noon, and from Demetrio, not the slightest lascivious touch, even when his aunt was well within reach. Only a nudge with a leg and a brief caress of the old woman's face. Incidents that took place moments before the hostess awoke.

And no drawn-out gossiping.

It would have been a waste of time for both mother and son.

A bold and hasty return to Parras. Then a dreary Noel.

Still, the effects of that memorable dance lingered for many a long evening and night, when Telma and Demetrio's thoughts mingled in bittersweet conjectures.

A vast illusion they willingly recycled, always seeking new angles.

Until Demetrio said: *I don't want to talk about it anymore!* His mind was, instead, pulling him in a more benign direction: Mireya from a distance like a circle with a ceaselessly shifting center: legs, breasts, ass, a cleaving—perhaps? The conjuring of a waiting nakedness, accompanied by a large number of banknotes descending, floating through the air, the whimsy of each movement—would it? could it?

But those Christmas days seemed long, so long that Demetrio spent hours in his room, entertaining himself with his sexual longings. Why not! He masturbated five or more times. What a greedy sinner! Such solitude exasperates and baffles, but he simply didn't feel like going out and wandering the streets of Parras nor talking to his mother about his plans regarding that angel named Renata. Finally, the New Year swelled with hope that would never be fulfilled or disappointed: hence: to leave, to feign ignorance yet know he was carrying the onus of an illusion. The material thing was in far-off Oaxaca. Nevertheless, first a toast. New Year's Eve: stiff, then soft and therefore remembered. Two solitudes embraced. Mother and son—contrite? The hug lasted a long time.

5

Romantic music in the penumbra, a bit of rumbling from behind the four walls: sequestered with memories. He deliberately made the volume overflow. Demetrio had no regard for the other lodgers' privacy. A mere quarter of an hour had passed and Doña Rolanda was already knocking on the door: her voice through the wood: *Turn it down! Please!* The good part: prompt compliance; the response: the act: down it was turned, without another word spoken. But the following night, the same thing—ugh!—and even more rumbling: the continued increase the result of love's pull or the lover's thickheadedness: an inexorable ascent or, better said, a brutal one. And again: *Turn it down! Please!* The third night of folly, it resounded even louder, and Doña Rolanda had no choice but to present him with the ultimatum that she would forbid him from having a radio in his room if . . . et cetera . . . and thus we put an end to the music problem. Of course, the music continued, but the volume: a wisp that only barely stoked the delirium of he who longed for the *ranchera* goddess. It's also worth mentioning that Demetrio had not been visiting Mireya. His longing for her and the oft-dreamed-of screws had steadily diminished during the return trip, a great doubt about the future of his love life having conclusively intervened. To make a sacrifice for a hope (unfortunately, always vague) as opposed to his need for a sexual workout, his apprenticeship, his fantasies, but . . . desire, that unscalable peak, that muddling and stirring blur . . . Abstinence, to be so wholly parched, the denial of all sorts of urgencies in order to fortify his tattered spirit. An expiation, perhaps, or a punishment—for how long? and moreover, in order to render what, exactly, clear? The truth was that while listening to those songs that waxed poetic about love's miseries, Demetrio made several attempts to write his first promised letter. He couldn't decide whether to write "Highly esteemed," "Dear," "Wondrous," or simply, "Hi, Renata," or the name by itself, next to a drawing of a flower, using five colored pencils. No! Such vulgarity, quickly shunned . . . Indolence. Inanity . . . Nonetheless, try, try, try again, knowing that sheer obstinacy would carry him to his goal, whatever that might be, which might provoke stentorian laughter that was nonetheless sympathetic . . . to enthuse her, make her forgive such . . . The agronomist managed to eke out only three sentences, not even particularly shapely ones, in an entire week. No reason even to quote them. They cajoled so blatantly that even he felt like a hypocrite, and the worst part: they lacked all credibility. His mission was to fill three sheets of paper, back and front—six pages in all, though at the rate he was going he calculated that it would take him more than a month. Dig out what was most natural in himself (climbing a mountain carpeted in treacherous snow), and express it, and—what words would sound really and truly sincere? what ideas that Renata could interpret as feelings rising from a limpid depth? Ah. So, no. Indolence won the day, and the other; the brothel, the awaiting brunette, the one to whom he need only say: *Hey, you, let's get it on!* Away, now! Resist. No, he didn't go. Abstinence is better . . . auspicious? Better to concentrate on his work in the orchard, as he was doing. In the midst of it all, Demetrio masturbated one night with great delight to the rhythm of the music. When he felt the semen seeping through his fingers, a mumbled sentence took shape, almost through attrition: *I am turning into a chaos.*

A chaos, indeed, what survived, awry, as an inexpugnable, growing glob. On top of which from time to time Demetrio remembered a few of his mother's sentences, especially those uttered in the course of that sad Christmas dinner, while both were eating chicken awash in green mole sauce, with a garnish of yellowish *guapilla* peppers: *You are the perfect age to get married.* Or: *I can't wait for you to give me grandchildren.* Or: *In Sacramento you will find* . . . Why listen to her? Little digs (pricks), irritations, itches, and redundant splashes of what he should be or what he should do. Fortunately, he found the counterpoint elsewhere, his triumphs, the remarkable ease of his job . . . Everything he'd left hanging had turned out as well as could be hoped . . . Except for one problem: the boss asked him for the checkbook. He didn't make a fuss. His point was subtle. His request came just as they were exchanging a New Year's hug. Then Demetrio's automatic acquiescence, and from now on he would receive his expenses on a weekly basis. Full focus on his work; again his recreation would be games of dominoes and evening cups of coffee. Those ancient calumnies.

Those decent and inane contours.

To be as he was before.

The other splendor. The more authentic one.

But, how long would he bear up under it?

If his compensation was to write raptures both extravagant and purposeless to an enigma, moreover, rather than a woman, his would be the emotional effort of a novice: a "maybe no" over here and an "I guess yes" over there, a "perhaps" in the negative, until he realized he had written a little more than a page. Many corrections, but . . . Well, we're still talking about disarray. All this in opposition to what had once been a genuine talent: the constant penning of letters to known but ghostly beings. On the other hand, he had Renata as an ulterior pretext, or an inanimate shape . . .

Sweating here.

Sweating there . . . hmm . . . Perhaps a cool breeze. An emotional titter.

Demetrio didn't want to make his life difficult, and at a certain point, without thinking twice, he made his way to the Presunción brothel in desperation.

He arrived only to discover that Mireya was otherwise engaged. The wait chafed. He wondered if her occasional client was an incomparable ejaculator, an unbeatable mover and shaker; a shot of rum in the meantime: ponderous sips, as if going slowly would help him bring order to everything he had made chaotic by prolonging his absence, now further prolonged—for how long? an hour or two? Sadly, two and a half hours went by . . . and there he sat. During this lapse he downed several more shots, three in all; hence a touch of blue-tinged giddiness, dragging him down, while he remembered Renata's sanctity ascending steadily toward that dismal ceiling of painted stars. Overhead, the blessed one in flowing white garments . . .

Overhead is the problem: inaccessible. The *ranchera* goddess spoke to him: *You won't see me naked until after we're married.* An immaculate and august edict, which though nonexistent the suitor already inferred because he would hear it in all its splendor if he visited the aforementioned: how long? Herein the knotty dilemma: it came down to the temporal (and geographic) distance, the gathering of steam to embark on such a vexatious journey. His annual vacation . . . not till August. Long months of indigence—still—so? There was largesse in the genuine if perhaps unwholesome proposition *Do you want to sleep with me?* And the predictable response, stamped on that dive's dark though dimly shimmering ceiling, those heights as artificial as any presumption that Renata, why not and to his absolute astonishment, would make: *Yes! Of course, I thought you'd never ask.* And he: *You really want to?* And she: *Absolutely! The only problem is that in Sacramento there aren't any hotels, so we'll have to do it in the hills. It will be beautiful. The desert wind will caress our skin. We should make love naked in the afternoon. I can't wait.* Nevertheless, the improbability, the demise of such an uncertain speculation, given that true (or enduring) love should be a battlefield. A feat or, rather, the expansion of a feat. A struggle so cruel and so prolonged that not just anybody . . . Then those words and the entire apocryphal scene falling onto the orange chairs, where those statuesque (now crushed) women were exposing the coarseness and wonder of their lower limbs, ready for . . . Extravagant payments. Nifty logic—eh? And Mireya: invisible, busy moving her own parts. She was taking her time because she was experiencing unprecedented pleasure—or not? Hence: another shot of rum? a perfectly good way to prolong one's patience. But no! and: what a pity! He could always betake himself to the other dive, check out La Entretenida. Departing in defeat but with his curiosity swelling. He left. First he paid, looking miffed. The best part was that he was no longer thinking about Mireya and much less about Renata, both had now become rearguard fixations. Symbols to return to later, at the risk of going loopy . . . Evil, good, vile twisting: here unhappy, there dramatic. Now for something new—much more expensive! The cover charge: almost highway robbery, and the prime attraction: suggestive lighting in a brothel with an abundance of foreign beauties. He was approached by women who did not speak our language well or who spoke it with unfamiliar accents. An improvement? These women were more aggressive. They sat down at his table without asking leave. He was obliged to say: *You, no . . . You neither. Go away! . . . I want to be alone . . .* The policy of the place came to light the moment he spoke those last words. No, he couldn't be alone. If he didn't hook up with one of them—sorry! he'd have to leave. The third one told him as much and a skinny waiter repeated it, a very short waiter with an arabesque forelock, who casually informed him that the entire cover price would be refunded if he decided to leave at once. A boon. A relief. At least, and—out of there! To his lodgings. To imagine Renata as she so divinely was (a sacred being—gorgeous! descending from the heavens and alighting on her feet—gently— for him alone!). To carry on, but not before he made corrections to the letter. Foreseeable wakefulness.

Insomnia's contribution: the risk of a hopeless muddle or the unlikely chance that all will flow brilliantly. It was difficult for Demetrio to find the point of deterrence, hour upon hour of toiling over praises as if he were trying to cram a square into a circle that was, in itself, imperfect; we must imagine the erasures, the sweats, the failure to descry any happy middle ground where he could assert his own importance and still strike a note of supplication where phrases such as "Really, believe me, you are the most beautiful woman I have ever met" or "What I wouldn't give to kiss the back of your hand" wouldn't demean him or, better stated, wouldn't make him the butt of Renata's perhaps concealed and scornful laughter. So as not to cram it full of lyrical treacle, the agronomist untangled the threads of his composition, written of course in such a stylized hand that it looked like a missive from another world, and set himself the task of recounting unusual anecdotes from his life, placing particular emphasis on his childhood longings and fantasies. He had once wanted to be a doctor: when he was young he played doctor with his friends; later, he dreamed of being a bullfighter and was enthralled by the idea, practicing alone with a bath towel while imagining an enormous bull approaching from a great distance. Oh, to describe the details of the snorting: the variety of noises the animal made: torrents of descriptive largesse, enough details to round out the tone and even a state of mind, and the diarrheic prosody of very long sentences. Albeit: effusive imbalance, to the extent that he filled both sides of ten pages and he still couldn't, no, who knows when. Then the brilliant unleashing, full of niceties (some fictitious, some truthful), seemed unstoppable until he was swept away by the monster of somnolence: galloping up from behind: horrors! may it be warded off till the final period be penned. He sought it. It was a strain. The signing off was a vulgar rapture. "Good-bye, my dear." Why "my dear"? What a subconscious! Still to come was the most arduous prolongation of his perfectionist—yes, that is what it was—integrity: to copy over with more calligraphic care the entire odd chorizo. Further corrections, increased frenzy: on and on, in spite of himself, knowing that dawn would soon arrive and with it the daily grind. In the end Demetrio didn't sleep a wink. Worse, he had no time to eat breakfast, either. Thus delirious, his mouth sour with fatigue, he forced himself to go (stumbling) to the orchard; he managed to remain upright for about three hours. Then he collapsed. We will not consign to these pages his period of repose in that tiny room crammed with tools, where his position could not possibly be horizontal. In the eyes of the peasantry in his employ, it seemed a bad omen: what's up with the boss? he had always been a model of industriousness. What's more, awaking quite giddy he casually stated that he was off to the post office. Almost in the blink and twinkle of an eye, followed by an almost improbably quick return that nonetheless did nothing to exculpate such inexplicable exhaustion, particularly in a person who regularly berated his subordinates with the oft-recycled harangue "Put a bit more backbone into it!" Catapult, now—a backhand? from them to him? No, not a chance. This strange behavior also included taking hour-long naps all week, well, a few seconds more or less; or rather: disorder, but also discipline. He took them at the wrong times: from eleven to twelve, smack in the middle of the workday. My, my! And his subordinates' deduction (take it as a glitch): their immediate superior was staying up late on a daily basis, or even: he didn't sleep, or very little, which was correct (for better or worse). In fact, to be precise, who knew. Who would know that he suffered all the stages of insomnia and that Renata was the true cause? Who would hear him lament: "I forgot to tell her the most important thing": his trip to Sacramento—when? surely in August? Who would watch him write a second letter, this one more informative . . . I? or the one who makes presumptions while prowling around? Or another who never errs? Let's go with the second, who was watching from who knows what angle as Demetrio wrote half a page with almost sickening care. A plethora of attempts. Why? As for his timid subordinates, they inferred nothing beyond what they could observe: the siestas and the subsequent parsimony at work. There was no second trip to the post office, not that week, nor the following. But here, on the possibly realer side of things, the evidence was evident: Demetrio had not had a chance to speak with his boss to find out the dates of his annual vacation in August, guaranteed by law—right? He needed urgently to know so he could tell Renata when he would come.

Nonetheless, the half page was ready as soon as . . . **The real is always paradoxical, for the view from angle x can never be more than a partial perception** . . . The meeting with his boss lasted an entire afternoon. The roughest part of the conversation is worth noting here:

"So, you have a girlfriend in Coahuila . . ."

"Yes, so it seems."

"You'll be able to see her only once a year, maybe twice if you use your Christmas break."

"I'm in love and I don't care if I can sustain the relationship only through frequent correspondence."

"Hmm . . . You are a good employee. It would be a terrible shame for you to leave such a good job for a faraway love . . . Hmm . . . It won't be easy for you to find another boss like me, one who trusts you like I do and pays you this well."

"Don't worry . . . For me, my job comes first. I am very happy working for you."

"I hope you don't lose your head, Demetrio: and remember, I'd even be willing to double your salary."

Bull's-eye! said on the sly ... A substantial raise, without his even asking for it, and this in addition to the not negligible 15 percent—already granted! A delight to hear! And the question: when would he get the raise? and the answer: as of tomorrow ...

As of tomorrow! Ooohhhhh!

Wow, how glorious love is and will be ... from afar!

6

Renata Melgarejo, a sizzling instance of decency on a grand scale, was the youngest daughter of Don Pascual Melgarejo and Doña Luisa Tirado. May this fact serve as a random point of entry that plunges us into the pure present, nor would it be too heavy-handed, at this stage, to recapitulate the outstanding episodes of Renata's childhood, for since birth she had resided in a space that took up a quarter of a city block and included an orchard, a fountain, a waterwheel, an enormous courtyard, and a chicken coop, in addition to an imposing building with six spacious bedrooms, a well-appointed kitchen and dining room, and only one toilet, with a cesspit, as rank as could be, quite as common at those geographic coordinates as was—and still is—the presence of a leafy tree inside the compound that gave it the right to be called home. That said, it is important to place Renata at the heart of an all-too-rigid family hegemony. She was looked after in ways that served her ill but were perennially in the service of spiritual purification that may have been worth tolerating; and, as for her predicament: her parents did not let her go out without their permission: because she was at the optimum nubile age; in order to dissuade the mischief of men; because beautiful women meet deplorable fates if they are given even the tiniest shred of freedom; these three arguments as well as a few more futile ones wrap up Renata's permanent circumstances. Her house was a lavish prison, ample and verdant, though with too few places to hide. It had also been thus for her sisters, who had had the good sense to marry outlanders: an affable escape to regions far from the family's rigid core, and—of course! the last remaining maiden should have similar good sense; she, the most beautiful one, for a thousand reasons; the young relic who had more than ten local suitors, all rejected *ipso* for it would tie her down to that suffocating small-town pettiness. For Renata, even the thought of living near her parents—nothing could be more intolerable!—for nothing would ever please those two creatures with their rigid notions. Vigilance, demands, reproaches, even when she was being courted by the best of men. Hence to marry and leave for a faraway place, as her sisters had done, and to their tacit advantage. One lived in Morelia, Michoacán; another in La Terquedad, Coahuila, a nearby hamlet, but nonetheless; the eldest was taken straightaway to Comitán, Chiapas; and another (the ugliest and therefore the kindest) was well-established with her large family in Comonfort, Guanajuato. Renata would be carried off to Oaxaca, still a wait-and-see, but the idea was already taking root, more or less, for Demetrio represented the highest aspiration, also for her parents, who after seeing his imposing and formal appearance, hmm—why think ill of him? They would find out everything, from *a* to *z*, from Zulema—who, really, was this prospect who had asked their relic to dance. Easy, soon, and then . . . Already her parents had subjected her to a basic interrogation. That Demetrio worked in Oaxaca but was from Parras, Coahuila; son of; relative of; that he was an agronomist; that he was saving up to buy a house there; who knows what the hell Oaxaca was, though the initial bonanza couldn't be all wrong. The prospect did not wear a hat, like those around here do. A distinction. A poor fit, though favorable, but . . .

It must be said that many outlanders visited Sacramento. Its fame was rooted in its unusual array of spectacular flowers, even though it was an isolated and somewhat tenuous spot. Where did those who came here come from? Remember Morelia, Comitán, Comonfort, La Terquedad. Remote outposts, and—how did the interested parties find what they found? A mystery . . . The amazing thing is that such goings-on had been going on ever since the town had been founded, hence Renata could not dismiss the possibility that prospects would hail from the United States and who knows what other foreign and remote countries. As it was, the exhibition of local beauties took place at church, on Sundays—what a nuisance and what a venue! because during the week was impossible . . . In her case, Renata's obstinacy coalesced at the wedding dance and from that moment on she dreamed morning, noon, and night about receiving the first letter from the agronomist. The more time that passed the more Renata had to refine her calculations: a month and a half more; three weeks more; four days more, or anybody's guess. Exhausting delight, which spread to other realms, and in the meantime the maiden carried out her domestic duties: mopping, sweeping, praying from time to time, what food might he like—ask him in a letter? All in good time, and in the meantime, these and other feeble proxies, though, when she thought about the missive, in addition to the expected flattery, some information. Hopefully Demetrio would let her know the date of his visit to Sacramento.

7

In, out; in, out; in, out. Rhythmic movements, slow and increasingly lubricated. Mireya had proposed an innovative position: she'd get on all fours to give Demetrio more wiggle room, that's right, for more commanding and prolonged wiggles, which also delayed ejaculation, causing pleasure to bubble up inside in a somehow more vehemently circulatory fashion. That was how they screwed and how they prolonged it. The bad part was not being able to kiss in that position, though they did enjoy a deliciously unparalleled slow pace that evoked a duet of moans of combined suffering and joy. The unfurling of the imagination: a creative surge that did not revert to directives. An effervescent scramble: yes and no, and a passing barely. Pleasure at the cost of precarious devastation, until Mireya proposed an even more tremendous game: fellatio, *Do you want?*—would be how it first was mentioned—*Let's! You can come in my mouth if you want.* Demetrio agreed, believing he would thereby experience the heights of sexual love, to him so modern—may the fun come in any shape or form! as if both were finally on their way to reaching rock bottom. He stood on the bed, swaying unsteadily, while she on her knees began to encircle the agronomist's gland with her tongue: deliberately suggestive. Then, in, out; in, out. A well-trained mouth. In classic fashion: a lot of saliva. Besmirched—down her front, conceptual? and so far away from any proper notion of decency. Nobody had ever done this to Demetrio, who for better or for worse experienced feelings of guilt. The idea of sin grew prodigious, even more so when Mireya, unexpectedly and with full oral penetration of said member, began to move from side to side as if denying everything, a maneuver that provoked Demetrio's immediate and prodigious ejaculation. Well, well! Her sublime swallow, which intentionally left some semen adorning the dark circle of her mouth; something like a thick whitish glob rolled down her cheeks, and his exclamation: *You look fine, woman, with that smeared on your skin.* All she could do was smile with pride. *It's because I love you,* she said. This was their gratification after so many weeks of absence. All good and fine. An outstanding experience! useful for a descent into normality, relaxed and breathy, silent, after such mutual, perhaps equitable, abuse . . . perhaps . . . What kind of double volley? Minutes later came their conversation, with an added dash of bashfulness. Sinful conversation, distended. They both seemed like caterpillars on the verge of transformation.

"So, my love, tell me why you haven't been to see me."

"I went to visit my mother over the Christmas holidays."

"Why didn't you let me know?"

"I didn't have time. She sent me a telegram telling me she was sick and that I should come immediately. My father died five years ago, and she lives alone, and . . ."

"You aren't lying to me, are you?"

"Why should I lie to you? What matters is that I'm here with you now."

"Where does your mother live?"

"Far, far away."

"Where?"

"In the south of the United States."

"Hmm . . . You know, Demetrio, I'm falling more and more in love with you."

"Me too."

"By telling you this, that I'm in love with you, I'm really admitting that I don't like this life in the brothel anymore. I want you to take me away from here."

"Where? I'm living in a rooming house. Soon I'll own my own house, though I haven't yet saved enough money for the down payment. Right now, I can't take you anywhere. "

"Get me out of this hellhole. I'm sick of being a slave to pleasure. I want to give myself to you, be faithful to you, have a family. I really will be a good wife and mother. I've never fallen in love before, Demetrio, but I have now, deeply. I love you. I love you madly!"

"Me too. Nobody has ever given me what you . . . Hmm . . . I promise to take you with me once I put the money down on the house. It won't be long, I promise."

"Really, promise?"

"I swear, and . . . hmm . . . I have to go now, but I'll come tomorrow so we can keep doing what we always do."

"Come back, my love, because it gets better every time."

To top it off, a long expressive kiss, that is: lots of tongue and lip action. Oh, let's just say that it became an enveloping spiral that aroused them anew and: a quick screw? Go for it! and, of course! an avid fellatio and other unusual positions in a mad and agitated dash, and let's take this opportunity to mention one detail: these girls were rented by the hour, hence the countdown. Mireya and Demetrio had already been together for three. Already the largest outlay ever. The second hour was double; the third, triple. The madam had already informed the agronomist of these fees, and only once before had they breached the two-hour zone. Only once! and you can infer the intense calculations, as well as their effect on habitual action. Finally, painless payments, rather, the resulting coldheartedness. Confusing—also—for Demetrio, who began to glimpse an obstacle, an enormous and very black one, expanding like a doubt that was taking its sweet time to edge its way over the cliff; like a long tape that would never break no matter how far it was stretched. Thinking hard in the taxi . . . The trip and its sparks . . . he would need to spell out so many and such complicated explanations and plan everything once and for all, yes, but—where would it lead? For instance: the house. It was yet to be seen if the agronomist wanted to buy it in Oaxaca, or where the hell else . . .

Not in Parras.

Not in Sacramento.

Better to wait, though the storm would continue to gather if he kept seeing Mireya . . . Fed up with explaining. Solemnity makes a mess of things. It never weaves in well. Better to peek into the most elemental things: become a wisecracker, whatever it takes, because after days of conjecturing, humor prevents the other from ever really penetrating one's own psyche. Humor is—would be?—a pleasant-enough defense, just misleading enough, in that it implies proximity while establishing distance. Life is—would be?—hilarious . . . This paradox must somehow be irrefutable . . . Intermittent and ambiguous reflections from one who didn't, as a rule, flesh out ideas as they occurred to him, hence the most precarious one could be the most efficient. And now to the praxis: daily experimentation with Mireya. At first he called her Bambi, as if to say "beloved whore." Demarcations: intentional banter, useful when she'd make her familiar demands: *Hey, don't call me Bambi*, whereby he could respond: *You should know that I'm a playful guy. I like to tease you, to make you feel how much I really love you.* Then, if she asked him: *How are things going with the house?* he could take a different tack by saying: *I'm thinking about buying a palace. You deserve nothing less—surely you must know that you have become a queen in my eyes?* Harmless snares. Strategies buried under obtuse explanations of cause and effect. Nothing explicit, thus harmony by employing the same measures love does to protect itself against the tedium of certainty.

Let us leave the anomalous lovebirds to their romps and pass in haste to Sacramento. Demetrio's first letter was in Renata's hands. A messenger boy, a mere child, brought it to her at noon, he being one of six local lads (about ten or eleven years old) in the employ of the post office. Doña Luisa Tirado watched the delivery of the missive from the kitchen. Theoretically, she kept cooking. She didn't want to appear nosy. She wasn't one to interrogate from afar. She didn't move, but her nerves . . . Howsoever that may be, let us try to imagine the daughter's mad dash: to find a place to hide; surely this the result of reflexive modesty, the desire to read unhindered. In her excitement she found a spot near the chicken coop, where she planned to bury the letter. First, the gradations of emotion provoked by perusing praise heaped on praise. Moreover, she appreciated the penmanship.

She savored it slowly.

The ample light falling on the sheets for an almost chromatic celebration. The ink as illuminating as the words. But the enchantment was broken when Renata saw her mother approaching with remarkably long strides. Busybody. Confrontation. Abusive . . . clearly no way to avoid the looming avalanche, because when she was still several paces away the doña brazenly asked: *What does he say? When is he coming? We must read the letter together.* That was the moment her daughter turned her back. She blushed, and, of course, the glimmer of a tear appeared in the corner of her left eye, a residue, to tell the truth. More questions ensued now from closer up, much more euphonic; utter nonsense. Moreover, let us note the dear lady's trembling fingers upon one of the bare shoulders of she who expressed what was all too well justified: *What you're doing is totally unfair, Mama! It's mine, and mine alone. I'm going to tell Papa!* Her mother removed her hand. The nerves of our impetuous fox showed signs of deterioration, nerves that clenched for a few seconds of silence only to reveal, finally, the all-powerful defense: *Your father supports me in everything. You have no choice. You must let me read the letter!* Resistance and cries: two weapons she used to hold the sheets, with brazen pressure, against her breast: Renata withdrew; if only we could hear without prejudice her whimpering and her *no! no! no!* Needless to say there was dismay on the part of her mother, who finally said she only wanted to know the date the nonpareil suitor would come. She still had a lot to read. So . . . we can infer . . . perhaps in the last paragraph . . . let's see . . .

May the information soon arrive!

The response: *Please. Let me read it alone, then I'll tell you.*

And the mother's (now sympathetic) retreat.

The thing was that once she'd finished reading the letter: no, there was no mention of a date. Renata's laments lasted a good long time, time enough to bury the letter and go moaning to her mother to inform her that no, no date . . . et cetera . . . Such a confusing medley of emotions, of defeat, when all was said and done. Renata's contrite postscript to Doña Luisa was frugal, of course! and now the counterargument was useful:

"You see!? You never know with these outlanders."

And other similar ones. More warnings mixed with further speculation.

"Don't you dare complain about me to Pascual! You'll only complicate things for yourself!"

Don Pascual had recently been quite down in the dumps, ailing. He had twice traveled in his truck to Cuatro Ciénegas to consult with the only doctor there, for in Sacramento there was none. Alas, what a nuisance! Twenty-six miles between the two towns. What's important to mention here is that the doctor prescribed an array of medicines, all quite strong, to be bought at the local pharmacy, owned by said doctor. But since Don Pascual refused to repose for even one hour during the day, despite his copious sweats and swoons, by two weeks later his condition had worsened. In the face of such fatigue he had almost asked for, he should clearly be spared the importunity of all that impending romantic nonsense, a profuse letter, delirium, longing . . .

Nonsense?

Or not?

Fortunately Demetrio's second letter arrived ten bitter days later. A rigorous half page, though one that brought joy and a date: *I will visit you on August 15.* Damn it, the hottest time of year. The trek through March, April, May, June, July, and then two weeks more still to come. Then another sentence, the necessary subordinate: the fumbling excuse: *My annual vacation begins on August 12 and I have only one week.*

Renata's quick glimpse: three days to get here, three to return, one day in Sacramento. Demetrio would stay at Doña Zulema's house. Summing it all up was easy: *If he's interested in me he'll make the sacrifice.* Nonetheless, a doubt, or rather, the future pirouettes of a doubt: will he really come? The situation presupposed an infinity of pirouettes, and to calm herself down, Renata, without giving it a second thought, informed Doña Luisa of the date, that the wait had indeed been worth it, or in any case—what to do? what to think? Now the old fox had her chance to play the part of the composed counselor:

"Write to him immediately. Tell him you will expect him, but don't be effusive with your emotions. Be friendly but cool. Don't reassure him. He'll like that. You'll see, it will make him more interested."

Talk about busybodies . . . In Oaxaca the training proceeded apace: in, out; in, out; in, out. And what about Mireya's fellatios: go for it! give it to me! on a daily basis, except Mondays, as we already know. The mechanics of peaking in pursuit of new peaks.

What was new was that Demetrio, caught in the undertow, had learned to lick her clitoris. Oh, such ideal reciprocity! His record was fifteen minutes, doing only that. What's *more:* he was constantly checking his watch while he licked away.

8

Nobody can predict when one illness might lead to another, nor when unexpected complications might arise from a given treatment. Sometimes allopathy completely cures a disease, ends minor complaints or prevents them; competent pharmacists, both dear and cheap, abound, and one must, indeed, take into account the patient's overall physical condition, none of which was done in the case of Don Pascual Melgarejo, an octogenarian unable to allay his ills: at issue was a vegetarian diet complemented by insipid dishes, some truly repulsive, others almost tasty, none that made him actually vomit. In any case he preferred the counsel of a local herbalist to the trips to and from Cuatro Ciénegas, a pedantic town, according to him, and this included the old folks and even the school-age children, so imagine what could be said about that town's portly doctor, quite expensive and, therefore, hyperbolic in his manners and his way of talking. All this to establish the seriously screwed-up situation of Don Pascual Melgarejo, who made an enormous effort to avoid the aforementioned expeditions, to wit: he overdosed on herbs, and nothing good was coming from it; he perspired, as we said, to excess, but he had no intention of surrendering, believing that if he did so, death—a rank and corrupt woman—would come for him at any minute, a notion he soon explained to his wife and daughter: *You can't trust the comfort of a bed.* Thus came the horrendous consequences, the diminished capacities, the failings that took a greater and greater toll, for example: his mood was down in the dumps, and his laments were nearly in the same lowly place: moreover, the need to learn, for real now, what urgency meant. As we've seen, he traveled twice to Cuatro Ciénegas on his own and carried out the doctor's instructions to the letter: the schedule for ingesting dose after dose of medicine; the correct nutrients, all in the proper proportions; everything except the repose. Never that: *If I lie down I'll die in the blink of an eye*, a verdict spoken in cavernous tones, unbelievable to Doña Luisa and Renata, who shook their heads in response. But his fierce obstinacy served him ill. One day among many he suffered a mortal collapse on the street, about two blocks from his house. Yes, alas! He was very dead—poor thing—nothing but a pile of rubble. A heart attack, as was later ascertained. Some local folks carried away that familiar corpse, which was, needless to say, deeply mourned by his wife and daughter. By others in Sacramento as well: professionally lamented and wailed with appetizing dread. Four days of mourning. Mourning in shifts. There were six of them—did he deserve fewer? Uninterrupted and melodramatic to the max, truth be told. As if these people were being paid for their painful performance, but no, not a dime, rather the result of pure ghoulish faith (if one may speak in such terms); rosaries that weary, wearied, would weary; by day, by evening, by night; a moaning mill that—oof! better not get too close. Zulema dropped by to offer her condolences and lasted all of fifteen minutes, then—the escape! astute; we have to assume the stench drove her away. So, to reiterate: a four-day wake, such foolish obstinacy because both Doña Luisa and Renata had to inform the four who were married. Telegrams. They had to come. The death of their father. And yes: they all arrived contrite, in addition to the woe of the rough road, accompanied by their husbands, also worn to the bone. Everything done properly, or at least in good order, the next step being to organize the open-casket funeral. Well, let's imagine the fond farewell wholly dominated by a stench akin to a dozen rotten eggs.

We won't talk much about the burial. This synopsis should suffice: there was a chorus of cries, over-the-top good-bye clamors. We'd rather mention certain events that occurred during the short respites from the wake. Sentences: written down one at a time by Renata, who left, then came, then left again, fidgeting in the room farthest away: her letter to Demetrio would not be long, half a page at most. But one sentence . . . and hours later, another, because she couldn't be away for, say, twenty minutes straight. Because her mother would reproach her if . . . Or rather: she left and came, and each time it took her a while to return to her task. Two and a half days to complete the concise composition, which will be summarized briefly as follows: Demetrio would be informed of Don Pascual's sidewalk demise; likewise, the period of mourning: three months of forced circumspection, with some easing by August. Renata used other words that surely pointed in the same direction. At the end were three semiromantic sentences: *It would be wonderful for me if you came to Sacramento. I need you now more than ever. But I have no choice. All I can do is wait till August.* And the radiant name—*Renata Melgarejo*—at the bottom of the page. The first letter she'd ever written was ready. But would Demetrio be able to read her handwriting? and if he couldn't? and if he could only sort of? She was not deft at the calligraphic arts— would practice help? We'd do better to highlight her emotional reserve. She wrote as if still listening to her mother's advice.

Here commences the give-and-take of a fraught conversation. A full-fledged family reunion. The first one to be held in the calm following the theatrics enacted at the graveside. Some spark would light up as they poured forth their ideas; the dining room had enough chairs for everybody: daughters, husbands, and Doña Luisa, who tried to talk about her future, in little bursts and a barely audible voice, poorly projected, which was understandable, considering her grief. The grief of a worldly woman who no longer had the energy of her better days, so that now—could she hope for a new life . . . with her daughter Renata as her sole domestic ally? At first she made mention of the eternal gratitude she owed her husband for the huge house she would count on forever: a prodigious appendage she could one day sell, though such extreme measures were not yet necessary, thanks to the large safe: this the bequest closest at hand. The difficulty: access, the combination to the lock unknown . . . no, never! it would be a waste of time . . . A secret Don Pascual carried with him to the grave. Such a pity! Alas! Though to view the predicament from a happier vantage, there was really no cause for lament. One of the sons-in-law, the brightest of the bunch, suggested they carry the safe to the roof and hurl it down onto the small patch of concrete in the courtyard, and then repeat as many times as necessary. The latch would have to give—it simply had to! A feat for the following day. There were more than enough hands, that is to say there were eight brawny men, all smashing . . . So—let's at it! right? Sons-in-law in action—all together now!—that's when they discovered a cement staircase; yes, with laudable foresight Don Pascual had had it built just six months before; it was narrow and had no banisters, for easy access: only sixteen stairs from the ground to the roof. Therefore the act of carrying the load up the stairs (beginning early in the day), then hurling it, and nothing, and again, and . . . Of course! Just imagine the sweating, the grunts and groans, the effort, each more lackluster than the last. On the ninth try—finally! The latch—yay! and out spilled the bills—yay! Everybody started counting. The evidence indicated that there was not enough for mother and daughter to live ad infinitum with a modicum of ease, or that there was just enough to invest in a modest enterprise: a restaurant: no! a grocery store, hmm, tick this off as one option; an inn, but for whom, the town had no tourism? Let's attend another family gathering held late in the afternoon, with chorizo and egg tacos topped with lettuce and tomatoes, indeed, and crowned (each to one's own liking) with a *guajillo*-citrus salsa. In the dining room, ensconced in a comforting cloud of oily odors, they continued to flirt with their fates. They had to come up with a business that would require neither too much toil nor lasting tedium. And they would all have to agree. Perhaps a full stomach would help: how about a stationery store? Not bad, though the understanding was that Renata would be the one to travel to Monclova for the merchandise, exclusively and comprehensively for the primary school, for Sacramento still didn't have a secondary school: maybe soon . . . who knows? A question of government policy, but did it really matter that much? So the discussion focused on Renata's duties, the troublesome train trips twice monthly to that nearby city, alone and obliged, moreover, to lodge at some run-down hotel because there was only one train a day. Then the hardship of carrying all those purchases in the boat and the horse-drawn carriage. But she declared that she was ready to make such a sacrifice in order to help her mother. What an idiotic or understanding daughter! Anyway, they would ponder the consequences all in good time. For now, the future for her and that worldly woman was a diaphanous glimmer.

The harsh clarity of the possible.

Under so-called control.

Though . . .

"Where did you hide the letter?"

"I will never tell you, and please forgive me."

This introductory dialogue was the first held between Doña Luisa and Renata when they finally found themselves alone. The rest of the gimmes and gotchas were some sort of increasingly heated verbal blather that didn't particularly distress either of them. Rather, both remained perfectly composed after an exchange of quips that translated into a hearty embrace; an exchange of vows to share a none-too-easy life. Gratitude and support: their forces united, as if by merging two mournings you could create one amalgamated spirit. From the mother, stalwartness for the remainder of her days, a determination to rise above her affliction, though it wasn't yet quite clear how; and, from the daughter, contingent mourning and its attendant longings. Demetrio's visit would be a detonation, but there were months yet to go. Moreover, that visit, which embodied so much hope, still lacked solidity when viewed objectively; it was, as it were, a mere hint of courtship: cloudy, uncertain, and in this sense, maybe Demetrio would disappoint her. On the other hand, if said creature turned out to be the true angel of salvation, and (God first and foremost) brought about the longed-for wedding and all the rest of it, there was also the possibility that the mother would go to live with them. In any case, all in good time, and in the meantime, a modicum of relaxation; only a modicum because for several days nobody lifted a finger to set the stationery store in motion. A merited enjoyment of the meager funds to be had. Sad enjoyment and almost silent. Convenient silence. Renata's scintillating strategy, for at a given moment she thought: *If my mother insists on asking me about Demetrio, I will offer her the reassurance that she will never remain alone.* And quite a lark to think of the three of them living in the same house, an idyllic and agreeable threesome anywhere in the world. Lest we forget: the wedding must come first. Future hyperboles that . . . who knows. A waxing and waning of efforts, stratagems, flutterings, resolve, all was yet to be seen . . . Et cetera. And an astute subtlety: Renata had rather poorly buried Demetrio's two letters near the henhouse, tossing fistfuls of dirt on top, a merely superficial layer, hastily accomplished. That's where she would bury everything that hailed from Oaxaca, or, more auspicious though also more complicated: at different spots around the vast domestic sphere. So here's a better plan: the excavations must go deep. Her own labor, or hire someone . . . No! she: in charge; she: without hesitation and with a pick and a shovel; she and only she and nobody but she.

9

August. Holidays. One week of resounding hustle and bustle: the agronomist must steel himself for the vexatious voyage that would, undoubtedly, wreak havoc because, doing the math, his stay in Sacramento would last less than twenty-four hours. Figure three days to get there, and, come to think of it, to make matters worse, a further abbreviation of the tryst: one hour for sure, two at most, three—impossible! then when considering that vibrant stock of minutes, he had to infer that the this and the that would be discussed, beginning with the most basic: *Will you be my sweetheart?* scorchingly brusque, and in the wake of some such response he would know what to say and how to behave. Always chivalrous, needless to say, though if his feelings were reciprocated, which he already took for granted, what emotional trifles would work to bind Renata to him very, very tightly. More of that later. For now Demetrio was compelled to calibrate the speed of the stopovers; such sketchy ideas formed in what he could see through the window of the small plane to Nochistlán: striations of clouds in the distance, and a splendorous bank of horrendous, gloomy clouds rushing by farther away. Thus he associated the tenuous white streaks with quick stopovers, whereas the woolly wads could represent the exasperation of an uncertain wait. But even if everything went smoothly, we're talking about a voyage of more than forty-eight hours. Thus his eagerness for the end.

The fifteenth. The promise. What would happen when they were face-to-face . . . It didn't help Demetrio to anticipate. Anticipation always labors under mistaken superstitions. Reality veers off, and surprises either fade or become monstrosities. So he tried to think about Mireya, her backside. Endless compendiums in her favor, to wit: discipline, the consequences of unhappy restraint, of seeing her only twice a week, explained away by being over-burdened by work. He imposed upon himself such abstinence be-cause the wench never stopped talking about how lonely she was, how they'd killed her parents when she was fifteen, how she had nobody in the world to protect her besides the madam and her bodyguards, how love was her only possible salvation. In short: frenetic protestations along with sex; recycled torments, way too much bother for the salacious agronomist, who, although he knew the whole thing reeked of smut, couldn't help but feel compassion. And love—misbegotten? To give it, to give of oneself with blind sentimentality. Sensuality tempted him; he believed through induc-tion that the wench was sincere, and while both were shedding tears, he came to the verge of the conviction that Mireya would be a magnificent wife and an exemplary mother; but the pressure, the problem that swelled up alongside that faint hope: *Wait till I have the down payment on the house. I swear I'll take you with me when I do.* That, memorized word-for-word, had to be repeated more than twenty times to his lover. For his part, he preferred never to utter those words again, for fear of lapsing into irritation. Because the two sentences were constantly making their appear-ance in his dreams. They seemed to be etched into a rock or howl-ing like an echo in mocking repetition from a distant dismal cave until he'd awake. A nightmare, followed by insomnia's hangover. Hence the change of strategy: tactful infrequency. A huge relief and the desire to become as well as to be: *Mireya, I really love you. Please understand that. I'm just asking you to be patient;* or even better: *I need only four thousand more pesos for the down payment. I'll have it in four months;* or the ultimate revelation: *I know exactly where we'll build our little love nest.* Falsehoods or clever ruses? She couldn't care less. Or so it seemed because one of the last times he was in her clutches, Mireya put him in check: *I want you to take me away from here once and for all. I'll go anywhere with you. I really love you, Demetrio,* and from him: *And what about the madam and her bodyguards?* Problem. Suspense. Retreat. *You're right, it's not easy to go up against those people.* The breadth of the suspense made any mention of their flight during the final fucks, thanks to the unforgettable fellatios, absent. Demetrio's triumph coincided with his landing in Nochistlán. The backside sliding out of sight just in time. The same went for one of Doña Rolanda's evening monologues regarding news of the founding of the Social Services Institute of Mexico. To provide the working class with free medical care. A benevolent government. The basic needs of the poor were beginning to matter, and—how great! She also said that they might soon build a hospital affiliated with this institute in Oaxaca. She read about it in the local newspaper and offered it up excitedly during dinner. As for the news itself—pay heed? believe? For Demetrio there was no news aside from what affected him directly. The world, or to be more precise, the country, or in any case, the trials, tribulations, and triumphs of an abstract Other mattered nothing to him, so he withdrew at that moment to his room—he remembered now with derision—; it was rude impudence. Better to be alone than listen to such idiotic speculations. Because any hint of abstract nonsense appalled him, even if it was of the pleasant kind. In that particular instance he caught only Doña Rolanda's vehement rebuttal: *That man is acting very strangely.* A trivial incident easily shirked. What else need he shirk? Good tidings. For on the eve of his departure he'd resolved things related to his job, all fine and good; to the satisfaction of his boss and his humble peasants. Already quite shrunken creatures and duly complacent, wandering around as if in a maquette placed

on some tile floor. A gale wind could flatten it: better it should! And
now the bus to Cuautla. The en suite. The inconvenience of traveling. Sleeping without resting. Lapses of reverie. Hopefully!

Nevertheless, he never managed to empty his mind.

Shreds of memories never quite settling.

Brief dream interludes that failed to break through the nagging
worry . . .

The indestructible: his money.

They'd doubled his salary. We have to add to this the 15 percent raise he'd received just before Christmas.

Which means he should have laid out the down payment for
the house. Something rather nice about this modicum of wealth.
But the piles of money coming his way were almost all going into
the bank. So it was.

And now for the most irksome part: the trip to Mexico City and
then to Saltillo. Two more stopovers: in Monclova and in La Polka.
Much hardship averted—it must be admitted—for they were all
tranquil events, yes, indeed, almost magical, due to the alacrity
with which they occurred. God was tending to him tenderly. The
many hours spent in the train were, in the end, an invigorating in-
terlude, a spiraling flow of repose. Even the boat trip across the
reckless river appeared imbued with the fantastical. The sun was
an emblem, almost soothing. Amazing! Not even the desert heat
put him out of sorts. Out, out, notorious monsters! Welcome, ye
angelical omens—were they pursuing him? Ah . . .

He carried four changes of clothes in his suitcase: one of me-
dium size, not too heavy. So the trip in horse-drawn carriage—the
glorious finale—was pleasant, despite the dust that accompanied
his arrival at Aunt Zulema's house. Sacramento—at last! after the
respite of two and a half days during which he could continually
reinvent himself.

Aunt Zulema's store: open and obdurate, it looked like a forg-
ery, an empty stage set, a desolate grayness from which the sub-

ject emerged ten minutes later, like a ghost, walking very slowly toward her nephew. Let's imagine the angle she espied him from. She was not a nearsighted lady, or rather . . . And he: a stunned contemplator, suitcase in hand, a statue, in principle, enjoyed by birds and insects because there were no passersby who stared and meddled. On the other hand (let us imagine her), decrepit solitude at three o'clock in the afternoon, until the embrace in the street took place. Then their conversation, interrupted to close up the shop—a cup of coffee! No! first the bathroom, as requested—oh, go on, then! And then again, a fresh exploration of the eagerness so akin to love that brought him here, and the news swarming with details about how Renata and her family were doing. His aunt was prodigious. Ah, her father had died a mere . . . *Yes, yes! I know, Renata told me in a letter.* Seems there'd been many letters over the past few months. Not many, only the necessary. The truth is, the conversation with his aunt was irritating him; she, so profuse and pigheaded, nerve-rackingly scratching away at the obvious. Despair in retreat, underpinned by an elemental defect in her hospitality: Zulema never offered him anything to eat, not a slice of bread, not even a cracker. Nor would she, and for him to ask . . . Demetrio chose to rise abruptly from where he was sitting in the dining room chair. Cut off. Get out. Clear his head. Sorry.

A parsimonious stroll that included the search for a tavern (how about some *carne asada* tacos?) and locating Renata's house: he would never ask his aunt, rather . . . it was more evocative to find it on his own. So he left. *Be back soon.* The town smelled of sweet marjoram. Odd. The evening heat was so extreme, it felt inhibiting; imagine, therefore, the savage sweating. Another wash, later, upon his return. Fat chance! There remained the fetters of haste. Everything the outlander would have to compress into distasteful actions: eating quickly and while sweating, everything seemed to be sweating: the walls, the trees, the tables, the food, the earth itself, and Renata's house seen from a distance, a rectangular delusion set against the barren doodles of the sky: a—humid?—counterpoint slowly growing dark. The house was located on the corner of the plaza; it was white. Not quite at ease, Demetrio wanted to sit down on one of the benches in the plaza. His proximity excited him, and more sweating ensued. Nonetheless, there was Renata lit by a naked bulb. A door was open. The respectable diva was a small thing in motion, her long curly hair was visible but not her waist and legs. Oh, such a paragon so eager to be a mother, hmm . . . tomorrow he'd be able to appreciate her fully. The store. His aunt had briefed him on the stationery store, and now that we've mentioned that good woman, let's assign to her, as the agronomist did, the task of informing Renata that the singular suitor from Oaxaca had arrived in Sacramento and what time would their date be, eh? Quite a favor. A matutinal task. In the afternoon, around five. Fast forward to the delight of she who would bathe and perfume herself like never before. Heavens! both must be presentable. But first aunt and nephew had to deal with how they would sleep. Not together. Why not? Well, just because! Yes, in separate cots in the open air, because of the heat; because Zulema had no fans . . . It would have been lovely to curl up with each other without sheets— dear me!—exposed to the fate of the regional breeze and the old woman's tremulous caresses: a fleeting fancy (not warranting a response) that wouldn't happen now—just because! Maybe later would come that irksome and dull indulgence. Zulema must have understood this, for she knew that with the morrow would come the declaration, the illusion . . . An illusion stitched with boredom: precisely what happened after a sordid morning during which Demetrio couldn't figure out what to do with himself. Then came the good part: depart well-groomed, counting almost every step. There was a script: he would sit on the bench in front of the door to Renata's house. The procedure described by his aunt, in turn described to her by . . . Renata would make him wait about twenty minutes: Doña Luisa's advice. *You've got to ride the high horse.* A means of increasing desire or, rather, artifice. That's why Demetrio didn't know about it, of course.

And, finally, the wait.

Zulema gave her nephew a bouquet of white calla lilies: the only thing she found in her neglected garden. The importance of an offering. But Demetrio got rid of the bouquet, tossing it into the bushes in the plaza. A mere ostentation prone to complications and what for. Words are better, however they come out . . .

But the wait . . .

Half an hour!

Damn!

10

"Go ahead! You mustn't wait."

"But if I do it . . . I don't know . . . It might be a mistake in the long run."

"Go ahead! Get pregnant! What are you afraid of? A child will bring you good luck."

Mireya wasn't quite as alone as she claimed. Once in a while she was able to shoot the breeze with a neighbor who had an abundance of work—thank God! She was a first-rate washerwoman, her name was Luz Irene, and she had a ten-year-old son who was in fourth grade (also thanks to God). A fact worth noting because it indicates a growing joy. Certainly we should picture a hovel of a room crammed with furniture, in the middle of which was a powerful radio . . . quite an achievement! On the other hand, the contiguous and ultra-run-down room next door—believe it or not—belonged to Mireya, who in spite of screwing so much (and with so many) still couldn't afford to buy an apparatus as showy as her neighbor's, not even a normal one, nothing, nor any furniture as shiny as that of the exemplary washerwoman, whose knowledge of life was vast, somewhat harsh, but quite judicious. A not-very-cheerful philosopher, or a dour woman well versed in the most elemental aspects of causes and effects. Or rather, Mireya should thank God she had her as a neighbor. They had spoken many times about the prospect of the tart's pregnancy. The harshest and most oft-recycled advice Luz Irene offered was none other than: *The child is what matters, not the father*, and the second, from a different angle: *We are human beings, but we are also animals.* The animalistic, held up like a key, opened doors onto all sorts of tender mercies. One could profit from people taking greater pity on a mother than on a single woman. At another point in the conversation Luz Irene, who with good humor scrubbed in her sink the soiled underpants of ladies and gentlemen, maintained that, as opposed to what most people thought (that is to say, "all the chumps"), a child never was and never would be a burden; that ever since she had become a mother she had been flooded with work, both from that concrete and unavoidable responsibility and from . . .

"But I believe in love, and even if it sounds weird, I believe in the couple."

"Love is a gift from God; He knows who gets it and who doesn't, just like He decides who is rich and who is poor, who ugly and who beautiful."

"Do you think a woman like me deserves to get married, have a family?"

"Only God knows . . . But you might as well try."

A wild and crazy imbroglio, the suggestion of fabricating evidence, a bubble that fate can pop or leave intact, especially regarding the birth of a child; once the outcome is there to see, that's to be seen . . . Who would take on the role of father . . . an archangel or an animal? Backward reasoning that led straight to numbing sorrow. For no matter what, the woman was the loser, this the premise and the conclusion. Another more telling premise, but also darker, was that Mireya slept with many men. Out of necessity, needless to say! but still . . .

"If I get pregnant, they'll throw me out of the brothel."

"That's the best thing that could happen to you."

"What?!"

"I can get you work as a washerwoman. To tell you the truth, I can't keep up with all I've got."

"It's a lot of scrubbing."

"Just look how well I'm doing. Any day now I'm going to open a grocery store. I'm already saving up. What's more, touch me. I'm strong. Touch me!"

To timidly touch that feminine musculature. To engage with the other's energy so fully, she could almost feel real sparks. Hence, vibrations whose emanations, indeed . . . Each vibration helped form a thought. A thread, too many threads: while Mireya was touching her, the request for a favor (that process) was forming in her mind, a brilliant and teeming favor: depraved and fortuitous, thus fragile. By the time the tart finally removed her hands from those imposing arms she had already formulated a plan she would now reveal: the request for a sacrifice of merely a few hours; this, her sentimental impudence: she asked Luz Irene to accompany her to the Presunción brothel, preferably on a weeknight; to remain outside watching, waiting, until Demetrio—the man in question—left. She belabored her description of him: tall and thin, young, about thirty years old, or a bit more. Nobody was quite like him, such an alluring presence. In other words, she'd hang around outside. It would be quite easy to distinguish what looked like a beanpole made of skin and bones though little of both, leaving the brothel, of course, and impressive—indeed! given that the Oaxacan world was peopled by the rather short statured, right? Then, after identifying him, to follow him, find out where he lived; the street, the address, the neighborhood—such vital information! A huge favor—she reiterated. And, the response? Luz Irene was mum. It was difficult to follow the wagging of her head, covered in an orange scarf: the horizon, the ground, her glances left and right, never eye-to-eye, or not yet, and in the meantime still not a peep. Finally, Luz Irene played around with the thorny problem of whom to leave her son with; someone trustworthy: but whom? A favor that incurs another favor and so on only to be subsequently settled: whom? She had a relative living in a wooded though squalid suburb of Oaxaca. Far out. Though it had been a long while since she'd visited her. She was a kind and generous person, hence: the language of persuasion: a manageable performance. Nevertheless, she went to see her to ask . . . Well, the favor couldn't be granted too soon. That was the first thing she expressed. An entire prior explanation that led to, *Yes, I'll help you*. Though . . .

"I think it's good for you to fight for what you want. I'm just not sure Demetrio will recognize the child and agree to be the father."

"Every time I see him he swears that he really loves me and that I give him what no other woman has ever given him."

"That's great, I just hope everything turns out the way you want it to."

The longed-for day arrived. With great prudence, the washerwoman took with her two bills of large denomination, suspecting that this favor might incur a hefty expense. There was a food stand outside the brothel that served pork belly with almost tenderized vegetables: a dish she hardly ever felt like eating. Its acrid smell like an ass widespread . . . What she did imbibe slowly were three bottles of cola. As she came upon the deplorable red-light district, she repeated under her breath: *Poor old hags*, and kept pitying the most unexpected details, thereby exalting herself in minor increments; she even spit out in a stentorian voice: *I am worth much more than all of this*. Anybody hearing her would have thought she was crazy.

11

Renata arrived at the bench aglow. She had walked ten yards. A moment earlier, Demetrio had announced his arrival with a fleeting gesture toward the open door of the stationery store. The house had three doors facing the street, and the diminutive diva emerged, without any hip-wiggling, from the one where three women and two children were shopping. Her lack of confidence was evident in her tentative steps. Was the future mother-in-law managing things from within?

The summit meeting, smiles from both in response to an invitation to be seated: he with suave gesture and she with spirited submission, perhaps strategic as well. Once settled, a tremulous silence descended. Demetrio noticed something strange about her: a natural face-to-face—no! why? maybe later . . . Doña Luisa had recommended that her daughter avoid looking her suitor in the eye, not at first, for that would be flirting. Hence, the modest damsel's eyes lowered in self-restraint, the pavement her only field of vision, a misguided sense of decorum rendering her like a wooden puppet, or to make her interest less obvious, among other things . . . The suitor, so as not to waste time, began to talk about the difficulties of traveling from Oaxaca to Sacramento. He said he had employed every possible means of conveyance: airplane, bus, train, boat, and horse-drawn carriage. He tried to be funny by mentioning that the only thing he had failed to do was mount a burro bareback and pedal a bicycle part of the way. Three days there and three days back. An exhausting trip. She expressed no awe, sitting there instead with her head bowed. Her response was, *Sounds exhausting! Was it?* which led Demetrio to immediately if fleetingly recall Mireya, who would have said: *What a feat! Congratulations!* and more admiring largesse. But with Renata it became quite clear that he would have to play the role of seducer, as if he were trying to sell her a product, and therefore, his task consisted of couching his intentions in syrupy phrases: another effort, this one really difficult, was the supercharged verbosity—indeed!—like swimming across the ocean: almost, or at least a lake or a rushing river, without yet knowing if this would please her. In the meantime the trepidant delight of the coming endeavors. The importance of everlasting love. The permanence of the joy of mutual understanding. A shared meaning of life. One bit of baloney after the other until he reached the longed-for locus: *Renata, will you be my sweetheart?*, using the familiar *tú* form of address, a subtle impudence she could not reproach, given the earnestness of the request, the very one she had longed to hear ever since that night of the dance, and she muttered: *Yes, yes, I will.* Forthwith: the impulse to grab that slightly calloused, white, and village hand: Demetrio in search of the sensual. Such a spur-of-the-moment outburst should have paved the way for this, at the very least, but the diva put a lid on it: *No, sir, not yet. I won't let you hold my hand until the next time you come.* Modesty placed front and center was such a gross hindrance. Oh no! to wait a year for . . . Too much desire. Too much punishment. He, scowling, put out, speechless. Her eyes weren't there to see his predictable reaction. But his silence was something Renata could interpret and thus she uttered this sentence: *If our courtship proceeds one step at a time you'll see that everything will turn out marvelously.* It will be, it is already, as if she overcooked love's certainty in order to appreciate, through longing, the value of time: if we understand love now as a sorrowful fabrication, now as thoughts tangled in dreadful constraints, and Demetrio, in the meantime, acting the role of the long and silent sufferer: exemplary? because if not, what claim could he make . . . that meant anything? No, only resignation, thanks to how quickly he found out that the first kiss on the mouth would be something as remote as the distance between the earth and the sun, their nakedness and his screwing her now light-years away. And as far as the hand goes, ah . . . During the dance he had already touched it, as well as her waist, and her hair with his cheek: a fleet and pleasing accident; but such modesty (now!) all in one burst . . . A courtship that delays in finding the license enchantment grants can transition with passion to the good parts. Restraint as nothing less than a circle swirling with deep water—right? Restraint: for months, years, a route that must go backward in order to go forward, and, phew! there came a break—an overdose of silence is risky—: Renata spoke about her father's death; the sudden change in the lives of two women who weren't used to earning their keep. She had to admit that the stationery store was not generating the desired benefits; the calculations had not been optimally carried out. A delicious (worthwhile) nut was being cracked open, with barely any cracklings of affection and trust that would allow Renata to boast about the hustle and bustle of that business challenge. The unexpected: biweekly trips to Monclova: the carriages, the sweats, endless hassles, brutal even down to the most unexpected details. Demetrio, as it were, played the part of the moved listener: so still he barely blinked as he heard a complaint that after reaching out suddenly contracted into a single idea: branches in one continuous curve: all that verbiage—out of necessity, and if not—by a beauty who kept her head bowed and began to cry— why? could it be from sudden joy . . . and if not, what? A courtship should be cheerful! or rather: future cheer; future long and soft kisses: a great subject for the study of sensations, and with the sudden release of the lips—cheerfulness at last! right? or not? In their heads—there?! *Ipso* her sweetheart asked: *Why are you crying?* and mechanically Renata answered: *Sometimes I'm quite a crybaby. You'll soon get to know me . . . I ask only that when you see me like this you don't pay any attention to me;* though where to look and what to say at that moment that would be appropriate: Demetrio tried. The surroundings themselves seemed discrepant: the trees in the plaza: witnesses, just like the little people in the distance: brute curiosity scattered about, which the suitor found intriguing, even more so upon seeing a young boy (head slightly bowed) just leaving the stationery store. Would he come straight over to the bench? It would seem so, because as soon as he touched Renata's arm, he practically issued an order: *Your mother says you should go home.* Renata jumped up as if spring loaded: *Goodbye, Demetrio. Write soon.* The end. So had passed one hour of sacred love. Not even time for her to ask him: *When will you return?* and for him to answer: *In a year.* Nothing, not even an encouraging finale, a hope-infused warmth. Nothing, then, except the parting of a sweetheart who had wagered her paltry pleasure on the clock. One hour . . . how dear. A disappearance that inspired growing desire. Nothing fascinating and unforgettable, or maybe a little, but—insipid? As he walked away her sweetheart thought about the three days it would take him to get back to Oaxaca. He thought of the hour—annual?—supreme and pale, a bobble melting into the distance. He thought about the stack of circumstances that would arise throughout the year, and to top it off, he had to find a nook in his brain for the idea that the sacred was unattainable. God was in a different sphere—likewise, true love, as was everything truly paradisiacal. Sex, on the other hand, a caprice. Ease at the expense of false loving . . . Pretense-sex, see-through-sex . . . But worthwhile love was nothing more than the dark and daring work of rodents, restraint, struggle—a nuisance or courage? Upon his arrival at his aunt Zulema's house, the strange suitor cut loose. He could hardly believe what he had just experienced.

The aunt—no need to guess—made herself comfortable: listening with lively astonishment . . . Yes! with a sarcastic look on her face she would listen to a story imbued with exasperation, and nothing he came up with could unhinge her psyche; a psyche quite seasoned in such scabrous affairs; an old maid's psyche that surely did not reel in anticipation of hearing graynesses over blacknesses and who would offer her point of view—knowingly—as soon as her nephew unloaded. Half an hour of contradictiousness: a rude concoction of rage and desire, and the culmination—here goes!: *You're going to have to work very hard to get what you want from that woman; it wouldn't make any difference if you lived in Sacramento. That's our way around here. I could tell you a dozen love stories from this region, and the most thankless thing about them is that they are all the same. You'll have to decide for yourself if you are going to stick with it or give it up. What I can tell you is that once Renata becomes yours, she'll stay yours forever. She will never marry another even if she is widowed, even if he looks exactly like you. Understand that! She'll be faithful to you for as long as she lives, and what's more: it will be eternal love. She'll put up with you even if you make her suffer. I swear to it! You could be a drunk, a murderer, a thief, even a deadbeat and a grouch, she'll stay with you no matter what. But in the meantime, you're going to have to suck it up.* All that was some sort of poultice, a conceptual compress that would be dangerous to remove. A fairly heavy flagstone, a simile of unconditional love. A fruit that's never too cloyingly sweet. Or also a torso taut with muscles and veins, or a stigmata that never decays. But most evident was the level of motivation Renata had managed to awaken in Demetrio. Having raised her bar to almost improbable heights, she knew that by not letting him even touch her hand she'd opened a gaping space of uncertainty. Perhaps that hour of terrifying proximity was the first and would be the last between them. That is, Renata was the one playing with the highest stakes, by far, because an outlander with those qualities, especially considering the trip he had made from the south of the country to see her, not the act of an ordinary creature, no, as it turned out an adventure without a what or a wherefore. Let's consider her, what she did after they said good-bye: she dashed off to pray to her private saints; she kneeled, mumbled lengthy entreaties that lasted more than an hour. Renata wanted her knees to hurt, some penance she must undergo, and—what the devil was she praying for? what? after having agreed to be, let us say, a hypothetical sweetheart and in the end feeling lonelier than an archangel—alone! on the other hand her mother's demands: which would only increase if Demetrio returned. And to return, for him . . . would it make any sense? Perhaps . . . The sad part was the year of reticent love still to come: a year of letters—how many changing plotlines? and in them she'd express the passion that could not be confessed in person; still to come: the immediate difficulties: Mireya with open legs; Mireya and her unique fellatios; Mireya letting herself be eaten; Mireya sweeping the floor and singing sweetly; who knows if a whore would be capable of giving him the good kind of love; still to come: getting her out of the brothel and taking her to live with him—where? that possibility, et cetera . . .

Twists and turns that set things straight. Theories that slowly run their course. Edifices left half finished. Margins of error when making a decision. What's incomplete versus what's finished, when finishing is a cruel detour. What conscience dictates: certitude or a ruse . . .

Demetrio fell asleep perplexed, he woke up perplexed, and Zulema knew it. In fact, she had the tact not to push harder on the subject at hand. She knew that her opinion had sounded a bit too decisive, more like a verdict. It was he who subconsciously repeated, after waking up, the words that for better or for worse had bored into his spirit: *You could be a drunk, a murderer, a thief, and even a deadbeat and a grouch, she'll stay with you no matter what.* To memorize this concept of salvation: a year-long task; a reductive duty, with thousands of reverberations. At that moment he had said: *Thank you, Auntie, for your advice.* Next: each to his or her own: she to the store of her devotion and he to embark on the dreary trip back. Here we must mention that Zulema did not offer him breakfast (insensitive hostess), though she did place her aged hand near his mouth:

"Kiss it!"

"Why?"

"Do it! It'll make you feel good."

"I don't see the point . . ."

"Come on! Don't be a fool. I know Renata didn't let you hold her hand."

"But you are not Renata."

"Pretend I am. Take my hand and kiss it."

Without knowing what he would get in return, Demetrio obeyed. He became a bemused kisser of wrinkled skin. Wrinkles that inspire tenderness. A warm sensation so similar to . . . and after continuing to kiss it slowly the depraved suitor stuck out his tongue and licked it lustily. It seemed like an obscenity, but then—ah yes! to lick and lick and lick the pith, so much saddened saliva, and in such high concentrations. The kiss lasted a whole minute. It could have been longer, but Zulema pulled her hand away and said:

"Now you can leave at your ease."

And Demetrio left with a bit of a cramp.

12

Now to Doña Rolanda: the befuddled welcomer. Let us imagine the arrival of a man who is falling apart: Demetrio and his flaccid height (collapsing): hoping to sleep for twenty-four hours, but . . . *A woman came by for you.* It was Sunday. Work tomorrow. His need to recuperate made him averse to hearing any nonsense. Please! The surprise came in stages, until it bored into his very core: certainly it was Mireya, though . . . ugh . . . Mi-re-ya?! the lady pronounced the name . . . How might his magnificent lover have discovered his domicile? In the meantime, to avoid second- and third-hand information, unlikely guesses, twists and turns—so many!: the lady attempted to accompany him (wordily) to his room, but halfway there Demetrio stopped her: *Listen! I am exhausted. Maybe we can talk in a couple of days.* Doña Rolanda was offended by her lodger's scorn. Did that matter?: perhaps in the end it would. However, just as he was about to fall into bed like a rotten tree trunk, Demetrio muttered one final sentence: *This has gone too far.* The following day he did not go to that dive, nor did he eat breakfast at the lodging house. Work. Pending issues. Gnashing his teeth against whatever he happened to eat. He ate green tamales in the market of Oaxaca. Two breakfasts—do you hear?! Avoid Doña Rolanda—disgusting! a torrential problem, and—enough already! Not till Tuesday afternoon, relaxed and ready, go to face her he must . . . Mireya, of course!, though . . . first, enjoy her . . .

After making love with fury and imagination, it would be unsuitable for Demetrio to unleash a barrage of questions, especially considering that Mireya hadn't uttered a word about her visit to his rooming house. Spent after achieving an extraordinary orgasm, she began to effusively caress her man. Her caresses felt more like clumsy tickles: giggles or pure joyous nervousness that, oh! *Wait a minute!* A form of distraction—triumphant? What was coming could be brutal . . . and in fact it was . . .

"You came by my place. How did you find me?"

"Do you want me to tell you?"

"Of course."

"Well, you see, the last time you left here I asked a friend to follow you. The next morning I went there, and the landlady told me you weren't in Oaxaca."

"What gave you the idea to do that?"

"Because I want to live with you. I've made up my mind."

"But I don't . . . not now anyway."

Such things catch fire, then flicker. To each of Demetrio's negatives there rose from Mireya a new and affable perspective. She exhibited a red-hot wit, despite her troubles and her panic; wit spiced up with nicknames such as: *my peach, my melon, my plum,* instead of *my love* or *my life;* fruits, it would seem, that do not ridicule. And though Demetrio tried to slither troutlike out of her grip, something, some sticky residue, remained on the thin skin of those palms, as it were, but so it was.

Let's offer some prime examples so that we can penetrate the very heart of this knot: what if she went to live with him at the rooming house . . . *No, that's impossible, Doña Rolanda rents rooms only to single people;* so he could rent a small apartment . . . *No, because I'm about to put the down payment on the house;* so in the meantime they could go live in a hotel, even a run-down one . . . *No, because it would be a foolish expense;* so he would tell Doña Rolanda (it was to Mireya's benefit that this name had been

revealed) that it was a matter of extraordinary circumstances . . .
*No, because she has very strong opinions, she is way too obsessed
with the rules she has made;* so he could slip her some money
that would change her attitude . . . *No, but . . . maybe . . . I don't
know . . . it's a matter of finding out how much she would want,
though I'm sure she would agree for you to stay with me for a
few days, two, three . . . I really don't know;* so she would go
in person and ask her . . . *No, not that, definitely not.* The esca-
lating propositions had surely reached their peak, whether out of
exhaustion or the curtness of the agronomist's replies, but what
Mireya did manage to descry was the image of a narrow path and
the course she had to take. Possibilities would pop up along the
way . . . The remarkable part of this whole hullabaloo was that
she hadn't had to mention to her lover that . . . well, let's see . . .
The following is what was tacit: she wasn't pregnant but she could
drop that categorical fallacy on Demetrio and, depending on his
reaction, set things straight and—set him straight! which would
be . . . well, let's see . . . set it straight? The pending invention, as a
last resort. An entire artful tale that she wove when she was alone,
and here we have it (let's see): it starts from the (truthful) idea
that at that dive, Presunción, prostitutes were not allowed to get
pregnant; if they did, they got thrown out; if ever there arose the
bizarre circumstance of somebody getting married, Madam and her
bodyguards, even the entire brothel, would attend the wedding (a
flowery falsehood), so such a celebration—civil, of course! for obvious reasons—no, no wedding in Oaxaca, though perhaps a neigh-
boring village . . . thus concludes the improbable; Mireya, however,
still counted on a barbaric fallback (a falsehood that bears fruit):
if Mireya got pregnant and the stud effected a foolish escape, the
bodyguards would pursue him and give him a thrashing, but not
before soliciting assistance from the police: sooner or later, but
effective nonetheless; that is: Demetrio beaten up, and even—
why not?—castrated: indeed! poor thing! not that; tell him—what

for? keep it in case there was some fervent refusal, or if Demetrio stopped coming to the brothel, then—indeed!—the search would be extensive, as she said. Anyway, this murky fantasy was confessed in detail to Luz Irene, who knew for certain what she had already intuited: Mireya was no fool, nor was she a pushover. Never! And the brunette's consummate charm was revealed without restraint. If only we could see the way she swayed as she walked . . . Two such delectable days in the brothel and outside her room. She wanted to be seen by one and all. As if that was what she needed! Two days, and then on the third . . .

Mireya arrived at the rooming house at nine at night. Demetrio was there.

First the confrontation with Doña Rolanda.

No, she couldn't come in, because she was a stranger, but: *I'll tell Mr. Demetrio that you want to see him. Wait here outside.*

Demetrio arrived frightened, confused, and for good reason. They held a long conversation outside.

Problems. Rejection. More problems.

Mireya had no choice other than to tell him about Madam and her bodyguards (those we've met), the beating (to be avoided, by any means necessary), and even the Oaxacan police force. Could it be that bad?

In the face of such a staggering description Demetrio had no choice but to speak to Doña Rolanda. He was bursting with fear. The situation was (to tell the truth) one of force majeure. *Wait for me out here. I won't be long.*

A discussion with the lady of the rigid notions . . . useless to try to persuade her. But when he showed her the fluttering bill: a bauble in a light, uplifted hand . . .

Aah!

And only for a few days . . .

Ooh!

The lovers lounged in the room whose foremost novelty was the improved odor. It just might have been the first time any two beings had practiced the act of screwing there: within the confines of rented respectability, where there was an abundance of saintly idols made of clay and porcelain, and a picture of *The Last Supper*. One must, in this respect, mention guilt. For as soon as the two locked themselves in the room, Doña Rolanda knocked on the door. She was carrying a large bag. In it she would place all those figurines who were, to her mind, somehow alive, though she left said picture. It seems that Jesus Christ and his apostles were so thoroughly engaged in their repast and the company they kept that they wouldn't have time to watch the disgusting things Demetrio and his lover might do. Doña Rolanda's act was quick and silent. She did ask permission to carry out what she considered "a liturgical and appropriate act," in her words, and: "Excuse me," and: "I won't disturb you again." The saints: displaced, as to *The Last Supper*—what can we say?: an act of carelessness and, indeed, partial guilt. Increasing guilt, because at night she heard the lovers' savage grunts—sex maniacs! Her curiosity to hear somehow connected with her compulsion to count three times a day the incredible sum Demetrio had paid her. Guilt-ridden sex . . . within . . . hmm, only in part, for Mireya had turned *The Last Supper* to face the wall. She had done so as soon as she stripped. Demetrio, for his part, after observing the maneuver, smiled but also crossed himself. And now, finally, without further ado, they went at it; during those days of plenty they enjoyed each other only at night. Let's imagine the agronomist at his job, from seven in the morning till five in the afternoon, and she locked in the room, getting all tangled up in ideas about how to finagle an almost fantastical felicity. She didn't want to be seen, either by Doña Rolanda or the other lodgers; and as far as being observed by passersby on the street: well, as few as possible. Even when she went out to get provisions she tried to scurry back, racing at great speed. No breakfasts or dinners in the dining room: well done! They clearly came to a mutually convenient agreement. They clearly shared the dregs of guilt.

We could say that Mireya and Demetrio's fears were growing by slathers. He knew that he couldn't keep working in the orchard, that his Oaxacan chapter had come to an end, that he was on the verge of fleeing with his lover to an unknown locale. Life as a couple—guilt ridden! and, bountiful! and, sinuous! and all the rest. This was the mischief happenstance makes, the unexpected arrangement destiny had handed him out of the blue: to live perennial sex to the hilt: screwing in the morning, perhaps at noon, in the evening, and in the middle of the night, and the ever-turning wheel of continual consent: oh, undulating tenderness! the never-washed-nor-aired-out filth, and of course the most plausible theory always obviated: that this was perchance the devil at work, but God in turn was elbowing his way through. He mentioned all these avatars every day to Mireya, who, for her part, declared her mettle three times: *I'll go wherever you take me*, and also more than three times added that if they stayed in Oaxaca things would go very badly. Just knowing that they would be looking for her because she'd left her job. Madam knew where her room was and, what was worse, her friend Luz Irene, though Mireya was sure she wouldn't reveal a speck of information. Hence the most dreadful conjectures: the bodyguards, the police, the supposed furious efforts of the ongoing pursuit. And at any moment—poof! Demetrio told her he would go to the bank to withdraw his money so that they could run away. If only they could leave tomorrow! Money in hand for the down payment on their love nest. A nest far away, of course. They would be left in peace if they lived in some border town, but the crowning effort would be to cross over to the other side, by any means necessary and as soon as possible, and there find a new reality. *Why don't we go to your mother's? You told me she lives*

*in the south of the United States. You ought to introduce me to
her.* Demetrio had made a mistake by mentioning that migration,
he hadn't remembered that . . . When he told her . . . Who can
know!? . . . And in that (induced) effort to dig up a name of the
town where she lived—did you gather as much?—what would he
invent to answer Mireya's insistence? That it was near Laredo,
Texas: with a difficult name to pronounce in English: a salad of letters all crammed together like sardines, that starts with an *f*, and at
the end there's a *t* and an *h:* a teensy place located . . . let's see . . .
about fifty miles from Laredo, you can get there in the blink of an
eye. Demetrio in checkmate or around the bend. Nonetheless, the
two of them would go there: the only place possible?! But before
that he, right now, to the bank. Not to work. Now to disengage.
Now to take the step, now to quit his job, as she had done . . . The
agronomist went out first thing in the morning to buy a suitcase
he already knew must be neither too big nor too small but soft,
yes, to carry—always risky—the banknotes. Mireya had wanted
to go with him, but: *You stay here. It's better that way. I won't
be long.* A logical fear arose: she expressed it, keeping to herself
the core doubt that had been growing for the last two days: what
if Demetrio took off with the money and left her in that genteel
environment, like an idiot?

Of some small comfort was: *I am also very frightened, maybe
two or three times more than you. We don't have much time left to
get out,* and he promised and swore to the ensemble flight, placing
love above all else. The seal of an excessively tongue-y kiss must
have meant a lot to Mireya, who, just in case, turned the picture
of *The Last Supper* back around. Then: intrigue and lassitude for
a man who could not set anything straight in his head, decisions
ricocheting, running roughshod over ideas about doing what was
right: Mireya had won out over Renata because she gave herself
without apprehension or restraint. The agronomist did confront
an obstacle at the bank: he couldn't withdraw his money: it was

a fixed-term deposit without any kind of flexibility or exception. Banking's inherent rigidity. Then his emotional theatricality came to the rescue: that his case was extremely urgent, an instance of force majeure, et cetera, and his almost tearful pleadings, almost kneeling, his palms pressed together as if in prayer: evil demons, those bank employees—utterly? and his tortured insistence paid off after forty-odd minutes, when one of them said that they could give him his money if and only if they subtracted the accumulated interest: *That's fine, give me only what I have deposited, but give it to me now, and in cash, please!* Next step: the agronomist opened his bag, which looked a bit like a briefcase because it was stiff around the edges, though with an air of something special: a modern object, brown and expensive.

Counting the money in private. Making bundles of a thousand pesos each, small change, in the end, but, to focus on the scene *de occultis*, the stacking of one bill atop another was seen by Demetrio as a mortification, the likes of which he had never felt before, as if he were closing one long chapter and opening up another even longer and more indefinite. So it would be from the very first moment he went out into the streets carrying that strange suitcase . . . The risk of being assaulted . . . God forbid! No, why entertain such terrible thoughts? And thereafter the possibility of being robbed would bubble up throughout the trip north: on the airplane, in the bus, on the train. But, to change the subject, he would not go to Parras even to save his life: a destination he lopped off from the start, like many others . . . Saltillo: cut; Sacramento: cut; Monclova: cut, and, while he's on a roll, how many more? Suddenly he espied as if out of the corner of his eye a place like Guadalajara: a luminous destination? During his hasty return to the rooming house, now with the bulging suitcase in hand—which actually excited a fleeting curiosity among certain Oaxacan passersby—he began to glimpse the dreary prospect of the voyage west. A Mexican west he did not know, vast and colorful on maps, a mystery host to an endless array of exclamation points, and even a sudden exclamation at odds with itself, a kind of dismay, because under a westerly wind the trees swayed, twisting and flattened against the facades: it was a gust, rising and falling, hair-mussing, a flight that carried neither garbage nor the infelicitous gliding of birds, and he associated the thought of flight with the airplane ride to Nochistlán, the daily one in the early morn, hence he and Mireya could not leave for the airfield that day but rather . . . When the agronomist reached the room where his lover was enjoying a siesta belly down: alack! he had to wake her up, for this was the ideal moment to depart. She, still half asleep, ran her fingers through her hair and said she was ready to leave at once; of course she saw out of the corner of her eye that shiny suitcase: the evidence . . . don't even ask . . . the money—finally! for if not—why the rush? hence, compressed wealth; hope stuffed into a rectangle that perhaps in the future would open, love—eh!—transformed. And the sudden prodding: *Let's go!* Demetrio exclaimed, and then added quickly: *This is all I'm taking with me. I don't want to carry anything else. Let's go!* Mireya had a bag with long shoulder straps. Two changes of clothes. She had left behind her meager belongings just as Demetrio would leave his, and herein we see moderation at two in the afternoon. Anxious yet stealthy steps. Why pay the rent or anything else, for that matter! More than ever the street meant total freedom. It would seem—fortunately—that Doña Rolanda was doing something of great importance in the kitchen—her back to the stampede? which was executed, finally! The lovers immediately caught a taxi as if thereby gaining direct access to something that approached a miracle. Destination: any old hotel on the outskirts or, better, the one closest to the airfield. In a trice they found a run-down hostel, whose only advantage was its proximity: less than a mile away, walking distance first thing in the morning . . . Let us say they copulated that night. Urgent frenzy that felt like juvenile mischief. Then came their dawnrising and their flight.

Part

Transfers

Two

13

"Mama, have you ever thought of selling this house and going to live in a city?"

"Is that what you would like to do?"

Two steaming mugs of *café con leche* awaited the slow delectation of Renata and Doña Luisa, though they, as if afflicted with tics, kept picking at the sweet rolls; most of the crumbs were ultimately ingested, though some remained strewn, like sown sediment, across the tablecloth. In the center of the table stood the basket full of said rolls: *plomos*, *conchas*, and *pelonas*. A warm afternoon repast weighed down with worries.

"It's just that in the last three days not a single customer has entered the store. There are fewer and fewer people in Sacramento."

By 1946—the year in which we find ourselves—Mexico was cobbling together the beginnings of systematic industrialization. The working class had emerged, and the exodus to the cities of people with vision had become a daily occurrence. Some areas, previously agricultural yet substantially populated, grew anarchically in a few brief years, as did those already dubbed urban. The phenomenon seemed unstoppable, even though many people still clung to the rural and, even more tightly, to small-town life. In Sacramento, as elsewhere in the region and the nation, hordes of workers flocked to nearby industrial centers, buckled down under rigid schedules, and came and went between their jobs and their

quiet hamlets on a daily basis; others, perhaps the majority, resisted, for the simple reason that urban life would drive them mad.
One could say that such a shift was akin to a purging, drop by
drop: some choosing not to uproot themselves to seek their fortunes, preferring to wrestle with the inherent limitations of village
life rather than get enmeshed in the alien concept of urbanization.
Be that as it may, the march toward industrialization gave rise to
endless job opportunities, and commercial diversification grew
like a circulatory system of unpredictable proportions. In the cities and large towns, the demand for labor was outstripping supply.
Manpower was in constant demand, but . . .

"Don't forget how competitive things are in the city. It won't
be easy for us to get by."

"It's just that I think . . ."

"Remember, we have the only stationery store in Sacramento.
It's the first time people can buy school supplies for their children
right here in town. You'll see, our clientele will grow with time."

One year or two: how much time does she want? And meanwhile, sales continued to plunge: whole weeks of utter idleness,
standing patiently behind the counter without so much as the
threat of a mother or child approaching. We should say that mother
and daughter adhered to unswerving principles: they would never
try to lure in a customer . . . Their counter was nothing but a table,
like any other—an innovative concept? By the same token neither
amused herself spinning in circles in the swivel chair designated
for the one on duty. The establishment looked drab and forsaken;
it exuded an affable, even romantic, rigidity. A set order: necessary:
because . . . Renata and Doña Luisa became caricatures more than
characters, for (right from the start) they had established a system
of turn-taking: two-hour shifts, tinged with annoyance due to the
excessive calm, though the relays were always punctual, right up
till closing time: watch in hand, at precisely seven in the evening,
never a minute later. Once that was all over, the fun part began:

sweeping, mopping, cooking, and, in Renata's case, in the days following her tryst with Demetrio, shutting herself up in her room to try her hand at penning a letter; at first there were but fragments, snippets of paragraphs, sentences strewn about; not to mention great pains taken over her penmanship. To tell the truth, she embarked on the task of writing Demetrio a long letter, but her corrections were so copious that she was obliged to start over again and again, each time laboring harder than the last, particularly with the explanation Renata presumably owed her sweetheart for having acted like a nun. Turbulent days composing: page after page dedicated to a plotline whose contradictions were exposed by the tiniest mistake. The extra care she took with certain concepts, and the additional aggravation of having time pressing in on her—for come what may she had to relieve her mother—led to a series of inevitable interruptions—watch in hand—just when her inspiration soared . . . She spent more than two weeks composing the letter (a total of seven two-sided sheets). It was distasteful to have to justify a philosophy of decency when what she most desired was to discuss the sexual arousal that Demetrio, unintentionally, had provoked in her with a light brush of knee against knee during their tryst. But no, not that, better to withhold, understood as the optimal method to achieve victory, and at that moment, a lightbulb went on!: she should go talk to Señora Zulema, Demetrio's aunt.

At church. On Sunday. Perhaps by happenstance. And if not? That's when another lightbulb went on: take advantage of her trip to the post office—it was a lot of work to fit her bulky amorous discourse into the envelope—and stop by Zulema's house. Her calculation: two hours was plenty of time, and this was her opportunity:

"Mama, I'm going to the post office to mail my letter."

"Don't be late."

"I won't."

"Don't you want to let me read it before you put it in the envelope?"

"Mama, it's none of your business . . ."

A crumb of rebellion and—three cheers for her! Which didn't mean she was in any way loosening her fetters, although Renata was now convinced that continuing to live in Sacramento was like being hurled into a pit of despair, a living death. In the meantime, the letter, the anticipated reply: days, weeks: the slowness, the timeless nature of her solitary chores; in addition, and in passing, she considered herself a pure soul trapped in a huge house and the world beyond it, where she had no chance at all of remaining anonymous. People thereabouts would somehow discover that on a particular date the beautiful (and diminutive) maiden had made her way to the post office to mail a letter to her towering beau and that, in consequence, problems had arisen between her and her mother due to the simple fact that she was in love with a man who still hadn't shown the stuff he was made of; that the stationery store was a total failure and that at any moment the money from their inheritance would run out; as well as other, more insignificant deductions, at which point, after mailing her letter, Renata betook herself to Doña Zulema's. She was seen, and hence the psst-pssters—what else!—with lots of loose tongues. Two faces, a single surprise (raised eyebrows and gaping mouths): in the aunt's grocery store—also customerless—: Aha! The visitor asked three questions, and the sole response worth mentioning is: *Don't worry, Renata. All I need tell you is that my nephew Demetrio was quite eager when he left. You are now, to him, a temptress, and a great ideal. Now, now, just give me a hug, oh, please!* A frontal, affectionate, and fulminating embrace, all viewed from afar! Yes, indeed! Ooh! Such a muddle of tenderness . . . In the end, Zulema was the one who disengaged in the nick of time: well, well, off you go, and may you go in peace. The shorter woman's puffed-up return. Ambler. Beauty. Dignity on the march: recycling (good judgment worked in her favor) a sentence that had to have been a boon: *I am a temptress for him and a great ideal.* Half true, half false, but who cares? The essence would keep churning away, way down deep, and the only bad part, of course, would be a long lapse before Demetrio's response . . .

In 1946, Sacramento had no telegraph service. How long would it take for this miracle to occur?

14

A very elaborate kiss midst formless gray clouds. The small plane tossed about as the pilot, feeling responsible, steered in vain. Its rising and falling was astounding, as was the tongue and lip action of the fleeing lovebirds, who kept up their mutual exploration rather than disengaging out of fear: for a mere moment, but no, not even that, the opposite: Demetrio began caressing Mireya's legs and breasts, to which she responded by zeroing in on the site of his member and inundating that area with a flood of caresses: such alacrity!: in full view of the astonished adjacent passengers, who were—how can we put this?—betwixt and between nervous and unnerved. So, no, disengaging was not forthcoming, despite it all, but rather an increase of mischievous manipulation, the search in tandem above and beyond with tongues and lips and, moreover, pure passion. Then came a chorus of throat clearings accompanied by recriminating stares. If the small plane crashed, that mortal kiss would become an eternal seal, or so it seemed to any passengers who might have had such thoughts. Therein the mouth-gaping shrieks commenced—of the dying, or whom? Fortunately, the plane's convulsions ceased just moments later, finally there was calm, finally there rose timid applause, now clearly called for. Yes, now, along with a normal flight pattern, there was a dis-engagement: finally, some decency, some prudence. The lovebirds smiled, then blushed: everything in order, until Mireya in a low voice dropped the following bomb:

"I'm pregnant with your child."

"What?"

"Uh-huh, I thought it better to wait to tell you once we were already on our way."

"Really! A baby . . . What a surprise! My love . . . Hmm . . . What do you know . . . Well, we must certainly give him the best education."

"Oh, dearest, I worship you."

However, not so much as a single kiss of gratitude. The other passengers were trying to find out if another long kiss would ensue, but no, not now, or they wondered why the man seemed so tense, for he suddenly decided to look out the window at who knows what loomings. The severity of an angry face—perhaps? Anyway . . . Landing anon. Imminent measures of some gravity (this said with a double meaning). And now we must skip ahead to catch up with them on the bus to Cuautla. More gravity: predominating: a sham. Mireya had lied. Surely it was nothing but a hackneyed trick, this pregnancy thing, a claim that provoked an onslaught of pertinent questions: a game of darts for a man in a tight spot, and getting tighter as he mentioned some iffy notions that anyway reassured the dark-haired wench. In this sense it's worth emphasizing the vague indifference of he who stared resolutely out the bus window (what might the scatterings in the fields evoke), then turned, like a ghoulish cat, to look at the belly of the pregnant woman . . . And after that—alas! where precisely should he turn: to the north, the east, the west, straight down the middle, or where . . . The border, the state of Tamaulipas—yes? If Demetrio could find a job there . . . No, but the trick would be to get her a passport (first hers), perhaps a residency permit, something of the sort, then go to the agronomist's mother, to that place near Laredo, Texas. He must already have a passport, and he should show it to her . . . Which obliged him to lie, right there, on the fly, saying that this and other personal papers were stashed in the suitcase with the money and, needless to say, it would be pretty daft to open it then and there, and what, anyway, was the rush. Next scene: the tender attack, whether or not he was happy about the baby . . . Yes, yes, of course. A bitter and oblique response. And obliquely, in the heat of the moment, he formulated two questions: *Why didn't you tell me you were going to get pregnant?*, and then: *How much longer before our child is born?* He hoped Mireya's answers would be quick and succinct, which they were, as follows: *I wasn't careful. My doctor gave me the news.* And the second: *A little less than eight months to go till the birth.* More insistent: would they reside with his mother . . . Of course, for this was the very best solution in such a predicament: *I want you to know something very important: my mother is a very generous woman. She will help you throughout your pregnancy and later with the baby while I look for a good job.* And the money in the suitcase—eh? Almost all of it was earmarked for the down payment on the house . . . how obvious.

The onslaught of questions slowly sputtered out, the thoughts and silences turning into undertows and aftershocks: thus their separate obstinacies sharpened, chafing, though all appeared vague and at crosscurrents, until Mireya came upon a clearing in her mind: *I don't want to live with your mother.* Kerplunk! We insist that her declaration was as contingent as the journey itself. To wit, let's frame the scene as if we were viewing it from a certain height and through a lens: dapper Professor Demetrio (under duress) dealing with a pupil who needed repeated explanations as simple as they were definitive; the pressing needs: a house of their own; independence, as well as, and needless to say, distance. Yes, as it were, it would be fine to meet his mother, but Mireya suggested that she would like to live in a city with a dependable hospital, a

Mexican city, that is: on this side—never the other! She also asserted that she would need two full-time servants and other minor requisites that may well have felt like prods. And her missteps kept multiplying. Hostility, but . . . longing for a taste, seeking the mouth that kisses, and as Demetrio didn't want to look at her, imagine how stubbornly he stared out the window, and all Mireya could do was stroke his neck, from behind—how embarrassing! and so it continued without a hint of even a rude response. On the contrary: a vigorous recoiling, a deeper and deeper retreat: Demetrio elaborating a quite injurious plan: first and foremost, to disentangle himself: oh dear!: gradually deciding how: an uncertainty that would have to last till a none-too-easy determination grew darker and darker. The sun was long in setting. It would have to be carried out shortly after boarding the train to Saltillo. Night was, would be, different. They would both sleep in their seats, first-class seats, to wit: cushioned and cozy: sinking softly, and much farther down than on the bus. It would come and . . . The agronomist, in the meantime, established a rule that he would no longer kiss her on the mouth, no more frolicking tongues or lips, nothing, not even a puckered peck. Well, maybe an inadvertent one, okay, but no holding of waists, nor clutching of hands, for any length of time. A victory over discomfort. Chilly exchanges, few words. We find ourselves now on the train platform in Mexico City, where Demetrio finally spoke lightheartedly: *We are going on a very long trip. We might be on that train for thirty hours, even more. Tomorrow we'll be in Saltillo, and I'm thinking maybe we can live there. Saltillo has everything: servants, first-rate hospitals, jobs. Things will go swimmingly for us there. My idea is to stay in a decent hotel, and from there we'll see.* This wasn't what he meant but rather something much subtler: the pretense of very certain courage.

Night. A long and continuous slumber! Utmost to arrange, before boarding, the purchase of sedatives so they could sleep at least ten hours. They wandered around and found, and also bought, sandwiches as well as a generous helping of *dulce de leche* candies and candied peanuts. Necessary baggage, a semblance of abundance—undoubtedly!? Once seated they ate their fill, and the train departed. They would sleep sitting down but—careful!—: not snuggled up against each other, only their eyes told the adjacent passengers—what?, let's see, that they really loved each other? No, no point in that. Just the shared sweats, the bother of wiping away ticklish trickles in full snooze: how awkward to awaken like that! Demetrio's strategy consisted of maintaining a certain distance, which enabled him to rise from his seat whenever he pleased and thereby avoid, needless to say, waking the brunette. Hence the contemplative strolls up and down the train corridors. To caper at will . . . ah: he would dare, he would do it, he would get off at one of the next stations, but not before ascertaining that Mireya was completely unconscious.

The aforesaid should also be considered in light of other details: once they were filled full of sandwiches (two each), and traditional sweets (three each), they swallowed the sleeping pills as planned. Mireya took two: the prescribed dose, according to Demetrio. And he, well, he only pretended to ingest his. He did not swallow what she did. Rather, he held the pills on his tongue, tolerating the bitterness as well as he could or, more precisely, until he saw his sex goddess asleep. Eight or nine minutes passed, a lapse filled with disagreeable disintegration, a matter of discipline, until finally— out, out, you tiny yellow pills!: remove them and place them in his shirt pocket and all set and remain calm, had to, because when he asked the ticket inspector how long it would be before they got to the next station, he heard him whisper, an hour more or less, God willing . . . So, an hour of intellectual proliferation. The fading of the Oaxacan chapters. What had been a plethora and might never be repeated. Nevertheless, the almost outstanding future: to live with a whore—what?!—besides building her a house and continuing to struggle for a happiness that, how could it ever be; a heroic feat, indeed, such a red-hot entanglement everlasting and so to do one's duty, comply! Comply for years with the crass obligation of screwing consistently, and when their old age came upon them, to what end alas. Moreover, the kid? What would become of him? Ugh! Nervously awaiting the birth to see a resemblance, if any: his eyes, her mouth; his nose, her eyebrows, or some other less obvious physiological repartition, that, yes, ultimately, or maybe nothing, and then what? Mellifluous life . . . A growing doubt . . . Little certainty that mattered . . . Not that, absolutely not, right? It was not in Demetrio's interest to do something so far removed from his sentimental convictions. Nevertheless, he began to caress the hair of the sleeping, defeated woman, as if he were petting a cat, and it was palpable that in the depths of that lascivious soul there resided a spirit filled with goodness. The occult part of an occult faith that can reach great heights. Perhaps hidden within was the lushest honesty, but the scoria . . . so many layers of depravity . . . sex that refines eternal vibrations . . . So no, flat-out, no, right? To leave her there asleep would not be tragic but rather the natural upshot of a steamy transaction. For his part, he hoped Mireya would arrive safely in Saltillo. Certainly finding herself in a bind—indeed— she wouldn't be so foolish as to not find a job as a first-rate whore. Dignity, pure and marvelous, right? Even Demetrio had faith that she would become a queen overnight, an unparalleled goddess of pleasure, in whatever house of prostitution she found. With such a body . . . In fact, and viewing things from a different angle, the moment she awoke, her lover wouldn't be there, but she still had four headcheese sandwiches, six *dulce de leche* candies, and four bags of candied peanuts, as well as a surprise of some consequence: a big wad of bills. Demetrio, before detraining at the next station, will have carefully placed the aforementioned wad in her bra. Therewith, we reach an appropriate place to tie things up.

And now we can open, unfurl . . .

He waited at the top of the stairs, money-filled suitcase in hand.

Lights were visible in the nocturnal distance: a forlorn hamlet. His arrival, like attrition. At that station, virtually virtual, seven people descended, among them Demetrio, who once his feet touched the ground quickened his pace without planning his route in the slightest. There was a flicker as of embers in the distance and a bright gas lamp in the station . . . In 1946 only 40 percent of the country had permanent electric lighting . . . Here, therefore, none: not even a shy sixty-watt bulb, only (and perhaps to the agronomist's benefit) the merest glimmer: a flame cipher, or barely a brushstroke: such weaknesses everywhere, all the more reason to fling himself headlong into the hazard of the haphazard. Quickly now, propelled forward by the dread of Mireya perking up and pursuing him in a panic: a futile pursuit through the darkness, fruitless clamors; and Demetrio's tentative advance, wishing only to secure for himself an enveloping and beneficent silence. One thing he knew: not to return to the station, where the brunette might be lying in wait.

Such a thought brought heavy perspiration. Onward, onward: trouble: barking dogs: an explosion of barks, but no sign of agile bodies eager to bite, and Demetrio: cautious: where could he go risk free? Avoid the mud huts, scattered about or clumped together on the wavering horizon. The only adobe building was the train station. Would knowledge of the hamlet's name be useful? Should he find it out? Better to take to the hills.

If the constant barking frightened him, hearing a voice would have frightened him even more, for to be found soon, a shamefaced discovery, especially with that suitcase full of banknotes, for then: aha, a holdup, aha: to explain why he'd fled: the simplest deduction if captured by more than one. Also, a holdup in such a forsaken setting: divvying up the loot in the dark among the lucky locals: an oblique hypothesis . . . so improbable. Or maybe they'd call to him from afar: *Sir, we have your wife here!!! Come get her, please!!!* Or even: *Sir, your wife is crying. Don't leave. Don't abandon her!!!!* In that case, undoubtedly, the brunette would wait at the station until they caught the irresponsible wayfarer: the hunt on horseback, and Godspeed! and with a pack of dogs to sniff him out . . . At such a thought, Demetrio hastened his pace as much as he could: bad, good, and again bad or rather unhappy, for he could hear the pounding of his own heart as well his own footfalls: would speed resound?: this question slowed him down, then more beats and more steps if only to establish a definitive distance from any such mishap. Before him lay the curve of the night, punctuated by a chaos of stars. No more flickers of huts, nor qualms arising from them. It was good to see a hint of the moon in the crown of a tree. Our wayfarer had to pass that apparition for any relief. He still had a long way to savor it, though suddenly he stopped, because carrying that suitcase . . . No, he didn't want to look back, it would be a bad omen. Hence, he set his sights north . . . where else? The remaining traces of light showed him silhouettes of cacti, huisache, and a rough and tangled tumbleweed, and farther on—perhaps—a jumble of scrub. He knew to avoid such shapes because coiled snakes were known to doze beneath them, his ranch experience now coming in quite handy. As for wanting to sleep, he would have to do so on a flat patch far from any underbrush or spiny shapes, on the hard ground, seen for what it was. But, where could he find such a spot? How much farther had he to go? Demetrio walked about two and a half miles and finally . . . He could use his suitcase as a pillow. We must take into account the cold winds, and he jacketless and . . . To sleep exposed but with the certainty that nobody was pursuing him. Otherwise he would have already been found! Demetrio thought he discerned flashing lights behind him: rude and provocative shouts ordering him to stop, or else . . . Well, let's imagine shots from a rifle or a pistol, aggressive houndings, a clamor from behind—is that all? In the end, rejected hypotheticals in favor of commodious accommodations, to stretch out fully across the hide of the earth. He'd surely have aches and pains the next morning for not having lain on any padding whatsoever. Demetrio in the guise of a log, and overhead, a world of unknowns: coyotes might approach while he slept. A sniff or two, then gone: contingencies. He would remain rigidly still if he happened to open his eyes. Maybe keep within reach . . . To be attacked would be quite unfortunate, but why steep oneself in fear?

Next: the glow of a piquant sun. At the caress of its first rays Demetrio made ready to rise and start walking. Achy grumblings, indeed, but how much greater the suffering if he failed by the end of that day to reach a town, one with a hotel. A tall order, but if we consider it under a different light, maybe returning to the train station wasn't such a bad idea, now that he was convinced he'd encounter no trouble. In fact: from that moment on his intuition would be his guide. So vast were his surroundings that merely locating a hill would offer comfort: and: to walk in that direction. Cottages here, train tracks there. He decided to head in the direction of the nearest hill, and as he walked he began to recite the Lord's Prayer: so—phew! not since he attended church with his parents as a child, he didn't even remember it, he made it up as he went along, and as he didn't want his entreaties to be bogus, he simply muttered again and again, *God, help me.* Now we can take an even broader view: a man measuring more than six feet tall walking through the desert carrying a suitcase. Miles: three, five, to which we'd have to add the first signs of thirst. Fortunately, he came upon some cottages at the foot of the aforementioned hill. He received a peaceable welcome. The arrival of an enormous and unexpected visitor who, of course, asked for water. He spoke Spanish—really?! How could a local peasant imagine that a man of such magnitude would speak this language of ours without stumbling? With a different accent, to be sure, but not haltingly. And they posed the question that you and I (and others) can already guess: what was he doing in those parts, and so—must he lie? We'd guess as much, though that he did so with misgivings.

The need for an untruth, even one pulled out of his sleeve. Here are the good bits: they were chasing him; he ran like the devil, leaped like a gazelle (though carrying a suitcase, packed with personal papers); he changed direction ten times to shake off the three or four villains (perhaps killers; no, not that, because they didn't shoot at him); they probably called off their pursuit when they finally lost his trail. And in response to a key question from a young sombreroed man as to the reason for the chase, the recent arrival said his pursuers had confused him with another man of his same height, one who had fled in a different direction, one who was carrying a hefty sack, indeed, and the contents—eh? what were they? and the answer: *I don't have a clue!* The sprinkling of questions soon abating met with a bittersweet counterpoint of lies? Yes, which he had to maintain until he reached a village: a fully fluent supersized scammer, aware that any sharp query, formulated by any tomdickorharry, would be like an itch that would mean a pathetic scratching: almost a swelling. So, at least at this impasse, luck in the abstract seemed to take the form of a redeeming angel, the one who had accompanied him from the moment he got off the train. Because the peasants believed him, out of pity, or tenderness, but they believed him nonetheless, or better yet, they forgave him, so much so that nobody dared ask him to open the suitcase. A pistol inside: a real probability, or an unhealthful mystery. Better to meet the unknown with meekness. Better to enter the realm of respect, and a small dose of decency, don't you think? Nor did he receive any indirect abuse, no suspicion, nothing, for as he appeared, he appeared to be a good man, just to hear his woeful voice . . . The luck of the crossroads!, merciful . . . Back to the important subject: when the visitor asked the whereabouts of the closest town, a peasant said there was one about twenty-five miles away, and another offered to take him on his burro to a dirt road where passed trucks and people on horseback, if only rarely. A head start of six-odd miles: some sort of favor, but—oh prodigy of prodigies! For Demetrio was born under a lucky star, and now its luster was beginning to be felt, a beneficent and honed luster it turned out to be.

A burgeoning lie becomes a crass albeit pleasant reality. Watching that duo atop a burro retreating into the distance must have greatly amused those peasants. Poor burro carrying a dwarf and a giant, an unexpected oddity in that open country: the giant's feet constantly brushing against the ground, inevitable: glorious dust, a yellow seam sewn by hooves and feet: an image soon to become a faint point before it disappeared. Few questions along the way, rather comments from one or the other but not about the pursuit. The conversation, such as it was, was too oblique to matter; in fact, there's no point in mentioning even a sentence at random, or rather, if you'll forgive me, perhaps only those spoken upon parting.

"Well, sir, here's where I leave you. I hope all goes well by you."

"Thank you very much, really. I am very touched by all you have done for me."

"Good-bye and good luck!"

This apparent conclusion to the episode was the sign of an almost unbelievable elucidation, in which the coming mishap implied roads going in all directions: how could Demetrio be certain that trucks and men on horseback passed by here. His four-hour wait was weighty (as bad as that sounds), and nothing, and then hunger and anguish, thirst as well, for the sun had baked him dry. He was sweating, he was trembling. Then he remembered the money in his suitcase—would it sweat? A drenching. A softening. What was going on in there? So he opened it, just to see: yes: humidity, the dangerous eventuality that the money would be worthless if it began to fall apart. Gripped by such fears, the wayfarer grew more and more concerned at the unlikelihood of a truck picking him up to carry him to village x. Unless all that stuff about a village was those folks' idea of a joke, uh-oh, he was talking himself into an ill-fated end: going the way of dry toast . . . Getting toasted, indeed: iron willed and gullible. Something extraordinary would have to happen before evening: salvation like a hanging bough, but for hours not even the distant hum of an engine, nor of horse's hooves, nor of any phenomenon that might bubble up into a mirage. The process of penitence, for having done what he had done, while his body's stuffing was already wadding up from hunger and thirst, so much so that taking even mincing steps was as painstaking as trying to climb a eucalyptus tree would be for an obese man.

Evening came and nothing.

Night came and nothing.

Falling asleep in spite of himself, impotently . . . Making do with the gravel of the road . . . Better to be resigned to vanquished immobility than attempt . . .

Hope that torments then slowly swells the soul . . .

Again the suitcase (with no give) for a pillow—phew! though now corrosive and pervasive hunger and thirst prickled him everywhere, even his thoughts, which already made diminished sense and were jagged and sharp and malevolent.

And his lucky star: was it melting? Just one of its points drooping, perhaps turning black, because the following morning, very early, a rickety vehicle drove by carrying two sombreroed men, who, upon espying that vast human form facedown and expired: ah! a death in the middle of the desert, sunstroke be the cause. The men descended from their truck to see for themselves the horror they imagined. They found the giant half alive though nearing the end, for it took several long minutes for him to respond and engage in conversation. Neither of the above-mentioned opened the suitcase—just so you know. Phew, at least one of the points of Demetrio's star hadn't melted entirely.

"I want to get to a town . . . I need a hotel . . . I'm hungry and thirsty . . . Help me!"

Almost exactly twenty-four hours without water or food, which wouldn't have been so catastrophic were it not for the horrific sunstroke the giant had suffered: the loss of strength in tandem with psychic deterioration and new diseases that for all we know had no cure. On the good side: life: a counterflow, in itself the only friendly light and still on this side of things . . . His saviors made but spare effort, alternating between helping him walk and letting him wobble, just to see if he could go it alone, before settling him into the vehicle's staked bed. A rush decision, after all. A rush to cover the large body with a blanket to protect it from the blasting sun.

"We'll take you where we're going: San Juan del Río; there're three hotels there."

"Take me to the cheapest one."

Okay, so why didn't they put him in the cabin? That's easy: because a monstrosity of his size wouldn't fit, and he lacked the strength to hold up his own head and neck. There were no questions or preemptory answers. The guessing game as to the locals' motives trailed far behind, or we'll leave for me—or you—to play. The fact was, it was to Demetrio's advantage that there neither was nor would be any conversation.

How preferable, this lack of curiosity! The lucky star of the supposedly dying man was slowly putting itself to rights, scintillating, becoming—unscathed? Now the journey really would be made under shade's treachery: until . . . or that was the intention, for the agony continued, because the sun's rays penetrated the blanket, in spite of its heavy weave, playing havoc over that crumpled square. The itching was hardly tolerable and . . . San Juan del Río an hour later. Then the unveiling, which wasn't carried out by Demetrio but rather . . . On to the hotel: the truck parked in front of, let's say, a wooden-facaded oddity. It must have been quite dramatic for the old hotel clerk to see that stinking hulk walking and stumbling though not, no, not falling, toward the counter. She would have to ask the bum to pay for the night's lodging, given that the sombreroed ones had already left.

"Of course I have money, otherwise I wouldn't come here asking for a room."

The clerk didn't believe him. In the event that he couldn't show her even one banknote of large denomination, no, not even the worst room would she rent him. The resultant anger of the supplicant, who dug into his pants pockets to find—ooh!—one-peso coins. He had a torn ten-peso bill: fatal humidity, and—darn! what fortitude it took to open the suitcase and extract a wad! in light of which: why, of course, in this case! and at your service, what's more, a room facing the street: a fairly seedy street: without trees or lively colors to cheer him up: and thus it transpired, though, well: genuine privilege and rest: two words that were irrelevant, given the circumstances. Most urgently he needed to eat, bathe, drink water, and buy a shirt, a pair of pants—what a nuisance! Hours yet before the bliss of the mattress would be his . . . Let's watch Demetrio walking through the streets of San Juan del Río: a stooped pestilence going this way and that. His return after obtaining the basics. Back and forth, carrying his suitcase—too risky to leave it in . . . he would never part from it. True, he returned to the hotel with a modicum of dignity, for he was sporting a new, flowery shirt—he so much enjoyed showing off this extraordinary extravagance, if only to bolster his spirit— and the locals took notice. A startling form with his head swinging low: never before seen: a reeking stranger bedecked in colors, cool threads, hmm, more like a woman's, or those of an effeminate giant. Indeed! That strange monstrosity also seemed about to collapse in plain view; in fact, he staggered a few times: oh! but if we keep his lucky star in mind . . .

He had his sights trained on Parras. Demetrio had no other choice. Needless to say, the maternal mantle would be less than welcome. Ten years ago he'd understood the what and the wherefore of the blessing of being the only son. When he decided to find his own place in the world, his father was still alive, and, of course, that pair of old codgers and their overprotectiveness would have harmed him. So this homecoming: did it carry a stigma of temporary defeat? Yes, temporary, searing, painful, but, anyway, back to his plans: he would board a train to Saltillo, and now for a parenthetical datum: in 1946 the exhausting journey from Mexico City to Saltillo took place every other day. The engines ran on firewood, which explained the slow pace, as well as the plethora of steam from start to finish: an extended blur as long as the train itself . . . So not till the following day: an awkward contretemps. At the hotel they told him that the train stopped in San Juan del Río a little before midnight, but not tonight and hence the need for patience at that moment in the past, which in a few more minutes will be antiquity: forced tedium of a plot that can't get off the ground. It would have budged slightly if Demetrio had gone out in search of amusement, but he didn't, for the town had no brothels; cafés, cantinas: yes, though carrying a suitcase anywhere in the vicinity, but no . . . Well-lit locales, scourges that had lowered him—as we know and to all appearances—from a semivertical life . . . Now consigned to oblivion, momentarily, all the good stuff that had happened to him up to the very moment he had descended from the train at that gloomy station and all the bad that led to his being, as he was, between four strange peach-colored walls, overlooking that decrepit street, and, moreover, night, and, moreover, craving sleep. A mattress at his disposal: recuperation: twelve hours of flat-out recuperation: and even better: six more on the train, the one that would take him where he wanted to go. That's where he was (to situate ourselves) when he awoke at dawn and couldn't fall back to sleep, which anyway had failed to bring him any kind of revelation. Moreover: the revelation came during this nocturnal vigil, when he thought he saw Mireya's ghost wandering down the train corridor. He saw her face in the shiny contours of the train car: a mortifying intermittency that vanished forever with the dawning of the first light of day. Many hours yet till Saltillo, and he even thought that the brunette might be waiting for him at the station, having divined her man's trajectory and patiently waited, so he adumbrated a plan: keep going till Monterrey: the perfect way to avoid an untoward encounter. In fact, and finding him (as well as ourselves) in Saltillo: indeed! aha!: through the train window he saw Mireya sitting on a bench outside, or did it just look like her? or was it a ghostly sham? She was eating an apple. It was her! for sure it was, Demetrio hid, recoiling, squeezing himself into a tiny ball . . .

Fortunately, after fifteen agonizing minutes, the train departed the station. For fifteen minutes people were getting off and on: the people being the crucial part: a crowd, indeed, but no Mireya among them, or maybe he didn't see her, but he had to walk through all three passenger cars to check if . . . and no—thank God! The giant returned to his seat with a smile. Then he grew serious, a bit contrite, due to the inconvenience of extending his trip to a place he didn't want to go. Monterrey—what a bother! Another whole day of aggravation, perhaps two. Another hotel, more closed doors: where—what amusement there to find? The best thing—or maybe not?—would be to count the money in his suitcase. Which he did ten times and in the meantime concocted a plan to invest it—in Parras?

"And that flowered shirt?"

"I bought it in Oaxaca."

"No, son, take it off! You look like a queer."

"I don't have another one. My suitcase was stolen in Saltillo. I was careless."

"And your other suitcase?"

"It's full of personal documents."

When exhaustion mixes with haste, the most unexpected mistakes are made. This became the handle Demetrio resolutely clung to. We're talking about a lie with branching consequences, branches that become increasingly resinous, so as not to say sticky and bitter, when clung to for long. First came the mother-son embrace, following Doña Telma's surprise, incomplete (though growing).

Why was he in Parras at this time of year? We understand they had a lot to talk about—subjects tending toward a reassuring futurity rather than a piecemeal recounting (these, as you know, being whoppers), until night came upon them. Nevertheless, Demetrio feted his newfound talent for fibs, amusing himself with his fictitious inflations: the primary fallacy being none other than that he'd been unconscionably fired from his job; his boss was a beast; two days before, he had fired five other workers on a whim; the man, like all rich men, was impulsive, capricious, and worst of all, quite desperate, wherefrom he derived all the other many reasons for his wear and tear, but one of the reasons he was forced to flee Oaxaca, which he offered up with a straight face, was that his boss's assistant wanted to give him a thrashing: an envious and impudent man, a devious manipulator of a group of peons on the ranch in question, someone who for a long time had been plotting to take over his job and who, from one day to the next, had become the boss's right-hand man. This story had many fissures, but his mother didn't bother digging, she didn't see the point in pressing to the bone what already appeared to be loose, false, and all the rest. Instead, her son's arrival, in and of itself, thrilled her, and with teary eyes she confessed how lonely she had been and, well, just as she was about to launch into the familiar melodrama about her age and her many supposed illnesses, Demetrio stopped her, all he needed to do was utter one semisweet sentence: *It's so good to be with you, Mama,* for the woman to be appeased, though her appeasement was short lived. As we'll soon see:

"Did they pay you?"

"Of course!"

"And the money?"

"I deposited it in the bank."

Another lie Doña Telma did not question. If their exchange was prolonged, stretched out, we can readily imagine the subjects they focused on most: new horizons, oh, yes, maybe with her money and his: why not!? To conjure up something grandiose and original, something that would inject them both with new life. That's when the flowery shirt cropped up again: a Oaxacan purchase? Huh? No, alas, three-quarters of the truth: a hasty purchase in Saltillo, the first garment he'd seen in the first shop he'd happened upon. The house of lies began to crumble. It would collapse entirely the moment the woman peeked into the suitcase. That occurrence . . . yes . . . a fine line: a question of good planning. Let us first assert that they settled on no enterprise that reached the heights of their pretensions. Also, Doña Telma gave her son some of her dead husband's shirts and pajamas, until the son could buy . . . et cetera. Then the suitcase (the intent): to take a peek at midnight, when Demetrio was in his lucid dream sleep.

15

The envelope was fat: special delivery. Doña Rolanda adopted the stance of an enthralled reader, her flashing eyes eagerly trolling each line. Both sides of seven sheets, fourteen pages to enjoy, or a compost of varying moods. A vengeful violation: what she shouldn't have done: carefully breaking the seal of the envelope to avoid tearing the contents. A complex task. A violation because her boarder had fled without paying her, without offering any excuse, and without giving any indication of his return.

Flight of the evildoer, and with that indecent and profligate woman to boot. His clothes—not even that many—left hanging. The churlishness of the flight was comprehensible, comprehended only a few days before when two policemen and a very fat woman as well as some peasants and a small, very old man who said he was his boss came looking for her giant boarder. To all and sundry the same response: Doña Rolanda was in their same predicament, even though they considered her an accomplice; reason enough for the poor woman to invite them into the fugitive's room: *You may stay here as long as you like. You'll see he won't come back.* Then she added: *You can search the rest of my house to assure yourselves that he's gone. What's more: he was here with a woman who looked quite vulgar. I'm certain he left with her and, well, without paying me.* More details, more questions: circumstances of great concern. A deeply disgruntled Doña Rolanda informed them that in order to settle things once and for all (hopefully!), they were welcome to watch the house for days, weeks, months, as long as they needed to catch him upon his return, should that come to pass. And thus began a search, a meticulous one, the policemen eyed everything and likewise the very fat woman; similarly, though on a separate occasion, the peasants and the diminutive boss proceeded apace, also posting a guard out front, one on the day shift and one at night. Imagine, if you will, how enormous was their suspicion for them to extend such largesse for three days. Doña Rolanda knew full well that the uniformed men were the guards of an expensive brothel. Tut, tut!

An oddly invigorated and pouty mix: one part depraved leisure and one part hard work: peasants and policemen involved in the same affair. Perhaps they'd eventually become friends, for occasionally they shared jokes with considerable mirth. Finally, the wary watchers became convinced that Demetrio was gone for good, having left only his clothes behind. Everyone understood he would never come back to get them.

The letter arrived afterward, so we can say: in blessed peace. About the violation, we can say: bold, for it compensated Doña Rolanda for the money her boarder had failed to pay. And to read it standing up in the middle of the courtyard, page after folded and creased page, that admirable penmanship profiling everything wholesome and adorable about a distant damsel explaining why she had nixed a normal holding of hands between sweethearts. A perfect facsimile of true love that was expected to perennially nourish desire; well, she didn't say that in so many words, but something similar, for better or for worse, thanks to her ostentatious candor. The damsel made reference to the many long kisses to come; a profusion of corporeal devotion, also down the road, but only after their union had gained gravity, still years to come: distant blessed perversities. Far-off marriage. Strong bonds or an unbreakable knot, but in the meantime, alack, careful, careful, grow, achieve. Hmm, pitiable decency that always starts down below; pitiable because mostly it fails to achieve its goals, and into this subject the authoress threw herself with passion; as for Doña Rolanda, she noticed one evocative idea: *I don't want to lose you, Demetrio, but be patient with me. That's how we women from this town are. Remember that I'll never be able to replace you, not with anybody else. If I lose you, I'll never be able to love another.* There was a lot more recycled honey, even absurd honey, naive, but of a purity that was perfectly poignant. And around page nine Doña Rolanda looked up from her reading because her unflattering conclusions had just about achieved full expression, one in particular (the third) she grumbled out loud: *That man doesn't deserve such a woman.* Then, in a lower mumble: *That man is a miscreant and an ungrateful wretch, a swine who will hopefully come to a bad end.* Whereupon, even lower: *How could he possibly have traded such a true woman for such a lowdown whore?* Finally—long live decency!, and I needn't note here the more painful pronouncements. Doña Rolanda was pretty angry and thus wholly convinced that her boarder would never return. God willing he wouldn't!

16

Lie . . . Acrid teeming lie, vile, bartered, ineffectual. A lie made to taste then immediately spit out. O lie that unravels at midnight, as when Doña Telma, just as wary as could be, took the defiant initiative to enter the room where her son was sleeping; she spotted the suitcase at once: on the ground, to the left of the head of the bed, just where the one now supine had placed it shortly after his arrival. Easy now, and . . . to open slowly and search therein, to make no sound that would stir Demetrio; he detected nothing besides what was palpable: his own mysterious interior gurgling. The action in black and white, more or less. Inside, she felt hard objects, rectangular lumps that grew soft around the edges, maybe playing cards or banknotes or strange documents or something of the sort. She took hold of one and pulled it out, then left as warily as she had come. Outside the room, darkness prevailed, so she went to find a candle: groping her way to the kitchen: there were six in one drawer: yes! remember that what she held in her right hand was still undefined . . . to shed light on uncertainty . . . in 1946 in Parras, there was electrical service from five p.m. to eleven p.m.

Sometime after two in the morning.

We need to grasp the ominous slowness of these actions: searching for a large box of matches: somewhere—but where? way in the back. Careful not to let the crackle of match-lighting reach that room and, once accomplished, the surprise: a hefty bundle of banknotes and, hence, the lie . . . why? Then the deduction: how many more bundles? She was fingering a fortune. In other words, Demetrio had run the risk of traveling with an astounding quantity of assets; Providence had protected him: big-time!, but the weird part: why didn't he tell the truth immediately, a truth that would not have upset her? or, why the hell did he say he'd deposited his salary in the bank? Doña Telma's return to where she had to return was, now, fairly noisy, now she carried a candle and deliberately stomped about to force the liar awake. More stomping around the room itself, even the implementation of a ridiculous flamenco footfall, but not a peep from the sleeper. Then, believe it or not! the worst came to pass: she shouted in his ear: *Wake up! You lied to me! Wake up!* And, needless to say, Demetrio opened his eyes. Doña Telma shined the candlelight on the banknotes in her hand before she exclaimed, enraged: *I guess there's more of the same in that suitcase.* And he: *Mother, why are you waking me up? You could have waited till tomorrow.* Doña Telma mentioned the deception, the salary, and the bank deposit—what for? Then, shining the light on the open suitcase, she confirmed her worst suspicions: a bundled fortune. Then came the rebuke, but Demetrio countered with two arguments. The first, we can imagine for ourselves without considering the consequences of piling one lie on top of another: that he had received a much larger payment, the rest of which he deposited in a bank in Oaxaca. Anyway, a bitter, devious, inefficient lie because of the imprecision he had uttered the day before. And the second: *I am no longer a child you can scold. Now I think I shouldn't live with you. You didn't let me sleep, damn it.* In the face of such a harsh accusation, the poor woman had to beg forgiveness and place the bundle back where it came from, with a mere: *I only ask that you always please tell me the truth, otherwise you know how upset I'll be.* The son was well acquainted with his mother's latent and convoluted paranoia. It was one of the reasons Demetrio had fled the bosom of his family and gone as far away as possible in the first place. Also, his father when alive was a snarling man, insufferably vexatious. Anyway, let's now say that the mother went to sleep, whereas no matter how hard the son tried, he couldn't drop off. Why live in perpetual stupidity? Stupid to return to Parras. Stupid illusion. For if he had foreseen the changes wrought by her widowhood, or by her beleaguered solitude, above all by the loneliness of village life, no—it's now been proven—people don't change, they pretend to, but in general there are never any seriously surprising alterations; people don a variety of masks, feints of pleasing transformations, but . . . No, Parras, no. Perhaps Saltillo, Monclova, Monterrey, Torreón. No small towns, because they are insane hellholes, and—where could he go once and for all? To a jumbled metropolis, which ultimately might be the most accommodating: to feel anonymous and free, to have the opportunity to botch things up an unlimited number of times and not be reproached by a single soul: respect or indifference? Whatever it was, but—yes!—peace within reach: and: from deeper down: Demetrio had not foreseen the dilemma of deceiving his mother, of convincing her of—what the deuce? Understanding—structural? Bah! Mere crumbs of understanding, residues of what for. Indirect rebukes, not that either! Nonetheless, what good would his insomnia reveal to him: nothing but an unfettering, or idle clarity about what he had already supposed: leave, leave, lose himself, recuperate, and that's when Renata's image rose before him: saintly companion—for better or for worse? That immaculate beauty finally faded at dawn because slumber descended wholly unconcerned by what had just transpired, and seeing that her son had yet to emerge from his room, Doña Telma resisted acting imprudently and did not awaken him. Let breakfast get cold—no problem! A change, yes, though next . . . that same old level, a cutting comment that could be interpreted as a reproach . . . No, nothing thorny came up . . . Respect or indifference? Caution, a steady ascent . . . Around noon, conversation and food. The son announced to his mother that the very next day he would travel to Sacramento to see his sweetheart, that this was surely the best tonic for his nerves . . .

"Will you return?"

"I don't know."

"I promise, you won't hear any more scolding from me. Again, I beg you to forgive me . . ."

"Don't say anything, Mother. Soon I'll figure out what I need to do."

"If you want, I'll hold on to your money. I think you are taking a huge risk by carrying it around in that suitcase. You really shouldn't."

"I'm taking all my money with me. I don't care. I want to live near my sweetheart. I want to get married soon."

"But you don't have a job. If you don't start working, that money will pour through your hands like water."

"That's my business. I don't want you to ever scold me again."

Separation. Choice. The rest of the day mother and son exchanged nary a word. Demetrio took a stroll around Parras. He needed to feel alone in order to think things backward and forward. The bad part of that tree-lined town was the paucity of restaurants and cafés, and not a single spot that was even remotely depraved; rather, the tacit aspect of the tranquility: more sacred relief than you could shake a stick at: three small plazas with cute benches and well-scrubbed kiosks. Streets made for the most primary of pleasures. Sights and sounds like extra decorations that made (and make) the seeing and the feeling seem haggard. Nevertheless, to stroll without faith, take a seat in some spot, and slowly slowly convince himself that this was not for him, that such a small-minded world would ultimately fill him with supreme disgust; it would be like consciously shrinking himself in order to quickly attain the philosophical outlook of an old geezer; it was to remain uncontaminated, at least not infected, by the unknown, or to cling

to a few fixed ideas that had to be neutralized with neutral ingre-
dients, never anything perturbing; it was the nonemancipation and
the nonaudacity and, most of all, the senility of it all, of his soul,
for example. Perhaps a fettered spirit. A young spirit whose flight
had reached no higher than a hummingbird's: to wit: to peck only
at the known, at what was most obvious, and from there thoughts
that zigzag toward the margins, to find therein more excitement: a
desire that must not be, how could it be, and till when. Demetrio
experienced more excitement on his train ride to Sacramento. He
couldn't, however, escape the rigid circle he had drawn for himself, unintentionally, in which, somehow or other, he now found
himself trapped.

Trapped. Never!

Why?

Nevertheless, as he approached that other negligible place,
swathed in the grandiose image of his saintly sweetheart, he
thought about countless entrances and exits. Once Renata was his
wife, she would be his unconditionally and would accompany him
wherever he wanted and whenever he wanted . . . et cetera. The
promise of a slave brimming with affection, flowing with honey,
drowning in honey . . . Well, well! Let us watch Demetrio with
suitcase in hand: a bigger one, which his mother lent him. Inside,
of course his compressed banknotes; on top of them, two changes
of clothes; two pairs of pants, one belonging to his father, which
his mother had hemmed for him; she stayed up late at the task. Let
us also watch Doña Telma's alacrity, her handiwork, punctuated
by bouts of tears; she dared not say a word about her son's pending
and inopportune departure. Cut, now, to the following morning. A
chilly farewell, no kiss, and complete relief for him (here an ellip-
sis) on the boat crossing the river. An exceptional reception. There
in her grocery store, like a perennial thinker, elbows resting on
countertop and palm propping up her chin, Doña Zulema watched
the rectangular vista that was her perpetual panorama: a frame

that contained two walnut trees swaying slightly: this the background; closer up: a crumbling adobe wall; even closer: the dirt road along which people who almost never greeted her walked. Then her nephew appeared in the rectangular door frame. The aperture: a miracle—finally! Doña Zulema—credulous? Yes, she roused herself and stepped outside. The shadow of an embrace: almost. *What's going on? I never expected to see you at this time of year.* And he: *Well, here I am.* Next scene: close up the shop and converse all evening and into the night. No, that last part, no, because the nephew was anxious to see Renata before nightfall. Doña Zulema—for a change—told him she would make him something to eat. Oh how splendid! Sudden hospitality after so much prior neglect. What a lark! And in the meantime he would wash by the bucketful, without caring if the water was cold, hot, or warm. Two events, if looked at carefully, that could be seen as joyous raptures: two promising predicaments, but as we can't see, we can only read—what elucidation remains! Happy tension—in black and white? Heavens! So let's place them side by side at the table. We'll stand ten feet away: just for fun? That would be fantastic . . .

A plate with four flour tortillas filled with refried beans, a mortar full of green salsa, and placed a bit farther away (strategically?), a steaming cup of *café con leche.* Grandstanding? Well, the hospitality was quite ostentatious, considering that before . . . remember? Very nearly bashful, stuttering summaries of the reasons for his presence. New and rather ghastly lies, and when cracks began to show, which they did, Doña Zulema had some elbow room to pose a hefty number of questions . . . Which meant there would be no time to be exacting, perhaps later, maybe tomorrow, but the most essential things, in plain view, could not linger on the tip of the tongue.

"Forgive me for saying something that you may find disagreeable: that shirt you're wearing is way too big on the sides and in back, and those pants are too short; your socks show too much. The fact is, you look awful."

That is, the father was fatter than but not as tall as Demetrio. And his mother's needlework was poor.

"I don't care. I'll explain everything later."

"But you're going to see your sweetheart."

"I'm telling you, I don't care. I must see her, period."

Wow! So he came from Parras dressed like that. Datum now added.

Come on! Flood pants and a shirt that was making waves.

17

The intention: to break the monotony, which is what one might fancy doing when uncertainty, mixed with sorrow, is magnified. Doña Telma alone, going from here to there and back to here in her back garden, was being watched by her two servants, who awaited orders. The heat was gnarly that morning. It seemed like the sun wanted to accentuate its sheen so as to augment the despondency of a few rather than inject joy into what's done. In that sense, and quite suddenly, the señora was afflicted by pangs of distress. Meanwhile, observed as she was by those meatheads, she managed to say: *Off to the kitchen with you! I don't want you watching me.* Then, more fired up, but with her head hung even lower, she continued her pacing. Analytical pacing, supremely painstaking, which soon turned into a process of degradation, until she finally convinced herself that her life was nothing but an assemblage of scraps, or a lack of fortuitous events. True, she was a widow with means and a house, but (completely) alone, as if she were a piece of poisonous offal. Could be because she was an incorrigible nag or because her destiny was a path that grew grimmer as it stretched further out . . .

Grimness now: entrenched. Thundering doom, a juncture that could lead only to a long monologue: days, weeks, months, years, of talking only to herself—mummification! The complaint and the cure being kneaded together forever, for years now, ever since her husband's death—a bit less than a decade ago—and even before that, when her daughters, one after the other, married those damn gringos, and she'd been all but forgotten, they didn't write or visit, only once in a great while, they never completely abandoned her, squeezing her in, but really, ugh! Demetrio: the only one, every Christmas, though . . . we already know the brouhaha: now that he had returned he had fled *ipso*, under the pretext of needing to see his sweetheart: what a cock-and-bull story! a bunch of baloney! In a typical Mexican story, she would shrink into a tearful creature and go chasing after him; hence, the very next morning she took off to Sacramento. That's right: to break the monotony so as not to sink even deeper into that tangle of guilt she had knotted for herself. Kneading the cure sans the complaints. A brave decision. To go alone, but not downcast, as if at that very moment an archangel had placed her in a harness and pulled her on to pursue her only closest blood-bond of deep affection, though with the humble desire to be forgiven; he—why not?—would demand from her a thousand apologies—great! fair enough! and finally, Doña Telma was willing to kneel before him, if necessary . . .

She announced her plans to her servants. She would be away from Parras for a few weeks. Vacation with a plot (not to be revealed). As for instructions: nothing unusual, the daily chores, for which—listen up!—she'd pay double. Better yet: triple: if they both remained in the house at all times. An interval propitious for runaway love and with the boon of an abundance of room. For they were so young . . . The possibility . . . yes or no? Whatever happened would be history's redoubt that Doña Telma would hold, even so, in light regard . . . to desire their understanding now and in the thereafter . . . *Don't worry. You can stay away for as long as you like*, the man said, who, needless to say, rubbed his hands with glee. If his sweetheart followed his lead, God willing!, and so on.

18

As soon as Demetrio walked away, a bouquet of lilies—given to him at the last minute by Doña Zulema—in one hand and his money-filled suitcase in the other, he felt awful. Glances and giggles surrounded him. It was his implausible height, like a walking bean-pole, as well as his seditious shirt and those schoolboy trousers . . . It was his ridiculous composure . . . It was—how could it be?, and the more the town's malice grew, the shorter the big guy made his stride. His arrival at the trysting bench and from there his shout for Renata to come out and meet him would be a genuine spectacle for the critical gawkers. Increased surveillance and a crescendo of laughter would subsequently affect his sweetheart much more than him; such was his supposition, so he made a full stop, sat down on the first bench he came to in the main plaza (the central and grandiose plaza, and the only one); disheartened, wishing to hide, he decided not to find out what was going on just a little ways away; yes, as bad as it seemed, he considered giving up, postpon-ing the visit till the following day and going first to Monclova to buy some clothes that fit, something more presentable, because in Sacramento you could probably find nothing but cowboy pants. Hence a whole day wasted going there and back. His course of action was clear. He had only to take a quick look at himself . . . How embarrassing . . . Especially because he had noticed noth-ing upon leaving Parras. Nobody had poked fun at him during the trip . . . Nonetheless—here it was! a gathering scandal that he alone could stanch . . . The problems were the trousers, the bright glimpses of sock, less noticeable was the shirt's roominess. In any case, he turned upon himself the most severe self-criticism and— what could he do! He'd have to return to Doña Zulema's house. An unpleasant retreat: ceaseless ugly jeers—was he required to ask for forgiveness? From anyone in particular? Sorry, sir, sorry, ma'am—nobody? That is, nobody confronted him up close, just as nobody approached him as he left for Monclova early the next morning . . . Jeers from afar, but a nuisance nonetheless . . . True, he was no longer carrying the bouquet of lilies, only the vexing va- lise. Perhaps the fault-finding multitudes believed that he wouldn't show his face there again, but . . .

A radical difference.

Extravagance on a Thursday afternoon.

Elegance can be intimidating if viewed in detail. The outfit as well as the overall effect, the heat notwithstanding; hence, quite conspicuous, for nobody in Sacramento ever dressed like that.

Demetrio went irresolutely toward his destination, but weak thoughts arose, one by one. To begin with, he had to make several stops. He placed the bouquet of lilies and the suitcase down in the dust of the street so he could remove a white handkerchief from the outside pocket of his jacket and delicately wipe off trickles of sweat: face, neck, and hands, and this thankless task awakened doubts, one of which was whether or not he should present him- self sweaty to Renata—how sweaty were the hairs on his chest . . . covered though they were? Very, because his personal rivulet was tickling him under there. Even his hair, so well groomed, would soon come undone: irremediably dissolute head, deserving of some distant chortle that he may hear later . . . nor did he have a comb handy to put the humid chaos to rights . . . and his elegant ap- pearance (in principle) was getting complicated . . . But he could not put off meeting his sweetheart another day. We will see, therefore, his stubborn lunacy, his audacity in the face of the worst possible censure. In his defense a great excuse he hoped he would not need to assemble on the spur of the moment. Anyway, he was already fleshing it out. The idea was that elegance was a pretense in a village where it was as uncommon as a swanky new car. And he reached the trysting bench and did not sit down. His (sweaty) elegance precluded him from hurling even one cry into the air, not so much as a whistle, much less shouting out the name of his beloved and telling her, moreover, that he had arrived on a whim. To wait, then, standing up: obstinate, tall, silent, flamboyant (he had to be). It was five in the afternoon and there in the constricted space of the stationery store Demetrio descried Renata's subtle figure: she was conducting business; likewise, the buxom figure of her mother, who was moving her lips—uncontrollably? Was she speaking . . . or was it all just futile action? Renata abruptly stepped out into the street. She was not gussied up, and one could surmise her astonishment from her somewhat stalking step. She drew nearer and— the last straw! words scattered on the ground, her words, for after glancing at him fleetingly, she lowered her head and:

"I'm very happy you've come, but I can't see you now. I am not presentable. Come tomorrow at the same time, if you can."

Once this blarney was over, she turned on her heel and ran away. Her mother was waiting with her hands on her waist as if to say: *Well done!* He was left standing with outstretched arms: the bouquet of lilies: void, useless, tomorrow another one. Bah! the amorous proposal snapped back as if it had been stretched out too far, and now, yes, the discordant giggles from afar embellished the retreat of the gallant, whose dandyism had done him no good. Laughter like barbs. Each step a gasp. Shame flaming from the lilies he still carried. As for the suitcase, what more can be said about it. Of course, the suitor longed to hide the bouquet under his jacket, but that would embarrass him even more. Circular then spiraling resilience. He refused to rid himself of that pleasant prodigy (throwing it—where?) because it would be proof of a frustration that tomorrow, at five in the afternoon, would be turned on its head, and, with a sharp pang, he wondered if the bouquet, especially because his aunt had given it to him, had brought him bad luck. When he arrived, she hugged him. She said nothing. She divined the course of events (rejection resulting from the surprise) and . . . A cry, meek, from her—of course! while he, with a knot in his throat, let her caress his disheveled head. Interior scene, so warm, in the kitchen rather than the grocery store, where the señora prepared *café con leche;* there was also a basket full of rolls, those familiar *conchas, plomos,* and *pelonas* for him to savor slowly. Bites as pauses. Words, all difficult and somewhat virile, rows of sweet relief. There must have been few: his: so-called sputum; though hers . . .

"I warned you, that's how women from Sacramento are, but I think it's worth your while to be patient."

"You know what, Auntie, I don't want to hear about it anymore. Renata and I agreed to see each other tomorrow. Now I want to be alone. I want to take a walk through town, climb a hill, I don't know, watch the sunset, and then see what stars come out at night; I think it will do me good to look at the moon for a good long while. I want to think, understand, because I am starting to despair."

"Do whatever you want. I'm going to give you a copy of the key to the house, and as you know, you can come back whenever you feel like it."

The moon. The scrublands. The gray and luminous hills. The desert ground to sleep on, as he had done days before, the suitcase: O pillow! O companion! Resolve. Apathy. Desire. But first, to dress appropriately: a short-sleeved shirt for wandering around, a T-shirt, in fact, a trifle bought just in case, or just because. In Monclova he had also bought a new suitcase for his new clothes, which, without a second thought, he had left at Doña Zulema's house. And where to next? Wheresoever to gird himself, to build up resistance against his circumstantial sorrow, but alone, absorb some kind of new and suggestive blessedness. So he ambled, dined in a tavern—a mendacious plate—then resumed his deliberate aimlessness. No dearth of onlookers watched him depart: hie to the hills, to hell with it all! The moon: light from a waning crescent (no trace of a path), and onward he trudged, trying to find his way. He wished that the night would silence all sounds then awaken his grief and sorrow with a tenuous tinkling. One footstep after another along the path to purification. It was not long before he found a small rise. There he sat. The sparse and far-off lights of Sacramento were also his own sparse flashes, already embossed upon the darkness. Drifting distances; he, extraneous: a fleeing spirit unable to glimpse a center or a refuge along the edges or a place beyond. His ideas failed to flow, but his soul . . . what weight? Barely any: a formless mass that would never be shaped. A hefty mass of flesh, a medley of legs, breasts, asses, and two faces: Renata's and Mireya's: heaven and hell, sanctity and sin, eternal and circumstantial, ruthless struggle and mere toy, but only one really deep intersection, an arid depth, and therein the absurd. If Demetrio kept thinking, he'd turn bright red and break out in tears, because any and every choice might prove fatal. Be that as it may, he had now firmly settled into the enigma of true love, love that placed the most impossible obstacles in the way, and to what end: to reach a cloud? the peak of a mountain? a star? Desire submerged in another desire and hence legions and thereby diminished, until ultimately it wouldn't know what it was or could be.

There perchance to sleep, sunk in abstractions.

May sleep fix without twisting the purpose.

May sleep strip Renata naked.

To see that saint naked. See her begging for sex.

If only!

Okay, okay, let's say that happened, that sleep brought him something of the sort. Maybe not the beauty's full nudity, but how about a sacred hand, offered forth: take hold! pa-leeze take hold! Renata ordered him in a quite implausibly beseeching tone: take hold, my love! And he did so as if it were a phantasmagoric piece of flesh. The more caresses offered the more doubts arose, the more improbable ripening, all for the worst . . . the entwined hands started to rot. When Demetrio awoke he stood up at attention like a soldier and quickly made his way back to Sacramento.

Maybe Doña Zulema wouldn't notice his arrival. Not a chance. She, so understanding, wouldn't dream of daring to ask him where he had spent the night. Surely on a bench in the plaza, or in some vacant lot, or in the hills, or—who knows! In fact, she remained resolutely silent: upon seeing him arrive she gave him a hug and that was all. He did not offer excuses, nor did he explain anything (it was nine in the morning). Though it is true that during the embrace he gave her a few very nice strokes on her head, her arms, her back, and:

"Do you want some breakfast?"

"No, I'm not hungry."

"What are your plans till this afternoon?"

"I want to be alone."

Alone. To waste time. Demetrio shut himself up in a room jam-packed with statuettes and pictures of saints. Such a moral, re-criminating menace: and: what he did was turn all their backs to him. They deserved it! or didn't they? Their ignorance versus . . . let's see . . . Our lover's levels of abstract thinking never went very far. Never, definitely, did they take a definite tack. Hence ensued the compensatory masturbation. Action rather than reflection. He fully savored the act and upon feeling the smudge of semen on his fingers he said to himself: *I'm becoming a chaos . . . but I don't care.* He wiped himself off with a corner of the quilt: disgusting!, and he rested—now, finally—and smiled, what a sin onanism was, how peculiar! A sin that consumes itself. Futile fount and for that very reason, extraordinary . . . and grotesque, and devoid of mystery! which is why later—once again? Thrice Doña Zulema knocked on the door, but only the last time did she ask him the following (take note of the respect, the not-opening, the not-being-offensive):

"Are you going to stay in there? Don't you want to eat something?"

"No, I'm perfectly fine. Leave me alone!"

He masturbated twice more, though, to tell the truth, these were not as pleasurable as the first. Then, at about three in the afternoon, Demetrio went out. He felt like washing with bucketfuls galore. His aunt filled up four, that was all she had. The nephew, however, remained a long time in the washroom and she took on the task of inspecting, by stealth, the other room. She saw the saints with their backs turned—what now? perversity behind closed doors? really? Her nephew, happy or unhappy, naked . . . perhaps . . . but . . . whatever's wrong with that? And, making a modest inference, she mused that masturbation . . . let's see, let's see . . . is natural for a man, as long as he doesn't take advantage of the privilege—what else could she conclude? Then—oh, darn!—the evidence: the soiled quilt; a whitish stain, which, when looked at up close—oh!: in it Doña Zulema saw the seed of children, grandnephews, but also of less-than-well-corresponded love, or despair, or spiritual sorrow, or—damn! why such a fuss. Three stains on the quilt, that is, three masturbations and—how disgusting! (already said) especially after making up the bed with new sheets and a new quilt. Be that as it may, no reproaches, no obsessing. What's more, she did not inspect the suitcases. She could have opened them, for both were closed with only a metal clasp, but . . .

Now we really must betake ourselves to the much-anticipated tryst. Exquisite presentation. Renata wore a quince-colored dress that sparkled with every move she made, and he a jacket and tie and, indeed, a Mediterranean-blue long-sleeved shirt; no, not a new bouquet of lilies—obviously! bad luck—remember?—; but his suitcase, now an inseparable part of him.

"What a shock you gave me. Why have you come at this time of year? I wasn't expecting you."

"Guess what? I no longer live and work in Oaxaca. I had a big fight with my boss and I decided to quit and go live with my mother in Parras. I will find work there."

"So, you didn't receive my letter."

"You wrote me a letter?"

"Yes, a very long letter."

"No, I didn't. As soon as I quit my job, I left for Parras because my boss paid me right away."

"Will you return to Oaxaca?"

"I don't plan to . . . But tell me, please, what did you write in your letter?"

"As I said, it was very long. In it I explained some of the reasons I want our courtship to proceed so slowly. I need to be sure this is serious. If you want me to, I can promise that I'll be yours forever, that you will be the only man of my life, that all my hopes will be placed in you. But, like I said . . ."

"You told me I would be able to hold your hand on this visit."

"Yes, hold it, Demetrio, but that's all, because otherwise I'll feel terrible."

"You needn't worry. I am a gentleman, and you mean too much to me to ruin everything. I long to learn to love you as you want me to."

"Maybe you think I'm stuck-up, but try to understand that I am a woman of principles."

"Yes, I can see that, and that's what I like most about you: your modesty, your sincerity."

"My mother is watching us! Look to your right, you'll see."

Demetrio did as he was told and . . . indeed.

"But take my hand, my love, here, below."

"My love." Where did that expression come from? From her soul or her conscious mind? And to obey and . . . already culminating in a feat: below. Desire: barely: a punctiliousness that summed up in a split second all the exhausting trips, everything turned topsy-turvy and reduced to a frenzy of initiation! Then crowned by a trembling and fascinated fingering. The concrete that sates, that calms. The here and now so small yet so glorious. Sanctified flesh worth examining eagerly though with restraint, this game of fingers and palms and endless limitations. Silence designed to stir up fervent feelings and promising portents. A moral path strewn with caresses of sluggish though benevolent beginnings, a steady climb, then suddenly:

"And that suitcase?"

"That's where I keep my money . . . Do you want me to open it and show you all the money my boss gave me?"

"I don't know, that's your affair. I wouldn't ask that of you."

"There are no banks in Parras . . . The truth is, I don't know where to deposit the cash . . . I was so anxious to see you, I carried it the whole way."

"Why didn't you leave the money at your mother's house? It seems very risky to carry it around."

"It didn't occur to me. I was in Parras for only a few hours, then I came here. I didn't even consider leaving it with my mother."

"You shouldn't walk around with that much money."

"I'll soon come up with a solution. I can find my way in the world. I have always been a very practical man."

Renata smiled, as if wanting to change the subject. We must remember that never, except at the wedding dance, had she looked him in the eyes. Decency as a heavenly abstraction yet one with an endless number of perhaps-too-concrete foundations, among which figures flirtation, ergo: head-on or, rather, defenseless insolence: never! what? still to come a long lapse before her eyes could feast upon those of her beloved, which would then mark an abject and absolute surrender: and—ugh! later, later . . . a later marked by a construct of desires so intricate it formed an impressive honeycomb. Nonetheless, with head downturned, Renata incited him to say pretty things, one after the other, what the hell!, and without improvised creativity, as it were: never would he act the fool and blurt out thoughts that might sound offensive, for being randy;

on the contrary, in the end, rather staid sweet nothings, credible, but—how? There should be no ripe emoting when one is humble in love, humble if a giant and in the presence of a beautiful woman, almost custom made, though somewhat short of stature; humble intentionally or merely a coward for restricting himself to a lexicon that projects pure sweetness, sweetness and extreme caution, even in his tone of voice. An attempt at emotional constriction would be useful. Like shrinking then growing through words. Demetrio wanted, he said, and then he faltered. To force himself to think about the power of velvets or silk, that's where it all started: oh, he was so insecure, and in the end he realized that the cadence of his caresses on that saintly hand would set a pattern for him that would allow something important to come out of his mouth. He could, but—was he pretending? He could, he was strutting his stuff, as if he were writing a letter with careful calligraphy; and Renata, though gratified, clammed up even more. There were many limits to the fondling (the border: the wrist; the forearm: never!) as well as verbal limits (never speak about a kiss anywhere; never speak about nudity—right? even indirectly), a careful search through simplicity, a temerity that was simply boring. A slow burn, but effective. A dreadfully proper middle ground—right? For a long time even keeled and stellar, until a boy came to tell Renata that her mother had said her time was up. The abrupt ending was that ugly. Remember the reserves of decency: its benefits understood. Yet, the promise: tomorrow again, there—ah! at five in the afternoon. Agreed. And each to his or her own . . . downhill, we might say, for both had managed to see, if not a towering peak, at least a small romantic hillock, made unforgettable by the contact, which there certainly was, that premise of hands that love each other. For Demetrio, arriving at his aunt's house was like arriving at a palace in penumbra, where a gray-haired woman, like a decrepit old housekeeper, came to greet him and insisted on embracing him because she saw him arrive almost with a spring in his step and almost smiling, and he, of course, resisted—leave me alone! don't touch me!—for this was not the moment to receive a doddering clasp. Doña Zulema froze. She trembled when she said that dinner was ready. No doubt, the aunt's diligence during her nephew's last two visits was notable. The ostentatious hostess had, as was only proper, demoted the store to second place and had no qualms about closing it so that she could play the part of the accommodating cook: she prepared *café con leche*, bought their daily bread, made a stew, and, most significantly: kept the cord of her discretion tied, that is: her efforts to reel in her curiosity, so as not to ask questions about the progress of the courtship nor insist once and for all upon a full explanation of what had gone on in Oaxaca. Regarding this last bit, the most curious part was her nephew's inexplicable zeal to hold on to the aforementioned suitcase: money? a pistol? what monstrous thing? Could be a question of self-inflicted punishment that resulted in the subtle affability Demetrio was beginning to value. No hint of reproach when the aforesaid decided to spend the entire night out. On the contrary, the tendering of a copy of the house key, the placing of great trust, and the longing for a celebratory embrace each time he returned. Perhaps Doña Zulema wished to see in that great big man the son she never had. Son-king or pampered prince, powerful though absentminded, or a struggling warrior, tender and somewhat inexperienced in everything. Nonetheless, during dinner it was Demetrio who aired a concern related to the future of his love affair:

"I don't know what to do. I don't want to go back to Parras or Oaxaca. I want to find work around here, but I don't know where to look."

"You really want to stay here?"

"Yes, because I want to be near Renata."

"Listen, there's a very rich gentleman in Monclova who owns, among other things, many ranches. Once in a while he comes here because he has a property near Sacramento that he's neglected, according to what I've heard."

"And you, how do you know him?"

"I've known him since we were children. He was a classmate of mine at school and he always stops by to visit me. He comes to my store for a refreshment, and we talk."

"Was there ever anything between you?"

"I never wanted him. When we were young he tried, but he finally realized that we were better off as friends and, well, I agreed with him there. He married very well, he has eight children and a ton of grandchildren."

"Sounds good! How can I get in touch with him?"

"I have his address in Monclova. It wouldn't be a bad idea for you to pay him a visit. His name is Delfín Guajardo."

"I'll go tomorrow. That way I can also deposit most of my money in a bank there."

"Money? What money?"

"The money in my suitcase. It's part of my earnings and my savings."

The mystery now solved. No further comment. No backhanded reproach about the risk of . . . never! In response, finally, Demetrio's impulse: to check his suitcase: to go, to know. He knew. And, as his gratitude remained unmitigated, he took the initiative to embrace his aunt. She was happy. A magnificent hostess, and something else besides: the taking-shape of enduring respect, as opposed to Doña Telma, oh, that meddlesome mother, so insolent. On the contrary . . . he just wanted to check if the fifteen fat bundles of banknotes inside the suitcase remained intact . . . Ugh! a crude memory of his accounting: and: the aunt could have taken two while Demetrio was bathing. Careless of him, in fact, at a glance, to have left it: yesterday: oh. Though, all told, he would have forgiven his hostess for swiping five bills or so, why even check? Better to plant a kiss on her cheek, a slightly salivary smack. Which he did: muuuuaaagh! And her delight redoubled; she: squeezed: then surrendered, a cuddled make-believe mother; she: her feelings and her charm abloom.

19

One less problem . . .

Around 1946 a wide road began to appear between Ocampo and Monclova. We are talking about a sixty-mile stretch, more or less, through the principal population centers of Coahuila's central region. For some time there had been occasional stretches with gravel that filled those who drove on them with hope for the future, but mostly rough ground prevailed, a series of disorienting winding roads that few knew well and that others, without even a basic layout, wouldn't risk. In any case, the direction you chose was determined by finding raised vistas, rather than the (always imprecise) points of the compass: to wit: what was in back of, or ahead of, or adjacent to, on the right or the left, and otherwise one's bearings, the difficult verticality, finding one's way by day, of course, for the threat of a fiasco if night fell smack in the middle of the trip, all that adversity and all that viability, but more adversity: those roads lacked uniformity, they got wider, then narrower, potholes abounded; so we can picture carriages, carts—and very infrequently funny-looking buses and cars, not to mention serious trucks and pickups—a to-ing and a fro-ing, which indicated that few dared make long trips. From Ocampo to Monclova: a challenge— who would do it?! Even from Sacramento to Ocampo, because if you take into account the innumerable and capricious twists and turns . . . well, let's start with the idea that a straight line from

Sacramento to Monclova was approximately twenty miles and from Sacramento to Ocampo about forty-five, but with so many curves, most of them unnecessary, and moreover poorly built, let's see—how many miles does that add? Clearly, as far as the dirt road was concerned, one must consider verticalities. Clearly, the sixty-five-mile-long ribbon of a road had to wind through three or four canyons and squeeze through a mountain gorge, and there indeed, the curves—hopeless! but the remaining stretch: the desert plain . . . True, the engineers had to use their best judgment to save miles, and, back to the main point, let's just say that the shorter the road the better—right? The practical must triumph, per usual. And the practical in this case was to get people off the train. Or, to allow people to travel farther and with less chagrin. So they could come and go in a day from one place to another without any problems, regardless of the distances specified above. That said, the pith of the previous digression was that when Demetrio traveled by train to Monclova he saw through the window some impressive motor graders in full operation working on the road, right in the Cañón del Carmen, between La Polka and Celemania. His traveling companion, a man of about fifty, told him that the road would be finished by the beginning of 1947, according to the state government. A huge step toward modernity. In the same breath he mentioned that after its inauguration a bus company would immediately place in circulation a large number of very well-equipped vehicles, and perhaps a short while later it would become a flourishing highway. Another significant advance. Finally. What follows now is Demetrio's resulting commentary:

"I'm glad the government is concerning itself with the difficulties some experience when traveling. As for me, it would be very useful if I could come and go in one day from Monclova to Sacramento. That would make me happy!"

20

She here and he there, as if ordained, perhaps because fate did not favor a mother-son encounter in Sacramento. At around three in the afternoon Doña Telma appeared at the very spot from which Demetrio, early in the morning and quite eager, had vanished. Perhaps at that particular hour of the day he and Don Delfín were reaching an agreement on the former's terms of employment, but no news of it here till tomorrow—hopefully!—and, finally, rather than elucidate what is most meaningful, let's instead focus on the unexpected encounter between the two señoras, as well as in the euphoria of their surprise. *You? Here? What for?* Doña Zulema was not—we must reiterate—a good hostess. She did not close the store, much less offer her dear relative so much as a cup of coffee: not so much as the courtesy of a sip at the counter of this commercial enterprise, so let's exalt her sloth above all. Hence, the woman who'd just arrived requested: *A sip of water, please, don't be so cruel.* It was pathetic, and the one thus implored produced two glasses of water, then proceeded to voice her thoughts on the subject of Demetrio; that his romance was moving right along; that he was looking for a job in the area, this the reason he had gone to Monclova. A deluge of facts of greater or lesser importance, which saddened Doña Telma: her oblique complaint—her foremost concern—her son's fury, how he left Parras without even planting a kiss where it should have gone: neither on her cheek (for example), nor on her forehead, nor on her hand. Doña Telma, however, did not want to reveal the reason for his rage. The point of gravity—full speed till there—under no circumstance; preferable to avoid what was shameful: the indiscretion of peeking into the loaded suitcase while her son slept; then when she woke him up to . . . Oh, forget it! may all that heaviness float; therewith the phoniness of the adjective "inexplicable" that was and continued to be a terrible mess from which it was quite difficult to extricate oneself, hence the melodramatic conclusion: *I think my son doesn't love me anymore. I am more alone than ever, because my daughters aren't with me, either. The truth is, I don't know what to do. That's why I came to Sacramento.* More and more miserable dribbles of sentimentalism, aimless, even groundless (Doña Zulema listening—perchance derisively?), or perhaps she was on the verge of acting forcefully, such as falling to her knees to beg for forgiveness the moment Demetrio appeared: would it be worth it? We'll leave that pantomime for the morrow, though: *I won't allow you to degrade yourself in front of him.* For now, how to move that big guy to pity? What madcap act would do the trick? Once and for all let's watch the scene that's worthy of a separate strophe unto itself.

It was a matter of a certain amount of obstinacy to keep one's eyes peeled westward up the street for more than two hours, even more to hold those particular four eyes thus and through that shop door, an obstinacy finally rewarded by the joyous glimpse of Demetrio's approaching figure, at which point both cried in unison: *Look! He's coming,* with Doña Telma kneeling (for a while already) in a ridiculously doddering gesture. *Get up, don't act the fool!* Nevertheless, the theatricality was enacted—of course! though with a bit less solemnity. So, when Demetrio arrived, the solicitous mother made a move to embrace him. You can probably imagine the droning intonation of her plea for forgiveness: verbal twists like sloppy swaddling, then muteness the moment the big guy shook off the embrace and began to tick off his news like rosary beads, indifferent to his mother's tearful pantomimes, all of which were undoubtedly observed out of the corner of the eyes of some passersby. For this scene took place on the bench; inside would have been preferable, but such qualms of privacy ran counter to the torrent of topics broached in the heat of the moment, consistent with . . . well, let's pick up some of Doña Telma's vociferations: *Look what I've done! I've come all this way to ask for your forgiveness . . . I, who gave you a suitcase to carry your clothes and money . . . I, who fixed the hem on your pants*, this being the range of vulgarities more or less worth repeating, until Demetrio countered, voicing his delight at being hired by Don Delfín to manage three ranches between there and Sabinas, that he would be generously compensated but that he would have time off only on certain weekends. In fact, his volley had a ways to go but Doña Zulema interrupted him with an order: *Let's go inside, please! I dislike exhibitionism!* They obeyed the director of the play, as it were, and now the same scene was enacted in the living room: his mother trying to hug him and he pushing her away with a flick or two while the volume of her relentless rant rose. Not on her life! though, fearful that this would continue, Doña Zulema issued another order, this time definitive:

"Demetrio, forgive her already! Pity your poor mother."

And he, still pompous and peevish, mumbled:

"You know what, Auntie? I've been thinking about this for several days. Now I just want to let some time pass before I decide to forgive her."

Doña Telma, crying out her eyes, took refuge in a bedroom.

Then Demetrio continued his story about how he'd deposited a large portion of his money in a bank in Monclova, in an account where he'd always have access to his—

"That's enough! Go to your mother and ask her to forgive you. I demand it."

"Neither you nor the Holy Father can demand anything of me. Right now I'm going to go sleep in the hills."

"The hills!? Really, Demetrio, don't be so ungrateful. Your mother is an elderly woman, you must take pity on her. You are making a big mistake."

Opportune words—were they arm-twisting? Two individuals on the verge of tears. Both flushed, by the way. And the emotional surprise—at last! The big guy went to his little mother.

There the lachrymose huddle.

Here, in the living room, the hostess atremble, proud to have played the part of the sensible despot.

Let it be known, then, that mother and son remained in that saint-filled room all night long. Also, that they prayed together and slept together. It was good they didn't dine. It would have done them harm. Also good that they emerged from the room the next morning holding hands. Both poised and apparently without any trace of ugliness still soiling their souls. To sleep together but without touching. As for the rest, the three at the table and eating a breakfast of fried eggs, bread, and *café con leche*. The conversation was decidedly pleasant.

Plans and more plans.

No restraint from anybody to anybody.

Flowing, fortuitous?

Doña Telma was resigned to returning to Parras alone. She dared not try to persuade her son to tell such an unfortunate ranch job to go to hell . . . And, to repeat: there was no occasion for either lady to express even the most oblique reproach. The reins, so it seems, were being loosened, *ex professo*. The two señoras, therefore, exhibiting some backward intelligence, allowing an ignominy to pass. Their combined synthesis of an unfortunate syllogism was this: that Demetrio would field the blows as they came. Neither Parras nor Sacramento nor Monclova but rather grim isolation—out there! where—who knows! in the so-called outskirts of Sabinas, Coahuila. All that was thought but not by those two gray-haired dames.

Good-bye hugs, finally, at early morn. Let's agree that the three of them slept outside, each on his or her own cot, and definitely without covers . . . For the heat at that time of year . . .

Ah, Doña Telma departing, carrying a light suitcase. She walked (let's mention the swish of her skirt keeping time with the shrugging of her shoulders) as if she wanted to shrink, let us say, under the authority of the sun. It would seem that her disappearance was going to be real, in spite of her having been forgiven and even though her son had curled up like a baby in their shared bed. As the brightness effaced her, there rose in the aunt and the nephew some kind of hypothesis that the señora had taken on a true maternal stance, that is, she was able to place herself in limbo awaiting circumstances that would bring her news of his good or ill fortune without her trying to affect the course of events. Perhaps she would never see her son again, perhaps she would see him soon, who knew, but in the meantime, while she was boarding the horse-drawn carriage that would take her to La Polka, and then to the boat and then to the train, she understood that her exhausting trek had had the desired effect, for she had planted in Demetrio a sentimental uncertainty, such as the possibility of returning, or half of a fiction that might never be completed. From then on resignation would work its magic and hence the amazed onlookers (Doña Zelma and Demetrio), for this was how they understood things. *I don't think we should keep watching her or we'll get sad*, the aunt said as she reached out her hand and gently pulled her nephew into the shop. Inside, the repackaging of ideas, though first a request: *Give me a hug, Demetrio. I want to feel that you love me as much as you love your mother and Renata.* The big guy resisted. At that moment, a hug would mean he'd shudder, so no, too cloyingly sweet, this setting things right—what for?, or due to something much simpler: he couldn't make light of his regrets, he had no reason to make a fuss about what still hurt, and so he plainly said: *Not now, Aunt. Maybe I'll give you a hug tomorrow.* Thus he spared himself the explanations and created distance and reserve and threw a little salt upon that sweetness that threatened to drive him mad. In a redundant show of respect, Doña Zulema took (three) steps back, for she also couldn't tolerate such a rejection; which led, in fact, to a side effect: *I ask you please not to go sleep in the hills while you're staying with me.* How to respond to that? with a bemused smile? Not even! Rather—as it happened—with a glance at the reed-covered roof, where—with squinting glances—Demetrio discovered three swallows' nests: already abandoned and on the verge of a collapse whereby clods would fall, perhaps—one day yes and one day no? To feel—what?—a slow disconnect. Anyway! What Demetrio did as he made his way slowly to his refuge was to keep watching the scattered treasures on the roof. Absentminded madman, though purposeful! To cap it off: seclusion. A masturbation was on its way . . . Cursed suspicions . . . Solitary sanctity, on the other hand, though his regrets didn't lend themselves to pleasure brought about by mechanical means, mere animal rewards, and even worse: no subconscious dejection. But Doña Zulema's intuitions were sharpening and—what good would it do? More merry harm, of course—or was that incorrigible amusement? What she did was knock on the door, trying to be quite gentle (pleasant knocks, pleasant voice): *Demetrio, I'd like you to share my bed with me tonight. I won't touch you. I just want to feel that I can replace your mother.* From inside came a "we'll see" and let's say that here concludes an episode of confusing endearments.

21

Solitude might be a threat of everlasting terror. It might advance then run out of steam. It might swell so much it frightens itself away. Be what it may, it is not desirable. A great effort is required to feel it as anything but a burden, so, what good is it? When she was young, Doña Zulema opened her heart to love, and she was struck by lightning. A cousin once removed was the indirect cause. This cousin bore gifts; he was kind. He: fire that mends by sharpening countless emotions; he was generous; he was complacent, he forever spoiled his cousins with wrapped and ribboned gifts. Pleasure. Selflessness, though to be precise, his favorite was Zulema, who didn't know how to respond as the gifts piled up. Without meaning to (what can one do?) she fell in love, a fall indeed, especially because this impulse had to be immediately checked, the brakes put on decisively, but no, because it was impossible to calculate such a natural and benign affection. Be that as it may, she took the prudent path: the obvious one, sans the audacity of flustered excitement; she chose to conceal from her cousin even the subtlest hint of romantic interest. Restraint upon restraint whenever she was with him: never look him straight in the eye. A radical reversal, an intentional detour: such was her choice; her goal, to banish any hint of coquetry. True, one time she dared look at him and even puckered her lips (somehow or other) to see if her cousin would catch a whiff of love, a discreet insinuation, but—nothing!

Their kinship was a ceiling whose luminosity could barely be discerned, an inflexible notion of arid affection, as constrained as grace itself.

And so time passed and so Zulema's fruitless passion grew. Her cousin, named Abelardo, who never realized what he had awakened in the lass, went to study medicine at a faraway university, without a thought of returning even for a visit to that remote rural outpost. In fact, his parents and siblings emigrated to other parts of the country as well. He became a doctor; then, still unsatisfied with this accomplishment, he took the liberty of specializing in an extremely difficult field that made him into an outstanding cardiologist, so outstanding that the practice of his profession rained riches upon him in torrents and allowed him to marry an admirable woman, ergo: from high society and the whole nine yards, one who deserves a house with a swimming pool, whence we can see that wealth dazzled him so much it debilitated him: buying in quantity, stuffed to the very brim. And with this admirable wife, named Esperanza, he sired ten children, who in turn produced approximately forty grandchildren. Clearly a prosperous tribe, if you consider that this entire jovial world strolled down the path of good (moneyed, in this case) fortune; sons and grandsons, corrupt and exploitative, but God fearing, as they should be. No doldrums for Abelardo, not for many years, not until he was widowed. Which made him sharply aware of old age and its ravages. An entire life of wealth that now, like a gigantic poultice, came crashing down upon him. What we're trying to get at is that he felt lonely and bereft, even if full of artifice, and there was no longer anything that brought him satisfaction. Let us say that death, an option always within reach and pictured as eternal whiteness, had become a constant threat. Suicide as a plaything, just like cowardice. Yes. No. Perhaps. What? Anyway, considering his high level of perpetual indecision, we'll opt to leave Abelardo in that trance and turn to what had happened to Zulema many years before. Ever since she was twenty she knew that the sacrosanct love she modestly poured into her cousin was utterly futile. By the same token she knew that she had committed an unforgivable mistake by not showing that love, to wit: by not letting him clearly understand that he was and would be the chosen one, hmm, an old-fashioned woman, because she had counted a couple dozen suitors (this sum included twenty years of prospects) and she had rejected them all.

From that we must subtract one dozen, the youngest suitors, for the simple reason that they were not prosperous; however, as far as the other dozen go, we include all those who offered her a serious relationship with the diaphanous prospect of being led to the altar, after which they would provide her with a life fit for a queen; well, no, not that either; which can be explained thus: the old tune became a drone after so many imprudent men posed the compromising question: *Why don't you ever say yes to anyone?* and she would respond: *When I was young I opened my heart to love and after that I closed it. I could not have Abelardo, so I won't marry anybody else.* We must stress the importance of this statement: Zulema was and always would be an old-fashioned woman. When she closed her heart forever it turned to stone, and—obviously! there but for the grace of God went she.

Now let's turn our attention back to Abelardo: the widower, the saddened señor who, with nothing better to do, held steadfast to the idea of taking his own life. There he was, up a stump with his folly, when one day an old relative came at his house and brought him news that though shocking contained a glint of hope.

"Hey, Abelardo, do you remember our cousin Zulemita?"

"Yes, sort of, but we're talking about a little more than half a century ago . . . Yes, of course! She's my cousin from Sacramento . . . Hmm, I remember I was in love with her, but she was my cousin and that was that . . ."

"Well, I must tell you, Zulemita remained very attached to you, so much so that she never wanted to marry anybody else. She had many suitors, but she often said that if not you, she'd never marry anyone. So she stayed single. When she was very young she opened a grocery store and that's what she lives on to this day."

"I suppose she knows I got married."

"Yes, but once she confessed that she had hopes you would be widowed and return to Sacramento to marry her."

"Ah, now I understand, she sent you to tell me all this."

"So it is."

"Well, if I had realized this before . . ."

"Abelardo, go to Sacramento! You would make that poor woman very happy. But don't tell her you're coming, okay? Just imagine what a surprise it will be."

A tricky hope, tempting from afar . . . Adventure, an injection of life. Spirit, exertion. Toward a stump that could not sprout, and now—new growth? Therefore, an obsolete trip: trains, boats, horse-drawn carriages, sweating, vexation, fatigue, and a sprinkling of folly to bring him back to life. Constructive caresses. Aged kisses like watery broths . . .

The dismal truth was that Abelardo's children visited him only when they needed money. Whenever he called to invite any of them over they, without exception, offered up excuses: that they were swamped; that they'd come later, which was synonymous with "we'll see when," and that "when" was never defined . . . Old age pays a high price, and there's dross as well, and will continue to be, we could say, excremental, and how to make oneself loved or what spontaneity was needed for him to obtain filial love . . .

Nothing, no irksome insistence . . .

And when he thought about it with a clear head, Abelardo decided that this Zulemita would look after him wonderfully well for a couple of weeks.

She would be generous if only because of that unrequited affection from so many years before . . .

His Eminence figured he should go to Sacramento without telling anybody . . .

A tenebrous disappearance . . . deliberate.

We could say that the urge itself to travel in the face of so many crazy obstacles would be a path to rejuvenation.

Base, struggling spirit.

I will come back, I will, but, what if I like how Zulemita treats me?

Two old folks helping each other live a little longer. Abelardo even played with the mad idea that his cousin—still in love?—would come to live with him in Mexico City.

It was yet to be seen if . . .

At least he would spend fifteen rewarding days, indeed!

Find out if senile love made for resolute decision-making.

There was also the possibility that his cousin would tell him to go to hell.

22

To descend one staircase then climb another that would take him much farther: Demetrio had found that this image portrayed—and summarized—his current plan. The hand-holding on the bench, as usual. No more than one half hour of decent love . . . A consequence of his showing up when she was not presentable . . . Thus the suitor had understood the need to schedule dates ahead of time. Because otherwise . . . too bad! . . . The subtleties of being out of favor, transformed into something that, fortunately on this occasion, became only a minor obstacle. Or rather the mother told the daughter: *Go ahead, but I'm going to call you in* . . . (already mentioned); resulting in: the consequences of haste: blocks of information from the suitor about his new job on the ranch out there in Sabinas; herewith we see the nature of the abbreviated because: his need to be near her so he could see her more frequently—how's that? As it turned out, the half hour passed in a trice. Then the immaculately platitudinous good-byes we can well surmise: no embrace, no fleeting kiss (not even) on the sweetheart's forehead: a most respectful one on the face (still so far away), nothing! then, damn, both their hands moving at chest level (arms bent) while he sketched out his plans to return to Sacramento soon to see her— see her! see her!! The looks in the eyes of two saints who, buried deep down in their spirits, longed to be a bit like dirty devils. But that's another story.

Finally, to avoid giving Doña Zulema the opportunity to air her lament about having remained a spinster (that night she had told her nephew the idyllic story about her and her second cousin, Dr. Abelardo Rubiales), let us set Demetrio down in Monclova, where we must picture a well-lit scene in a rural living room full of objects that conjure up the most presumptuous rusticity; the new employee, sitting with a bottle of beer in his hand, and his new boss, who never stopped eating canapés and drank nothing. They were discussing all the chores that needed to be carried out in the places under discussion. Demetrio would live at the ranch called La Mena, but he would have to pay daily visits to the ranches called El Origen and La Igualdad, for which he would have at his disposal a well-maintained pickup truck. A pickup truck he could also drive on weekends . . . ! *What a boon*, thought the one who had reason to think such thoughts, and still more: *On Saturdays I can go to the red-light district in Sabinas, if there is one, and have Sundays free to visit Renata!* To think so much: to get entangled only to get disentangled, easy as it goes, and, what a good job he had landed!

23

Two naked old people lying in a fairly narrow bed, caressing each other with almost trembling hands. They offered each other fear more than kisses on the lips. At first their quite puckered lips sought each other unstintingly . . . That is, first the fearful naked-ness that they both ultimately imagined as shamelessness: to see each other's drooping skin offered up to groping touches. It was important to be curled up horizontally next to each other. The bed creaked with each and every move.

This between-the-sheets finale ended up being more lachry-mose than throbbing. The sensual part occurred shortly after their encounter. Abelardo's arrival, with a cane!: rather weary from the vicissitudes of his trip from Mexico City to this deserted and deso-late place. Delayed recognition: the doctor (who boasted a quite graying quiff) was carrying his jacket over his forearm: he had to due to the heat: as he also had to loosen his tie and unbutton the collar of his shirt. An old-fashioned introduction, a bow, on the threshold of Zulema's shop. We will spare ourselves the slow verbal rapprochement and go directly to the embrace, which we should posit as the very marrow of the thing, because it was the first one they had ever exchanged: *Zulemita! . . . Abelardo! . . .* What good fortune! After seeing each other's wrinkles: it's been so many years! For her this moment was more than unexpected, it was a sign from the above and beyond: God had willed it, and willed it well. The entire panorama of a lifetime, made to wait . . . Waiting behind a counter, always backpedaling, the heavy daily dullness, what could have been and—likewise—the waxing of what had been an irreparable youthful error . . . A life that stippled till it made shine what would literally become a deep fissure at the peak, this while they embraced. Finally, that the embrace would be the longed-for summation, above all for Zulema, who resisted letting go; and she won the day because when it came to physical strength she had much more of it than he, and what's more: she was holding him up—careful! the cane lying on the ground. And words of love now as flowing as song: words repressed for half a century or more. To not let go of his aged wrist—no! Even if he tried, his efforts were, if we may say so, pathetic! . . . Whereby Abelardo had no choice but to demand, with plaintive tenderness: *Let go of me, my love!* and she—how wretched!—had to do as she was told.

More catching up in the kitchen. Everything that had settled like pirouettes of fog over long years and without a chance of clearing, all Zulema's fault. *That relative who came to tell me about you should have done so when I was a student. Now I am a widower and I have children and grandchildren,* Abelardo proclaimed, then added in a phony tone: *I always loved you, Zulemita, even though you were my cousin.* There was no forgiving herself the blunder, now immense, the result of her recondite small-town candor. A regret to be churned in her stomach juices, never to be expelled.

But there they were, facing each other. No point in talking much now. They chose to wallow in carnal delights. Naked—anon! the silent exchange. Zulema took the initiative and unbuttoned her blouse. In response, he dropped his trousers. A jumble of garments strewn across the floor. Portents of ultimate disorder, even more so if viewed from above: *O collage!* Nevertheless, what we now see are the difficulties of divestment, more for him than for her, because standing on his feet without his cane—how was he supposed to keep his balance? But he did—really! A matter of dignity, of heroics, except his shoes: their removal—a risky business? That should take place while they were seated on the edge of the bed. Zulema, on the other hand, naked from head to toe in the kitchen. The rest can be inferred. Promptly, then, came the pleasure of the naked embrace, so full of tenderness and so abiding, though: it couldn't move forward, for Abelardo simply couldn't, confound it, no matter how hard he tried, and what a pity that he was unable— proof positive—to induce even a subtle erection. Nor did she particularly crave vivacious penetration. Hence the solution was to curl into cuddles from head to toe, extensive pathways for meandering hands that—onward! erred then found their way again. Anarchic displacements or, rather, trembling activity that slowly turned into very concrete circles drawn with index fingers on bellies, chests, arms, faces, and that's all. Their sexes—no way!— rather to respect them, to pay homage to his impotence. The naked sacred attaining a higher ground, and thus three days were spent. Zulema closed the store on his suggestion. When we say "three days" we wish to emphasize the consistency of their routine, which included eating, sleeping, and talking, this last one wrapped in each other's arms in bed: an ascendant life fitted onto a flat one, that is: always naked, with an ever-increasing tendency toward the detailed familiarity with such a plenitude of wrinkles, but also in their many or few achievements during the long years they had been passing through. So, the finishing touch, bodies for the long haul (now), as well as lives whose paths diverged like two branches growing from the same trunk. Essential trunk, blood: cousins, disgrace, penury, and the impossibility of knowing that never—never! God forbid! even when it was not unheard of for some family members to marry and have normal children. Anyway, holed up for three days during which the amusing—and fascinating—part was to watch Abelardo naked and using his cane to move around from here to there; of course she couldn't laugh, for she was ecstatic, and he upon seeing her broad hips, her dropping flesh, likewise her breasts, like balls of socks, he had to hold back his urge to let out a giggle, a weak, sickly one, because on one of those afternoons he confessed to her that he hadn't been feeling well for the last few months, and this certainly was quite crucial, for on the third night, while both were sleeping in perfect peace, she awoke around three in the morning after feeling that Abelardo's body had grown quite cold. She touched him with her usual tenderness and was overwhelmed by terror; she shouted, shook, then placed her ear against his chest, and no, no beat. The aged gallant had died . . . Aaaaayyyyy . . . No matter, she tried to give him mouth-to-mouth resuscitation, a kiss with consequences, and nothing—nothing! He showed no sign of gratitude. Then came Zulema's subconscious howl hurled to the winds. Her closest neighbors were far away and in between were courtyards, orchards, thatch. So unless she immediately got dressed and went out to the street and screamed like a madwoman, disturbing all the sleep surrounding her, the best thing would be to await the dawn. In the other room . . . to attempt to doze in the other bed . . . She couldn't. Poor thing! What unfortunate love! What a dire circumstance!

Subsequently, her neighbors were polite when . . . Herewith an et cetera that compressed the action: two-pronged assistance: prepare a wake; bring votives, candles, flowers (the most fragrant), from early till late in the day. The greatest difficulty lay in constructing a wood coffin and finding a spot in the graveyard to dig a grave. A collective, sweaty chore—indeed! so much so that the wake took place without a coffin. An old stranger covered with a sheet. An excess of prayers. Weeping? Only one, she, who didn't want to hire mourners according to the custom. Zulema was quite afflicted. Her cries were genuine: arising from deep down inside—how could they not be! for her laments stirred up a thousand things. Just imagine her incisive question: what does God have against me? Fated to wait an entire lifetime for her one and only beloved and when finally he arrives at her house brimming with affection—plop!: death: the paradox. Still pending was for someone to inform Abelardo's children and grandchildren of his demise, but the informing relative was not in Sacramento, and telephones and addresses—if he even knew them—never! So how? A quandary deferred . . . A quandary to address in stages, this dissemination of information, all in good time, for his children and grandchildren had ventured into far-flung corners of the Mexican territory, not all, just to be clear, but anyway; their desire was none other than to visit the grave of the eminent doctor. One of the sons ordered the construction of a pompous tomb. This was a matter of dignity, for it was not fair for a gentleman of his stature to be buried like a dog. And now as an aside, let us add that Doña Zulema was, as far as can be expected, a model hostess, so much so that she tired of being so, after welcoming (nonstop) his relatives over a five-year period. By the way: strangers kept arriving, and each one gave her money. A business, inadvertent, or divine compensation, still insufficient, considering that the tawdry tale did not even give her the gift of a child. Abelardo left her nothing but three days of lapsed love and—sorrow! for she found few people who were willing to hear in full detail about her one and only real and lasting misfortune. Demetrio, yes, that night, on the eve of his trip to Monclova and then on his way to Sabinas: he heard, and heard, and heard, without asking any questions: exemplary attitude translated into Zulema formulating an ulterior proposition:

"Demetrio, allow me to take on the role of your second mother . . . As you can see, it is what I need most of all at this point in my life."

"Okay, I understand what you are proposing . . . It's just that for me it's important to know what being my second mother means to you."

"Only that you may live in this house whenever you want; only that when I die you will own it."

"Great, that suits me just fine."

"If you end up not liking your work on Don Delfín's ranches, you can return here. You will be near Renata, and you can invest your money and work in Sacramento."

"Really?"

"Yes, and from now on you should know that my store is yours."

"But my mother, Telma . . . hmm . . . I can't just forsake her."

"She's as forsaken as I am . . . But do as you like. You could, for example, bring her to live here, she could sell her house and . . ."

"Look, Aunt, I have to think carefully about everything you are suggesting . . . But from this point on I accept you as my second mother—by all means!"

Part

Three

The Need for Sanctity

24

It's hard to know whether the earth, midst its thousands of millions of rotative and orbital movements, had tilted a bit or veered slightly off course. Such speculation is germane considering that the weather in October 1946, at least in the central region of Coahuila, was hotter than hell. The population's consternation was so pronounced that nobody expected the weather to change till November or December, many even fantasizing that Christmas celebrations would be accompanied by fans and perspiration. Which had never happened, but now—phew!: climactic displacement was a reality and perhaps not till January, or even February, would it begin to grow cold, not so cold as to need a heavy coat, but still. Some even thought that the real cold season (the normal one) would not begin till March or April of the following year, and a few, carrying things to an extreme, thought it would never again be cold on the face of the earth, and there would never be rain (not even in jest), and blahblahblah: and as no one knew the exact cause of the phenomenon, almost everyone attributed it to divine retribution. Perhaps human beings had been behaving so badly that they deserved the worst: a perpetual and bruising heat, brutal—right? Hopefully not, others thought: God might apply pressure but is incapable of destroying what he himself had created.

Anyway, the heat hovers over everything else in the sense that the thousands of stories unfolding herein will be subject to a perpetual drip. Hopefully not, we think, but only because it is convenient to think in these terms.

So, let's skip ahead once and for all past the wondrously imaginative predictions of the locals to reveal—perhaps therein damaging the logical unfolding of a plot—that in December 1946 the weather turned around abruptly from one day to the next. First came a deluge (with murderous hail) throughout much of the region, which in turn almost immediately ushered in very cold winds, mostly from the north and the west; that's how it was, and we shall deal with what follows all in due time . . . In the meantime, we might fancy a fan.

25

To learn to drive. Demetrio nearly started panting when he heard these words from Don Delfín's lips as the principal requirement for the optimal administration and supervision of the three ranches. Daily trips in the pickup first thing in the morning except Sundays, supposedly his day off. We should say that he was supposed to finish his rounds shortly after midday. In Monclova there had been mention of these duties, and the exciting news began to sparkle the moment Demetrio heard he would have use of a pickup sui generis, brown, quite used, that was waiting for him at La Mena Ranch, though here's the obviously surly part: the roads in that region were not uniform: they tilted, they narrowed, sometimes they seemed to vanish only to pick up again who knows where. All this seen on the way, for Don Delfín was taking the new employee north, where: first La Mena, and then whatever comes next . . . Rough riding, in the meantime, in a pickup, jet black, latest model . . . In 1946, on the stretch between Monclova and Sabinas, there were only twenty miles of pavement on what would later be called the Carretera Central. The rest, sixty miles perhaps, was gravel, a wide grade but uneven and, therefore, dangerous. Especially dangerous was a detour right next to a gigantic huisache tree, like an expressive and watchful ornament, from which hung abandoned blackbird nests. An unmistakable point of reference, as was the fifteen-foot drop the boss-driver accomplished with true dexterity, which led onto a dirt road straight to La Mena; still to go was a long stretch, many curves, and much fatigue. The field for driving practice, a perfectly unproblematic plain to swerve about on: first, second, third, reverse, almost never fourth: the roads didn't allow for such speeds. Don Delfín told Demetrio that there were three barrels of gasoline at the first ranch; one more at El Origen and another, if needed, at La Igualdad. And here, all aquiver, is another bit of information: at every ranch Demetrio would find peons dexterous in the automotive arts. Practical wise men, with basic knowledge of whatever they needed to know. Because breakdowns . . . no precautions taken ever end up being a good bet. One lovely obstacle after another, spread about this territory beyond the reach of Mexico's industrialization. Abiding life, almost like in the Stone Age: a matter of adjusting to the purely primitive with the single solid idea of somehow enjoying it, well, now to return . . . Among the many responsibilities assigned to the agronomist—once and for all let's set some clear boundaries: we call him "agronomist" to stress that these were livestock ranches and that they wouldn't plant a fig, not a seed or a tree to save their lives; hence all Demetrio's agronomic baggage was utterly useless—and now, yes, to return to the evolving story, we wish to point out that his primary responsibility was to transport supplies, the most urgent ones, as requested by the peons on both ranches: El Origen was to the northeast of La Mena, whereas La Igualdad was to the southeast: at a slightly veiled diagonal. And the daily dust storms kicked up by the pickup: a romantic image for those (very few) who took the trouble to watch the arrivals and departures. By the same token we must say that Don Delfín had a hard time holding on to driver-managers, but we'll get to the deeper reason for that later. In the meantime, one of the many chores involved the transport of goats and lambs, and once in a while a cow or a bull; breeding animals who were treated like kings, or slabs of meat to be sold in Sabinas and Nueva Rosita; there were other job-related oddities there's no point in enumerating. We simply want to mention that the peons managed the full range of information. Though really: imagine once and for all the endless hustle and bustle, and—on the other hand, what an avalanche of difficulties awaited Demetrio! The fact is, the more his boss talked during the trip, the more paralyzed he became. So many particulars, so many unknowns, yes, of course! because of x or z.

When the boss and the new manager arrived at the aforementioned ranch—let's call it the "head" ranch—the former let flow an endless stream of declarations; the points he made were incisive and parsimonious, and unfailingly incriminating; herewith the most resounding: *You should bring a woman to live with you here.* And then: *A place like this can be lonely and tough.* And then: *I want you to enjoy yourself, in spite of the hard work, though without a woman, who knows what you'll have to come up with:* that last touch, on the heels of other similar ones, must have really struck the new employee. A collection of bitter juices churned in his gut: Renata; marriage? bring her here! if she would agree, needless to say; but, darn, the monstrously tempestuous; the ill effects of accelerating, and not; in the meantime, and for a good while longer, strategic patience, knowing that in such a place, one day had the dimensions of one week, and one week seemed like one month, and one month, one year, solitude under these circumstances as spiritual elevation that would keep rising to who knows what heights: more and more purified severity: white and unscathed . . . from a lack thereof, but also from a guise of servitude . . . Okay now, let's move on to what we can discern. La Mena consisted of three adobe structures, a corral, and a windmill; a scattering of roosters, hens, chickens, and one or another naked child roaming around. The goats and lambs prisoners in . . . Demetrio wanted to know as soon as possible where he would reside, but Don Delfín (diviner) told him he should first pay a visit to the other ranches so he could memorize the day's run on the roads, with the understanding that any detour on any of the many side roads that branched off from the main road would get him lost. *There are only three curves from here to El Origen, and all three turn to the right, whereas on the way to La Igualdad there will be six curves, two to the right and four to the left . . . Remember that the roads to both places are wider than the many side roads . . . Be careful!* In training, from the start! little by little, of course (trifles upon trifles), and off they went to El Origen. First they answered the peons' greetings—stick figures and busy bodies—by raising one hand, as they had done. *It's six miles from La Mena to El Origen and eight from La Mena to La Igualdad.* The heat increased (we are in the aforementioned October). There was no defense other than to constantly swab forehead, cheeks, and chin (this last the most drippy, wouldn't you say?). *Here you will sweat as you never have before . . . I recommend you carry at least three handkerchiefs in your trouser pockets.* Upon hearing such nonsense Demetrio asked: *And who is going to do my laundry?* And a smiling Don Delfín answered: *The wife of my peon at La Mena. Her name is Bartola and he is Benigno. I'll introduce you to them soon. They will be very important to you.* And now, so as not to drag this out, we hereby present a summation: El Origen had one adobe structure, no windmill, an insignificant corral (a smallness that evoked compassion), whereas La Igualdad was nothing but two adobe buildings (meager progress), also no windmill, though a cheerful corral, larger than the one at La Mena—what for? with more heads of cattle—my, my! They went through the introductions: lightning fast, as if by the way, for the deepening of mutual acquaintance would go hand in hand with the working relationship; learn each other's names: as an initial requirement and, here comes another of Don Delfín Guajardo's declarations: *We'll see how you do when it gets cold. It gets pretty bad around here. I'm warning you.* Uneasiness? Misgivings? You be the judge.

Hence, what's already been stated: he finally learned how to drive: at first the apparently obscure, and then—off he went! Yet to see if student and master quarreled under the murderous sun (let this then be the emphatic beginning of a briny life), both bathed in sweat, Demetrio more than Don Delfín. The good part was that the agronomist quickly learned the ins and outs of driving that pickup that had been sitting at La Mena for a month. It's also worth mentioning that the peons knew a lot about automotive mechanics but nothing about driving—unheard of! Because the boss stubbornly refused to teach them. Inexplicable waning notions, beyond which let's make clear that the powerful old man had an expression on his face of permanent disapproval: one that was scary, for nobody could divine his hidden reasons. The peons knew—just as Demetrio soon would too—that this grand gentleman was the owner of fifteen ranches (a dying empire), and this was the extent of what his mysterious expression revealed . . . Anyway, we were talking about the agronomist learning how to drive the pickup truck in only a few hours. By the afternoon—take a look at him! Alone, without a copilot—come on! Crepuscular applause, somewhat lackluster, but fortuitous. Uncommonly talented, that one: nobody like him in years, none of the previous managers, who'd learned their brakings and accelerations there, as well as the great problem of pacing, not a single one like Demetrio, who needed only a little practice. Next: to view the quarters where he'd make old bones; he beheld cramped discomfort and meager furnishings. A stage set consisting of a bare cot, a washbasin, a table, a few dishes, and a crystal radio the size of an adobe brick, which required two fat batteries. A novel private world and forced appreciation. And now for Don Delfín's agreeable good-bye. He left feeling quite proud and not before handing a great big wad of bills to the new manager, who was astonished as he watched his departure, while in an alternate register amazed at having in his hands a quite uncanny quantity of cash, which Demetrio stuffed into his suitcase at once; he had no choice.

Being the manager meant he was in charge. Up to Demetrio when he'd issue the first order, just as the sun was setting . . . Also, the useful relationship with Bartola and Benigno, the only inhabitants of La Mena apart from an unknown number of snot-nosed kids . . . So he roused himself to go see what he should see, and in order to smugly tell them to make him something to eat. He acted too hastily, because the chubby little woman was about to bring a plate of beans to his quarters. In any case, his arrival inside, where the family sphere had all the comforts of domesticity *de occultis:* ergo: no tantrums in the background from the naked children (there were three, he discovered), only a few sounds from them moving about. The adults' terseness was noticeable, for they did not initiate any conversation. Boundaries, hermetism, and the sudden gravity of two captivating words: *Drink, eat:* a reverse order, issued by Benigno, and that was all the encouragement the manager needed to set things in motion, like this:

"I don't understand why Don Delfín gave me so much money . . . You saw the size of that roll . . . I think it's too much."

"He gave you that much because he probably won't pay you again for months. Maybe not till December, or even later," Benigno said.

"What?"

"That's what he does with us."

"Why's that?"

"Because money's no good for anything out here on the ranch . . . It's his way of keeping us enslaved. Once a month he brings us sacks of beans, oats, and flour."

"That's all you eat?"

"Sometimes lamb or goat meat, but only when he gives the okay to slaughter one . . . That happens at least once a year."

From there they went on to the grisly, or bellowing—we could say—details, for anything extra they ingested was restricted to snake or rabbit meat (an abundance of which could be found in this desolate wasteland, according to the peon), and soon the topic at hand did an about-face, for the big guy was an urban creature and liked to constantly change the subject: dissipation galore, or deliberate disconcentration. The question arose whether they had ever considered living in a town or city, and the immediate response was—never! a word both deep and euphonic that also contained a shred of logic both definitive and conclusive: *If we lived in town we wouldn't know how to use money . . . That scares us because we don't know anything about numbers.* In the face of such a well-conscribed truth it seemed futile to push the peon past who knows what boundary to give further explanations, and no, only the weight of the hardened squaring, congealed, as well as the discomfort if . . . hmm . . . How to clear things up? Somehow they let Demetrio know that they had no desire to prolong the conversation, that their routine determined their terseness: early to bed and that's that. Rising at dawn was more pleasurable than anything else. But there was one more volley: a tidbit of information dropped in passing that broached the most shameful deficiency: neither Bartola nor Benigno knew how to read or write, whatever existed outside this rustic scope of their life was and would be very difficult: obstacles like too-sharp thorns, so much so that any unplanned movement created an upheaval, and anyway—why? oh fie! Why try to join a society that is so unforgiving? The confession was hesitant, so how to interpret what only barely, or what almost; one could affirm that illiteracy was synonymous with fixed deep-rootedness, or merely a roughshod philosophy born and bred and dead in the opacity of a small, almost unpopulated world, an— enough!, and—phew!, the guest (of sorts) understood grudgingly after consulting his wristwatch. It was eight p.m. So late! Horrors! And this: a watchword: get used to not enjoying what nights can bring: the relief of—socializing! damn, which was also the (spiritual) relaxation so necessary to make space for the doldrums of the day: no way! not here! and no way to order the peons to stay awake; an indication of future problems . . . with the boss—when he came? The radio was a consolation to help the newcomer relax, to listen in irremediable solitude to songs and news that really did seem more alien than ever, faraway clutter, which would no doubt become less and less appealing, though for now . . . Well—good night! and so let's appreciate his urge to go and fiddle with the volume and tuning knobs. Salvation radio, night after night . . . the project of slowly falling asleep. A partial victory, in the end, but . . . In 1946 the only radio station that was broadcast nationally was XEW, the Voice of Latin America. However, there was no shortage of clamorous crackling and hissing that interfered to a point of ruining the original broadcast. An important thing to know because plenty of nights an English-language station would cross paths, then take over, and that's what Demetrio suffered almost daily; we say "almost daily" because we are evaluating a stretch of time characterized by a fastidious routine. Nonetheless, clarifications are in order. Which is why we must find a temporal counterpoint. Therefore let us turn to Monclova, when Don Delfín and Demetrio were just coming to terms. The transcription should have fallen squarely into a notebook in which the new manager was writing down every step he would need to take once he got settled at the ranch; one of those, very important, was the list, with names (for social reasons) and addresses, of the eight butchers in Sabinas and the four in Nueva Rosita. The distribution of the butchered: one lamb per week, as well as three she-goats. Meat on the move. A sure sale, in any case. A lot of money to keep—where?, nowhere, therefore—in the suitcase? The shining advantage resided in Don Delfín's coming to the ranch every week: on Fridays: an essential habit in order to, among other things, collect the cash from the weekly sales: that's it: let's repeat that this is an advantage because otherwise Demetrio's mangy quarters would soon become an absurdity, to wit, a warehouse crammed with bills. Manifold futility at the mercy of an arbitrary windstorm—and what conjecture would become reality if a storm swept the bills away? The loneliness of the ranch lent itself to such imaginings, for already the utterly unusual was making incursions: fortunes flying over the desert: when? never? The first time Demetrio went to Sabinas he asked Benigno to accompany him. He wanted to be sure not to lose his way along the supposed fifteen miles from one point to the other, for the moment he started the truck the peon warned him about the large number of forks off the main road, hence: *Come with me. You can help me find the butchers.* Unfortunately, Benigno didn't remember the precise location of those establishments. It's just that, trying to find your way in that urban muddle . . . In fact, the peon had been only four times to Sabinas and only once to Nueva Rosita . . . In 1946 Sabinas had a population of approximately thirty thousand inhabitants, whereas Nueva Rosita was a town of fifteen thousand, or perhaps fewer. But both places had spectacular commercial activity.

This work trip turned out to be a kind of holiday for both. So: *Come. Do as I say. Let's go.* And yes, agreed. Yes, flat-out compliance, by virtue of the fact that both would benefit from a temporary disconnect—from what?—the monotony of the ranch, less longed for by Benigno, but the manager: how about it? A different environment; the world, culture—bah!, his presumptions had to be exaggerated . . .

Of course, before unpacking the knicking and knacking of selling and buying the meat, it's worth sorting through the core of the sparse exchanges along the way: *You might not want to learn anything about numbers, but you should realize that money gives you freedom of movement.* Freedom of movement? More dependency, more anxiety, because numbers are limiting. A different kind of servitude, perhaps an even darker one, because of not knowing the true value of things. A reality calibrated to the quantity of coins and bills. Another corral or a different prison, but a much less happy one—or not? and since there was no escape, better to have someone higher up who resolved all the problems: a god, a boss, and therefore further submission to a perfect fit, to stay out of trouble—and uncertainties? In case we have interpreted the peon's words otherwise: that is to say: harum-scarum, it is worth recording here his conclusion: *No matter what, we are slaves to somebody or something, and I prefer to know who it is and what the one who gives me my living is like; as long as he treats me well, right? why dig any deeper?* Then, the counterattack: *But wouldn't you like to be like your boss? He is rich and powerful.* In the face of such a bold truth there arose a tiny truth: *You do realize, sir, that I don't know how to read or write.* A sharp deficiency, the final blow, and a return to silence, not without Demetrio blurting out a crushing commonplace: *There's no doubt about it, we are who we are,* would you listen to that! What? Demetrio saying such things. Or rather, once and for all he had to attain a mental toughness that could dispel all sorts of humble arguments. Or rather, his own—how prodigious were they? or rather—what did they settle? So, no further attempts at conceptual largesse, better not to get angry for no reason, but rather to clearly recognize his role: he was nothing more nor less than a masterful manager; he was, therefore, a person who should know about numbers and an infinity of other organizational procedures (what words!) that would put this lackluster ranching business on a firmer footing. Know thyself, in order to fit oneself in and—hey! know that this peon, like those from El Origen and La Igualdad, didn't count. It's a matter of language, that's all, and—what is to be done? None could be his assistant, because none was a problem solver, besides about trifling issues related to provisions. O crass circumstance . . . so reductive! which also made him feel (now, really) alone—alone! a lonely madman? Unless he had a woman by his side . . . Renata (fixation), still unattainable . . . Longing in the ether, damn . . . Because he was neither a missionary nor an apostle . . . And the course of that vital truth—put to the test? In fact . . . it was important for him to

know that not even at moments of direst despair should he expose
his most mundane thoughts, considering it much more appropriate
to emulate the behavior of the peons: their terseness, their lack of
expressiveness, their perhaps saintly subjugation.
Blood on his hands: on Benigno's. *Come on. I'm sure there
are sinks in Sabinas that have some good soap.* And just like
that the peon—what a bother!—made the trip. A brute question of
haste . . . Moreover: dawn had barely broken when Benigno began
killing animals. In less than two hours he had slaughtered a lamb
and three she-goats. Such murderous dexterity put Demetrio on
tenterhooks, for he made the following calculations on the side:
this ranch hand could kill thirty-two animals in eight hours, as well
as slit their bellies, cut them up, and skin them; and if he added up
the number the ranch hands at El Origen and La Igualdad could
slaughter in the same amount of time . . . A contest between them,
someday, with a prize for the winner, not money but food: an abundant ration of canned goods wouldn't be so bad; the notion of a
feast in the middle of such scarcity; but based on what Don Delfín
had said when they were there in Monclova, the sale of meat was
by special order, so this time the meat would be sold to the butcher
who offered the most; imagine that for a whole month—nothing
to sell! ever since the last manager escaped on foot and at night
through the desert. Even if there had been orders, there would
have been no way to fill them—how? Clearly selling live animals
would be more convenient, but the butchers in Sabinas and Nueva
Rositas were too lazy to do the slaughtering. So, to return, here we
have the meat on this reckless trip, in the sun, of course, because
it was daytime, and yes: the carcasses covered with a blue blanket:
a subtle way of buying time there in the truck bed . . . In 1946 there
was not even one refrigerated truck anywhere in the length or the
breadth of the Mexican territory . . . Hence the complex aspect of
this troublesome situation was to transport the meat packed in ice,
oh yes, only from where to where, eh? because to get enough ice:

where . . . And the impossibility (right?) of . . . Well, anyway, we'll now close this muddle with a happy fact: Demetrio and Benigno did not have to wander through the ignominious labyrinth of the streets of Sabinas; all they had to do was find x butcher to buy their goods, which had been covered. The transaction in itself was formidable because the butcher (the owner) placed a huge order for the following week: four lambs and eight she-goats—a heavenly delight! or that's what we would call it.

26

Let's mention the drought so we can go straightaway to the only two letters Renata buried near the henhouse. Regarding the latter, later, for it held quite lively interest, and as to the former we can state that October, November, and two weeks of December had already passed and no rain had fallen in Sacramento or the surrounding area, not even in the distance did a bold and threatening cloud appear above any hill, not even did a lost burst of lightning bring a furtive flash to gladden a few hearts—nothing at all! nothing but a solar invasion, with the accompanying clear skies, everywhere and always, whose tones of livid injurious blue began to fill the few inhabitants in those parts with terror. In fact, the nocturnal and diurnal heat seemed to gnaw with multiple rows of teeth, awakening the sensation that at any moment the inanimate might begin to stir.

We can talk about the animate (mobile, legged) only in terms of caution and despondency, or the search for relief in the shade. People, animals, insects—where could they find refuge? There were deaths, mostly in the hinterlands, which became most definitively a horrific expanse, more and more uninhabitable. This serves as a point of reference from which to ponder the increased sluggishness in Sacramento: no signs of whips or spurs, nobody wanted to budge because that meant suffering for the mere sake of it. And as far as business was concerned: sales plummeted, specifically at Doña Luisa and Renata's stationery store, which was now quite clearly a business of secondary importance, because they didn't sell food; in fact, for weeks they considered having a go at selling an array of cold drinks, but, to begin with, they'd have to buy an ice chest, then get three blocks of ice every day and start chopping away from early morn . . . In 1946 there was a small ice factory near La Polka, a place called El Cariño de la Montaña; there are reports that every day great quantities of these blocks were carried by cart, and that it took three trips by boat to transport the entire load . . . However, the sale of cold drinks had stiff competition; the ten grocery stores in town each sold an unimaginable quantity of such drinks. Packaged coldness—it should be stated—did not guarantee a profit. In fact, all businesses were hurting. The fault lay in the weather—but was it only the weather? The fault lay in the exodus of people to unknown burgs (otherwise called industrialization): the ripping apart of the small-town social fabric, and now let's focus on Renata and Doña Luisa and extract a snippet of a diffident dialogue: a dinner with dishes piled high with eggs and chorizo to ponder piecemeal the possibility of moving, for example, to Monclova or Monterrey, assuming that Sacramento would soon be doomed: add to this the fanning that kept time with the eating: manual nimbleness shoring up adversity. On one hand, the urgency to flee: the beautiful one putting pressure on the obstinate mother, who claimed she'd rather die in Sacramento than venture into the unknown: *I'm not going anywhere, even if it is for the best.* Moreover, she said that in a small town she felt protected; she mentioned relatives twice or thrice removed who lived there, as well as her very close friends who lived nearby: *Everyone, at the end of the day, would take pity on me. Whereas in the city* . . . The advantageous gregariousness of the small scale, the tribal, the cyclical nature of a consolation that stiffens one's resolve: right? After this affirmation the conversation took a different turn: *Unlike me, you have the option of getting married, going somewhere*

else . . . However, the fact that she'd heard nothing from Demetrio
came to light: that he hadn't written; that he hadn't come; that
maybe never again, in spite of living so close. And supreme disappointment became evident: *I haven't heard anything from him
for three months. Maybe I could ask Doña Zulema if she has had
any news* . . . Her mother gave her permission to . . . The next day,
Renata went to her. Profuse perspiration, rather crass: the effect
or the fruit of the way there. Even more sorrowful was her return,
after hearing that his aunt also had heard nothing from the one who
had sworn and sworn again to frequently visit the town. Another
chat during which: *Maybe he has a girlfriend there*, Renata said
with a blush: ugh! on the verge of tears: Doña Luisa, with her indis-
tinct spirit, saw this and went to pat her back, a lot, as if she were
patting a deficit or as if she were fine-tuning a single sentence with
each touch, one that would be the key, or whatever you'd like to
deduce, to rise above a gush of sentimentality and: *Keep in mind,
you'll have no end of other prospects.* Others? What for?

Next step: digging up the letters: the fat one and the thin one.
A (strategic) maneuver at noontime. Digging more with nails than
with the whole hand to get to the not-very-deep bottom. The aridity
aided her: finding and hoping. Rereading under that authoritarian
sun—in the middle of December! To pronounce each word out
loud would be like pleading: *Demetrio* . . . *Demetrio, come! Come
love me!* If only that effect would result from that cause. More
likely Renata would stuff the tender pages under her mattress: right
in the middle so that when his beloved lay down he would feel her
weight in that faraway ranch. Naked imaginings: yeehaw!: that's it:
an ambitious "yeehaw" as a response to a hot and steamy reality,
and then a glimpse into a nighttime bedroom scenario: Demetrio on
his back, hugging a pillow, a wool pillow, pretending it is Renata's
succulent body: in, out; in, out: further in and not all the way out:
a deep-seated position, yes, so that the sperm would soon gush:
so that immediately the scion would start to sprout (pretty nice,

isn't it?), O masturbation! understood as a libation. A vibrating plea: *Don't forget me, Demetrio. Feel my body even if it is a pure and vague illusion. Feel it like this or like that, as if I were keeping the rhythm you tell me to keep.* After this mental entreaty, Renata went to lie down for a while in bed. First she placed the letters where we said before and tossed and turned to see if . . . She cried out with unwholesome pleasure . . . She wouldn't even think of masturbating: only motile sanctity, ever more feminine; more denigrating divinations. Well then! at that moment a few drops of rain began to fall on the roof. Large drops, we should say: hail? Increasing: really joyous, because the random symmetry of sounds was so merciful! At last! Huge heavenly onslaught in the middle of December. The outburst decreed by God lasted for three hours and a tad. It was a—contorted—miracle! whose consequence was colder and colder and now, indeed, the logic of terrestrial life: winter, as it should be, seen as a camouflaged accident, which put in order a disorder that was also fortuitous.

Needless to say Renata and Doña Luisa celebrated Christmas modestly, but with the consolation of shivering while they ate their chicken dinner.

27

In, out; in, out; in, out: frantic and frenetic midst the nausea the big guy felt in those primitive quarters. Sex as corrosive expansion; sex as a thrust from something far away; an urge with an exasperating sting. That debut onanism on the ranch, the result of despair, for three months had passed without so much as a touch, not even a graze, down there, not even a toying with—never! not even when he washed by the bucketful: soaping around his belly button: the lather necessarily falling toward his scrotum—always a possibility? when that action produced stimulating tickles: ah, dealing with that problem was what the (final) redemptive bucketful was for: water to the rescue, and that was that. Thus sanctity should be understood as routine abstinence, abstinence that sets the spirit aflame in order to transform it into some kind of foil, or also into a knot that was only kind of untied; the beneficial sensation of being in control, translated into a quarrel with oneself, ongoing, although Demetrio had discovered during his many trips to Sabinas and Nueva Rosita that there were brothels in both places, in that region they were called *congales* or *zumbidos:* to wit: cathouses, almost clandestine (better), but till then—we are at the beginning of December—he had not had the nerve to pay any a visit, among other reasons because hooking up with a whore meant a sleepless night for sure, for those houses, according to what he had been told, opened their doors only after ten at night, and the return trip to La Mena, and the early morning chores the next day . . . Nevertheless, the person in question didn't realize that the peons themselves would forgive him a slight excess of this kind, only for the obvious reason that seeing him so saintly, so single, so single-mindedly devoted to the comings and the goings—making sales! as well as his apprenticeship, though only as the hoister, of the slaughter of the animals, the slitting of throats, the skinning (also selling), the bringing to pasture (more and more), and the keeping quiet; as well as his connection—a counterbalance—to civilization through the radio and its songs, night after night: a soothing softness even if it was distressing. It was Benigno who told him he should go to the *congales* to appease his bachelor longings; for his part, he wouldn't breathe a word to the boss; he should go, let off some steam, whenever he liked, for as manager, he was getting results never seen before: he was taking a lot of initiative selling meat and hides: quite pleasing progress, all noted by Don Delfín when he received the weekly take. But Demetrio resisted any disparity. On the contrary: what he needed to do was purify himself to avoid confusion. Once, he confessed to Benigno that whores scared him; he even admitted that a long time ago he had fallen in love with one and that such foolishness had ended badly, for he was no longer able to distinguish between a good woman and a bad—where, then, could one find the truth about love? That since then he had had filthy ideas, which led to the terribly shameful. What he did not confess to the peon was that he had a saintly sweetheart in Sacramento—why spill out the private? For his part, keeping that secret made him feel more blessed, more energetic, even though he had made no effort to go visit she who would certainly be his lifelong wife.

Reserve. Silence. No revelations of anything subconscious. Careful: keep the light to himself, and for that very reason (come what may) create an air of suspicion. And in the meantime: in, out; in, out; the corporeal pillow; nocturnal depravity transferred to an always future figuration: Renata in full ecstasy offering up words of gratitude. Hopefully! So many sentences he invented and placed inside that candied mouth . . . But Demetrio was fooling himself—or was he? For lately he'd shown stamina: let's imagine him as a lecherous robot, placing the pillow on the bed every night and: aye aye! taking off his underpants and trousers, and, to put it prudishly, he didn't always flail around like mad until the white band of streamlined snot appeared . . . How disgusting! Filth. A tumult in his conscience . . . Surely Bartola noticed his besmirchings when she washed his few washables; in fact, yes, hence the peon's coercive words—as already stated—: again mentioning the *congales* that were there to be visited: temporary relief—why ever not! However, we must make room for an onanistic upheaval: one night Demetrio decided to place the pillow on top of himself. He had to try a new position if only for a change. To see if it would be more effective. The movements were more difficult, that's true, that bit of exasperating distress led to—or so he fancied—it starting to rain: a miracle! and the rain got heavier. Sublime unexpected storm: and yes: the heat fled headlong, so abruptly, and likewise winter arrived—maybe because the big guy put the pillow on top of himself? So it was: let's just accept it. There may have been other causes, but . . .

And Demetrio, as if bewitched, and because in his present state he couldn't ejaculate, chose to go to a *congal* in Sabinas. He went during the week, to wit: he didn't give a damn about interrupting his rapturous work routine, arguing to himself that Don Delfín had many times congratulated him for his dedication and his . . . et cetera and et cetera . . . Now let's set him down in Sabinas having a cup of coffee at a tavern. A deliciously cool afternoon.

Later at night, the cold, a speculative disintegration: and he's off; whether he'd regret it or not; whether he should ask directions. Fear vying with urgency. They'll tell him once he's in the neighborhood. That's why he had to drive around: searching in the outskirts: perhaps it wasn't so obvious; until someone told him that at such-and-such a house, one that did not even sport a red lightbulb. And Demetrio knocked several times on a corrugated metal door. It took a while for it to open . . . remember how clandestine, so he—is it already obvious?—had to think up an excuse because the purpose of his visit was solely to get a woman he could fuck. From behind the closed door they told him that they rented women by the hour, not more: okay? What he already knew, somewhat indirectly. More details translated into restrictions that inhibited the solicitor, who was on the verge of saying: *Thank you, I'll come back next week.* But he dug in his heels on that threshold of a hell, if it really was one. It's worth mentioning here that it all transpired through the corrugated door. The madam didn't open it until she had set the exorbitant fee: one peso and fifty centavos! in comparison with the prices in Oaxaca . . . a comical bargain . . . finally a faceless agreement: a nuisance. Demetrio was trembling when he entered. He saw a small room lit with half-burnt candles that looked pretty gloomy, inhabited by monsters or something of the sort.

Whores as living ghouls, alas.

What he saw—ghastly! and suggestive of worse.

Wandering about, like a superfluous emphasis, was a pack of black and gray cats, but not a single white one.

The whores, three on show, were very fat ladies with unkempt hair, all wearing nothing but an apron; grotesque nakedness otherwise: no underpants—really! Seated horrors. All three were wearing flip-flops instead of spike heels, and, which one should he choose? None! but his horniness . . .

Under his breath Demetrio asked the madam if by some chance she had a female specimen a bit younger and with a nice body and:

"They're all I've got . . . But I can guarantee you that they do good work . . . They are professionals."

Such a long time without an imbroglio . . . the distasteful as a substitute for—the palm of the hand? . . . on the ranch? Descending doubts, though not at an avid downhill speed. The ascent, like a fluttering certainty, is never complete, of course, as far as fulfilling whatever need. Go for it! He hired the least ugly and least fat one, probably the youngest, judged on the fly. Then came the sinful march; culmination, that is, unimaginable, in a tiny room whose nauseating effluvia weren't in the least exciting . . . Demetrio was even ashamed to take his clothes off. She just had to take off her apron and—ready to go! Stripped naked! And straight to business—oh, my God! The bad part: total consternation, as you can imagine: what kind of erection if . . . ? But a screw did ensue. It was like penetrating something very deep and very gelatinous. It was a struggle to find contractions that never, well, let's see: the chubby woman didn't even manage to touch his arm: kisses on the mouth—not on our life! Though, examining things more closely, what would that sausage with puffy lips (heavily lipsticked) and a snaky and (perhaps) scaly tongue taste like? Moreover, the woman kept rushing him. She wanted that semen to come as if out of a modern electrical appliance, latest model. Verbal aggression not worth reproducing here, for Demetrio, feeling more and more like the victim of an idle simulacrum, brusquely disengaged and with true dis-ease got dressed, the quicker to escape from such pestilence. Here we can offer an analogy: it seemed like the big guy had just been released from a pretty tricky coyote trap.

Fortunately his investment in that experiment had cost him only one peso and fifty centavos.

An infectious, monumental, depressing adventure because it gave him no glimmer of clarity as to the direction his life was taking. Curves and straightaways, though many more curves and perhaps some regression that could be interpreted as a harbinger of a precipitous conclusion, so much so that on his way back to La Mena he felt as though he were approaching an abyss.

The headlights of the pickup, in addition to shedding light on the familiar route, seemed to place in his path armies of nopales and huisaches: rising abruptly out of the earth or descended from the heavens: no! for God's sake—not now! Interlopers! Frauds! A world of thorns. Certainties that when passing were merely glanced sidelong, fade-outs rather than fortuitous disappearances or the semblance of a current rushing backward. The (illuminated) illusory was so real, so apocryphal because so fleeting. Then, when he arrived at La Mena, he would have liked to see a single lightbulb, one electrical surprise to counteract, given the splendor of the mass of stars, but—what a fool! what a doltish delusion! it would be forever before electricity would come to that region. Not next year, nor the following, not in a lustrum, nor in a decade. The bulb relief—O remora! A highfalutin fantasy: a teensy and allusive stigma of what might or might not happen three decades from now . . . If only there were a bulb (just one one-hundred-watt bulb, let's say) Demetrio would acknowledge that this ranch was his ideal place, and he, of course, the wise pioneer chosen by God to build first a hamlet, then a village, and then a city: a fervent founding father, but the darkness—primitive, shapeless, constricted thus rank because so narrow: now errant, now repellent, now the dregs of the dregs, and, therefore, a reality that not only dejects but imprisons. When he saw how uncertain all this was, especially when it was almost midnight, Demetrio realized he couldn't live there much longer. Neither alone nor accompanied. Renata, in the meantime, resurrected. Sexual meekness that required a maximum of spiritual meekness, a future in dribs and drabs in exchange for true power. What a paradox! The big guy had taken this job to be closer to her and in the end he was much further away. The lack of communication, the workload increasingly heavy. He could neither send nor receive letters, and a trip to Sacramento, without knowing the roads well: ah, he would get gruelingly lost. He didn't even try. It would be so risky, tempting perhaps, but . . . Renata instead inspired him to focus on his job. If he killed a goat, there in the thick of the blood Renata's smile appeared. If he milked a cow (he'd already learned how), he encountered the oneiric semblance of her beauty in the spurts of milk. If he heard songs on the radio, his darling appeared to him suspended in the breeze. And during his trips to Sabinas and Nueva Rosita, Renata's face, above the clouds, began to appear, and the intense green of her eyes dyed the white and blue of the sky. Then dissipation. Then the magnetism of her voice saying: *Come, come love me. Don't abandon me.* In fact, some time before, in an about-face and with unexpected force, Benigno asked him:

"Did you have fun in Sabinas?"

"No way. I had a terrible time."

If only he had made the effort during one of his daytime trips to those half-town-half-cities and asked ever so casually if there happened to be a more upscale *congal* . . . No, not that, not now: stubbornness fortified in a sorrowful interior . . . He didn't want to find out (ignorance and its acrid ups and downs were better), for he also didn't want to touch himself down there and thereby create confusion: never again! It's just that without love, sex was disgusting and fraudulent, gratuitous suffering, disgusting gratification. So, on the plus side, the longing for indestructible purity and endurance. And the reinforcement of his fixation on one sacred ass, the one he predicted would overflow with beauty and mystery, the notion of a tunnel with flexible walls, but still steely and quite slippery, something like a divine—yes?—chalice placed in the middle of a bizarre altar; vulgarities (almost) for a boost, also so as not to give much of himself to anybody: to wit: Demetrio was becoming more silent. He no longer sought conversation: the essential, a kind of casual dissipation. True that Bartola made him food, but the only word he offered in return was "thanks," a mere euphonic abstraction in spite of the fact that she brought him his plate of beans, or eggs with salsa, as well as flour tortillas and a glass of milk, to his quarters; the family stopped inviting him over, but the manager's refusal operated with more vigor: fists raised, pounding the air; also, boorish stomping, even kicking up some dust. Even on Christmas Eve, Demetrio preferred to dine alone, perhaps so as not to recall his mother, nor his second mother, nor Renata, nor—whom else? A mental blank: a discipline of sorts: barely a blur: an oblique achievement. When New Year's Eve rolled around, he chose to drive the pickup about three miles away from La Mena to avoid any hugs for—Happy New Year! To gaze at the stars, to glimpse vague signs . . . He fell asleep in the cab of the pickup, hungry by design, bundled up warmly (he'd bought loads of clothes in Sabinas), wearing—who would see him?—a thick wool hat with earflaps, and a double-knit scarf, and—of course! his privacy tripled. He didn't even chat with Don Delfín when he came, when he handed over the weekly take: astonishing numbers—so precise! and otherwise just the stern yeses and nos, one or another sentence spoken as if to summarize a civility after hearing a particular command. So there wasn't even a (diplomatic) Christmas embrace, nor one for New Year's (so graceful). Who could explain his disdain?

Wise discretion peeling inner layers open.

What kinds of riddles and dissipations . . . other than the words?

Total devotion to work and nothing but.

And thus two months passed . . .

March brought a freshening . . . perhaps a clearing, suitable for carrying out a mission.

Suddenly Demetrio played with a happy idea: to go see Renata in the middle of the week, even though it would take him a couple of days. He left in the early dawn, right around three . . .

He ventured, he got lost. Since the manager didn't know by heart the long detour that connected La Mena with the wide dirt road that in turn connected Monclova to Sabinas, he came to a graded crossing of four roads, and the mistake: he took the last one he should have taken, ending up in a hamlet called Hermanas:

far far away: on the outskirts of the enormous municipality of Ocampo. So he turned around: angry: blast it! He was even angrier when he realized that, without meaning to, he'd taken yet another road that had brought him to another hamlet, called El Pino Solo: a rustic slime heap, almost spectral, because very strange people lived there, people who wanted (almost) to kill just for the sake of it. However, his vexation did not arise from his fear of being imminently and definitively killed, but rather because the pickup had by then burned more than half a tank and who knew if the gasoline would last until he arrived safe and sound in La Mena, moreover— which way? which was the shortest route? In fact, night came upon him like something grotesque. It was cold as hell in that desert without a glimpse of butte or hill. Hunger gnawed as well. It seemed like his guts were beginning to stick to his backbone: a bellowing belly, and—who the hell was going to give him something to eat? If he didn't happen by a ranch on his way back, he had better get used to the notion of ingesting plants: creosote and lantana didn't taste so bad and they were, in fact, quite nutritious. After sleeping, terrified, in the aforementioned cab, he continued the following day like a lost and rollicking fool full of faith. Yes, faith, for he prayed in his very own way. He never tired of repeating, more than a hundred times: *God help me!*, a phrase that became more and more syllabified and, deliberately, more prolonged and melodious; just once he added to his entreaty the following sentence: *You know I'm a good man!* and at a different point, blarney of this sort: *If you help me get to La Mena soon, or to El Origen or La Igualdad, I promise I'll bring flowers to the church in Sabinas as soon as I can.* Flowers? what a magnificent gift. Perhaps God, upon hearing that such a great big being was going to give him such a colorful offering, had no choice but to take pity on him and thereby help him find his way. He reached El Origen in no time. His adventure was but a deceptive detour. The tank still had gasoline—oh!: a miracle in this region, so far removed from the progressing world. Even he, who had desperately swallowed a few handfuls of (inevitably encountered) lantana berries arrived quite restored at . . . He was never thirsty, hard as it is to believe! Although, a while later he did feel the aftereffects of what he had experienced, SO TREACHEROUS, hopefully never again to be so lost.

Anyway, we now find ourselves at La Mena, which we might rightly call a noisy place after taking into account the recounting of the manager's troubled travels. Two bitter days and: let us say "noisy" because the sole family there welcomed him almost with cheers: what for? Let us look, then, at the basics: the children jumped happily up and down: virtual nonsense? or better to explain it as follows: Bartola, upon seeing him return in the pickup, imagined a horror, almost a goner, so she brought food and healing herbs, though—healing? food? None of it was necessary. Demetrio had returned in one piece. God had seen him through. Hence she exclaimed jubilantly, and Benigno mimicked her heartily, gesticulating four times in the air overhead: the result, now for real, an aha! his was rather jarring, and the children's leaps that gave the final touch—right? are we done yet? Simulations that—phew! Nonetheless, once calm had been restored Demetrio began to recount in detail what had happened to him: a story lasting an hour and a half: a narrative with punctilious detours, which may have seemed insignificant globs but turned out to be quite substantial, so much so that the family was disappointed when the manager said: *Well, that's all I have to tell you.* Too bad, as they all would have wished the tale of those troubles to continue, but what Demetrio wanted was to rest . . .

Ergo: recuperation for . . .

The "I'll never do that again": sublime.

Understandable.

What wasn't understandable was any explanation of why Demetrio had kept silent for almost three months and then recounted his adventure with such eloquence . . . It even seemed he had held back his speech for so long in order to be able to lavishly squander it on a script that had already been chosen by Providence, that is—by whom? Such things, if conceived of as enigmas, can only correspond to God's will, because only He knows what He composes and decomposes, perhaps because He is always lonely and bored and wants to make up stories . . .

Could that be?

Before Demetrio went to bed at noon, Benigno cautioned him: "I think you should have gone to Sabinas and from there taken the main dirt road to Monclova . . . When you don't know the desert roads by heart it's preferable to play it safe."

Aha!: a sigh in response. And good-bye and thank you and, does "should have" exist? Yes, though it only attains amplitude in the imagination and in games of hypotheses. The "should have" exists in a dream, for it presupposes a marvelous discrepancy that could be anchored in the future, whereby, without further ado, we turn directly to what the manager dreamed at a very slow pace. We will, in fact, summarize it, as long as we make an effort to present it as a disorderly derivation, disposed of, usually, in dribs and drabs and, so, let's take a look: Renata and Demetrio met in an unknown city—which could it be?—one with lots of very high buildings and imbued with the everlasting fragrance of the sempervivum. There they met, by surprise, at the tip-top of one of those monoliths: such a surprise for both of them: you are and you are not; yes, I am; me too; so, let us hug and kiss on the mouth until we are tired of holding each other so tightly; agreed; and—what are you thinking about? that it wouldn't be so bad for us to live in this sinful and modern city, this is the center of the world; yes, it's true, beyond this city nothing would matter to us. Then they embraced only to turn their attention to the activities of the tiny people way down below; a while later she said: it looks like an infinite anthill, we are also ants and this is happiness. That's where the dream ended. It's advisable not to encourage the improbable. Nevertheless, when

Demetrio woke up he knew he had to go to Sacramento as soon as possible. Likewise he realized that it didn't make any sense for him to keep working as a ranch manager; he knew he should leave the following day in the pickup: at dawn? that's right . . . It's just that life on the ranch was driving him crazy: oh, rustic sanctity without any air to breathe! without a glimpse of anything beyond the same beyond!

28

Filling up the tank. Benigno offered his assistance to the manager. The children witnessed the action, but not Bartola. Demetrio, of course, said it would be a routine trip to Sabinas and Nueva Rosita. He would take three dead goats and two live lambs to the butchers: what do you know! a special order, which he should have filled three days earlier, but we know why that didn't happen. Likewise we know—and it shouldn't be painful—the (not heartrending) fact that he was going to leave forever. May the damned be damned! Not he. He was a calculating man. For many years now he had had his sights set on getting ahead: more and more society to obtain thousands of subtle solaces and millions of extravagant, though ultimately cheerful, burdens! The pulse of life in a vortex is never dull . . . If it could be in that dream city, the one with the tall buildings . . . The condition: companionship. Renata and her eternal love: win her in order to sate her. We could say she was a tiny phoenix waiting in the wings. She and he would rise together. And . . .

Demetrio left La Mena after saying to Benigno: *I'll be back by noon, as usual.* But the peon, who was quite intuitive, suspected something quite bitter, though to what reasonable extent . . . He said nothing—why should he? A suspicion is never more than a thin slice, just a question of catching and tossing it: it won't go very far . . . As soon as Benigno saw the pickup drive away, he went to the manager's quarters. Proof: the aforementioned had not taken his suitcases. Fleeing with the shirt on his back: an implausible layering of garments. Fleeing with a wad of bills: of course, for in Sabinas and Nueva Rosita you needed money. Hence the considered conclusion: *There's no longer any doubt; the manager is not returning.* Though this unhappy judgment: *I gave him the go-ahead to leave.* Causality . . . unintentional. However that may be. worth placing a period here.

The purchase of a suitcase and clothes in Monclova: on the road Demetrio was already fleshing out a plan that contained cynical elements, which must have excited him through and through. Whatever else, he had to consider the long-standing relationship between Don Delfín and Doña Zulema, which restrained him like a brake of contingency, creating a dilemma that was limiting if not downright narrow. The limitation was that he couldn't steal the pickup: a matchless venue. Stealing would mean driving to Sacramento in the vehicle: indeed! the skillful and arrogant driver. In fact, he presumed that the wide dirt road that connected Monclova to Ocampo and passed through Sacramento and other towns was ready, time to give it a go, and herewith a microhistorical fact: around the middle of March 1947—finally! (stated with jubilation, though better not to exaggerate) . . . The weird thing would be for him to arrive smugger than ever at his second mother's house. But he couldn't lie to Doña Zulema: that he'd bought the vehicle out of necessity; with his savings—no way, José! that was stealing, whereby Don Delfín, once he'd discovered Demetrio's as well as the vehicle's absence, would go complain to his lifelong friend: *Your nephew is a thief and with all due respect, a son of a bitch.* Then he would add emphatically: *Why did you recommend him?* And his second mother would be hauled over the coals when . . . Further fairly probable torments weighed heavily on Demetrio's mind as he drove, an entire tense crisis that, in the end, led him to the inevitable: to leave the pickup there in Monclova, half a block from Don Delfín's house. A rash act at midnight. The thing was to

find out if . . . he didn't really remember the exact location of the
house, just that it didn't have a front porch; the front door opened
right onto the street: a paved street—of course! and then he remembered some useless details: there was a large store in front
of, and a eucalyptus tree on the verge of a broken sidewalk—yes?
perhaps?—and a movie theater without a roof, with posters for
Mexican movies stuck on the white plastered facade: more or
less the image Demetrio had formed of the street when he had
been there; other vague details: ones he would not see at midnight, for even if he reached Monclova during the day he'd have to
wait for total nocturnal calm (urban, dangerous, or so Demetrio
imagined). His plan: to rent a hotel room for a few hours so he
could lie low. Anyway. Then, as he refined his strategy, he considered the benefits of the door: oh, to slip a message under it:
a plot synthesis . . . et cetera! . . . to wit: a telegraphic missive
in which he would outline his primordial motive for quitting his
job. It wouldn't be so bad if he wrote, among other things, that
it was impossible to work as a manager without a woman by his
side; the gentleman would understand—wouldn't he? He himself
had recommended that he bring one—remember? Find a pen and
some paper. Later. The first obstacle: to take his money out of the
bank. Then board the train for the usual trip to La Polka. Then
the crossing on the boat and the horse-drawn carriage. Then the
final one-two punch: invest in a business in Sacramento: a grocery store—what else?

The agronomist was so utterly absorbed in his plan that he
passed right by Sabinas, as if he were on the moon. He didn't ask
anybody how to find the main road to Monclova. As he was already
quite familiar with the city it was not difficult for him to find what
he was looking for.

And he headed that way almost subconsciously. His lucky star
(his assistant) was again shining, though—let's take a look: he forgot that he was carrying two live lambs and three dead goats in the

truck bed. He remembered only a bit farther on: when he'd already been driving for half an hour on the magnificent road where, obviously, there was little traffic: one or another daring semitrailer: yes!; maybe a four-door sedan, with a visor over the windshield: of course!; as an aside we might mention the occasional person on horseback; a truck; another pickup . . .

A tentative return to Sabinas to sell the stock: no! now that he was buoyantly on his way to total freedom (more his than ever) he could not stand to think of returning for the sole purpose of getting rid of what would cause him so many complications in Monclova.

To avoid such a fix he found a different fix and injected it with a dose of mischief, if you like, an impetuous solution: place the dead goats in a row—skinned, as was only right—by the side of the dirt road; and the hides in another row (three and three, yes): finders keepers: the charm of well-calibrated irresponsibility; not forgetfulness, rather a tangled game . . .

That's what he did: O guile! And as for the live lambs: a fate they could fete!: leave them to their own devices: let them run off into a very spacious and wild happiness. Hopefully nobody would claim them. A future without corrals. Hopefully!

Bargain-basement compassion for the sake of a positive portent: to watch those children of God walk away, together, like brothers who love one another and always give each other mutual support. Good-bye, lambs. Demetrio crossed himself and—let's go!

When he reached Monclova—where's the bank? Quickly found: cash in hand: withdraw the money in its entirety, which when combined with what he already had: congratulations!, modest wealth: independence; a cinch because he had no trouble getting the (sorrowful) bank employees to give him the noteworthy wad. The bad part was figuring out where to stash it all. His trouser pockets were not big enough: and: he asked for an opaque bag. They gave him a cloth one, solid and of goodly size, which he placed in the glove compartment of the truck. He would lock the cab when he finally got out, to wit: as soon as he had parked it. His most pressing wish was that Don Delfín would not be strolling about the city, so that he wouldn't see . . . et cetera!

Straight off to rent a hotel room: an unproblematic step . . . luckily or because of the brilliance of his star (in the sense of twinkling) . . . A circumstantial rest, after finally showering under a stream: ah!

Demetrio was living the wonders of this metropolis, not much of a metropolis, to tell the truth, but . . .

With sprightly step he then wandered around downtown Monclova. He had to buy some good clothes and a suitcase with lock and key. Immediate success.

When he got back to his hotel he asked the receptionist to lend him a pen and a blank piece of paper, unlined—eh? That's it! Everything was working out perfectly. The text: a kooky substance reduced to its conceptual essence: let's take a look, for it was charming:

Dear Don Delfín:
Along with this note I am leaving you the keys to the pickup truck, which is parked half a block from your house. I just want to say that I got unbearably bored at the ranch. My work as a manager was very interesting, but as I could never bring a woman there, it's better for me to leave. I am grateful for all your efforts and your trust in me.
Demetrio Sordo.

The note could have been more concise, but that's how it came out, and that was that.

Certainly no previous manager had had as extensive an imagination as he. Undoubtedly they'd all fled on foot from La Mena, surely toward Sabinas, and, though honorable men, they were also pitifully decent fools! Demetrio, on the contrary—judge for yourself—wanted to be decent—saintly?, yes or no?, only in a more original, hence more effective, way.

For now, we really must end this with the act announced in the note written in a rather showy hand. Let us evoke (illustrious!) midnight as if it were echoing all around: surround sound—whirring because warped—which tended to provoke terror whose decanting eased said maneuver: leave, leave, leave, flee without running, back to the hotel, once the mischief had been made. Somewhat neglected sense of safety entrusted to the aplomb of his stomping footsteps. Another chapter was beginning. So he should start off with historic relief (smiling with the knowledge that his face would have an aquiline appearance, the same he viewed at length in an oval mirror) between four walls that smelled of florific glory, and, well, tomorrow would be the day of the joyous flight.

Once again the figure of the big guy carrying a bulging suitcase that just fit all his belongings. He looked almost vintage, almost unreal, almost toast.

The Monclova train station wasn't as crowded as it had been on other occasions, hence the reasonable assumption: *I guess they're already running a lot of buses along the new dirt road . . . Little by little people will stop using the train . . .* How could he be wrong? But the train went much farther than Ocampo and company. It took the route to Sierra Mojada, so—would the trip be pleasanter?

Demetrio felt like a traveling prince. Empty seats. Oh joy. The few passengers had the pleasure of being able to partially stretch out on the cushioned . . . The slowness of the train didn't matter, rather . . .

What to say about marvelous sleep.

What to say about the unusual smell in the car: almost encapsulated, almost anesthetic.

29

"What's happened now? Why are you here? Did you already quit your job?"

"Yes, I quit, it didn't suit me at all."

"I knew it . . . and, well . . . Welcome, my son! . . . but . . . what are your plans?"

First the obligatory embrace. Doña Zulema was jubilant, perhaps because this was a surprise she had somehow expected. You can surely predict a coming recurrence, but even if this memory fails you altogether, because that happens sometimes, let's just say that the flavor of the conversation emerged at the table. Another recurrence: the hill of rolls—*conchas*, *plomos*, and *pelonas*—washed down bit by bit with *cafés con leche* (everything landed in their bellies in the end), and in the meantime there was a jumble of distorted facts, no more than 20 percent of which corresponded to real events: Demetrio astonished Doña Zulema with his nearly six-month-long saga of ranch life: inconvenience as the principal premise and conclusion, inconveniences that made the old maid laugh with her mouth wide open and her tongue hanging out. She, celebratory. He, a blowhard of such extravagant lies that he himself began to give way to laughter. Then both succumbed to relentless guffaws: distressing rather than joyous, for Demetrio had only to utter two words and immediately there followed a burst of jocularity, and her response was equally alarming: an unstoppable attack of spluttering. Even when they drank they coughed, so: phew! they quieted down so that they could catch their breath. The amusing tale had sated them.

His account of killing goats and lambs, of milking cows and occasionally pasturing a mixture of livestock just before sunset, all described so piquantly that the truth seemed more like a tale of a grotesque paradox than the accretion of daily suffering. The same goes for the trips to Sabinas and Nueva Rosita, upon which Demetrio placed a ratifying emphasis: ergo: rattling along with dead meat bouncing about in the truck bed: just picture it and— ecchh! What a peculiar kind of elegance! and hahahah: so: a joint sigh underpinning the unspoken though perfunctory goal of gently returning to serious issues. Such as his plans. Back to Doña Zulema's question, regarding the store.

"Well, as I said, I'm loaded with money and thinking about starting a business here in Sacramento."

"What kind of business?"

"I don't know, but that's what I'm thinking about."

"You could help me expand my shop."

"Yes, I could."

"Take your time to consider my proposal. All I can say is that if we work together we'll have the number-one grocery store in town. But take your time, I mean: till tomorrow. What do you think?"

"Seems like a good idea, but first I have to discuss it with Renata. I want to know what she thinks."

Wash again. Get decked out in clothes that fit well . . . then . . . Now we come to a domestic innovation: Doña Zulema had bought a huge cedar barrel that looked like a round bathtub, into which, butt first and by minimally contorting his folded body, the big guy fit like a charm. On his first try. Though before that came a disconcerting event: ambulatory adult nudity, only his—what's the big deal? as he was the apocryphal son, he could do this and much more: and therefore: a moment of precarious delicacy: reflections

paving the way toward the prospect of a local business that hopefully would . . . Water up to the chest. Overflowing, one could say,
with warmth and many hours of sudsy sluggishness. Demetrio had
never taken such a relaxing bath, and he felt—because he was enjoying the outdoor chill—like a rhizome, his thoughts vertical and
all in a row, all the while observed, out of the corner of her eye,
discreetly and despite comings and goings, by . . . Doña Zulema
took advantage of her beloved guest's stupor to tell him that they
had come to her house selling these huge tubs; a couple of men
from San Buenaventura (a town near Sacramento): modern traveling salesmen, drivers of a truck with a stake bed full of tubs.
This wood artifact was the fruit of a fertile concept: the master
bath. And—indeed! a person could remain submerged in the water
for hours. Hence to bid farewell to the nuisance of buckets. Now
bathing was, indeed, an unparalleled pleasure, as much as shitting
or making love . . . the sensible pleasures of modernity: more and
more inventions to come . . . And the aunt's comments: *Ever since
they opened that road, many salesmen have been driving their
trucks to Sacramento. On the one hand this is a good thing, but
on the other . . . Well, what I mean is that my sales have gone
down.* His aunt had taken the correct tack for laying out her plans.
Folded and soaped up as he was inside the barrel, Demetrio held
forth about the benefits of expanding the grocery store: products,
renovations, shams, changing people's tastes in order to create
new motivations for consumption. Their competitors would be
those on the road, now in automotive vehicles, and after lavish
commentary he managed to spit out a fundamental sentence: *I urgently need to buy a truck.* This established him firmly on her side,
and she flung up her fists in a gesture of victory; verbal flingings
followed, along with delectable wordplay, syntactic inversions, a
few of which we will spell out: we will live together; we will grow
together; jests and largesse, but so many threads must be tied up:
which the naked man did when he said that this ambitious project

depended (here he goes!) on Renata's opinion, because knowing
that she, as well as her mother, were standing on their last legs with
their stationery store, still to determine what could be arranged: to
help out there, for instance: that inflated circumstance we know
about: ergo: anxiety here: Demetrio: fickle, unsure, frankly lacking
clarity . . . And the elucidating meeting still to come. His sweetheart: a Solomonic judge?

Demetrio's impeccable attire did not help one bit: snow-white
long-sleeved shirt, gray cashmere pants, patent-leather shoes, and
an arabesque-style hairdo with loads of pomade. He stood next to
the usual bench: he never sat down! Three messenger boys walked
by, one of whom he hired for the mission. Finally!: Renata, soldier-
like, had to present herself; her commanding lover had summoned
her. Beautiful afternoon, with a great deal of glancing at trees, as if
to emphasize the surprise. Renata: the obedient automaton stood
some seven steps away from her Prince Charming and said in a
bittersweet voice:

"I'm very glad you have come, but I cannot visit with you. I am
not presentable. Come tomorrow at the same time, if you can."

"Yes, I can, my love . . . See you tomorrow."

Scripted? Recycled? The same excuse as the other time he
showed up like that; the exact words; a play or a movie: oh! from then
on Demetrio had to dispel any hint of surprise. It was nonsense, unless he wanted to hear some pretentious prattle . . . Which wouldn't
be bad . . . But wouldn't be good . . . To begin with: a warning, or, on
the contrary, a beefing up of intransigence, though without ruling
out that the third time would be different: the extraordinary beauty
might not show up; she might tell him through the messenger boy
that he should stop courting her . . . In that case! so as not to run
an experiment using smoke and mirrors, plagued by conjectures
and paradox, it behooves us to add here a second scene from a
different angle, but with Demetrio in a similar position: left hand
touching the back of the bench, standing—of course! without turn-

ing his head in either direction, he told a messenger boy that blah-blahblah . . . Before Renata's resplendent entrance (hopefully she won't be long, thought her suitor), we can report that he now wore an olive-green lamé shirt and gray astrakhan pants; likewise we'll add that he had taken a three-hour bath (one hour longer than the day before) in the comfort of that cedar tub, and he knew word for word what he would say to his beloved. Now with the spoken phrasing partially specified, we can fully recount one part of the conversation they held as they sat contentedly on the bench and sucked the words from each other's lips. We will dispense with the explanation Demetrio gave (let's imagine her interjections as chatty questions) as to why he'd quit his job: here goes: the limitations of ranch life; the unbelievable amount of work; the impossibility of writing letters; the blocks, yes, the lack of ideas, even though, in Sabinas and Nueva Rosita, there were post offices, but the "overwhelming obstacle": the open and professed indolence—made obsolete by doubt? Anyway, we can deduce the plethora of questions: her gravitas, her turn now, how much she suffered because she'd heard nothing from him, and—herewith the essential!, because now we are at the most important part, maybe a bit before, but . . .

"Renata, my love, in addition to the pleasure seeing you gives me, because I truly love you, one of the reasons for this visit is to tell you that I have saved a large amount of money and I'm thinking of investing in a business here in Sacramento."

"You want to come live here?"

"Yes, because I want to see you every day . . . That way it will be easier for me to lead you to the altar."

For the first time Renata lifted her face and looked straight into her lover's eyes: blessed splendor: and: a dubious pleasure that began to gain boldness and confidence. To look at each other, to know each other: enormous green eyes: feminine magnetism mingling with tiny brown eyes, very virile, and thereby the subtle

amalgam of visual ecstasy and the fluttering of lids that accentu-
ated the connection and the tightening of the sensual knot and all
the time Demetrio, underhandedly, caressing (clawing) that divine
hand: the steely left, for the pulsations were so strong they could
be felt even in that hasty caress (bad, good; bad, good), which was
soon joined to the verbal, when her jumbled words emerged:

"Demetrio, I don't want you to live here."

"Why?"

"Because I want to get away from my mother, just like my sisters did when they got married."

"What will your mother do on her own?"

"God only knows."

"I'd venture to guess that she won't let you marry me."

"Here in town we have many relatives once or twice removed.
There are others throughout the region . . . Somebody will look
after her."

"You think she'll want to live with relatives?"

"We've already talked about it, but she still hasn't agreed."

"I guess she won't let you get married as long as she's alive."

"So it seems. She doesn't like you because she knows the day
will come when you will ask me to marry you."

"And what do you say?"

"I love her and I love you . . . To tell you the truth, I don't know
what to do."

"I think it's better to have a plan that would make her happy . . .
You'll see, we'll find a perfect solution."

"You think so?"

"You'll see, I promise you . . . By tomorrow, when we meet, I
will have thought of two or three options."

"I hope none of them means you want my mother to live with us."

"No . . . Not that."

Cut!: the impertinent messenger boy. Interruption at the acme,
just when they were getting to the really good part: and: *Your*

mother says . . . et cetera. The celebratory moment would come in twenty-four hours: condense all the proposals and the finding of a solution into the space of an hour: worthwhile moments weighted down so they can then be lightened: it wouldn't be easy, but . . . You can already imagine Renata's parting shot: *Let's meet here tomorrow at the same time.* And a sharp edge appeared, one that prodded Demetrio and pushed him, one (rather blunt one) that from that moment on would lead him to the sublime muddle of matrimony toward which, as if accidentally on purpose, he was slipping, slipping as he sank, but which made him feel neither hot nor cold. He struggled with handicaps; initial stupor because as the gallant and Don Juan he knew himself to be, he had always assumed it was his duty to take the initiative, as in: *Do you want to be my sweetheart,* and then the magnificent one: *Do you want to marry me.* But Renata's indirect step forward: what role did that leave for him? considering that not even a tentative "yes" had been forthcoming from either, nor a date for the wedding, nor, well, only the nebulous—vaguely strategic?—groping. Perhaps Renata stepped into that amorous purview because of her sweetheart's long absence after that other absence: not even one letter, however brief, and now some assurance: obliquely . . . Or it was her subconscious on every level . . . Or it was an accidental detour . . . Demetrio, in any case, had to confide in his second mother; the opinion of a veteran would reestablish the guidelines of that surprise; love was rising from a depth that, because transparent, was partially contaminated.

Problems, itsy-bitsy problems, great big problems: substance that arises and clarifies little.

Now let's see: his aunt was already scheming—ultraobvious in her wowed face—when she saw Demetrio enter her house; he was scratching his head (odd): an unusual beginning. They spoke, he unloaded, as if he'd been carrying three sacks of beans on his back: reality with detours and provisions, the "pros", let's say, of endlessly serpentine love, and the "cons", let's say, snipped to bits. This time there wasn't any *café con leche* or bread. Only cold water, soothing at least, because Demetrio was determined to be as sincere as possible, a confession without prevarications was painful, like exposing one's guts, all red and inflamed. On the one hand, the antecedents to marriage: on track, whiteness, sentimental bluntness; on the other, the impossibility of living in Sacramento (bye-bye to the buoyant investment: the one he suggested from the tub), Renata's reasons for which, put forth as obstacles, had to be pecked at, a large spread-out shroud whose edges extended (not far off) to her mother; both their aspirations ended (or should have ended) in her: such expansiveness was definitively circumscribed by her refusal to remain alone; maybe her relatives could take care of her: bugger!; the worst getting worse, and in the meantime the bewildered beau presented one gigantic serious circumstance after another—all his own speculations—thus prolonging what should be a happy conclusion of everything under consideration, while Doña Zulema began to cleverly shape a somewhat objective solution, not a solution of every problem from *a* to *z;* should she say it, interrupt, let tedium overwhelm her apocryphal son, one minute, three, four, and at an opportune moment, she burst out with it:

"Look, son, if you end up marrying Renata and you decide to live elsewhere, I'm willing to speak with Doña Luisa. I can propose that we live together, either she can come live in my house or I can go live in hers; and instead of having two stores we'll make one: school supplies and groceries—what do you think? both of them would grow."

Spectacular idea, even more so because his aunt kept adding details, or plasters, if you wish, so that good fortune would stop and shine down upon their union, ah. Finally something solid—appealing?!, instead of a solution that—would it still take long to come? Let's see, the mere fact that she suggested something that sounded practical meant that decisive explanations would be forthcoming. That's when Demetrio, in a semijocular tone, said:

"It wouldn't be such a bad idea for me to go to Parras and try to persuade my mother to come live in Sacramento . . ."

Let's examine this idea so we can elucidate with fair or foul efficiency what the betrothed was betting on, which he didn't state at that moment but would if the conversation continued the following day, in the store—right? anyway . . . The sale of the house in Parras: a fortune—yes siree! Then the three ladies living here together: blessed progress: a whole network of aspirations that helped him espy an always straight path. Doña Luisa's house was the largest, so the noble triad could be there: a convenient packing in—though for how many years? The last to die would be the winner: aha! All of this laid out with great tact. The store resounded with all that novelty. Further enhanced with elaborate decor (the three old ladies encouraging each other, day after day, and all the other fortuitous adventures): one sensible idea after another: either from the second mother or the apocryphal son: and: the real premise: the three old women strengthening their (gooey) family bonds, to allow for the other: love, no longer a battlefield! . . . by remote control! yes, yes! yeeeesss! of course! the only thing left was Renata's opinion and then immediately to carry the idea to the next stage: the mother, that one, that Doña Luisa . . . with her whims and her wonts . . .

Let's go without further delay to the bench, where, after having bathed like never before in the cedar tub, Demetrio now flaunted a satin shirt with tiny polka dots and brown canvas pants. Renata appeared in a diaphanous dress, orange to a fault and with yellowish-gray edges, the fabric—serge or silk?, the thing was she looked so hot she seemed to be on fire. In a trice the handhold, decent as ever; and Demetrio and his full disclosure: his extraordinary proposition, elaborated; then the climax: that Doña Luisa and Doña Zulema would live together, Doña Telma as well, she in Parras— what do you think? because with the assets of all three . . . It was even possible that none of them would have to work: such lavish wealth—don't you think? and forward-looking twists and turns, laborious and, of course, quite favorable for a fanciful and always reassuring (triple) flight, as he constantly added elements, until Renata, with a gasp, proclaimed:

"It's not a bad idea, but it all depends on what my mother decides."

"If she makes the right decision, we'll be able to get married soon, I know."

"I hope so."

Upon hearing this last sentence, the suitor, already feeling like a husband-to-be, fell into a rapturous state: he lowered his head with sublime ecstasy, and, true to his nature as a bold transgressor, he also—just because—pressed his lips together to form a kissing horn, a bit like a mushroom in full bloom, and—bam! smack onto the back of Renata's right hand: that most supreme kiss: supermeaty—wow! but in the absence of any saliva to seal the deal he stuck out the tip of his tongue and began to lick with supreme tenderness: the exploit of a pro who was putting his all on the line with this tenacious salivation. Renata watched this enraptured act in shock; she allowed it to continue, hoping that the caracoling tongue action would eventually peter out as it wound round and round; until she yanked her hand away and cried out in horror:

"I thought you were a gentleman . . . I never want to see you again."

And off she ran to the stationery store. She was indignant, copiously tearful, like a little girl who'd seen a bogeyman, or somebody even worse. Fear: shooting rays, and her refuge: the arms of her angry and quaking mother. She had come out to meet her daughter as soon as she'd heard the piercing shriek. A sidewalk embrace. Many witnesses: all children. Now we turn to Demetrio, who was still sitting on the (trysting) bench, not understanding a darn thing, as he watched right in front of his eyes, almost like a thawing, the tawny embrace—for it was evening—of mother and daughter: indeed: a minute-long cry in arms; the orange-wrapped

sobbing beauty, and then Doña Luisa, turning around, gave the big
guy a furious look and spit this out:

"Go away, you scoundrel! You disrespected my daughter! Go
away and never come back!"

But of course! and without understanding the extent of the
damage done, Demetrio, with dignity, changed his physical position and walked out of the plaza. He was watched critically, as
well as with alarm: many saw; many whispered: now children and
adults: more and more, while in the stationery store:

"Calm down, dear, calm yourself."

"Yes, Mama, I will."

"Now, please, tell me what he did to you."

"He kissed me and then he licked the back of my right hand."

"Scoouundrellll!"

Demetrio was able to walk with excessive slowness: his head
down—darn right! repentant—no way! But it didn't even occur to
him for—what had he done wrong? Though through his confusion
he had to admit: increasing black bile. And: *What if I'd stolen a
kiss from her lips?* he thought. A naked kiss, a quickie . . .

The ignominious slap . . .

Spit?

What else?

No, don't look back, just define it . . . An impassioned summation . . . A magicked end . . . A searing sentence, against him, to
bury the death of love . . .

He came late. First off to rake over his complaints with his aunt,
who, upon seeing him arrive such a wreck, offered him water, a
jug; water she'd taken out of the well just a half hour before. She
had no rolls, neither *conchas* nor *plomos* nor *pelonas*, just sliced
bread: she took a loaf from her grocery store and—would you like
a slice with some butter and jam? Such imprudence . . . No! No!
Only water: ergo: Doña Zulema was all ears, though: you can well
imagine the big guy's verbal stammers . . . It was impossible for

him to articulate anything coherent. Moreover: maybe she should have reduced him to tears, it would be good for him, but he was so macho . . . He preferred to keep stuttering as his red face got splotchy and his shaking continued unabated . . . Under the circumstances Doña Zulema waited for him to settle into the calm, but that: uh-oh . . .

Is it over? What did you do to her? What did she tell you? Were you disrespectful? Such likely questions would be the immobilized aunt's foremost observations. Perhaps he was crying inside, for he silently shook his head and at one point brought his fist down upon the counter. Later, he uttered an explanatory sentence, as if with supreme effort: *Renata got angry because I kissed the back of her hand!* A moment later he added: *She said she never wanted to see me again.* Most dramatic of all was that Demetrio didn't wait for Doña Zulema's reproach but rather, feeling already very much like a scolded child, chose to shut himself into his room and lock the door, and there he remained until the following day. Based on what she could hear, he indulged in mad mutterings: perhaps a corrective soliloquy, incomprehensible to his aunt, who pressed her ear against the door more or less every half hour, and even then. Nor did she dare suggest he come eat supper. Respect overrode fear and, above all, ostentatious suffering. His aunt went to sleep perplexed because she'd heard only the bare bones. In fact, she would have liked to hear the unhappy conclusion: if there'd been a slap or whatnot . . . No spitting, because Renata was decent . . . Or—was there only verbal aggression? Venial, though categorical, words . . . Let's proceed, then, to the following day: Demetrio left his room in a swoon—was he hungry? A guessing game: silence accompanying his aunt's robotlike preparation of coffee and the frying of a couple of eggs. A depressing effort: he nibbled slowly. His head forcefully bowed, hence we can presume no glances passed between them, it would be futile to look at each other, better just to say, for example: *May I have more* café con leche, or to straightaway refer on the spot to . . . Not a word—understood?—: and after wiping his damned smooching mouth with the napkin, he rushed back to his room. Seclusion. Mumblings. Ideas that didn't set things straight, though they did take root.

In the afternoon, after bathing neither in the cedar tub nor by the bucketful, though impeccably dressed, he gracefully betook himself to the trysting bench. He wanted to ask Renata for forgiveness, see if maybe. Doña Zulema, immediately and with investigative élan, followed him, closing the store behind her. She maintained a constant distance from each of the big guy's quick steps: praying to God, all the time, that he wouldn't turn around, wishing perhaps to gain clarity from the prayers she was sending up, not yet. And now the scene itself. Demetrio asked a child who was playing in the plaza to go tell Renata what you, Doña Zulema, and I can already guess. The child went and returned quickly and: "Renata says she can't come out and to please not come again."

The ultimate definition. As Demetrio carried out his contrite retreat his aunt hid behind a tree and from there saw her nephew returning with his head hung low and his fists clenched. She, prodded on, hastened her step so she could open her shop as quickly as possible: of course!: she would stand behind the counter knowing herself to be, let us call it, an actress: her chin leaning crassly on her theatrical hand and her bare elbow resting upon the aforementioned surface: distinguished stillness in waiting: a wait that didn't last long, given that soon Demetrio's figure formed a faded outline: at the door: sadness and rage. Now he really did want to spill his guts:

"It makes no sense for Renata to tell me to go to hell only because I kissed her hand . . . I don't think I disrespected her. I don't feel guilty in the least, my kiss was affectionate, completely affectionate! I could never behave in bad faith with a woman I want to marry. And you know, Auntie, as I told you two days ago, we've already spoken about getting married, you were even willing to live with her mother . . . Anyway! Now everything's ruined. Now Renata doesn't want to see me—and why?! why?! I don't understand . . . Anyway, she was the first one to bring up getting married, I planned to propose to her much later . . ."

The big guy's enraged huffing and puffing put an end to his harangue, and from one of his eyes there sprang an unborn tear, which he didn't wipe away, despite how macho he was, but his bitter feelings finally betrayed him, the tear rolled, trembling, down his left cheek: no way!, because—really—how shameful! Then Doña Zulema spoke:

"Demetrio, I think you made a mistake . . ."

"A mistake?! What mistake?! I treated Renata just fine and that's why I don't want to stay here one minute longer. This puritanical town horrifies me. I'm leaving!"

Or rather, as it was late evening the aggrieved man would go sleep on the top of the hill. His aunt was unable to stop him. Instead she watched, moments later, as he stuffed his dirty clothes into his suitcase, and after a spirited shutting he grabbed the handle and took off down the street. Why watch as he walked away?

Part

The Game of Decorum

Four

30

More and more cars and trucks. A teeming trough. A miracle of motorized and motile phantoms. To tell the truth, and looking at the phenomenon from a different angle, the production of intractable tractors grew in dribs and drabs; whereas bicycle production—a minor news item—appeared to be, by all accounts, incalculable, even though burros were still exceedingly useful. Just think of carrying cargo, which bicycles obviously couldn't do. Given the foregoing, we really must assert that in 1947 the Mexican automotive industry was at its apogee. Cars, trucks, and tractors were being assembled as quickly as toys, and the demand was growing constantly, in no small part due to the excellent conditions the automotive companies were offering for the purchase of said conveyances.

Not counting the use of tractors (not yet), let's take Sacramento as an example (and place ourselves smack in the middle of 1947): one could count six cars and eight pickups, whereas at the end of 1946 there had been only two pickups. Let's also take Parras (much more populous than all the other towns in Coahuila), where there were twenty vehicles at the beginning of the year in question and thirty by the middle of the same year; a tripling, then, because in December 1946 there had been only twelve. We needn't do a breakdown of cars versus trucks, for all we have to know is that there were three tractors. All this said, let us betake ourselves to Parras, that universal cultural center superior to, let us say, Tegucigalpa, or—what was the previous comparison? anyway, that's where we are in virtue of the fact that Demetrio was living at his mother's house; he, whom ill fortune had dogged throughout the central region of Coahuila, arrived and told Doña Telma that life had dealt him a few bad hands, though as yet no blows that had felled him fully . . . That ranch job had turned out to be a fiasco . . . He didn't tell his mother anything, at first, about what had happened with Renata, he simply said that in order for him to live for any length of time in Parras he would need to buy a pickup truck. The mother was happy to help in any way she could, though her son's savings sufficed (ha!): he bought one in a jiffy (a bit used and without a stake bed) in Torreón, he wouldn't go to Saltillo even if his life depended on it, and now, indeed: Demetrio's truck could be counted among the vehicles in Parras. He still had enough money for some boring investment or other. In the meantime let's imagine him as unemployed by choice. Indecisive and smug or, if you prefer, a perpetual seeker in pursuit of not employment but rather new horizons; the search for plots in outlying areas where he might plant an orchard, that is, when the blessed new beginning . . . Months passed and there came no decisive move toward either investment or employment.

Be that as it may, Demetrio was up late every night, for a very ad hoc club had opened in that huge town, a place for diversion—a miniature hell whose name lent itself to a thousand interpretations: Centro Social Parrense—but that in essence served as a cantina and a place to play dominoes and billiards into the early hours of the morn. Above all else, decency, for neither women nor children were allowed in, soldiers likewise, though anyway there never were any in the vicinity. Playing relieved tension. The joint, very roomy though quite dark, opened at five in the afternoon and closed at one in the morning; and—careful now!—only four alcoholic drinks per person were allowed. Whether a defense of decency or merely a sham, you still couldn't get drunk: hence the club's success, for it had public, as well as municipal, approval, such as it was. In this respect it must be said that the mayor of Parras occasionally went there to spend a few congenial hours shooting pool and dealing dominoes. Also, by the way, it is fitting here to add that the Centro Social Parrense was for members only. That is, one had to pay a rather hefty fee to join, as well as modest monthly dues. By the middle of 1947 it had forty members. Although the monthly dues drove some away, others were always on hand to replace them. Hence a steady number: a few more, a few less: ergo: may more players come, and we'll see if they last . . . We mention endurance because soon the under-the-table bets began. Demetrio fell headlong into this so-called trap and began to realize fabulous winnings. He rarely lost. Once, he won two thousand pesos in a week: that was a huge sum in 1947, and with minimal effort. We emphasize the obvious: gaming, especially playing dominoes, was turning into an insurmountable source of income and he, therefore, into a fearsome player, who, undefeated, challenged many: which many took him up on—good thing! let's play!—whether as trembling contenders or devoted clientele, they never came out ahead. The result: a rather sordid fortune. And now, returning to the quotidian, let's take a look at his cohabitation with his mother, who never tired of asking him about Renata, to which he responded: *My love life is fine.* Or: *We're taking a break to think things over. Her mother doesn't want us to get married. She's afraid of being left alone.* Or: *The mother is the obstacle.* Or: *I promised to go see her in September. By then I'll know what she's decided.* Or: *I've written her three letters and she hasn't answered any of them.* Or: *It will all be resolved by September, but I think our love is on the right path.* Or: *Believe me, please. I never give up.* Credible pretexts piling up or applied like a poultice that would soon become excessively soggy, for Demetrio showed neither signs of affliction nor the least urgency to travel thither, despite his pickup truck. The truth, awkward because so inexplicable, or rather the mistake of that accursed kiss on the back of her hand, would not be recounted until his mother, with her dose of adult and feminine intuition, would apply sweetly insistent pressure, which she was on the verge of doing, but . . .

His mother was endeavoring to not upset him. She dared not tell him that it was about time he invested his money if he had no intention of getting a job. Nor did she suggest even subtly that he was depleting his savings. Instead, she indulged his every whim, her only goal to make his stay in Parras pleasant and thereby obviate any absurd notion of him abandoning her anytime soon. A mother's love—with a dose of humility? Let us admire her fortitude in the face of his lassitude, for once he told her: *You know? I am making a lot of money at the club. In just a short while I've become the best dominoes player in Parras* . . . To which she only penciled in: *Do as you wish, but be careful.* And, in fact, he did exactly as he wished. Every week he went to Torreón, to the cathouses: there were four classy ones, the place was teeming with beautiful whores. So, go for more than one!, though—he knew all too well—he wouldn't be stupid enough to fall in love with any of them. Moreover, the distance, understood as infinitely reckless, even though by 1947 there was an excellent dirt road from Parras to the junction of Paila and from there a flourishing highway to Torreón, but no; there and back week after week . . . with nauseating faith, certainly derived from confusion . . . Hmm, may the past rot: a thick stew whose defiled dregs will molder: a lingering scruple with an unbearable stench . . . Nonetheless, Renata: that breath of a future life . . . Sure, it was on the verge of collapse, but . . .

Traces of regret . . .

At one point his mother told him that if he did decide to invest in something, she would like to participate, for she still had a lot of money . . . *You still have a lot? I can't believe it* . . . In response came a spontaneous and affectionate, because snug, hug, and that was all.

31

Let's pause for a moment. We have reached a point we deem fitting for the elucidation of an assortment of worn-out ideas, to wit: the five basic allocutions Doña Luisa imposed on her daughters to ensure they'd behave properly with their suitors. The first had to do with not looking their beaus directly in the eyes, for that would be a sign of flirtatious impertinence. The second concerned the filthy nature of all things carnal, meaning that the beau should never dare kiss any part of the beloved's body, for kisses in general led to the worst of perversities. The third was more radical: it involved failing every once in a while to keep a promise: if, say, they agreed to meet on a certain day at a certain time, the girl should not show up. The beau's misgivings would establish a pattern for judging just how interested he was. Any forthcoming reproaches, especially angry ones, would prove the aforementioned's lack of self-control and mean that a breakup was advisable. The fourth regarded the timing of trysts, which should be strictly limited and held within sight of the mother. Like, for example, on a bench in the main plaza, directly in front of the house. To run off elsewhere, to hide, well, that would be a dangerous decision and, needless to say, injurious. The fifth, and final, and most thoroughly outlandish one was the most difficult to follow, because, in order to prove the extent of the subject's love, it would help at one point or other, to say, for example: "What you did is not okay, so I don't want to see you again," or even: "You are a scoundrel," or "You are a pervert," or "I thought you were a gentleman," or something similar that would be insulting and, as a result, bring about a definitive break. Nor should the beau's immediate apology suffice. He must be required to apologize over and over again (first and foremost, over an extended period of time); his failure to do so showing clearly that his love was in no wise true. There were other maternal pronouncements but the essence of the advice was constant, so any different interpretation . . . No other! . . . That is, about fifteen years before Doña Luisa had written this short but substantial list on a piece of sky-blue cardboard. The handwriting was, let us say, quasiperfect, in part because she used an indelible India ink, a special one that in spite of the passage of time continued to shine . . . who knows if the daughters, having memorized this advice, became faithful adherents. The mother informed each one in turn that this was how she had conducted herself with their father before she had gotten married. Courtship with a host of restrictions, but a happy and joyous marriage, where never—and she crossed her fingers to swear to it—did anyone shout, much less show any sign of disrespect: naturally, she never tired of repeating this refrain: *You have witnessed our union for many years. I want something similar for you, because if marriage is suffering, it's not worth getting married.* Then she would assert that the bond between her parents had been similarly wonderful, without any signs of emotional to-dos, adding moreover that her mother had given her similar advice when she had reached a marriageable age: she had not drawn up a list, but she did abound in similar verbal inculcations, because likewise she had an exemplary relationship and because, turning to the grandparents, great-grandparents, great-great-grandparents, and beyond, she knew they had all been entirely happy: this her duty, to be thus perennially, or even better, emotional security without any ups and downs. All of Sacramento was like that—unscathed?: almost-almost: unique customs, as discreet as they were grandiose. And now to the particulars: the first daughter, Mercedes, followed the script to the letter and triumphed, though—was she still triumphant out there in La Terquedad, that hamlet in Coahuila where she lived?; the second daughter, Ernestina, the same; the third daughter, Glendelia, the same; but the fourth, Torcuata, well, she had been a bit of a rebel: once she went with her sweetheart to the hills; some children, accompanied by an adult, saw her kissing her mustachioed beau on the edge of a cornfield: they exchanged incredibly tongue-y kisses and some quite passionate fondling in diverse places, though never beneath their clothing. In any case the witnesses spread the word, and it was the father who decided that Torcuata would not marry that mustachioed man, but he, who really did love her, persisted for almost four years until he managed to lead her to the altar. What we're getting at here is that ever since, they'd lived in Morelia and were very happy, though, looking at it with a more dispassionate eye—how certain can we be?, and moreover—how certain can one be of the everlasting good fortune of all four? The fact was that the four sisters didn't come to Sacramento on a yearly basis, nor did they write their mother a continuous stream of letters, or rather—what about it? invisible happinesses; scant information; no complaints but to tell the honest truth—where? in what intimate terrain? Perhaps they'd rather take pleasure in or suffer their relationships than remain near the harsh nucleus here: right in the marrow of such corrosive decency: ergo: where the fifth daughter, Renata, was stuck, confused, crying her eyes out every night: how much? just a little or how much, really: with her guilt in gradations of regret that by now, the what if, the what if instead, the what if she had strayed from the script . . . let's see . . . and instead of saying to Demetrio what she had said, she had thanked him for the kiss on the back of her hand and his salacious licking, but—honest?! affectionate?! No limits, no disengagement. Until she herself came to the conclusion: *the kiss yes, the lick no.* A painful assessment, going against the grain, though . . . The lick, no . . . Disgusting. Aggressive . . . In the past few months Doña Luisa and Renata had been harmoniously in contact with their local kin. As word of the amorous split spread like wildfire, there were various conjectures and fabrications, some quite alarming, others inoffensive enough, though most implicated the mother's unfortunate intervention when with her verbal theatricality she had insulted the outlander, who had done nothing inappropriate: a kiss on the hand, admittedly extended, but to make such a scandal, such an unexpected commotion. Renata, to begin with, was guilty—for making such a nuance manifest? turning it into a capital offense with her violent disengagement and her tears and her flight and the wrath of her mother, who had not had the prudence to manage a situation that in others' views and judgment meant nothing and, well—why had such an insult risen to her lips? After digging deeply into the matter during those afternoon teas, the arguments always crumbled to the rhythm of the sipping of *café con leche* and the dunking of sweet rolls, and the conclusion finally had to come: she saddled her mother with the blame, at least for her sudden irrational outburst: her response lacking proportion and instead . . . It is known that the actions of third parties in a conflict are always valuable to the degree that they exercise a calming influence, but . . . let's see . . . Doña Luisa did not acknowledge the accusation: no! what for?! never!; hence the coarse words an uncle spoke, words that came nowise as a surprise: *The problem is that you don't want Renata to get married. You are afraid of being alone, isn't that so?* Her mother had to admit that said uncle was correct. He had so much harm stored inside him that were we to follow him we would easily predict him saying something like this: that old age is a symptom of inevitable frustration, however it comes about, and from there even more malice so why even mention it . . . Solutions, therefore— conscientious ones?: which ones?: one, at least, that would seep in deep. It was a supreme comfort for Doña Luisa to hear that her relatives would not leave her alone. Several of them offered her their homes and a few swore they'd be willing to live with her in her house. Hence her freedom of choice should Renata get married continued to be reaffirmed and spelled out—though would she get married? Let it be known that she remained silent throughout these emotionally strained meetings. If someone inquired about the kiss on her hand (for this was the core of the commotion and the crux of the gossip), she had recourse to her viral reasoning: the kiss yes, but the lick no. Upon hearing for the first time that nasty conclusion, the mother exploded: *He licked your hand, didn't he? He's a scoundrel!* Then: a further increase of indignation: from her alone. Inductive tyranny, emanating from disgust, nothing more, as far as Renata was concerned, who, in this particular case, had ceased to let herself be influenced by those maternal allocutions. The tyranny of her rigorous decorum, which, after being made public, became doubly painful. The tyranny of the rupture. The tyranny of disrepute, even though her mother's insult still hovered, heard by—whom? That "Get out of here, you scoundrel!" sensed in the bewilderment that still echoed throughout the plaza. So, their discussions included the issue of who was more guilty: 40 percent to the daughter and 60 percent to the mother . . . the arithmetic wasn't precise, but it didn't matter, after all . . . Now, as far as regrets were concerned—who had more? Renata began to consider writing Demetrio a letter: five pages of—fastidious?— exonerations, but her mother stayed her: *Wait, dear, it's not for you to ask for forgiveness . . . You can be absolutely certain of that.* It was that salacious smacker who should be struggling. For if not, what was the point of trying to change the course of an affection. Be that as it may, Renata began to write in secret. Her theme: her helplessness, in the wake of that stupid interpretation of a kiss that was perhaps legitimate, but—why the lick? What was the goal? Oppressive slowness, so slow due to the lack of even one convincing, or at least persuasive, notion. In fact, all words seemed hostile: and: the writing was awful because she didn't know what was underneath, how deep it went, how, that's it: how to justify such a violent rejection, which her mother, in turn, had amplified. The amorous collapse was insurmountable—or was it? and how to help it arise from . . . Hence her attempts to write, and the immediate and complete erasures. Days and nights of darkness and again playing with words and again nothing, only disconnecting and coarse calamities continuing to accumulate, whereby one wrong word distorted all the others, whereby: better wait for later: when feelings and intuitions grew clearer: Renata, the more she faced this ambiguity, the more paralyzed she became. Patience, therefore, and natural vision and yearning: hopefully soon!

Many of her relatives told her that her duty was to get her sweetheart back; the question was how. Others, much like her mother, recommended waiting, caution, in order to establish an effectual new arrangement, in the sense of her acknowledging how much she was willing to compromise. Others, fewer in number, suggested she forget the whole thing; at which point Renata would express herself in stentorian fashion: *It's not so easy to destroy what I have built.* Ah. Fortunately chance provided a counterpoint, just when it was most essential: the incentive to make a hefty profit out of the stationery store. With the beginning of the academic year upon them, the sales of school supplies skyrocketed. The palliative consequences of this circumstance. An exorbitant amount of work. The trips to Monclova (now by bus, which meant the trip was quick) for enormous amounts of merchandise to stock up on here, where people were waiting in line: morning, afternoon, and even some at night! Work piled on top of work, even on weekends. Satisfaction, midst the rough wear and tear, surely enhanced by the boundless bustle. The avalanche of sales continued into the middle of October—of course!, then a gradual easing, but still . . . The evidence was that the beau gave no sign throughout that entire period of celerity: not even one miserable (tantalizing) letter nor a fleeting appearance on the aforementioned bench. Nor did it occur to Renata to go visit Doña Zulema, only to be distressed by some bit of news: that Demetrio was engaged to another (where?) or had taken to drink due to his sorrows; but the letter still to write . . . When Renata finally did pay a visit to Doña Zulema, the latter confessed that Demetrio had cursed Sacramento as he left. The unforgettable final sentence was: *This puritanical town horrifies me!* He didn't say where he was going. Nevertheless, his aunt did drop a hint: *If you want to write him, send the letter to Parras. At least you can be sure his mother will get it and keep it.* Renata wasted no time before responding with: *And what if she opens the letter and reads it and then hides it?* The aunt smiled as if a ghost were tickling her arid armpit: *How many dirty things are you going to write? If you speak to him of love and even indirectly bring up the idea of getting married, he just might change his tune . . .* In a somewhat insulting, though gentle and even syllabicated voice, his aunt said she was willing to intervene on their behalf, as she needed to talk to Doña Luisa anyway: *I would be very diplomatic or, how can I put it?, quite tolerant, or, well, not at all argumentative . . . The one thing I do know is that this relationship can still be saved.* Salvation from the bottom up, tread by tread, about three hundred in all, like climbing to the top of a pyramid. Renata squeezed the waistband of her skirt and asked Doña Zulema to give her the address in Parras—wow! she knew it by heart, so: the process of writing it down on a slip of paper; then she left: grinning at first then subsequently sort of sad: her cheeks sagged: her fine-lipped mouth almost like the tip of an arrow: the slight elevation against the double descent (lovesick): blackness below and above a vitreous brilliance (a flourish?). Smoldering ember: of sorts, enough to notice that she still didn't know what to write. Never grant a full pardon, because . . . the premise . . . The kiss yes, the lick no . . . That sentence could come at the beginning . . . Let it serve as a refrain throughout the rather twisted discourse. Leave the writing for later, right? because writing was like laying down a foundation in a straight line, avoid having to hang a strong roof—solid? how? The only solidity would consist of a blunt proposition of marriage, then children: many: a baseball team (ha) with a few on the bench (ha), but . . . the foundation and the urgency, a combination that would strengthen the undertow of a, perhaps foolish, desire: the pleading sweetheart: Oh, on her knees . . . hypothetically?!, and thus a lifetime of disadvantage; though the other path would be, perhaps, the mistaken one of pride . . . if only there were others . . . Better the ruse of patience, until it became an enormous (though not daunting) question, something that would collapse on its own, and then . . .

To prefigure the letter's voyage: a fantasy: that in transit the ideas would shift, sweeten. That day Renata was ready to write only the opening salvo, but what could she say that wouldn't sound pleading or pardoning. Maybe even ask her still-sweetheart why the lick or what was behind that surprising smut. Start off by telling him that it had been a mistake . . . Anyway, that he should come back: right now! hurry! you've been forgiven. Virtual rearranging reflections: everyone: her mother, she herself, nearby relatives, all would overlook that stupid misstep, which in the end wasn't that serious and maybe merely the result of an affectionate and inconsequential overflow.

On the way home Renata kept recalling Doña Zulema's words: thorns, splinters, twists, and with dismay and displeasure she kept returning to the first: *This puritanical town horrifies me!* The town is to blame and not—so there!—only Renata and her mother. Therefore, a misunderstanding, which to be understood as it should required a ton of conjectures and explanations in the minutest of detail to be poured into that letter, the only way to avoid defeat by an unfortunate trifle . . . Explanations, and more explanations: to sum things up, and . . . Renata did not know how to face the enigmatic blank page. In fact, she let a long time pass, because she also found it unbearable to hold a fountain pen: weeks: three, four, five: November: torturous cold: beginning of December: almost there: almost Christmas Eve; that year of misfortunes was coming to an end and the letter: the beginning: oh, to wish Demetrio all the best for the New Year: that's it! already written in the green-eyed gal's head were the message's opening sentences, but first she wished to inform Doña Luisa of her decision:

"I want to write to Demetrio."

"What are you going to say?"

"I just want to wish him a merry Christmas and a happy New Year."

"Don't even think of making the dumb mistake of asking him for forgiveness; he's the one who disrespected you."

"It will be a very short letter."

"Are you really still interested in that good-for-nothing? Remember, he licked your hand. That's really disgusting."

"I don't think he's a good-for-nothing. Remember, he returned the next day and said he was sorry and I didn't come out, I didn't forgive him . . . Now I do want to forgive him in writing."

"I don't think it's right . . . Maybe if he came here, or wrote you, but he hasn't."

"So, I'll only wish him a merry Christmas and . . ."

"My advice is not to write him, better to wait until he makes a move . . . If he really loves you he will."

"How long do I have to wait? A year? Five years? How many?"

"One year, maybe a bit more."

"That's too long for me."

"A lot can happen in a year, both good and bad."

"Well, I want to write him and, as I said, I'm just going to say hello. I'll remain cool, I promise . . . It will be my last attempt at a reconciliation."

"You are stubborn, Renata. You'd be much better off if you had more dignity. You should follow your sisters' example."

"This will be my last attempt . . ."

"Okay, I'll try to understand how you feel . . . I only ask you to show me the letter before you send it. Agreed?"

"Agreed."

Hurrah! All Doña Luisa had to do was show a tad of flexibility for Renata to flesh out her scheme. Her idea at first was to fashion a benign narrative of their relationship up till then, the romantic policies, prudently expressed, or with a slow dotting of all the i's and a crossing of all the t's, in the guise of outlining a feeling she would then have to describe in detail (so much explaining, how would she ever), but—careful!—, in the meantime such a fastidiously elaborated rational discourse, how many ideas would be worthwhile and how many futile: would they be compressed or expanded, or how to remove fibs but retain feelings . . . Anyway, now Renata had two tasks: to write the laconic letter with good wishes that—bad news—her mother would read with loads of prejudice: we can take for granted the scruples that would arise during revision—an ungrateful task, the whole thing to be shredded after the maternal review, indeed, let's admit it once and for all; whereas the other composition: profuse and secretive: a long (the original) letter that Renata would stash in her panties on her way to the post office, which had to be the good one, the only one, the one with stamps and seals, the one she would have to write with lyricism, even if without great calligraphic care or adequate segues between the ideas. It's just that if she took too much time (prolix verbiage covering the length of both sides of five or six sheets) she would awaken her mother's suspicions, too long this undue delay; hence one afternoon's work, full steam ahead, for two hours, or less, a letter that she would hide under the mattress: there to be (indirectly) stashed . . . Ugh! and, that said, let us now turn to the phony letter, which had to be exemplary: three or four sentences, five at the most, and as a final flourish she would close with an "I miss you, Demetrio," as well as her name at the very bottom (in stylized script), "Renata Melgarejo" . . . somewhat pretentious scribbles from start to finish . . . Anyway, once she had completed that quite prodigious product, the green-eyed gal took it eagerly to Doña Luisa, who made only one cautious correction: instead of "I miss you, Demetrio" she should put the more blatantly brusque "Cordially yours," nothing more!, hence the (nauseating) nuisance of copying it over and . . . Let's now return to: the real composition!: the straightforward outpouring of emotions: waves crashing against each other, so to speak, or fortuitous stumbles and stammers, meaning the fearless expression of variations on "Yes, I love you, but . . .": pure momentum—of course! and as quick as a whip, but when she finished, it was as if she'd run a marathon, she was gasping for breath and on the verge of an infarction. Then she filched two envelopes from the shop and ran (a bit awkwardly) to her destination, with Doña Luisa's permission. First she had to hide in the bushes in an empty lot in order to . . . It's enough to assume the concise letter was rapidly rent: shreds like confetti and the even quicker removal of the real letter from her panties: the fat and bold and slightly damp one—ooh! which would surely dry out completely before it reached Parras.

After dropping the letter in the mailbox, she was left with her resulting pangs of conscience, her wish for the letter to arrive directly into Demetrio's hands . . . Hmm, Renata was certain he wouldn't be able to make out her handwriting, but it would be enough for him to read her name, writ large at the end, as well as the "I still love you, my love," another flourish, and that was that.

32

He seemed like a god, it was unbelievable, by the middle of October, Demetrio had lost only ten rounds of dominoes out of the three hundred–odd games he had played at the Centro Social Parrense. At first it was the sly, perhaps sinful passivity of the game, but soon he derived frolicking fun from betting small sums, then defiantly raising the stakes to liven up the entertainment, viewing it almost as a way of life, as legitimate as going to work every day, a life Demetrio was adapting to better than most: becoming ever more skillful as night after night he employed new winning strategies, in addition to his absolute trust in his own lucky star, which meant he always drew good tiles no matter how gently or roughly his rivals shuffled them; hence every player wanted to be his partner to guarantee x amount of winnings and, to sum things up, the big guy won tons of money and daily deposits ensued . . . In 1947 in Parras there was an establishment that offered the services of a savings-and-loan; two years later it had become more sophisticated after moving and hiring more employees; it still wasn't a proper bank, but people called it a bank, for none dared call it a savings-and-loan . . . Anyway, back to Demetrio, who we said was making hefty deposits, a total of fifteen thousand pesos in thirty weeks: just right for a more or less grandiose investment. The brakes were put on, however, in two ways: the most important being an agreement among the most frequently defeated players:

a group of twenty confronted him and told him that nobody was willing to play against him anymore, especially when a juicy bet was on the table: *We're tired of losing*, said the brawniest one. To Demetrio's great disappointment he could no longer strut his stuff and had no choice but to do something productive. The second time the brakes were put on was more crushing: Píndaro Macías, the mayor, outlawed gambling, not only at that club but also throughout the entire territory over which he reigned. This was because the big boss had played and lost. He had become a (daily) gambler and, never particularly adept at that particular art, well, there you have it; he also considered himself a visionary with long antennae, and he surmised that to continue to allow gambling of any kind would inevitably lead to social decay, which would translate into an infinite number of regrettable events, so he pulled prohibition out of his hat and ushered in, naturally, the downfall of said club. It made no difference that the pair of proprietors had purchased six new pool tables and several more of ping-pong, for if no betting was allowed—what was the point? So the club closed temporarily, a reopening remaining a possibility until further notice. In consequence, Demetrio withdrew his money from the bank (the fifteen thousand pesos and a bit more of his other capital) so that he could ponder, now in earnest, his business aspirations . . . What would be best? At one point he even had a notion to open up a high-class cathouse, the first in Parras, for better or for worse, but . . .

The risk: exuberant!

Where would he get high-quality whores?

Bring them in—but from where? Too difficult!

How many permits? How many expenses?

Evaporation and a mordant grave for such an impossible and indecent idea—right? A tad of regret after the posing of many objections. Immorality as a crappy way of life . . . What a muddled venture!

It could be said that with money in hand Demetrio glimpsed

the thicket of sex, in Torreón: undulations he well deserved, considering his stamina and despite those weekly trips, a few days each; a hypothetical plan to set in motion his underused machinery, but first let's take note of his mother's badgering, especially one crucial event around the middle of September, when she reminded her son about going to Sacramento: to wit: what he had promised her and seemingly had no intention of carrying out. The big guy employed no end of pretexts to sharply dissuade her: that he'd go later—okay?, later; naturally, she, for a long time already, had sensed an affective uglification, we could call it, because when questioned about Renata, the aforementioned did his utmost to avoid falling into her unbearable snare of questions and answers, mostly through churlish and curt remarks: *I'll go in October . . .* Or: *We had a little misunderstanding and I want to wait . . .* Or: *I need to feel really good to feel like going . . .* And more shadowy means to make it stop, but the mother, not satisfied, forced from him a confession. She did it tactfully, as if she were stroking thorns; always leading with tenderness, and success like a blossom: to sit together and talk parsimoniously. She cornered him cautiously. Demetrio spoke, spoke as he moved—with Doña Telma pushing him—backward, until he reached the supposed vulgarity of the kiss on the back of the hand, and, yes, the heartfelt lick; perhaps it was the eagerness of the novice to kiss passionately what never before, nevertheless, the unexpected explosion, how strange it had all seemed to him, because her mother had also insulted him. Demetrio wanted to be as explicit as possible, so he mentioned that the day before, he and Renata had spoken about getting married, and then the unexpected had occurred, as well as the consequences that had already taken place (double-dealing Doña Luisa): the pathology of a Puritanism that served no purpose, on the contrary, it messed things up, holding out, always, the path of forgiveness, which also served no purpose. At that point Demetrio had nothing to say other than that he had gone to see Renata the following day and no, just no, and Doña Telma, herewith:

"I know those Sacramento women. I am certain that Doña
Luisa and Renata planned the whole thing the night before in order
to find out how deep your love for her was. Maybe mother and
daughter thought you would make a wrong move because you had
spoken about marriage, you might put your arms around her or
caress her or squeeze her hand a little bit too hard; any of these
gestures would have been normal for you, but you chose a precipitous kiss, with no bad intentions, I know, especially because
of where you did it. In any case, Renata must have interpreted it as
indecent and especially because of the lick—what a shame!"

"So, what's your advice?"

"You shouldn't give up . . . You should go to her. You'll see,
she'll forgive you."

"What a pain! really . . . I must admit, at this moment I have
absolutely no desire to go anywhere."

"I understand how you feel. Just remember that she is still in
love with you, but she wants you to fight for her, she wants to be
absolutely sure of you before she takes the next step . . . Hmm . . .
I know all about those Sacramento women."

"They are too complicated."

"But they're worth it. As soon as she's yours, you'll see, everything will come right."

What's to say other than that this onslaught left Demetrio bewildered. It would seem that Puritanism had unknown tentacles,
arising from the most unexpected places, which had finally pinned
him down and paralyzed him. He now saw that nobody he told
about the incident of the kiss and the lick would take his side.
Hence, to accept defeat, admit his mistake to the four winds, and
thus avoid ever being squashed; and the admission of guilt—would
it save him?, perhaps, but in the meantime distension to the point
of obliteration, or as the chance to be dissipated to a point of satiety, and to elude his mother, once and for all, Demetrio ended
the conversation like this: *I'll decide whether or not I should go to
Renata. Now I need to take care of myself. Please don't pressure*

*me and don't bring up this subject again. Because right now I'm
going to Torreón. Just so you know, I'm going to sin! What? I'm
starved for sex. I want to lose my head! I'm dying to . . . and . . .
well . . . I'll probably be back the day after tomorrow.* Stunned,
Doña Telma slowly lowered her head: "I understand him," "I understand him," "I have to understand him"—et cetera; she could repeat
it to herself a hundred times, as if she were poking her breast with
the point of a knife. A temporary setback—did she know that? And
here we have the beginning of the skit: on the road, once and for
all; the knot that almost came undone every time Demetrio placed
his shoe on the gas pedal; the truck and the gasoline were his lively
assistants that gave him a boost—right? another boost would be to
whistle out of tune the whole way so he'd feel like a lad about to
be initiated, for he was on his way to commit the greatest misdeed
of his life, something like, let's see: what if he hired two beautiful
whores so they could take turns massaging him and doing him?
That's it, one would shower him with caresses while the other got
on all fours—yes! and then the other way around, and that way,
long-lasting sexual antics: the whole night, no matter how much
it cost. When he arrived at a cathouse called Los Laureles—very
costly—he immediately called two women over: one blonde and
one brunette. However, the joint's policy required that he order
a drink before choosing. So, while he downed one shot after another Demetrio thoroughly planned his anticipated seclusion with
the duo: step-by-step, assuming they agreed; at the same time, he'd
be open to their suggestions, this or that change of position, more
efficient arrangements, whereby nobody would feel at a disadvantage. They: concubines; they: sheaths with opinions as if they were
mocking a simpleminded puppet, someone who found comfort
elaborating a pleasing idyll only to grow weak before taking even
the first step, because while they sat at the table he didn't touch
them once, a long way from an array of what could and should
potentially be done: a thoughtful, lascivious, sinful trio, though for

Cirila and Begoña, which is what they were called, what mattered
was to get the client drunk as quickly as possible. Hence the mischief of shamelessly ordering mixed drinks they barely sipped, the
trick made manifest: obvious to anybody who knows the ways of
any cathouse, but he: how many straight shots of tequila did he
have to imbibe before he became unbearable? Eight, nine at the
most: an amount, once reached, that made him lose his balance,
fall off the chair, and pick himself up with great difficulty, but once
on his feet he said again: *Let's go to the room! I want the two of
you at the same time.* Oh, really? well, out with the bills already:
ergo: the spender rendered unconscious, and next they called over
the bouncer to drag him to the room of sin, the concubines following behind, amused and mocking. Slow motion once inside: a real
fuss to undress somebody not used to drinking so much alcohol.
In the end, the man couldn't perform, not even half an erection
could he muster. The worst part was that he'd paid in advance,
an exorbitant fee, for these two cynics who, after seeing him im-
paired, called the bouncer back to have him thrown out on the
street. They carried him as if he were a rag doll. A collapsed and futile mass, and: how could he drive the truck in his state? Demetrio
had no choice but to ask someone to call him a taxi that would
take him to a hotel, a cheap one, please. This episode entailed a
long list of grievances, culminating in a long overdue explanation.
The taxi driver informed him that none of the joints in Torreón's
red-light district allowed sex with any of those statuesque women
until you'd first drunk torrents of booze and paid in advance with
a hefty roll of bills. He also told him that if he just wanted sex he
should go to the seedy women, the worst of the worst, all over fifty,
perhaps some chubby young ones and, to top it off, they stank,
those sitting on their rocking chairs, each one in front of the open
door of her own mangy hovel. There were lots along a three- or
four-block stretch. The thing was that if he wanted fine flesh
he'd have to drink like a donkey and . . . which has already been

said . . . money attracts money, right? as well as disgust and definitely drama. *Like so many others before you, my friend, you've
been had.* After uttering this reproachful rant, he hurled at him a
hail of insults, and who knows how much they affected Demetrio,
for his reason seemed to be drifting like a slipstream: he heard
sharp words—but which ones? The discourse was—could it be?—
inebriated. The little he caught became faint in the face of fleeting
memories of Oaxaca: there everything was straightforward, no sly
malevolence, only direct consummation, whereas here . . . longings
left unquenched that get reabsorbed and mess everything up . . .
Money evaporating in proportion to aggravation provoked, knowing that if he returned to the red-light district he would have to do
so with great caution: not pay in advance: duh!? Suffer, err, and
top it all off sleeping in a hotel, ergo, impersonal sleep, even more
so because the room was—cheap? Demetrio didn't know how
much he'd paid the taxi driver or the clerk at the . . . A fortune—
tough luck! And there he remained till noon the next day. When he
awoke he had no appetite, only pure dismay. His priority—can you
guess?—: go find the pickup. His hangover had left him transfixed.
But he found a taxi and, did he remember where . . . ? He paced
painstakingly through the red-light district: four blocks; very few
people in the streets; the big guy's lucky star better start to shine
soon; if only it would magically appear—now!—his vehicle, among
the splendors of chance (few, many, just the right number): leaden
destiny, for God's sake! and, after walking around like an inept
detective he finally found his pickup, it was all in one piece, and it
even seemed to have acquired a new sheen. He took off, of course,
for Parras . . . automatically . . . Well done! The magnet: sanctity—
what else could it be?, or at least caution was pulling him back. The
devil would pull at him later . . . But now let's have a look at this:

His arrival at the house of rustic beauty. His silent mother, big
like him, wanting to embrace, let us say, a distress: and: the parry:
such scoundrelly persistence. Right away Demetrio's retreat so he

could pull himself together. There was noise in his head and twisted (red) threads, so to speak: confusion, unmitigated, or one obstacle after another: intrinsic, or—what the hell were they? Some kind of logjam lay in wait for this semisinful man, a logjam that threatened to drown him in one single and frantic obsession: sex, at any cost: once, again, then again and again, recondite recycling. However, when he saw all those saints in his room, porcelain beings that seemed to grow bigger the longer he watched them, he muttered this: *"Demetrio" is synonymous with "nobody's fucking me."* And he fell asleep. His dream did him no favors. Mireya appeared, as if against her own will, shining from the jewels that bedecked her. She was the queen of the red-light district in Saltillo, where he found himself. When she saw him she said in a malicious voice: *Well, well, I finally find you . . . You might like to know that your daughter is twenty years old*—had that much time passed?—*She's studying medicine at the best university in Monterrey. I pay for her studies with my work as a high-class prostitute. What do you think about that? Now, get out of here, because if you don't, I'll have my men tear you to pieces. Go away! You're a pathetic fool!* Demetrio woke up with even more encephalitic din. He began palpating his temples with his fingertips, trying to soothe the internal whir. He had meager success. Little by little—thank God!—the noise went elsewhere.

What the big guy needed was a long and deep cleansing, and that's what he got. The lathering had to be like an incursion into territory where all memories, good and bad alike, become futile. More and more beneficial suds. An inkling of a new beginning where it would be ordained that he could do whatever the hell he wanted, as long as he acted strategically, per the reigning paranoia, whenever he acted boldly. It had been a good idea to get rid of the brunette, but—Renata? that haughty yet suffering decency . . . hmmm . . . let her suffer; may her error ramify; this was the already prodigious and accepted revenge of a macho and now let's turn to something else . . . See-through-sex; provocation-sex; struggle-sex. So many gradations of falsity that would soon become achievements. Then came what was not desirable: he emerged resplendent and perfumed, and his mother stood in the main hallway and intercepted him and—what do you think she said? Her indiscretion erupted . . . She was in such a state of anxiety . . .

"Demetrio, tell me please if you sinned while you were gone."

"Yes, indeed I did."

"How do you feel?"

"Look, Mama, leave me alone, or I'll go away and never come back."

"It's just that I'm worried . . ."

"Well, you needn't be, because I've been an adult for a long time . . . What's more, I'll tell you right now I'm going to keep on sinning . . . I'm very fond of all and any sins."

How could the lady reproach him? She understood, finally, about him being an adult: it's about time!, and the irremediable strains of maturity: his! he was beginning to rot, whereas she was better off positioning her tearful self in an unfamiliar weepy dimension, because she wept in front of Demetrio: her apron—absorbent? A shudder that hearkened back to when she rocked her only male offspring in a pure white cradle: a pink baby, a sleeping peacock, who then became an incorrigible toddler: O avid restlessness, that then led to him studying to be an agronomist, as his father had recommended, and now, tough luck! to have to see him become a flagrant sinner who walked out without kissing her good-bye on the cheek as he uttered a bitter sentence: *I'm going to Torreón. I like the cathouses there. I'm going to sin.* Hasty and contemptuous communication. And the pickup and the gasoline: everything ready, of course, for . . . He left whistling, he wanted to sing, but—what song? He didn't know all the lyrics of a single one. So, random fragments, O uproarious crooning!, or a feeling of boldness to peel off layers of doubt, don layers of enthusiasm: free and delightful swaying over the course of miles . . . Happiness is always fortuitous . . .

Let's watch his relapse: his arrival at Los Laureles, because he wanted to get it on with those impressive concubines: that Cirila and that Begoña, both unforgettable. Herewith the arrangement: in order to get them to come to his table, Demetrio would have to pay an exorbitant sum (a new rule) to a man with a very flat Carmelite hairdo (that is, with a part down the middle). However, the big guy refused to pay, arguing that it was very bad for him to get drunk: that he was not an alcoholic; he couldn't tolerate all that nausea and vomiting; and the most whimsical: that alcohol would prevent him from having a decisive erection, to which the man with the very well-groomed do replied that if he wanted only sex he had to pay triple the amount: fifty pesos for each female: o-ho! such a sum was almost highway robbery, or maybe a splendidly pleasant altitude he'd have to reach, for at stake was, let us call it, an irresistible otherness, and Demetrio said, okay, I'll go for it! Hence the pay now, play later, though the "play" part required a brief wait, whereas the pay became a proud display of bills: an insolent Demetrio under the glow of multicolored lights: mistake . . . to excess. The brief delay led to a further complication: the man with the hairdo called Cirila and Begoña over and they hid behind a violet curtain. The last thing he said to them was this:

"You're going with that client from before. The guy is loaded, so you know what to do."

Yes: they promised great things (per instructions) and, right from the start: cloying affection, handy for softening up the pseudo superman; a devilish start that led to a quick disrobing behind closed doors: a naked trio who began to eagerly grope each other . . . If only we could see the bare-assed outlines . . . Cirila gave the commands; the other played the role of the compliant slave: that is: let's see . . . Begoña was the first to practice fellatio, which started at the client's (unwashed) testicles: then crept up slowly to the glans by dint of tongue action, then the risings and fallings that began at a very precise speed, while the other, in corroboration, planted a big kiss on the lips of the aforementioned, who experienced, how could he not! a continuous nuanced bubbling throughout his entire body. Next, Begoña, following the instructions Cirila gave via hand signals, climbed on top of, what we might call, the murder victim, so he could penetrate her, followed by a slow trot on horseback. That part was easy and, man, what a delight! In addition the kissing in perfectly syncopated rhythm continued, a sublime lark conducted by the director's right index finger. Let us here note that a hasty ejaculation by the big guy would have been quite inconvenient, for it would have spoiled their well-planned and executed plot. So: no increase in pleasure, instead somewhat extended endurance, though not in ascent, or let's call it an opportunistic (ahem) "petty elongation," or, to wit, the two managed to get Demetrio to close his eyes and that was when Begoña announced she was going to the bathroom for a minute to pee. The pleasure continued full speed ahead because Cirila immediately climbed on top and inserted him into her, and her movements were so beguiling and rhythmic (much better than Begoña's) that the big guy didn't even think of opening his eyes. Quite clever, this trip to the bathroom: a fucking foil, for Begoña was rifling through Demetrio's pants—could you have guessed?—: that bare-assed babe swiftly removed the man's well-endowed wallet and dropped it into her handbag. Then the sinful kissing continued: a kiss that reopened the mouth of the man who used to be rich: she surpassed the other, in this respect, so we are now talking about sexual plenitude: the magma of the savage—and therefore ecstatic—interlacing. Then came the semenic eruption in Cirila's lubricated insides. Whereby we can assert that Demetrio had never before experienced such almost otherworldly pleasure. The consummation waned and the sinner, dazed, was exhausted, but the concubines ordered him to get dressed right away: *We're leaving. And you, my love, can't stay in the room alone.* In consequence: a vibrant rush, the departure of the trembling trio. On the way to the salon the bewildered client assured them he would return the following day: *I want to do tomorrow what we did today. I loved it!* But the concubines scurried away between the scarlet curtain panels. They said neither thank you nor good-bye. When Demetrio reached the room where the music played, the man with the Carmelite hairdo intercepted him and was persuasive in the following way:

"Looks like you had a good time, but you must leave immediately."

"Why?"

"Because Cirila and Begoña's boyfriends have just arrived and they have to go to them. If they find out their women were with you, they'll probably fill you full of lead. They're gunslingers and, well, very jealous . . . hmm . . . very violent. So I recommend that you . . ."

"But I want to come back tomorrow. I really liked it!"

"You'd better leave and not come back. There are some pretty dangerous people around here."

The sinner grew livid. He failed to understand such magnificent logic, but he hastened his step under the weight of an increasingly heavy suspicion. His fear, though peaking, was still fallible, for he wanted to be brave though didn't know how: his doubt, his nerves: one feint, two, three, merely his (fleeting) intention to return, but . . . The world outside seemed to pulsate, and he, still under the spell of the uproar of the voluptuous, made an abrupt about-face and found himself face-to-face with the two bouncers of Los Laureles; one of them pointed a pistol at him and said: *Outta here, you chump . . . or I'll kill you right now!* Hmm, leave—why? otherwise—death in the dumps?

It was then, while in retreat, that Demetrio patted his pants pockets. Some dark instinct propelled him to reveal a truth that, in this quite real fix, must have been horrible, and it was: because his

wallet—oh no!? Unbelievable discovery, and—oh no! Plundered—
when? During his sexual fervor, and through an oblique kind of re-
construction: aha! when what's-her-name went to the bathroom . . .
that the sign, that the surmise . . . Never to be recovered—needless
to say!—the abrupt (and well-deserved) downfall of a simple sinner whose only recourse was to leave for Parras that late at night,
because if he didn't . . . a simple sardine (that's how he felt) caught
in a delicate though unfriendly net, and it was useless to ponder
the what-ifs when the outcome, when all was said and done, would
be the same, or worse. He therefore proceeded to his pickup in defeat. Fortunately his keys were still in his left pocket, this the extent
of his consolation; but what about gas: would he have enough to
reach Parras? A drop-by-drop dilemma, which would drip though
not ooze, the liquid s-cum of an unforgettable sexual adventure:
the ineffable delight seeping (simply) into a fiendish curse: not one
red cent! And then: he couldn't remember if he had had ten thousand pesos in his wallet, or more, though in either case his wealth
had evaporated in a matter of seconds, the consequence of his
nonpareil sin. So was it—divine punishment?, vengeance hurled
against his perversions? It is important for you to know—unless
you disagree—that his thoughts might get out of joint if he kept
mulling his misfortune, which wasn't done messing with him, because once on the road he feared he'd run out of gas. Evil shadows
lurked, and, in fact, when he saw the star-studded sky he knew
that something up there was speaking . . . If only it were astral
mirth, a resounding word descending . . . It wasn't long before the
pickup stopped on its own, that is, deliberately. That's what had
to happen on the road to total rack and ruin. A sinister stop, in defeat, because—who would rescue him at that time of night? Every
sound increased his disgrace, all to no purpose, a mockery in the
midst of desolation, or an ever-widening lie . . . Demetrio's only option was to sleep in the cab, though sleeping was a futile deferral,
for once the new day came—then what? Delaying the solution: the

infamous: a hardening, damn it, infusing further doubt . . . It wasn't till about six the next afternoon that a stake-bed truck stopped and, well, let's look at it this way: good people must show up, but not necessarily when you need them: to wit: they are the people who solve problems without asking for anything in exchange. Surely such a miracle can take years, or months, or—who knows! but herewith anew and very askew, Demetrio's lucky though damaged star shone through, though the circumspect señor wanted to charge him for the gasoline. Which meant the big guy had to tell him what had happened from beginning to end. A story with a surprise ending? Of course, and because the señor was cracking up at the whole sexual welter and the other part: the sinister corollary of the dearth of funds. The theft—while astride a throne?! and the rest—in the mire! At a certain point Demetrio asked him:

"Hey, why are you laughing?"

"Because if I'm going to give you five gallons of gas the least you can do is let me laugh. But if you have a problem with my being entertained, then I won't give you any."

Then the señor laughed again, and quite explicitly explained what Demetrio would have to do if he wanted his help: he described how to plead on bent knees, joining his poor hands in dire supplication (ha), as well as a maelstrom of final flurries. No way! The guy was a reasonably good man who was holding all the cards, above all, his laughter sounded like a motorbike, though, if we are to be more precise, edged with forgiveness—so what could Demetrio do?: forbearance: scolded dog that he was! A long chiding though not very thorough, more like a drip that tickled, or, if you like, any exaggerated surmise. Let's see if it's appropriate now to say that the stranger's laughter seemed to throw salt on open wounds: which lasted days, psychic fraying translated into a silence that made his mother suspicious, for day after day she watched her son in saintly seclusion. He ate little. Ever since he arrived in that sorry state, stepping out the door seemed dangerous, footfall by footfall! Colossal fear, tremors, consonant tension. And the dear lady longed to find out what horror had befallen her lamb in the cathouses of Torreón. *You can trust me. Tell me what happened. I'll just listen. Unburden yourself.* This attempt at persuasion would be repeated more than five times and in different ways, and the result could be none other than his contempt: all and any way: however he wished: such as: turning his back on her, or giving her a sour pout, or muttering nonsense, or, you can imagine the rest, until . . . Who knows what devil prodded the big guy to blurt out his wretched story. He spoke as if he were in a hideout, avoiding anything that would shed light on the extent of his folly. In fact, he decided not to describe the sexual. With his mother he had no confessional playbook to follow other than traipsing from one surprise to the next and summing it up strategically bit by bit. Hence his opposing inventions, nurtured by the supposed innocence of a person still apt to be astonished who realizes that everything is disappointing, beginning with the cathouses of Torreón, where thieves and murderers abounded. That is, some guy stole his wallet at gunpoint. That was the only anecdote (an auspicious invention), the rest was nothing but a pile of sketchy notions, as cerebral as they were abstract. A drastic and meandering simplification so that his mother would understand only the cruelty of the theft and his attendant anguish, about which she, without holding herself back, proclaimed thus: *I know how terrible you must feel, but that's what I'm here for, to help you through this.* Nonetheless, Demetrio, at some point after his confession, began to elaborate a grievance that had its origins way back when his father used to beat him; whippings for any reason whatsoever; the terror of living without hope, knowing that whatever he did would be wrong; the sense that the simple fact of growing up was a threat, the weight of which would soon crush him, as if life were perpetual confusion and he had no choice but to toe the line if he wanted even modest security. Or rather: never even attempt to stray. That's why he

studied agronomy, because his father had forced him to, because
the señor owned land that his only (submissive) son would have
to manage. Manipulated, though only temporarily, for Demetrio
finally rebelled. He fled—when he graduated, of course!—from
his house, with an ideal of freedom that didn't—nor ever would—
have any foundation. The purpose of his life revealed itself only
in puffs of mist and . . . enough already! His glimpse of what was
essential was as normal as it was overwhelming: get married, have
children, work like a burro, and have not the slightest spirit of
transgression. A vertical trajectory as unobjectionable as a plant
that bears fruit, although being alone and doing things he didn't
like, for example: agronomy—how could such triumphs hold his
interest? Demetrio had followed a script whose sequel was uncertain, if not straight-out false. By his age he should have been an
opulent man, swelling with countless honors and endless pride,
but . . . who was to blame—he or somebody else? or, whom could
he rouse with the extent of his affliction, though to put a fine point
on it: failure . . . simple failure? failure because he'd been robbed
in a place he should never, under any circumstances, have been?
When his mother heard that word she entered the fray: *I think it is
absolutely clear that you have not failed. You are a professional
with a future and you also have savings in the bank. If they stole
a portion of your capital that doesn't mean you're ruined. You
must also understand that it is your good fortune to have me, I'm
a widow with some money and . . .* Such redeeming niceties and
that appeasing blahblahblah were not sufficient. Enough with the
harangue. Demetrio stopped her with an "I know, I know, enough,"
then added that he wanted to invest and to work with great resolve,
but he didn't know at what. Nothing fit the bill entirely and, oh, such
sauciness—from an overprotected fool? *You like games, you could
invest in a pool hall, there isn't one in Parras, a pleasant place
where people could also play dominoes and cards. You'll do well
even if there is no betting. I'll help you.* Unexpected illuminating

twitch! Smiles that shine. Light that floods the scene and sketches overhead a spectacular hunch. Thank you, Mama, for . . . Now to come up with a name for this business. A sudden about-face: a complete change of mood . . . A hunch, ready to pluck! . . . A fluke supported by a good dose of spunk (to wit, the so-called lucky star shooting sheets of lightning) to pound the pavement every day to find a well-situated locale in Parras, large—needless to say! and with easy access. Oh, uplifting resolve, which would in turn be the recipe for shedding light on all manner of dark corners.

And, off we go!

Enthusiasm never before seen: Demetrio was so eager he forgot the dross: sex for hire: the carrion of spectral silhouettism: blurred flesh: brutalizing pleasure: enough already! He left it all behind. Vomiting. Suffocation. And then, sacred love: Renata's green eyes observing him from afar . . . Decency awaiting. His thrashings: part of vile prehistory, as is agronomy. The nature of (past) ugliness that he could spit out like so much chaff, and et cetera.

Right?

Another lapse? Another attack?

To hell with it!

Another future, then.

For Demetrio, December was a month of arduous work. Much was accomplished as if by dint of magic, because, well, we'll mention only three things he dealt with: in less than a week he found a large locale to let, located in the heart of Parras, right on Ramos Arizpe, the town's main thoroughfare; second, and related, was the hiring of two young men quite eager to work (for all of which his mother confidently forked out hefty sums); third was the most troublesome: the purchases, the trips to Monterrey in his pickup (now with a staked bed), in which Demetrio brought back three very fine billiards tables packed in thick cardboard—strategically flattened—as well as an abundance of billiards paraphernalia: cues, cue holders, cue supports, cue balls, timers, chalk, counters, lamps, boards: and imagine the trips necessary to purchase the dozens of little knickknacks. Then: dominoes tables, tons of chairs, two (long) wooden benches. The whole business was ready two days before New Year's Eve for the inauguration (God willing) the first week of January 1948. By the way, we'll mention that mother and son celebrated Christmas and New Year's Eve dinner euphorically (and with a plethora of victuals, a lot of foolish nonsense). Doña Telma received epistolary best wishes from her faraway daughters: Merry Christmas and . . . tra-la-la . . . It would have been fantastic if they could have come to Parras for the holidays: but, impossible!; but, thanks: that word was written in two telegrams sent to Seattle and to Reno; but (once again), well, they were thinking of her and that should be enough to make the señora cry with happiness.

Exuberant start to the year. A new and dandy life—hopefully! The inauguration was held on January 7. A huge crowd of future deadbeat gamers attended. It's probably better not to think about how much tolerance was needed to allow all those haughty maidens and matrons to attend the event; the women would not play, not then, not ever, because it was frowned upon, but, hey! this was a local social event, full of splendor and general approbation. Therefore, it was packed. And, moving on to a different role for the prurient, it's worth pointing out what you've probably already figured: the primordial rule: there would be no gambling, no, none of that: make-believe at the service of gentle evening recreation. Let's mention the hours of operation: from four in the afternoon till ten at night. Finally, the mayor was responsible for taking the first shot, he missed, but . . . the apology and then the rejoicing. Then the stentorian toast, and onward with sinful fascination!, it's about time; many signed up to play in the midst of the racket; the women left once this got under way. However, ten at night: that's all: remember! The most important part of the whole affair would take place in the following few days. They queued up, along almost half a block, to play. The first to get in wouldn't ever want to vacate their tables. So we have to consider the numerous challengers. He who lost, left: and, back in line . . . outside? Some played and others didn't; or, to be precise, there was always dominoes, though: a queue formed for that, too, a much shorter one, foolish challengers, about which: well, of course! we must point out that most of the clients were there for the billiards: a novelty: ergo: carambole rather than bravado or "La Bamba"; whereby Demetrio soon realized that he should buy three more billiards tables in Monterrey. A weekend shopping trip. He went with his two young assistants. However: what about dominoes, in abeyance, and now we must picture him for real: after the three new tables arrived, the big guy had to get rid of the tables and folding chairs destined for dominoes. As a result: only pool tables!, better!, more prosperity! As far as the rest is concerned, let's note the added attraction of the sale of cold drinks, no alcohol, no, not that.

In the midst of this unparalleled merrymaking at the beginning of the year, Doña Telma carried out her household chores with much more enthusiasm than ever before; she cleaned deeply, things that may have seemed insignificant, like each and every leaf of the potted plants. May all dust disappear completely: how many hours a day did it take her? or, how many orders did she have to give her two servants before they fell in step behind her enthusiasm? Her cleaning perfectionism was consonant with her state of grace.

Because she saw herself as an admonishing spirit who was giving her son a lifesaving solution that would hopefully hold for years, Doña Telma strove daily to bring out the shine in her own environment, matching the abundant drive of her son, who came home every night both exhausted and jubilant, full of ideas so brilliant they seemed preposterous, even if any attempt to carry them out would have to be somehow or other elaborated. More and more flashes of genius pouring into an endless spiraling eddy. Unstoppable progress, therefore, as well as money and enlightenment. The mother's triumph resided in her conviction that Demetrio would live by her side for, hmm, and just when she started thinking about lustrums and decades, a letter landed in her hands, or rather, the lump of a letter: addressee: Demetrio Sordo, and sender: Renata Melgarejo.

Breaking one spell with another, when viewed from a different angle, led to a problematic detour, considering that Demetrio was already on his way and to suddenly stop: a whiff of love—could it be? causing momentary dis-ease, or a favorable concern to which he should give full sway.

After fondling it for nearly three minutes, Doña Telma decided to peruse all that prolix passion. A tentative trespass, however, when it came to opening it. Hesitant or eager or pressingly perverse or tantalizingly slow, and how to proceed without messing things up. Egipto Cavazos, her servant, gave her a useful suggestion, recommending that she use steam to avoid damaging the seal. The need for delicacy in the operation was obvious; so Egipto offered to attend to this detail, and, well, we can imagine his dexterity, not to mention his presumption: *I'll do it very well. Don't worry.* Likewise the subsequent resealing, which also had to be precise—of course!, but also secret . . . In Mexico around the beginning of 1948, there appeared a stamp that said Express Delivery and another that said Ordinary Delivery. The latter, which had existed before, though without the degrading adjective, was what the new stamp wanted to distinguish itself from, though the distinction went unnoticed, for there was none, hence the term "express delivery" was nothing more than a pretense people mostly ignored. In reality there was a difference of less than two or three weeks between one kind of delivery and the other, depending on the distance from the point of origin. In this case Renata used the new service, which was supposed to be faster but wasn't, for the letter had taken almost two months: from Sacramento to Parras! that is—within the same state! We can imagine the journey: once the letter arrived in Saltillo—this is a guess—it was brought to a halt, perhaps a bureaucratic one, in order to give priority to the most urgent. Nevertheless, a delay of almost two months! Why? Imagine if Renata had sent it by ordinary post, how long would it have taken? One month longer at least? Conclusion: mail service was a nightmare. The so-called ordinary assumed neglect, a leaving-for-later, or merely a dead calm, or outright indifference; as for the express delivery, it was the same—wasn't it? or maybe acting very deliberately, or imagining the postal workers watching the (ordinary) letters pile up for days in the semidarkness and feeling quite smug about not rushing around, or worse: viewed as a work of found art, or something of the sort. All we have to do is look (with a magnifying glass) at the date it was sent . . . Ah . . . We said "with a magnifying glass" because Doña Telma used one but understood little. The handwriting was so bad it looked more like irresponsible scribbles, way-too-small and illegible letters that seemed to have been written in haste and with a whole host of inhibitions. The señora, however, was able to follow a certain amount of logic through the capricious combination of several key words, such as "marriage," "love," "loyalty," "forgiveness," "children," "kisses," "lick," "mistake," "come," "Sacramento," "I love," "Renata," "Demetrio," "happiness," and therein potential good fortune.

A plot that abides by defensible sentimental conceits in which the more cramped and illegible the damned scribbles the better intentioned they might be.

Or perhaps it was a stern rebuke, and Renata's forgiveness came with many demands.

Or a definitive break.

In the meantime, the nervous resealing: Egipto in charge of this challenge. Precise, so as not to spoil the stamp. And so it came to pass, and the next step came that night when Doña Telma told Demetrio: *This arrived for you this morning.* The latter opened his eyes wide. His surprise swelled. Just to see the name of the (promising) remitter: aha: this should be read in private. Therefore, he shut himself in his room and tore the edge of the envelope and read excitedly as he turned each page, and just like Doña Telma, he understood very little. Oh, such grief! At moments, no doubt, the big guy wanted to turn to his mother to help him read that Babel of letters penned with rapid strokes, for he knew that to attempt it alone, it would take weeks to decipher what . . . let's see . . . perhaps with a magnifying glass . . . Okay!, the only favor he asked of his mother was that she lend him the tool in question, and obviously she had no choice but to look surprised: good actress: her hypocrisy worked. The thing is, the magnifying glass simply magnified the jungle of lines, but . . . Now it's time to transpose this whole nuisance to a conversation between son and mother in which the former confessed what we already know and she, once again a good actress, proposed trying to read it herself to see if . . . Or that they should read it together . . . An uncomfortable solution, or what other choice did they have . . . Demetrio agreed to the suggestion, of the joint deciphering, and it now behooves us to sum things up, also to mention the fact that not even together could they . . . they struggled, interpreted, even favorably: and: the letter—blast it—: impenetrable: why?

"You should go to Sacramento."

"What about the business . . . ?"

"You don't trust your employees?"

"It's too soon to trust them."

"If you want, I'll get Egipto to take your place. As you know, he has worked for me for many years; I trust him completely. He's never stolen even one penny from me."

"Well, okay, I hadn't thought of that, but . . ."

"Go! Now! Go claim that woman."

A heat-of-the-moment push. Spritely automatism. Blossoming illusion, leading to a hubbub of fits and starts: Egipto, Egipto!, a serious man with a brash mustache. Serious—let's hope!—and (according to Demetrio) an honest skinflint . . . with a future? Faith, trust, and then a trickle of only good things; thereby AGREED, and that was the end of it . . . Doña Luisa's excellent suggestion, as she smilingly caressed her enormous offspring's arm, right along his bicep. And now let's excerpt the most outstanding part of the conversation: knowing full well that the poor handwriting had prevented them from getting to the bottom of the sweetheart's story, his mother ventured to make a crucial suggestion: if Demetrio resolved to go to Sacramento he could kill two birds with one stone: once and for all he could propose marriage to the green-eyed gal and on his way through Monclova he could buy the engagement ring. As abrupt as an avalanche. True, there was the ring size: hmm: he had a model close at hand: Doña Telma's ring finger: such parity, perhaps a bit bigger or a bit smaller, for—naturally!, rarely did a woman have fingers as fat as a man's; so no point in taking measurements, all he had to do was take his mother's wedding ring in a box and purchase one of a similar size. The señora heard as much and immediately took off the ring, then searched among her baubles for a box. She found one right away. Ready! and: *When are you planning to go?:* first things first: instructions for Egipto. Introduce him to the young employees of the pool hall: Liborio and Zacarías. The daily accounts, the liabilities and the assets. Careful with the suppliers! Demetrio would be gone for a week, more or less. In addition to all that, his mother posed a large question: *Would you like me to go with you?*, then added that if Renata accepted his proposal of marriage, she would go to formally ask for her hand, et cetera and et cetera. We repeat: all as abrupt as an avalanche, to which Demetrio agreed with an obedient nod, for his anxiety eased when he let himself be guided. Two days of activity: fine-tuning the arrangements: at the pool hall, mostly, for Egipto Cavazos's eventual leadership carried a certain degree of risk and for the very reason you've already guessed: sleight-of-hand theft, chaos, lack of authority: you choose and decide which. And now let's turn to his mother's concerns as far as the domestic and temporary regency of the young maid, named Gonzala. That the poor dear would receive a bundle—not too thick—of bills for daily expenses. That if she had any problems, Egipto was at hand. As for the rest: throw caution to the wind! Embrace uncertainty, not without first placing oneself in the hands of God and a troupe of saints. Then the accord between mother and son: they wouldn't take the pickup, better to go as usual by train. Hers was an order, not a suggestion. Here too you can choose the reason why we saddled Doña Telma with this one. One reason we'd like to propose is safety. Anyway, we can already picture them seated and in motion. Nobody should be surprised that his mother spoke in torrents as if she were dictating a script to her son, all about what he should say to Renata. Then came the chore of memorization . . . Well, let's state explicitly that Demetrio softened up because it served his purposes.

The purchase of the ring in Monclova, gold-plated to impress the green-eyed gal, one that really shone, even though it looked a bit like a cheap trinket.

Deceit, when all is said and done. A major expense, which Demetrio hastily paid with arrogant pride.

Next came the virgin voyage on the dirt road.

For the first time the mother and son rode the bus from Monclova to Ocampo. Sacramento was the seventh stop out of a total of fourteen towns. A distance of twenty-seven miles.

And . . .

"I'm certain you will marry Renata. I have prayed for this to happen as soon as possible."

Certainty breeds generosity.

33

No, no, innocent displays of impudence just wouldn't do, something like wholeheartedly shouting out his beloved's name from the bench until he saw her emerge quite dignified from her house to meet her beloved, or bringing a fairly showy bouquet of flowers and lifting them up and holding them aloft for a quarter of an hour, or a bit longer. Let's just suppose Demetrio stretched his arms up as high as possible to show off that cumbersome bundle: you can judge for yourself what a sacrifice, what a show of repentance, but the former as well as the latter were ruled out. Better to come up with a single amorous maneuver: the most prudent one: send a messenger boy with a note, something like this written on a piece of paper: *I beg you a thousand times to forgive me for having licked the back of your hand.* Also ruled out. What's the point of humiliating oneself if every humiliation is still an extravagance. Another option would be for him to sit on the bench for hours and hours until Renata came out dressed to the nines. When Doña Zulema made the "hours and hours" suggestion, Doña Telma pointed her index finger at her as if the beginning of the correct answer were about to be divulged; Demetrio, in the meantime, looked surprised. The trio had been speculating about possibilities for how the suitor would present himself, something that would be touching, but above all discreet, no blatant displays, and, well, right when the "hours and hours" idea came up, Doña Telma shot a mischievous glance at her son, then proposed the following:

"It wouldn't be such a bad idea for you to spend the night on the bench, in the event that Renata doesn't come out to see you . . . You shouldn't call to her or write anything, just arrive and settle yourself in. You'll see, your silence will be your triumph . . . What's more, it would be good for you to bring your suitcase as if to say that you plan to stay there until she comes to you, even if it takes one or two days, and nights, or more. Just remember, if you send her a message you'll spoil everything."

Obedience—just like that? without a hint of recomposing. Hrumph, sleeping outside wasn't that bad, although . . . In 1948 in Sacramento there was only one policeman, and he had a pistol but no uniform; a sixty-something señor who wore a cowboy hat instead of the official cap. A fetid cubicle, fifteen by fifteen, located in back of the council house, had been used only twice as a jail cell, when the then-fifty-something señor recruited four volunteer deputies to trammel just one prisoner in said cubicle. We bring up these two incidents because both times the confinement lasted one night and was due to a minor infraction: spending the night on the bench in the plaza. Both were outlanders who couldn't find anywhere better to sleep and had planned to leave at the break of day. A crime, though—which one? This was brought up by Doña Zulema, who went on to say that for ten years nobody had been incarcerated, not even for more weighty infractions. So, Demetrio need not be concerned about sleeping in the spot previously suggested. He might be reprimanded by the policeman (now in his sixties), but that's all. A reprimand without consequence— right? a tenuous prohibition, that's all; moreover, Sacramento was so peaceful that the only dubious deed could be the commotion the bees made when they built their hives, to wit: a stinging attack if some birdbrain dared venture near where they labored.

Such was Doña Zulema's hyperbole, wishing (in addition) to make herself agreeable. Bear in mind the look in her eyes, just like in Doña Telma's, which was to push Demetrio to "not think so much, just do it," because he—oof!—with his yeses and his nos . . . It's just that, how long would he have to stay on the bench? And he wouldn't be able to change his clothes, or bathe . . . Then: would they bring him food?

"I don't think it will take Renata long to show. You'll soon see," Doña Telma said.

And now, yes: obedience—just like that? It was the following day in the afternoon that Demetrio—suitcase in hand—walked toward the trysting bench. There he brought his silent veneration, his sweet resentment, to magnify what would be, in the end, forced humility. In fact, he didn't sit but rather partially reclined, wishing to feel the hardness as if he were lounging in a pretend hammock. He made not the slightest gesture toward Renata's house, or rather the stationery store, where people came and went (not many, not even that), and hopefully the green-eyed gal would soon notice him . . . Others did. The sixty-something policeman did, that sharp observer simply shaking his head back and forth . . . We must add that the policeman continued to shake his head on several occasions and every so often. That is, he paced back and forth through the town center without straying far from his object, for he suspected the stranger had decided to sleep right there where he'd already found repose. True, a reprimand, evidently quite respectful, would not be uncalled for, but he would have to wait until later at night to see if yes or if no. And he insistently remained: with foreseeable consequences. Well, his sweetheart simply didn't show. Stubbornness, dignity. In a roundabout way the policeman had found out about the possible romance, just a bit and nothing more, and anyway the outlander was not wholly unknown to him, but it was the first time the one under consideration had settled down in the spot in question with his suitcase . . . If at least his beloved appeared at that moment—at nine-something at night? Perhaps. And thus the minutes passed and nothing or just the same, and so the man with the cowboy hat turned to said spot to address the problem with a mere warning or the mere threat of jail . . . However, at that very moment the outlander got up and began to walk toward Renata's house. Pursuit and premonition, said in both ways: pursuit from the side—right?, when he heard footfalls? and the other, frontal: Demetrio saw a light on in the house's largest window. Renata and her mother appeared from the waist up: maneuvering? let's wait and see. So he left the suitcase on the bench and, cautiously and slightly bent over, took a few steps forward. The darkness outside was almost formidable whereas on the other side of the window . . . better to put it like this: Demetrio could see the señora writing down on a piece of pink paper what the señorita seemed to be dictating to her. Amendments: lowly propositions: postponements, that's for sure, because the definitive version was yet to be and—of course! as it seemed certain that mother and daughter would remain long at their task, the suitor would be visually entertained, though, well, we'd like to say that he had the good sense to position himself to one side of the window, spreading himself thin against the wall so he'd (almost) not be seen, for as it happened the women suddenly looked over at the bench. Oh: the discretion of their detections: their nervous inertia, let's say they saw very little. Their attention was focused on what Demetrio already interpreted as a missive meant for him, and which would surely be given to him the following day. An optimistic interpretation— naturally!, and . . . no, he wasn't sleepy; so he heard words, even two full sentences about love, forgiveness, or a more relaxed new beginning—hopefully! If he heard what he so strongly desired he would be able to sleep more peacefully, but unfortunately they kept the volume low. What a pity! And right there where Demetrio was standing, uh-oh, the policeman came up to him. A disturbance: which provoked a "shh!" An immediate shifting to one side, over there, please, over there; the ideal place would be under a tree in the plaza, that's what the now peculiar delinquent proposed so they could speak freely. No need to record here his allegation. Nor did it take long at all, because Demetrio took a bill out of his bill-fold, one of high denomination, which when seen by the policeman under what managed to reach them of the street lighting—why yes!, oh boy! the fix, permission to spend the night on the bench, as long as—hold on!—it was only for one night, with the understanding that if he stayed a second one the payoff would be double, and then no jail and, for God's sake—why complicate matters? Inevitable rural corruption, born of necessity. Corrupt policeman. Corrupt Sacramento—right? Now's a good time, therefore, to sum things up: mother and daughter were redacting until past midnight whereas Demetrio was overcome with sleepiness at about ten p.m. Never in his life had he slept on a bench in a plaza, but if we consider that his sacrifice should be exemplary, like a calvary, because of his supreme love . . . Fortitude. Dignity. The proof of a passion like no other . . . The suitor awoke with the first rays of sun. He was hungry, but . . . the lucky wait . . . The pink paper would arrive, and he was not mistaken. After two more hours on that unyielding bench, a messenger boy came to give him the delicate item, folded and sealed in a pink envelope. The flavor in hand. A colorful reading. Marvelous handwriting, and the content: herewith:

Dear Demetrio:

I am sending you this note because you must come to my house accompanied by one of your relatives before I can see you. My mother wants to meet you and find out a lot more about you. Remember, you insulted me when you licked my hand, kissing it first. As you must have realized, I was very offended. So, if you want to continue our courtship we must formalize it. That means, in case you need an explanation, that it must have a clear goal, but for that to happen you must ask me and my mother for

*our forgiveness. The family member who comes with you must
also show remorse. Our relationship has to change, it must be
leading to something that is good for both you and me, as well
as my family and yours. If you don't do what I ask, it would be
better for us not to see each other. What I mean is that there's no
point in continuing our romance on the bench, instead of here
inside the house where my mother can witness everything we do.
This has to happen soon. Think about this carefully, your decision is very important for me.*

    Renata.

The reinforcement of decency. The girl's mother could finally observe from close up the lack of groping. Or, rather, a kiss on the
mouth—never! nor on the cheek. Or, rather, to hurtle into marriage,
ask for her hand, a ring, a wedding date: ascent, or merely the turn
to the horizontal so that Demetrio could get a glimpse at the details
of the script: all fucking must result in children, whence the supremely obvious was derived: having to work like a dog to support
such a large, sacrosanct! pack, because that's the way things were.
Sex with responsibility. Sex with a gush that brings forth fruit, in
the name of a peace that must always remain muffled. Too many
binding fetters, or rather, one had to gauge it in some other way: a
paid prostitute in perpetuity, in order to attain the guaranteed benefit of sex and an almost improbable serenity. As well as the joy
of the children—beautiful? green-eyed? always smiling?, hopefully!
To put everything on the line, believing the witchcraft would be forever beneficial. A sharp turn. Path. Light. An all-embracing formula.
No more lascivious confusion. No more offal. Demetrio stroked
the pink page as if he were caressing with delight the skin of that
beauty in order to absorb it, as if he could glue it onto his spirit.
Annealed eternal love. Adherence and release. The truth was that
Renata was pushing him toward a defining sentiment that would
lead him onto the right path.

The sanctity of sex—abiding? Yes, yes, yes: relief, spaciousness. And now (ahem)—why didn't Renata come out in person to tell him what she had written? Could she have saved herself the long vigil, because—how many versions of that very brief message did she draft with her mother? The handwriting was unbelievable in its perfection, but—what for? for if they'd spoken on the bench they could have abounded in dozens of details. Plans, subtle revisions, and a grope here or there as well, sidelong and almost without meaning to. Bah, but she, as usual, had to play hard to get. She gave herself too many airs—her mother's advice—all to give him to understand that the acme of true love was still far away. More and more scrambling up steep escarpments. The air more and more rarefied but healthful nonetheless . . .

It was advantageous that Doña Telma was in Sacramento. She, as well as his aunt Zulema, would be overjoyed after reading the pink page.

Therefore, a conclusion in pantomime. Not another night spent on the bench, for the proof of his love had been long and monomaniacal, maybe even mature, if that's what we're going for—or what else?

All that followed had a touch of the ridiculous about it. Demetrio had to show the blessed letter to those women who were waiting eagerly to hear tell of his adventure in the plaza; however, before anything else, he said he was very hungry. So first came the rectifying assault on whatever was edible and easily dished up. Bread alone, no beans, no nothing, so: a cold plateful, though filling. No, the big guy shouldn't care about anything other than quickly extricating himself from his stomach's necessities and, chewing four rolls, two *pelonas*, and two *conchas*, poorly and in great haste, all he could say with his mouth full was: *Here's what Renata wrote me. Read it!* The truth was, it was a true delight to pull that all-important sheet out of the pink envelope, unfold it, and: let's see: two bespectacled readers, their heads almost knocking against each other. Doña Zulema was the one who read it out loud in a sarcastic tone. She must have found happiness amusing. All that followed had a touch of haste about it, or rather, of jostling, because all three wanted to talk at once. A jumble of quaint emotings within which the word "marriage" rang out most frequently. It's true the ladies were enticed by other good words, but the glint of the main one did not dim no matter how much garrulity was spewed. Demetrio could only listen to them and feel flustered, because their chatter seemed to be oozing out at a rhythm as swift as it was dissonant, leaving no room at all for a "listen, in my opinion" from him. If it was Demetrio's arduous task to keep track of that senile pandemonium, it would have been even graver for him to impose any measure, even more so when at a certain point Doña Telma asserted that the three of them would go to Renata's house that very afternoon. Clues in the message revealed the need for prompt action, and any delay would complicate further what already promised to be a true torment, because, let's take a look: just how long and how mollifying would be the explanatory episode that would precede the request for her hand. Then the *yes* or the *no* with the *buts*, perhaps absurd, or who knows what surprises Doña Luisa had in store for them. As for the big guy himself, suffice it to say that he wandered about in a daze. He hadn't slept well on that bench, so all this shared rejoicing seemed like a fantasy of cartoon figures who refused to keep still: their sheer drive, their sheer agreement as to who would bathe first and who next in the cedar tub; Demetrio, last, for he was the least important person on this occasion. In fact, his presence wasn't strictly necessary, or he could play the part of the dejected puppet, whereas they, supporting each other to the hilt, would carry the thread of the apologies that would lead to the highly desired result that Renata would marry him: he would then act out the unsurpassed role of presenting the engagement ring to his fiancée. A silent act—understood?—so optimal.

Demetrio sat at some remove from the kitchen table and watched with derision as the ladies made decisions without even consulting him, somnolent as he was: his approval, his disapproval, his glee, his anger. Nothing. Already a puppet. A wimp: affable or resigned? Yes, a rag doll when it suited him, for he would end up with his part to play at the moment of truth, on stage he'd let her rip, the element of surprise: emotive, most definitely. For now, reserve—the inverse! So, let them be: go right ahead, do as you wish! and . . . of course . . . so immersed in their activities, so full of themselves, so—what could he say to them? Go for it, believe what you will!? In the meantime he figured he should bathe as he never had before and dress up as he never had before; a suit and tie—right? A new hairdo: combed all the way back without a part down the middle—why? A ton of pomade—more than ever! What a notion and then . . . Now let's turn to the picturesque: three slow and winsome pedestrians, not indifferent to the eminent gawkers on the street: a bit perplexed or a bit like statues trying to figure out . . . The way to the event: where does it lead? better to follow the trio because soon they will disappear: a pleasant dash into . . . It was a question of falling in behind them: some did. But they came to a halt at a bench in the plaza, we can guess which one. And the conjectures on the side: oh: how many would deduce that the hand of Doña Luisa Tirado's daughter was at stake, she who would get naked and have children after she got married. Such a pity! The radiant flower was departing. A dark vision, but logical, and ulti-mately diaphanous, for soon other appetizing flowers would bloom and then others and others and so on. The natural had drifted too far away to think naturally, as the world turned on its axis without pausing for even a second. And the sequel to the transformations, with their wake of defeats and victories that were not now nor ever would be so definitive. To go and go and know without knowing for certain. For now, the crass picturesque: observed. The trio did not sit down on the usual bench. The big guy appeared to be telling a boy to let them know that . . . And Doña Luisa and her relic emerged from the stationery store. Timid and nonplussed, they approached the bench. We must say, the aroma of perfume permeating the skin and clothes of the trio had already spread into a wide radius around them. They dragged along yards of scent, which now ravaged the mother and daughter, and—phew! or could it be that they, who looked so poorly clad compared to the trio, decided to keep their noses in the air and that's why the flowery aroma became noxious to them. Be that as it may, whether fortitude forged from surprise or plain old woe or something even worse, Doña Luisa exclaimed: *All three of you are welcome, but you will have to wait here because my daughter and I have to make ourselves presentable. Not for more than half an hour, and then it will be our pleasure to welcome you into our home.* They waited almost three hours. The two bathed as serenely as could be, and not before they had first counted up their day's receipts. We must also take into account the slow pace at which they adorned themselves with fripperies and the preparation of a laborious tea. Also their art of table arranging, the placing of their least dinged pewterware. And other such trifles.

＊

34

Action at dawn: the theft. Over the course of that week, Liborio, Zacarías, Egipto, and Gonzala had become the best of chums. Egipto was the one who proposed the robbery. Let's begin with the toughest part: the pool hall personnel, those two wimpy, scatterbrained hicks, we know who they are: and: what about this and what about that, convictions, during the first nightlong conversation when Egipto repeated more than nine times the periphrasis: "It's a golden opportunity," just a question of encouragement. But those in charge of the pool hall were rather reticent, they hesitated, they swore, honor and dignity should always triumph over corruption, also they were Catholics who crossed themselves frequently, hence their sense of guilt never left them any peace, and stealing—horrors! Their policy was to toe the line and seek new horizons morning, noon, and night, always holding their heads up high. Nevertheless, "It's a golden opportunity," persuasion, temptation. During the second conversation Egipto emphasized how fucked their lives were in that harsh, unchanging landscape, with its perpetual component of darkness and unthinkable squalor; he waxed eloquent, that is, on similar subjects. All rotten; images, scenes, simulations, which all came down to how fucked they were, but no, not even then did he convince them. It took till the third conversation for him to be able to touch their souls: the future of their families back at the ranch—how about eternal smiles?, not bad, eh? To leave the worst behind them, like abandoning a filthy nest. Moreover, the robbery would occur at dawn. To wit: do it soon, before Don Demetrio returned. It was a matter of taking all the money from the safe and jamming it lickety-split into a bag, any bag. Then running off and vanishing—come on! It was not easy to push them into sin, he had to talk and talk, in a tone of voice that really softened the edges of the most horrendous ideas. *We won't take the balls or the cues, just the money, okay?* We must say, there was a lot, because the billiards business was growing at an almost demented rate, in just a few days—wow! so many vagrancy-prone customers. *It's a golden opportunity, don't you see?!* Finally Liborio and Zacarías, conscious that they were wavering and seeing the glint in each other's eyes, were persuaded to throw in their lots. They would cross themselves while they burgled. Midnight action. When all was calm, because in Parras there wasn't a lot of surveillance, and what little there was: why would they get out of bed at that hour. So: a stellar robbery. Yes, oath taken: from here on out, almost like a trick. Once those two eagerly agreed to go along with the robbery, Egipto invited them to the house. Celebration. A lavish meal for four, prepared by Gonzala, she who would steal Doña Telma's jewels, a huge quantity in a safe, an artifact that several blows would open. She and Egipto had already talked it over extensively, moreover these two were in love and for both of them the robbery would mean fleeing Parras to live their love somewhere distant and unknown—right? Then they would kiss each other as much as they wanted far away, very far away, perhaps somewhere with good weather. They imagined themselves, therefore, very much in love and bedecked with jewels, maybe even drinking delicious wine in supine satiety. Indistinguishable from the aristocracy, part effort, part merit. A shared dream discussed in frenzied details we'd do better to leave unspoken. During the meal Egipto outlined the scheme while they toasted and wished each other one hell of an awesome life. Nevertheless, a few casual details; to the beat of clanking cutlery and chewing, Egipto explained that everything they took from the pool hall and the house would be divided equally; split five ways because a man with a pickup truck had to be cut in; a man, also a thief, whom Egipto had hired two days earlier, and who was now in on the plot, pretty exciting development, this business of using passwords and the like. When to brake and when to accelerate (not much) the truck: like a shark in the dark, right? The hack couldn't make it, had other things to do . . . Everything was working out, thank God. It's true, few people would be able to resist such a thrifty theft; when the golden opportunity arrives nobody doesn't want to be a thief . . . To (gently) steal in order to gain access to a more praiseworthy life, who wouldn't, especially if no danger is detected. Naturally! anyway nerves get racked, so moving quickly is recommended, to get it over with, or whatever.

All four got along during the meal, which was delicious. Better not to list each thing they ate so as not to make the narrative too bourgeois, but it was all delicious.

Chorizo?

Buttery bits?

A motley mix of meats?

Wines so fine, the four were hanging from the rafters, once they were in their cups?

That's what we found. And we also found that they were pigging out. All the rest we must merely assume: a long dissertation about the meaning of an augural robbery: jewels and money, bigtime; corruption seen as fireworks, a fleeting and luminous spectacle, and its consequences: the lasting embers, those that linger long: life, period, embers, and again, casually, the word "corruption" appeared, so revealing, therefore, crush that word, destroy it, in order to raise it to the loftiest heights: corruption, corrup, corru, co, conquest, insofar as the theft itself would be the same as a silent then smiling flash of lightning. Finally came the good-byes:

many *good nights* many *thank you*s, see you tomorrow; careful! tomorrow at dawn the robbery will take place, so we'll meet at the house at exactly twelve midnight; agreed; say no more; good-bye. We will give only a few details about the sinister implementation: four in the morning; not a sound in the entire town, so the fortune Liborio and Zacarías removed from the safe, bah, just a matter of stuffing that many bills into a large oilskin bag, and magic and speed to load it stealthily onto the truck, then *vroom* to Doña Telma's house; there, the fortune the lady of the house left trustingly in Gonzala's hands was placed in a bag, apace; all the jewelry in another, yes, in the twinkling of an eye, and the escape from Parras, everyone scrambling in. So it came to pass. Worth mentioning that none of the five thieves were from Parras but rather from several different hamlets: past the farthest reaches of the desert, like scattered grains whose names, well, someday we'll name each hamlet, but for now only one: Paila—and that's all! Also worth noting something else: the thieves left the door ajar in the pool hall as well as at the house. Carelessly or with intentional malice so that others could go in and take what was left. The first to notice the doors open the following day closed them, that's right, in both cases they were quite decent. Bam! problem solved. Now all that's left to speculate about is where the pickup loaded with thieves would go; how they would scatter, questions that belong to the mysterious disappearance of all five, who perhaps ended up fighting among themselves in some desolate spot, under a sky of abstruse hues, between chestnut and orange trees; that there were deaths, perhaps; one person who kept it all, the smartest one, of course, let's dub it with "perhaps" and move on to something else.

35

Rehearsal. So much practicing of apologies there on the bench, the ones Doña Telma and Doña Zulema were ready to offer up in distressed tones, as if for a theatrical performance. One corrected the other, and vice versa, though not the big guy, who watched them impatiently but without a single word of reproach; he also kept turning to look at the house, to see if by now, but no. It was as if the delay made the coming solemnity more robust. More and more stammers popped up during rehearsals. Each word seemed to drag; each sentence seemed pressed on like a stamp; the rest was rhythm and delirium, a mopey flow. Three hours later Renata appeared, as if she'd been quite put out, though shining like never before. You had to see her: gorgeous, though a bit submissive. She was gesturing, "Please, please, come in," and the tense but enthusiastic trio advanced toward the site of the apologies: they didn't go through the stationery store (strange) but rather down an ambiguous hallway. The scent of eucalyptus grew stronger inside the house: why? there was no potted plant; then, following Renata's lead, they reached an (almost) totally yellow room; "Have a seat." The lady of the house would be coming soon, this said with great feeling. Her predicament, the airs she gave herself, which spread and which those still practicing their apologies in Renata's presence and in the other's absence could interpret, under their breath, naturally! and the lass heard them, and was puzzled, until, half

an hour later—playing the role of a supposedly portentous diva—
Doña Luisa finally appeared. Well, well. Sidelong ironic glances.
The jitters, in other words. A generic tension swirled, had to, because whose job would it be to break the ice. The lady of the house
with her hint of hostility—or what? One formidable cranky one and
a wee repentant trio, this the framework, but it was Doña Zulema
who began to hone in on what we can take to be a categorical exon-
eration as she modulated each idea so thoroughly that her elaborate
apology seemed to be but a small piece of a much larger anecdote.
The issue of the kiss planted on the back of the hand. The lick of the
damsel's skin as an expression of profound love, that sublime surrender transferred to the tip of the tongue, you must understand
the intent, a deeply felt decency that had spilled over into the saliva of that kiss. Doña Zulema had to explain several times that
her nephew was a man with the very best of intentions. A believer
in everlasting love and more and more such salvos, so many that
who knows how, but she began to courageously sweeten the subject and thus slowly departed from her script. Her speech became
a treacle tornado. His aunt was dazzling, prodigious, garrulous,
until Doña Telma, with studied scruples, tugged on her dress from
behind. A warning: somewhat doubtful, silent, to return to what
was rehearsed, and the mother, erupting: *We are very sorry about
what has happened. My son is the model of paramount decency.*
Theater. The speech practiced (of course) on the bench: back to
what was agreed upon. So that the penny would drop for the aunt,
and it did because suddenly she hadn't another word to say. Then
came a vacuum, in which nobody even clicked her tongue. In any
case, they glanced at one another guiltily, as if wanting to hide. The
room seemed to have gotten even yellower than it had been, more
infectious, sicklier, uglier.

For a while the apologies continued to proliferate, so much so
that the main point got murky; stagnation formed a kind of lagoon.
In fact, Doña Telma and Doña Zulema finally began to recite their

rehearsed speeches, in turns, with such precision that it could (truly) barely be believed; they were outstanding, agile, though without the slightest emotional charge, without pleasantries, and that's why Doña Luisa stopped them short: *I accept your apologies, but it should never happen again . . . Now, the one who should apologize is Demetrio, don't you think? It's up to him.* They threw the big guy a curveball; he was staring at the skilled craftsmanship of the floor tiles and after hearing himself alluded to, said, *Me?*, and then, *Oh, yes!*, whereat: *I offer the biggest and most complete apology. My intention, when I kissed Renata's hand, was sincerely affectionate, a tender kiss full of integrity. If I licked her skin it was because I thought of it as an act of devotion. At no moment did it occur to me that I was disrespecting her. So, I repeat my apology.* Doña Luisa smiled (smugly) and Renata did too, following her lead. This is where everything should pause. Then, like an undertow, the lady's apology, with resounding composure: *I also ask you to forgive me, Demetrio, for what I said to you. I was desperate.* Congratulations.

Nevertheless, the thorniest part remained: the brave act of . . . Well, aunt and mother turned their vulturelike scowls upon Demetrio; so did Renata; not to mention Doña Luisa. They were waiting for him to come out with what all this had been aiming at: asking for her hand with cloying ardor, all he had to do was utter one well-sequestered sentence to that effect, and they would buoy up the request, elaborating point by point what it would mean for Renata to live by Demetrio's side: the understanding, the affection, the peace, the secure economic foundation; but, well, feeling the pressure from the eyes upon him, the agronomist spoke like a good-natured person with common sense: *The purpose of our visit is (ahem) to request Renata's hand. I want her to be my wife before God and the law.* And the cornered fool pulled out the box that contained the engagement ring; he didn't open it, or rather: he walked around with it. Just imagine the gamboling up and down—how awful! Nonetheless, Doña Luisa, quite severe, threw a dart:

"What do you have to offer my daughter?"

"I have a lot of money. I have a very prosperous business in Parras. Moreover, I love her with all my heart. She will find that I am a man who is willing to make great sacrifices to guarantee her happiness and comfort. For me Renata is a goddess that deserves constant veneration. I'll give her everything she needs!"

The previous truth-telling paragraph paved the way for his aunt and mother to enhance the petition by assigning Demetrio attributes: a good man (and rising!): a very hard worker and unflagging and with a respectability proven by a thousand small things, and good natured, with a smile perpetually hovering over his lips, prudent, and, to top it off, endowed with a spirit of progress and more progress. Or, in other words: the best of the best, no holds barred. And hence their exordium continued until dilution threatened, because Doña Luisa lifted her finger, she wanted to speak, they didn't let her, such was the onrush of wonders, and, at a certain moment, raising her voice excessively, Renata's mother uttered this:

"Okay, my daughter can be Demetrio's wife after one year has passed. I give my word."

"What?"

"Just as you heard. Wait one year. My reason is that I still need Renata's help getting the stationery store off the ground. Around this time next year we will plan the wedding here in Sacramento."

A long time.

A long time to perfectly preserve an illusion. Twelve months of an enlarged enigma, a superconceit, unbreakable, let's say, that would nurture the steeliest desire. In any case there was a perfect fit: the ring, the offering; Renata, slipping it on; slipping onto her ring finger—yay! perfect. The symbolic yoking that was neither applauded nor commented upon. The trio still insisted that the wait be shortened, but Doña Luisa shook her head, girlishly, and held her ground with a little tantrum, stamping her feet in several ways. No matter: they'd won: the gratification of knowing and feeling that Renata was already Demetrio's wife, kind of, realizing that from then on there would be a new member of the family, a long-lasting (fresh, fine-looking) flower who already seemed delighted to consider herself a wife from then on. For his part, Demetrio wanted to celebrate by giving her a hug, a decent embrace, not too juicy, but—get a grip! if they did that they would lose so much, such humiliation, so: a show of fortitude, as if they were corroding each other, theoretically; desire so corroded it was on the verge of no longer existing, so: celebrate: never! The trio was leaving, not another word to say: the good-byes, hasty, all for the best: that's all, so little. But Renata (boldly) told her future husband: *Today I'll expect you at five in the afternoon, not on the bench but here in the house. Knock on the door, that one there,* an index finger indicating which, the clear sign: knock on the door they leave by. And the trio left, trying to find a spring in their steps, but no luck. It's just that a whole year of emotional propriety, what was already purified to purify it even more, candor and gabbing, Demetrio also understood that the billiards business would shine with success—hopefully! by that date, twelve months later, so much security, and in the meantime it wouldn't be long for truly domestic love and to sit down confidently in a very randy (and deplorable) way in the living room armchair. Renata had given him instructions: an exciting come-hither, that's how Demetrio probably embellished the invitation his wife had extended. He would return obediently, perhaps a kiss inside the house, one on the cheek, now, yes, but with no licking. Well, let's turn to the trajectory where silence won out over mutterings, although Demetrio heard one sentence, very loud and it doesn't matter who said it: *No way! Now you're trapped.* He, trapped? Renata was trapped, just like him: an image of a large jail cell, subject to growth or shrinkage . . .

Better for us to accompany into eccentric seclusion the big

guy, who when observed carefully appeared to be feverish, for at
the end of the day he was able to avoid the two-woman-strong dog
pack that was surely spewing endless advice. Therefore, when he
arrived, violence, door slamming . . . A room for him alone; yes: his
wish, to think to his heart's content, for a while.

So—trapped?

Let's not even think about their reaction, and they didn't dare
knock on the door . . . well, there was all that merry to-do about
the wedding . . .

But—trapped?

Demetrio's ideas spun in an orbit, recalling all his girlfriends as
if he were watching a parade of miniatures; miniature-girls; each
one, without exception, he'd done nothing more than kiss on the
mouth; charm in sepia tones, perhaps, nothing worth harvesting
from the past; lost loves that never involved nudity, and upon uttering that word he remembered Mireya, an unbridled fever of carnal lust; soaring sex, so rarefied, just to imagine it; everything seen
through the eye of a heron who could barely shake its wings. The
woman who possibly bore his child and was wantonly lost on night
x; the same woman who once in a while appeared in his dreams
laughing at him, calling him "poor imbecile," what you missed
out on, love like this and like that: sex as well as understanding
and infinite tenderness: what more do you want, you jerk. And if
Demetrio had allowed himself to be trapped by Mireya? Let's see—
what did being trapped or feeling trapped consist of? The truth is
that Mireya went from being a total whore to an awesome saint.
Struggling saint. Mothering saint. Sexual saint, embossed upon
the always-changing great beyond. Oh, most holy Mireya, gone
who-knows-where.

Then he imagined the whore rocking her baby sadly, an unlikely cooing, because in unreality it lasted an entire night. A whole
night of quite sensitive crying; the cries of a forsaken single mother
seen in almost floating limbo; rocking, faithfully rocking, a baby

who would probably view things in a dark light when he grew up; who would always have to put up with the vexing stigma of being the son of a single mother—ooh! she, such a whore to the core and such a saint to the discerning judge. She, who but for a magical mistake would have been his wife, but a church wedding—impossible! that was the problem. On the other hand, the green-eyed gal—what a difference! She was a different kind of whore, an emblematic one because legal. And he imagined everything he would do with her once they got married. He saw her upside down performing a difficult fellatio. He saw her doing a somersault in the air and landing precisely on top of him for penetration, no pain as the cowl slid over his erect member. He saw her in a swoon of pleasure, in the middle of an orgasm, her eyes upturned and her plaintive voice pleading for more. He saw her coiled then grow unfurling, that is, her ass and breasts got bigger, large, huge—man oh man! her mouth also swelling, the better to kiss with. Nevertheless, reality, in the end, was third-rate, so abruptly reductive. When Demetrio arrived punctually for his date, Renata immediately ushered him into the yellow room. They were alone, nobody was watching them. Her mother was busy in the stationery store. Moreover, they were already spouses . . . though only theoretically—right? and, naturally! Demetrio tried to give her a polite kiss. They wrestled. Just one on her pursed lips, or rather a responsible adult kiss, let's say, on the cheek, but Renata threatened to scream, loudly. Hence an alarm and thus he spurted out:

"Why won't you let me? You're already my wife."

"I will be when we stand before the altar in a year's time."

"I love you, Renata. Let me at least hug you."

"No, not even that. Things have to be done properly."

"But nobody's watching us. Come on!"

"Remember, I was well brought up, and it makes no difference whether anybody is watching us . . . God is."

"Do you promise you'll kiss me a lot once we get married?"

"Then, yes, but not before . . . I want it all to be beautiful."

"So, you promise me we'll even do dirty things when we get married?"

"We'll do whatever you want, but you'll have to go along with me till then. Don't ruin what we are trying to build."

As for the rest of it: sacred hand-holding and finally staring into each other's eyes for the first time, or rather: rupture, daring: the brown nourishing itself on the green, and vice versa. O furtive proof.

The process of discovery, that's what was on offer: eyes exploring eyes. To look at what's wild in the eyes, almost the world's toy, the color, that which opens onto and exposes the firmly rooted sunken length of a suggestion. Certainly silence abetted concentration and thus they enjoyed each other. Other details as well: the shape of the eyebrows and the distance from there to the eyes; then the shadows under the eyes, the cheekbones, all delicate trifles and, above all, good smells. There they remained for a long while studying each other's features. Neither of them had ever experienced that. A different kind of pleasure, more detailed. Example: the lashes—phew! They viewed each other's mouths more lasciviously. In fact, Renata was wearing lipstick, enhanced vermilion, kissable—no! but judging from the fleshy fullness of her lips she seemed ill at ease unless she was constantly kissing. A real mistake and a fantasy assessment. As opposed to Demetrio's mouth: thin lips, for whistling, not at all sensual, but longing to be so. A deterrent. The closest and most appetizing in reality was forbidden material. Sin was on the prowl and better to create some distance, if only because Doña Luisa, always shrewd and bitter, might appear at any moment, we can see her, even just her head popping in, first, in warning, then her whole body and saying:

"So, children, are you behaving yourselves?"

Tiresome, this decoy, why wonder. Distrust or excessive propriety. Also Doña Luisa told them that it was time to wrap it up, they could see each other again the following day at the same time: visits by minutes, we could call it. Meet in the living room, ergo: propriety: a small love, apparently, though grandiose if interpreted appropriately. So Demetrio left mostly contented because he had finally looked long and hard at Renata's face—what a beauty, truly!

When he got back to Doña Zulema's house he wanted only to shut himself up in his room. He didn't care to give even the most meager account of his date with Renata. Mother and aunt, in fact, asked, but he wagged his finger no, as if wanting to reject all their questions in a single sweep, about six stupid ones, or erase them one by one. He preferred to sink into his solitude, certainly quite cramped, rather than listen to banalities, even if all were instructive. When he did leave his room, because hunger was pressing his stomach against his spine, he preferred to go grab a bite at a tavern, and if we are obliged to expand upon this subject, there were three taverns and all three were on the verge of closing for lack of customers, just one or two throughout the whole day, not enough at all. So the food was poorly prepared at all three, à la don't-give-a-damn, or rather pretty or a lot greasy: creaky, crackling, thundering, or who knows what, and definitely—what a racket in the kitchen! when he ordered enchiladas or fried tacos topped with lettuce. But Demetrio, we repeat, preferred that griminess to homespun clean that translated into intolerable pestering. Between one torture and the other, he chose the tavern.

Now let's discuss in greater depth the four days Demetrio remained in Sacramento living out, as we know, his tiny but constant love with his future and sensational wife; he didn't eat even a crumb of breakfast, no lunchtime stew or supper at Aunt Zulema's house because, to tell the truth, he didn't want to talk to the ladies. Though he did mix and match the taverns: that one for breakfast, another for lunch, and, well, like that, then he switched it around: that one's better for supper and that one for breakfast, so he varied it: or rather his whimsy was an eeny, meeny, miney, mo, but what we can affirm is that none of the three taverns was any good, and also that's why one day soon they would have to shut their doors.

We understand that Demetrio spent the remainder of his time sitting (like a big shot) on a bench, mulling over his life, a way to kill what's killable by remembering it. True, he could do that shut up in his room, but out in the open air: advantages, the changing colors of the day, the tiny transformations—how many? That's when he looked at his wristwatch: five more hours until his date with Renata . . . Only three more . . . Now only two . . . Then to bathe in the cedar tub. The mother and aunt took advantage of those interludes to interrogate him, but his refusal, as we know, the dancing hands, oscillating. To never speak, not even when he was wrapping a towel around himself, not even when he was decked out as an impeccable dandy, not even when he was perfumed. In short, he wanted everything he discussed with Renata to remain secret—but what about us—what did they talk about in the yellow living room? About children, the ones God gives us; about how life would be in Parras, which was like an oasis, with such good weather; how they'd go on excursions in the outlying areas, in the pickup, what else, for he had bought a very good one, and they even talked about politics, that all politicians were a bunch of thieves, without exception; those public servants, were they helpful, once in a while, but, be careful! you should never trust them. They also touched on several trivial subjects, like fashion, like India ink, in 1948, its multiple uses, the latest craze in Sacramento, and still growing; what's more, they spoke about local customs, how people act in one place versus another. Renata also asserted that she was a woman of action—really? but Demetrio, one day, couldn't resist saying something like this to her:

"I don't know if I should bring this up, but I've dreamed about you naked many times."

"Me too."

"What?"

"In many positions, as if you were posing for photographs."

"What did you feel?"

"Look, the truth is I don't want to talk about it. It will just confuse me. Once we get married and receive God's blessing, then we can talk about all kinds of things related to being naked."

The truth is, they talked about the wedding, how Demetrio would send her money for the wedding dress; how she would arrange for the bridesmaid and groomsman pairs, *de lazo*, *de ramo*, and *de arras*; how he would come back in April to fasten everything that needed to be fastened, to wit: fastidious formalities; but it wouldn't be a very ostentatious wedding—would it? what for? And then came what they both dreaded: time to say good-bye. A cold good-bye indoors, in the living room. An eloquent pressing of hands, and nothing more, how awful. To also say good-bye to Doña Luisa. How polite! Everything to smooth the way, step by step. Now we'll reveal a question Renata asked her mother on one of those days.

"Hey, Mama, why did you put our wedding off for a year?"

And the inelegant response:

"Because I want Demetrio to suffer. My goal is for him to love you even more, and to understand that a woman like you is worth a hundred of any other. Let the scoundrel pay."

36

The first (long, celebratory) kiss after the wedding would hopefully be on Renata's marvelous lips, those two little round sausages, ah. Then let's imagine all the prohibitions, every detail spelled out on the train: frenetically: in blurts. We could say that it was a question of verbal regression, clamorous, on Demetrio's part, which gave too much importance to the embrace that the green-eyed gal definitely refused to give him. He had nothing to lose—or did he? Finally Demetrio came out with something he thought Doña Telma would like to hear. *I didn't talk to you because I didn't want to hear from Doña Zulema at all. I don't want any advice from you, either. If that's what you're going to give me, not even one little bit, so I'd rather keep quiet.* Whereby we see the mother listening, until she got fed up. The big guy was fed up, too. The list of restrictions was too long and irksome, but to give her opinion on anything—humph! not on her life! Rather, she stifled herself, the good lady didn't utter so much as an ahem, and thus they traveled for hours, lulled by the train's seeing and sawing. Until Demetrio himself, in contradiction to his fed-uppedness, asked his mother for her opinion, one, the first, because he was very frustrated, he had been going down a path full of confusion that had led him to offer her the ring. A bond forged in darkness—right? There was no retreat, because then—what manner of man would that make him! *You're trapped, all that's left for you now is to feel fresh when you reach the peak of love. That's what you've been struggling so hard for.* And so, what was wrong with a kiss?, one on the cheek?, a small, decent kiss?, a hug, too. *Renata will give you everything you want, just wait. The wedding will be soon.* The wedding, the culmination of a process, the vertical path, always exhausting. Now would come the ruddiness of pleasure that would never fade. In the meantime that inflated hope that helped him know how to live out the illusion. It was worth waiting for what would come, for the fulfillment bit by bit of the best of the best. Doña Telma was more prodigious than necessary; Demetrio found no way to silence her. An opinion transformed into a speech, but also a litany of ideas that were worth listening to. Philosophy of the lowlands made to sound highfalutin. Even once they'd arrived in Parras and boarded the horse-drawn carriage that would take them home, Doña Telma continued speaking with inspiration. Overflowing eloquence—to be believed?

37

This begins where Doña Telma's speech ended. It ended when she discovered that Egipto and Gonzala were missing. A quandary, a surprise. They'd escaped, it seems, with the money, which wasn't much. Even so, desperate screams ensued, louder and louder, there must have been vibrations everywhere, up and down the walls, and now for the part you are not going to believe: Doña Telma looked under the beds. The servants fled with all the money and of course they pinched some other things as well. The lady went to the safe, which was, as she intuited, open: her jewels!, gone! Macabre emptiness, because the thieves had also taken several very beloved gold coins, as well as some valuable presses, metal scraps, and tools. Hence, the lady's cries burst forth; she cried out with good reason, in the end, all that tremendous moaning heard by Demetrio, who came to embrace her and showed great compassion. *My jewels, those two took everything I most loved.* Then she said that she had already suspected they were secret lovers, and the worst part was she had nowhere to turn. Egipto was from a hamlet in some godforsaken place, and Gonzala was from another, far away. A problem to go to each hamlet, even getting there would be no cakewalk, moreover their relatives would protect their loved ones and who knows anyway if they would even know about the robbery; no, perhaps they hadn't even gone back there. In the end, a perfect crime, irrevocable. All lost—and now what? Good thing the inheritance had been deposited at the local savings bank. Then the larger conjecture: Egipto as well as Gonzala had worked in her house for more than twenty years. They never stole a cent—why now? Because of the love they had sworn to each other?

The opportunity to do it right.

More than enough money.

They could even buy a house somewhere.

But the barbarity of this act still had a much wider reach. A major robbery, in the end. Doña Telma suggested that her son go to the pool hall to . . . Already Demetrio was thinking that Liborio and Zacarías were likewise two filthy thieves, or if not they would be able to give him some information about what had happened at the house. A modification, an increase in horror, because at the pool hall certain balls and cues and (to top that off) some chalk were missing. He went to check the cash register. No, or rather, empty, not a single bill or coin. More thieves, as we see, but let's see if they had anything to do with Gonzala and Egipto? Theft here and there? Really? All on the same day—right? So maybe two separate crimes, or maybe the four had made some kind of pact— but how? There might have been a meeting, a supper, perhaps? Demetrio was already piecing together an approximation in the air: layers of mud (on top of each other), the cash all gone, and another thing, they must have done it at night. But the big guy didn't waste more time making further conjectures but rather went out to the street and shouted at full throttle: *I've been robbed! I've been robbed! They robbed my pool hall!* He ran about wildly, indeed he did, going around in circles as if he were playing a game. He stood there screaming in the middle of the street, then suddenly turned south, toward his house, but not. Many passersby were watching the scene and they were moved and they approached to touch the body of the shouter to tell him to "Calm down!" and other things of that sort, but Demetrio kept on in the same vein: shouting wildly, as if he were taunting fate by spewing barbaric

things such as: *I'm going to hang those thieves! Their names are
Liborio and Zacarías!* No matter how much they tried to console
him, nobody managed to calm him down, and he continued spitting out incoherent babble. With their combined forces, however,
they did carry the giant, but only for half a minute, after which
Demetrio violently bolted. They wanted to take him home, which
was only—how many blocks away? But he told them to let him go
because he would walk on his own two feet and just fine, thank
you. The thing is, once he was put down (roughly) on the ground,
Demetrio stopped shouting. On the contrary, he showed a curious
kind of dignity as he walked away. A respectable upright man, casually straightening out his shirt and pants. It was a good thing that
he had become quite sober, as was appropriate, and he stayed that
way until he reached the house. A few followed him, just because.
Imagine, then, the embrace between mother and son. The defeated
duo, alone. Or, rather, inside the house and with the door closed.
Or, rather, they cried a lot. Yes, there was a big because.

The coincidental robberies. The unimaginable. Too much trust
given to those who didn't deserve it. And Demetrio lodged the most
serious complaint:

"I always have to start from scratch, always, always, always. I
want to come out ahead for a change."

"It's not the end of the world. We won't be starting from scratch.
Fortunately, I still have money saved. Though I never thought such
a thing could befall us."

They kept talking sorrowfully, standing up, without losing
their balance, and embracing each other, though soon they loosened their grip. There in the middle of the courtyard their desolation pointed in a certain direction. Then the pair began making
futile speculations. Here's one example: why were others able to
lift themselves up with no problem, while they, no matter how hard
they struggled, just couldn't. *God doesn't love us*, she declared,
then immediately added nuance to her affirmation, beginning with

the following banality: *Or, He loves us with tough love.* After elaborating on the advantage of being close to God, his mother proposed they go to church to pray for more than two hours. Demetrio, without hesitating, agreed and rejoiced, for it was of utmost importance to thank the Almighty that they hadn't been completely scalped; for the robbery, in both cases, had been somewhat prudent. It was not a catastrophe, it just was, and—what might have happened if they'd stayed in Sacramento for two more days? or a week? eh? For now, let's watch mother and son walking with their heads down, leaning on each other with good balance and clutched hands. Many passersby saw that saddened pair take one step after another. But what they mostly noted was their entrance into the temple. Their rustic humility that would be rewarded in the great beyond. Anyway, finally they kneeled and then began a kind of harsh penitence, parabolic, parodies of Our Fathers and Ave Marias: whatever they knew partially, thus: a gallimaufry of somewhat dim-witted prayers, and wedged in there were mother and son requesting that nothing dark happen in their lives again. In the end, their prayers were spicy enough to burn their tongues. There was generosity and even pain, for they remained kneeling for three hours, and their knees . . . ayayay . . . Then they left, almost stumbling over themselves. The walk back was more difficult. Mother and son were thinking—in between the *ay*s—about everything they had to do. Renew their trust in people, but—to whom, what nature of folks, would they give it? The truth is, things were complicated, really, supercomplicated.

Part Five

Each and Every Matter and Manner

38

Oh my, the queue. We wish to emphasize the number of people looking for a job. More than twenty-five were counted. All men, and Demetrio requested solid references from each: a letter—signed? the name of the reference, and, if he lived in Parras (rather than some nearby locale), precisely where. Sometimes he was swayed by summary impressions; an agreeable smiling face, a placid voice, mild manners, and other such niceties. When someone struck a chord, he was asked to return that afternoon. More revealing exchanges ensued, a deeper digging into the details. That is, to be more precise: in the morning there was a queue and in the afternoon there wasn't. Three days were sufficient to find someone who might fit the bill. He liked three people, so he focused on them. Next step: inquiries: find out where the reference lived? Go there. Take the trouble. Talk to him, and in each case this was done. A scrupulous mechanism for the selection of the most virtuous. He would have liked Renata to be with him, an already official wife with a good eye, that is: a vast switch of dimensions; women, their premonitions, the notion that they are never wrong. He conducted his investigations laboriously, but the two young men he picked, in the end, seemed to have been sent to him by Providence. Consider Demetrio's lucky star, perhaps for a time hidden behind clouds, or consider the hopeful prayers in the church, the penitence so well enacted, or, also, let's remember that it was high time things began to go well for him, in any case these two young men: as the days went by, Ángel and Aníbal, overflowed with industriousness. In fact, they were willing to work more than twelve hours a day, even on Saturdays and holidays, for a quite paltry salary. What joy!

As for Doña Telma, she made less of an effort selecting her servants. Naturally she made sure they were not young, preferring grown women doggedly devoted to the drudgery of domestic duties: washing, sweeping, mopping, cooking, each chore performed to the utmost and with serious intent. No, there was no queue, but there was a high frequency of knocks on the door in response to the more or less arresting announcement the dear lady hung in one of the windows facing the street. A high frequency of questions lasting about four hours on one day, a sufficient span of time to say this one and this one. Modesty was the telling sign, servants should not know how to either speak well or string together a long (elaborate) sentence, far less two, the worst would be if they could connect two ideas. Horrors. Intelligent—what for? Obedient: yes!, like absolutely noble burros. Results in a trice. Without gratuitous strife. It was never okay to argue, or more specifically: when an applicant argued even a little she thereby disqualified herself. Hence we can say that Doña Telma spent little more than two hours choosing two servants (stout middle-aged women, single—how fortunate!), who would be her daily companions and we say this because she had a room for them with two beds. Extraordinary accommodations. Doña Telma, nowise prudent, did not ask for detailed references regarding who, in fact, Amalia and María Fulgencia were, she took her impression from their looks. No, she did not investigate. She did not go to talk to their references, who did exist and lived nearby, a question of walking ten blocks, maybe a bit more. No, nothing but trust, understood pejoratively. Better, therefore, to put her trust in God and Saint Jude Thaddaeus to ensure that her intuition functioned to a tee, whereby: the proof: their behavior when at work. No order she gave brought a scowl to their faces. On the contrary, they obeyed happily and, well, that's enough about that.

Things were also going well for Demetrio. Once again the overly idle flocked to the pool hall. A prodigious business. A money mill: think of it as an unstoppable force: truly. The employees Ángel and Aníbal seemed never to flag in their hard work, and they always wore a broad smile. Nevertheless, a week after reopening the business for local recreation, the big guy realized that he had to make a trip to Monterrey to buy more cue balls, more quality cues, more fine chalk.

So, off we go! And the big guy left with his two model employees. By truck: an exhausting trip. They would not spend the night in the Sultan of the North, as Monterrey was called. Seven hours there, along a dirt road, and seven hours back, along the same one: a more or less jumpy ride. Their watchword was to buy and to come back. No recreation or even reasonable leg stretching. Such admirable criteria.

And they managed it all almost in one breath, in a manner of speaking, but yes, indeed.

Before the trip to Monterrey there was a banking issue: the mother withdrew money and warned her son as follows: *I have very little money left from the inheritance. We must make no mistakes in our investments. The pool hall must do well.* We shall deem everything that came before a series of false steps. Now the appropriate precision, for there was no longer any choice. A vantage point from which to glimpse uninhibited growth. This is what mother and son talked about during their dinner for two: *Every peso you spend is critical.* Whence arose, in a sudden burst, the huge cost of everything wedding related: yes, yes, naturally, there must be a feast, but only for a few guests, but . . . ; as to the bridal gown, no pompous exhibitionism, no bloated presumption, but not a shoddy garment, either, something middling, but . . . ; as to the honeymoon: travel, hotels, meals in restaurants, oh, nevertheless, Demetrio thought they should choose one spot and there have their movie moments. A hotel, with a pool. Hopefully! He thought of Piedras Negras, the border town, who knows why. Not Sabinas, nor Monclova nor Saltillo nor Torreón, not Monterrey either or anywhere else. So Piedras Negras—why? Perhaps because it was a place nobody talked about . . . anyway, we'll see . . . More and more discussion, never without Doña Telma's insidious and recalcitrant warnings: *Watch every peso you spend. This is our last chance.* But strutting—even embellishing—his stuff, Demetrio rose from his chair and cited the dependability of his lucky star (and the blahblahblah started—oh mercy me!), insisting that anything he did was bound to turn out hunky-dory. All the more so because they had prayed for hours in the church, on their knees—right? remember how much pain there was during the prayers, and still they remained. So we can now move on to what happened in the following weeks. December came and, Congratulations! Christmas and New Year's celebrations, quite delightful; January came and, Congratulations! February came and, a few ups and downs, but generally good, very good! We now find ourselves in March 1949, in full marvelous ascension. As far as the house goes, hmm, Amalia and María Fulgencia were exceptional; the same goes for Ángel and Aníbal in the pool hall. What splendid hires!

Let's talk against the grain about Demetrio's great confidence: mental adjudication: all white, maybe pink, but no other color loomed in his future, for sure: what he'd found, what he'd contributed, all could now finally be seen as rhizomic. No putrescence, therefore, need be descried—ever! And one day with perfect composure the big guy told his employees that he had to leave Parras: a four-day trip, five, six, maybe less. They would be responsible for the business, that is, everything ship-shape, same as they were doing every day, so much so that he sometimes didn't even stop by. Which explained why he asked for details the following day, so he could deduce a precise picture of his assets. An uphill ride, as usual more difficult than downhill. But we were talking about his trip to Sacramento. In any case, Demetrio went to church without telling anybody. He prayed, just in case. The penitence was wretched, almost artful: on his knees, on the ground, and crawling toward the altar (such a show), his arms spread in the shape of a cross. The forced entreaty: what began with pain would have to end the same. The sacrifice was exemplary, though looking at it up close probably not necessary. It's just that Demetrio wanted to avoid another robbery: *No more robberies, My Lord, have mercy . . . Please listen to what I am saying, I am begging you fervently.* A farce? Almost to a tee. How sincere could he be when at one point in the middle of a prayer Demetrio let slip an unintentional chuckle? Who knows what came into his head . . .

Anyway April arrived and with it the trip to Sacramento: of great importance. The scale of what he was about to carry out. First he asked Doña Telma for her blessing, and his mother, proud and empowered, hmm, crossed herself with aplomb, yes, well, you should have seen her, this fact alone made her feel grandiose, because she would remain in Parras more regal than ever. Did she also have a lucky star? While we're at it, we all have one, it's just that we don't all think about it. Rather we think of God's will, which is something else, or the saints'. But what we'd like to make clear here is that thinking about our lucky star, every day, would be a horse of a different color, as they say. One—yes or no?—of an alarming unheard-of size, perhaps the commanding size of an archangel.

39

We needn't stretch our imaginations too far to take as given that Doña Zulema welcomed her nephew with open arms. We can also imagine the exultant cuddles. This business about her being the second mother comes up immediately; to put it in strong terms, she came right out with it; which made him—the apocryphal son? Confusion, and the more they clung to each other the greater the confusion, an almost libertine reflection; hindered love: fluctuating between which norms; more confusion, and therefore, even stranger. Oh, the twists and turns of affection, though the passion was directed elsewhere, as we know: Renata, still at the beginning. So Demetrio abruptly pulled away. From that moment on he never again wanted to catch even a whiff of the old woman's odor—how disgusting!, and he expressed himself with such honeyed delicacy that even he surprised himself at having said what he said, which is better omitted because it is too sweet. We can well imagine the grandiloquent excuse, full of whatever it was full of. Then, while expressing gratitude for such withered hospitality, the nephew asked if he could take a bath in the cedar tub; he also asked his aunt not to say a word about Renata, for she knew that the affairs of the heart were coming to a head. For Doña Zulema, however, keeping quiet was rather esoteric, though she wisely abided, how understanding of her; how wounded, if only because she couldn't speak . . . Anyway, she was left with the urge to utter a neologism, though not even that . . . Demetrio spent a long time outside in the tub. Let's assume the nephew arrived in Sacramento around two in the afternoon then subtract the minutes of the embrace (cuddle), a first press as of an inaugurating nectar—or what can we call something that blooms? Then the bath that lasted about two and a half hours. A lot of, let us say, lazy soaking. But let's expand upon the priors. Surely the sweat must have mingled. There was also subtle impregnation; now, dropping in, let's try to watch his naked egress, let's say, an instant seen by the aunt, a second of sight before the bashful nephew covered with the towel what shouldn't be seen. All told, distant affection, impossible, but let us forget the forgettable and go once and for all to the model figure Demetrio cut a bit later. Model-husband; model-lover; the model who took a string of pearls out of his suitcase: the perfect gift for Renata. Then Aunt Zulema made a definitive, but appropriate, comment: *On no account are you going to give those to your future wife. The superstition is that for each pearl there will be a tear. It is an ugly prediction. Please, throw that away, anywhere. It brings very bad luck.* Superstition? Belief? One must never challenge the devil's wisdom. The most dangerous thing one can do. In fact, Demetrio went and threw the necklace out on the street, and whoever, poor thing! picked it up would go belly-up. The prudent thing was to go to Renata's house bearing no gift. So let's watch the big guy arrive quite carefree at the stationery store, where—thank God—there was a swarm of customers. The fiancé had to wait until they'd all been helped, and when mother and daughter were alone Renata ushered her gallant into the living room, accompanied by the holy mother-in-law. Then: *Wait here alone. Enjoy the living room. Look it over carefully. My daughter has to get dressed, spruce herself up. Don't get impatient.* The fiancé ensconced alone in that space. It comprised the family's approval. That is, Demetrio was already one of the family. Phew! what a price to pay.

294

The big guy sat with grave intent in the large greenish armchair in that still-strange and yellow living room. A new position,
as if he were a pseudostatue or, better, an incomprehensible stiff.
Waiting, waiting knowing how alone he was, almost drowning in a
somewhat depressive state of mind.

Hmm, the more time passed the more wicked ideas cropped
up in his head.

And a ton of minutes passed, hence—here comes the scab of
his bawdy life! Oaxaca: the symbol, lechery *a la costumbrista:*
against: suddenly: in Torreón he almost died. He saw the barrel of
the gun pointing at him: he, who was now a well-groomed, ultra-
decent husband.

Half an hour, a bit more, before mother and daughter appeared,
quite dazzling.

Pleasure at the sight of his conditional wife: Demetrio smiled
after a short pause. But the whole time he was wetting his lips with
an onrush of saliva. Quite abnormal, let us say, this action that
soon discomfited the two women.

Renata knew why Demetrio had come.

Sensible, for the gallant promptly pulled a large roll of bills out
of his jacket.

The most practical of the practical.

The mother-in-law was alert. She didn't want to miss a word
the betrotheds exchanged. Darn it she was meddlesome.

The first thing the proud husband announced was that Renata
could buy an extraordinary wedding gown with that money, with
some reckoning, of course, because these funds would pay for
everything related to the feast, though it depended, to wit: how
many guests would there be? The sisters and their husbands
and the closest family members in Sacramento, Lamadrid, and
Nadadores, no more than sixty people, mother and daughter said.

"You two will be in charge of that."

Also the cost of the Mass. Moreover: an anthology of details that piled up as the three spoke, but with that wad of dough the big guy avoided any rows, in fact, mother and daughter paid him no heed while they counted the money out loud.

Problem: the onerous amount of work . . . for the two women. Counting the bills took so long that Demetrio's thoughts turned to his and that ill-fated Mireya's son; he imagined him healthy and with a respectable vocabulary by now. Yes, quite the talker. Yes, quite the walker—achoo! Naughty, for sure, but just then Renata exclaimed that it was so much money . . .

And Demetrio puffed out his chest, feeling quite stuck-up, and said only, "Yes, yes," then stretched his neck up a bit farther.

Next they moved on to an issue of supreme importance: the date of the wedding. Doña Luisa said, "One moment," and left then returned in a flash with a calendar in hand: let's see. Closing the stationery store came up, as a factor in and of itself. So: the best would be to aim for a Saturday in October; naturally! though it could also be November, not December, so . . .

Speculations were skittish, for all three were tiptoeing around much too much, without any overpowering reason to do so.

In the end: the first Saturday in November. Agreement, obviously symptomatic. The fifth, yes, fifth of . . . Five was a lucky number. The wedding would be held in the morning. It would be a good idea for Demetrio to arrive a couple of days early, just in case anything unexpected should occur—or not?

The most important issues were apparently resolved. But the mother-in-law didn't leave—damn it! Clearly that pest would not let her daughter talk to her future keeper: never! For Demetrio had said that he wouldn't be returning to Sacramento before the wedding. His business there was demanding. The women pressed him for information on that subject, the reason for his diligence, why so busy.

And what Demetrio was inclined to reveal:

"It's a pool hall. And it's thriving."

This slightly squelched the women's jubilation. Imagine a pool hall as a black stain. A fomenter of daily dalliance. Disappointment, (almost) depravity. There was a partially aggrieved silence, noted by the future husband, and clearly revealed in the resigned droop of their heads: what a pity! However, he offered up one explanation that maybe . . . *The pool hall thing is temporary, afterward I'll invest in decent businesses. My mother also disapproves, but she understands my strategy.* Such a sincere explanation deserved a partial pardon. The women lifted their heads, buoyed by the tiny ray of hope that shined through. To all appearances he'd strayed, though here they espied a timely corrective. Temporary perfidy: right?, what was the time frame? Something like six months was a lie that could be believed. Renata believed it, and her mother, well, probably she did too. In fact, one must look at the positive side of pool halls: a business that underpinned what would be solid solvency. And Doña Luisa declared: *I hope this pool hall thing is indeed temporary.* And he nodded—in response? Let's watch Demetrio's hypocritical affirmative: what a notorious movement of his head! Then: upon seeing that the lady was not going to say, "Please, excuse me," he decided that the moment had come for him to depart, he would return the following day for a visit (okay?). In any case, as he walked out and continued doggedly down the street, the following wove itself into his brain: he would not give up the pool hall because it made him a lot of money; with Renata (requested and granted) by his side, what did he care about his mother-in-law's recriminations. Or rather: he would be the head honcho once he got married.

Therefore: his idea of starting a cathouse in Parras was as spurious as any fantasy. And what about other depraved enterprises that would make him a pile of money. He wanted to become as corrupt—why not?—as he could. He wanted to join forces as soon as possible with people in politics, so he could steal (in a nice way) with the full weight of the law behind him, and he told himself:

Yes, I want to be corrupt, and wealthy, very wealthy later on. I want my relatives to respect me. Suddenly, there appeared in his ambulatory obfuscation Mireya's son, his son, too, and all grown up. That bastard (fairly muscular) son confronted him. He grabbed the lapels of jacket x to upbraid him for having shirked his responsibility toward him before he was born, and what could Demetrio say, no way could he say that his mother was a whore, it would be too hurtful to state it so straightforwardly. Well, that gloomy idea soon fled his mind, only for the shining word "trapped" to appear, indeed, trapped by the green-eyed witch—beautiful? naturally she was very beautiful, as well as unsoiled, as well she should be. Trapped by decency, forever. And, although he was corrupt (in his own way), he would appear to society as a decent man for having married a decent woman; an ignorant woman, illiterate, quite unfortunate, but with marvelous moral principles—how does that sound? He soon dismissed such ideas, however, as if rejecting them as too fastidious, then felt like a proud king, a king who should now leave Sacramento: by bus, by train, any way he could, because he didn't want to talk to his aunt Zulema, who without a doubt was going to harass him with a rosary of compromising questions. Toxic woman, already diminished by fate; and that's when he thought of the pool hall. His business, understood as the vast idea of a truly free genius. Hence corruption came knocking, giving free rein to leisure, and—what should he do? A doubt, the robbery. Bah, no doubts, rather lethargy, a bow to the coming ease. His waxing lucky star, we repeat, kindled his aspirations. Perhaps so.

40

His son was still making appearances on the velvet ceiling of the train car, a dangling insinuation, graying. We should mention that it was a first-class carriage, and it was nighttime, and they were unreal scenarios, the shadows barely doing the trick. That son went wandering through the corridors when silence held sway, there to see the oversized proof (yes or no, between the brows), and he had no difficulty recognizing what he was seeking. And grabbing the lapels of the large gentleman's jacket, he said: *Just so you know, my mother has suffered a lot because of you. She's had to go to bed with many men to make ends meet. Poor thing. She, who wanted to love you, but you abandoned her, and you suck.* Then the supposed son disappeared, thank God. By the same token it must be said that Demetrio did not sleep well, because the son (almost like flashes of lightning) kept appearing, throwing gobs of spittle then disappearing with a devilish guffaw that continued to reverberate for a long time. Then a daughter made her appearance, the poor girl quite pretty, for who knows if Mireya had a boy or a girl. Anyway, the girl was also grown up and, very even tempered though quite feeble spirited, she sat down next to her father to tell him a few things that might have sounded indignant: *Many times I've hidden and watched my mother making love with one or another of her clients. Without her noticing, I try to see, to learn. But the truth is I don't learn much because she copu-*

lates very mechanically. She's never fallen in love with anybody.
She never speaks your name and when I see her crying I know
it is because God took love away from her. Maybe also because
she knows that nobody will ever truly love her. And, after saying
that sort of verbose glob, the (grotesque) daughter began to vanish. So Demetrio—did he sleep? how could he get comfortable?
He managed: for minute-long lapses. And he arrived in Parras in
a daze. It was the afternoon. When the sun's edges were almost
gone. A swath of disturbances. A succession of last straws, all corrosive and infamous. Daughter and son: in relay: harrowing malice,
enough to make one stagger. The whole time he wanted to douse
the unreal and the ruthless (no to apparitions) (no to parleys), but
he couldn't.

How to escape those wailing voices, or how to definitively bury
what was by its very nature inanimate, that is, the judgment of his
crimes? He would have to go to church, alone, a guileless devil
who had no choice but to kneel for hours on end. Pray—how? or
a convincing argument, what God had given him, that explosive
trifle: eternal love. And: *Lord, you have given me Renata, I want*
to have her with me till I die, so don't let anything bad happen
to us, I beg of you. Followed by the whizz-bang of the entreaty.
Tomorrow, deeds of devotion—naturally! but now to the practical,
the verification he sought. When he arrived home he at once saw
that his mother was happy, for the servants she had recently hired
were superindustrious: Amalia and María Fulgencia: a miracle, how
cheerfully enterprising they were! The domestic sphere looked like
a floating fantasy. This according to his mother, who was exaggerating to be sure. Doña Telma really was exaggerating because
it wasn't such a big deal, or maybe in her joy—was she spewing
nonsense? Anyway, Demetrio decided to go to the pool hall so as
not to hear more hyperbole, for now anyway—right? and he was
tired. In any case he went that night: crowded pool hall, merrymaking, smoke, pestilence, money-spending vagrancy, that was

what mattered. And Ángel and Aníbal fast and furious, well organized, come what may, they never missed a beat. Greetings. Ah. The outcome: the glory of careful bookkeeping, finally, in a still-dizzying atmosphere now devoid of people.

All on the up-and-up.

The employees: smart. God was now fondling him.

A robbery. No! Relief. Tranquility.

So the following morning Demetrio was obliged to go to church and offer thanks. Yes, as well as beg that Renata . . . et cetera.

Naturally the final pantomime would have to be exemplary.

How long to crawl on his knees and with his arms outstretched in the shape of a cross?

A good long while, you ass, someone from the next world might tell him with derision and aversion. We can, therefore, predict everything Demetrio did. Three laps on his knees around the nave of the church, inside, of course. A difficult act that—was it even worth it? His knees were bleeding: ow-ow-ow. He couldn't walk quite right for three weeks. The slowness of his movements alarmed the servants, his mother, the employees of the pool hall, not to mention a vagrant or two, for nobody understood anything about optimal balance, a concept used by a circumspect *curandero*, and which Demetrio repeated everywhere. What! "optimal balance"—could it be flattery he swallowed whole?

His mother tended to him daily. Nighttime ministrations were even more supercareful, for she used miniature cotton compresses and other secondary dressings. Luck before ingenuity. Treatments very early in the morning and very late at night and very who-knows-what. Nonetheless, slowness, gentleness. So-called love and so-called relief. Relief from suffering. So the scabs would form as soon as possible, the solution. Herewith we have the mother: a fly-by-night *curandera*, quite devoted, even, poor thing, breaking a sweat. Everything subjected to a "now we've got it," which was working. That inexperienced petitioner was quite put out, however, by this stooping compliance. That ferrule discipline. And three weeks went by and still the big guy was walking awkwardly, you should have seen him half bent over every time he walked from the house to the pool hall and vice versa and nowhere else; limping sickly was the price he paid for things to go superwell. Because the pool hall, well, although it used to open at four p.m., later they decided to open at one, and Ángel, Aníbal, and Demetrio studied the possibility of opening at ten a.m. and closing at midnight—every day!, except Sundays, that is, for one mustn't forget, not ever, the weekly Sabbath . . . So, here comes the reason!: how to deal with all the customers who came at all hours of the day! Many young bucks planted themselves at the door of the pool hall awaiting the happy opening, as if it were a grocery store; a whole hour ahead of time, believe it or not. And the spectacle of idlers eager to hit a few balls, to the sonorous sounds of shooting . . . No way around it! one day they simply had to open at ten a.m., and from then on . . .

Nose to grindstone! And . . . what about a raise? A small one. An all-too-subtle percentage that—damn!: crumbs. Well, now you have him: Demetrio was unremitting: his face was getting harder, as wealthy people's faces do: handsome, interesting, self-sufficient, his two eyebrows like two triumphal arches and his mouth squeezed more tightly into a ball: signs of ceaseless success, a form of disdain, an attitude of thinking of himself as the cat's meow. Much later there would be, let us call it, a "visualization" of the employees' merits: those! tush!, so honorable. And, from a different angle, since things were going so swimmingly—money by the cartload, a gift from God, rolling in the dough, day in and day out—he foresaw the possibility of investing in new businesses, maybe even citified ones, the urban brought to the small town, but which ones, which one: a dive—exciting! unique! that space envisaged so long ago. Oh, out with it: a cathouse with beautiful whores, good lighting, and rooms in the back. Ambition. Like the ones in Oaxaca: good old Presunción and the other, La Entretenida; also, with guards, but not aggressive ones: everything tending toward discretion, not like in Torreón, where he came within a foot of losing his life; no, not that, rather a joint that one would want to go to, to patronize . . . Oh, still a hazy dream. Though . . .

If he talked to the mayor. Invest fifty-fifty . . .

Partners worthy of something supersalacious . . . Still limping slightly, Demetrio made his way to the town hall. By hook or by crook he would get an appointment with Píndaro Macías. And he did. There to lay out his plans, dotting all the dirty i's and crossing all the t's. The mayor listened attentively to his diligent description of this seedy world. So many details, but the mayor, smiling stintingly, said, "No!"

Emphatically, it would seem. The "no" reverberated loudly.

Because Parras was not ready for such a radical change. People would rise up, first against him, then against Demetrio.

But even such well-established perversity: no!

Parras would have to grow to triple or quadruple its size for such a place not to be seen in a bad light.

And another stream of reasons for the rejection, though Demetrio would also be interested in starting up some other kind of business. More corrupt, less corrupt . . . Let's talk . . . Another time . . .

Demetrio left the mayor's office with a thunderous suite of ideas. Going into business with this mayor, hmm, better to become his good friend. Tactics piled on top of tactics. Perfidious and subtle utilization, and, of course, after, after . . .

Another meeting—when?

A difficult, because delicate, step.

Now it's time to shrink time, for good news was going to flow like a wafting breeze (a weightless one), which is to say, nothing terrible was happening that would delay the multiple manifestations of a thousand and one simple situations. Nothing black, nor murky nor gray, hence whiteness, if you like, in all that he had to suffer or surfeit, made everything, therefore, turn out like never before. The mountains of money at the pool hall; for better or for worse each week the cash register filled to overflowing, and at home such remarkable pleasure: each day harmony more deeply entrenched, like a rosy and benevolent blob, something as normal as the sun shining large, or the sky clearing all about, or sweet aromas rising from who-knows-where, or when everything we see inspires us.

And the days passed with no apparent sadness: spring—how joyous!, and summer—how peaceful! Add to that the truth about accretion: the charm of knowing that money makes even the most unpleasant things charming and that the servants Amalia and María Fulgencia, as well as the employees Ángel and Aníbal, had not lodged a single complaint for months, not the slightest, nothing, how fortunate, confound it. *We're doing very well*, Demetrio commented to his mother with a surfeit of cynicism, and they said, cheers! clinking together their mugs filled with *café con leche*. It is perhaps fitting here to say that at that time Mayor Píndaro Macías occasionally frequented the pool hall, he played his games, and he lost over and again, but his leisure time—how delightful! He was not good at billiards because he had little practice hitting the ball; just consider all his responsibilities as municipal leader . . . completely overburdened. Nevertheless, the frequency increased, not so much to play, but rather . . . What if he managed to do some crooked business with . . . ? Persuasion one small step at a time, persuasion recognized immediately by the successful man, then later ascertained, when the mayor told the big guy (straight out) that he wanted to talk to him in a relaxed and leisurely fashion, in his office, alone, about business, tantalizing demons, more and more suspect. Demetrio went out of inertia and listlessly listened to the lengthy proposals. Improvised twists and always unprecedented expectations for business deals that were not totally transparent. Surely he tired of listening, but as soon as he had a chance to respond, he was arrogant and almost smug when he exclaimed:

"I'd like to do business with you, but only after I get married. My wedding will be on the first Saturday in November. I will be gone from Parras for around three weeks, so we should talk around the beginning of 1950."

"Where will you have your wedding?"

"In Sacramento, Coahuila. A much smaller town than Parras, very close to Monclova. It will be a simple affair. But if you'd like to come, please . . ."

"No, no, I just wanted to know where the wedding will be. No, thank you, I cannot go, I don't have time."

"Anyway, I want you to know I'm interested in working with you, but . . ."

"That's fine, it's not far off."

"I just want to say that you can go to the pool hall whenever you like. I will leave instructions that you not be charged."

"Well, well. Thank you!"

"If that's all, and with your permission, I will take my leave."

Office intrigue upon his departure: spying bureaucrats watching Demetrio's every move (not limping, luckily). They thought this alliance with the mayor quite peculiar. His second time there and—how many more? And if ghoulish plans were afoot—how bad? Let's end this with a less assonant dread. Disparate, rough hewn, something that was beginning to get tangled in the shadows, little by little, imbroglios of maggoty folk, nothing more. Because Demetrio's reputation was already the subject of much comment. His business, the pool hall, it was all like some new and grandiose wave. A local harm evocative of My Lord Jesus or Sainted Virgin, and growing and voluminous and what kind of business was it anyway—would he close it? Did he and the mayor make a deal—or not? or was it an arduous diatribe—or what?

Better to say that the date for mother and son to go to Sacramento was approaching. For the first time they would drive in the blue pickup belonging to . . . They would arrive with pomp, surely. Airs, more airs of unbridled solvency. In that same vehicle the newlyweds would go on their honeymoon to Piedras Negras. An event that had already taken on a well-defined hue. Nevertheless, doubt lingered in the background, for no matter how honest and competent the two servants and the two employees were, it was risky to turn home and pool hall over to them, trust blindly, as well as give them money for . . . That's why Demetrio took precautions and paid the mayor a visit (unannounced). A favor. Whatever it would cost—their first business deal? Friendship comes first—doesn't it? That he hire eight policemen, four at each site, in shifts, to guard both properties while they were gone. Moreover: what was the daily rate? Calculations. Pencil to paper. The mayor had fun adding and subtracting, then erasing, then he wrote anew with greater resolve, and then, finally, the total, eloquence itself: advance payment of the full amount for at least three weeks, to avoid misunderstandings. The following day the money delivered. It wasn't so much. But yes: men in uniform would keep watch night and day over the appointed places . . . And to inform the honest employees about the surveillance—understandable!? It was the prudent thing to do, given what had happened to them.

The date was approaching.

The jitters . . .

Happiness conceived of as the painstaking paring of an exquisite idea.

On the way through Monclova, Demetrio had to buy a black suit . . .

For now: they readied the trousseau: so much spread out on the truck bed, such elaborate packing, and yes: mother and son left one week ahead of time. Doña Telma, intentionally annoying, pressured the big guy to settle whatever he had to settle and . . .

Rattling and, finally, happy trails.

41

The roll of money glowed, stuffed as it was into a barely visible cranny; high, separate: the roll still whole, and almost magnetic, just to look at; like twisted rays: what an imagination—could that be? It was tempting to touch the bill-stuffed projection. A brush, an inadvertent stroke from Renata, who stretched out her arm, a surmise, then finally the arrival of some certainty when she realized that it would cover even those details one thinks of only after the initial accounting . . . The unexpected minutiae remain for the end, and can often be of considerable expense.

And one day among many Renata took hold of the roll. The spending would now begin. We must also say that little by little, over the course of a few months, relatives living in Sacramento had been approaching Doña Luisa and Renata. They knew about the upcoming event (full speed ahead) and, of course, more than enough helping hands were tendered. Also obliging were some clients who offered any help that might be needed in good faith. And the roll: come on!: time to take some practical steps. What would the first one be? Knowing she was facing a mountain of quite simple issues, let's mention three that stand out: first the food, quite a predicament, because you had to figure on the slaughter of a lamb and a pig, for example, though it would also be a good idea to ask the obvious question: who would the butcher be? Then deciding on the first course: tomato pasta soup or celery soup;

then dessert: what sweets would they have—nothing too expensive? Second: decorating the church: with what? How about carnations, lilies, or gardenias, or some other kind of flower, and the question: where to get that, or this, or something else even more improbable? and also—who would do it? And third: the wedding dress: which beauteous garment would do?, what trim and whether more or less of it, and the price: which shop in Monclova: hence the need to go, and come: exhausting: carrying an enormous box. This task was Renata's alone, as opposed to all the others, which could be assigned to third parties. Other issues would crop up in dribs and drabs. Nevertheless, we see that once she had the roll in her hands, Renata knew that the first order of business should be the purchase of the wedding dress, so she extracted a hefty number of bills and put them in a safe bag. The next step was to go to Monclova by bus, spend the night in a hotel, not an expensive one, but not a very cheap one, either. It would take her more than one day to pick a dress.

We understand what a nuisance it was to make the trip, although, on the other hand, the gem she bought justified the sweat. When she arrived home she wanted to spread the dress out on the bed. It took her mother half an hour to give her approval, though when she did so, ah, she began to cry like a baby. Let's understand her, let's try to understand her . . .

42

Renata's sisters were arriving, four women (four blessings) and of course each one accompanied by her respective hale husband. Different travel plans, hence the anticipation, the suspense, the diurnal and nocturnal appearances, and—what a scene!, beds for all, so many bedrooms, even some left over, though don't think for a minute . . . Then all the usual rushing about; endless errands, not only the fuss and bother for the wedding feast, but also three meals a day. The more people in the house, the greater the expense: the unforeseen, it turns out, as something tacit. Each sister gave the impression of being a problem-solving phoenix, better to put it in no uncertain terms, for that's how things were, the adjectives also suited their husbands. Let's take some examples: they had to gather fifteen square tables and, let's say, a total of some sixty chairs. The logical question was where to get the tables . . . let's see . . . Relatives lent one or two, some customers also, one by one, or two by two, or mix and match, until reaching the magic aforementioned count; next was to count the number of arms in action, for whatever there was, there was: lots!, and thus they spent three days gathering the fifteen tables, placing them in one row of five, then two other rows of the same number: let's imagine, then, and from a bird's eye view, the resulting square bracket on the patio. A square bracket exposed to the wildest winds, which didn't matter, but rain—in November?, hopefully it wouldn't rain, not even the merest touch of a squall. Always a risk, though, and—done! . . . The paradox was for the water in the sky to remain there, as if the sky itself were waiting for the wedding to release its load a few hours thereafter. And the lovely thing is that it turned out exactly as the mother and daughter, as well as the four sisters and their husbands, thought it would: *Don't rain. Please don't rain,* that was the prayer under their breath, and no, no, really, no. The request did not depend on the appearance of a saint, it was a secular plea and that was the odd thing. Aha! the longed-for event was coming to pass. And now let's turn to the china, a colossal feat of borrowing from so many sources. You can include anybody you like, as long as they lived in Sacramento and as long as they offered their help. The result was necessarily a hodgepodge, many kinds of forks, spoons, knives, plates, and cups, and you can add whatever else you'd like. The ease with which all this took place depends on the fact that any customer who lent them anything would be invited to the party, as is only proper, and this unanticipated nuance affected the number of guests. In fact, with each borrowing came another guest, until at one point the mother said: *Not one more guest! We'll make do with what we have.* They already had plenty, it's true, as it is also true that Renata and her sisters no longer needed to go house to house with requests, so many procurements after so many days. Enough already!

43

Let's consider Demetrio's proverbial visit to Renata's house. A monarch was arriving, one who would be greeted by many maids all in a row: a reception line and smiles all around (diplomacy). But we'd do better to leave that for later, better for now to dig our teeth into what Doña Zulema said cheerfully when Doña Telma and Demetrio arrived at her ancient abode. Just like that, almost without so much as a polite welcome, she said that she had offered to help with the wedding preparations; that she had made herself available a while back, almost pleaded on her knees, somewhere between humble and obsequious, to the now quite largely looming Doña Luisa, who thanked her so graciously, no, there was no need—not at all!, and this should be understood because Doña Luisa stated that Demetrio's generous contribution was enough of a boon and, as a result, everything else would be handled by the other party: the two women, first and foremost, and the entire family subsequently, as well as some of their customers. But let's turn to another key moment, that of the arrival of Demetrio and his mother in the shiny blue truck; a blue you'd have to see to believe: modern metallic blue: full fledged blue, and to be fully enjoyed. The trip there was the nasty part: such a jumble of roads! However, the big guy's sense of direction never failed and hence the (fleet) feat of arriving, exhausted, sick and tired of the bouncing, needless to say, which was now replaced by boasting. The motorized prodigy, then and there, the sight of which would soon send Renata into raptures.

And with no further ado—let's go! Driving that solvent and haughty blueness through the streets of the town, Demetrio, the one and only king, though: what's on view is the luxury, not the proud driver; what's on view is the shining but cautious advance. That's how it went, believe it or not. The fact was, Demetrio felt haughty, what with all the unwavering stares, all the way to Renata's house, where—just watch him!—he whistled, a loud whistle, hence, presumptuous. Naturally they'd come running out of the store: Renata, her mother, and two of her sisters, a rip-roaring whistle, long though not piercing. Then, the evidence: the over-the-briny blueness that pulsated and continued to pulsate, like a shooting of hues into the air, really very attention grabbing. And herewith the consequences that came about just right: Renata, her mother, and her sisters, all amazed, as well as the two husbands, soon added to the mix. All in all we have to imagine astonished paralysis. Six watched as the arrogant big guy descended from the vehicle then strode with a steadfast swagger: in their direction, then said, "What's up?" And we must say he was received with an almost reverential welcome. They invited him into the living room: everybody! The man's height impressed the sisters and their husbands: that future family member who had, so it seemed, a plethora of riches. Moreover, because he himself talked about how his business was making him mountains of money, a business he held up to the heavens and spoke about to all who wished to hear, although he had the tact not to mention the particular business it was: *Just buying and selling*, this simple fact revealed, even if it was a mysterious and indirect hint at the nature of his affairs. Finally, the family left Renata alone with her great love, and just as each felt the urge to formulate a question, they abstained and the whim wisely vanished. They did well to behave discreetly, ergo: back to work! let's get on with it! Subconscious praise on its way. And Renata and Demetrio once again alone, now knowing that they would soon stand in front of each other naked and amorous; love like a bubble that would have to burst—finally?! because the truth was, he was eager to kiss his beloved on her cheek, a husband's legitimate right, but she, repulsing him, reminded him that it was better to wait, that it wouldn't be long before they could get on with their heavenly depravities. Demetrio wanted to shout in despair but ended up resigned, keeping in check an audible pout. Then, all on his own, he changed the subject, as if the cheekiness of a kiss on the cheek had become meaningless to him: with or without a lick? Bah. The thematic replacement was the truck:

"I drove it here so we can take it to Piedras Negras for our honeymoon."

"Piedras Negras? What's that?"

"It's a gorgeous border city. You'll soon see."

Piedras Negras: a phonetic affront worth memorizing. Renata eagerly enunciated the pair of words repeatedly. As it happened, her relatives repeated the name later and imagined the distance between it and Sacramento: hence, an ideal occurrence: *Piedras Negras, Piedras Negras, Piedras Negras,* like posing a question that conjured up an infinity of answers. This happened in a big way during an episode we won't even recount, for now let's focus on something very concrete:

"And those tables arranged in a square bracket?" Demetrio couldn't refrain from asking when he looked out the window onto the patio.

"That's where the wedding feast will be."

"There'll be a meal?"

"Yes, at two in the afternoon on November fifth, after the Mass."

"What will we eat?"

"It will be a surprise, but everything will be delicious, I promise you."

"And the bridesmaids and . . . ?"

"Don't bother your head about any of it. You did your part by giving me all that money, and now you needn't worry about a thing. We are taking care of all the details."

"What time should I arrive at the church on the day itself?"

Let it be known that there was only one semi-impressive church in Sacramento.

"A few minutes before eleven in the morning."

It could be that this crucial exchange of information was a way to say that Renata and Demetrio shouldn't see each other again until their wedding day. This is how the big guy interpreted it, hence he anticipated the instructions his beloved was surely about to give him.

"The next time I see you will be in church. Over, forever, is this timid love that doesn't suit either of us. Good-bye to love on the bench and love in the living room. Good-bye to immaculate bashfulness. We will now live a love with flying colors, with all kinds of kisses and all manner of touch. Soon you will see, my own dear wife!"

Fortuitous good-bye? Imaginative leisure as long as they didn't see each other. A broad swath of hours like a spring stretched as far as it would go. Only a tight squeeze of the hand and a see-you-later: so: two ideas as one, almost-almost. Then: one more fantasy-filled day. A fluttering array of multicolored lights. Two faces in the clouds getting closer and closer to exchange a long and slippery kiss.

44

What luck! The wedding day itself dawned rainy—in November? who would believe it, or who thought that if it didn't rain the marriage would have (no holds barred) a disagreeable destiny. To hell with such superstitions! They always get in the way.

The customers started arriving about one hour before the Mass and stayed to help. Figure about twenty, let's say, counting by fours: soaking wet. The tears of the tempest looked like mere fluff dusting their clothes, a whitish sheen, accumulated shimmerings of light drops, more noticeable if the shirts and blouses hadn't been white, lucky devils. Then came the relatives hailing from Nadadores and Lamadrid, and they were many. They filled the entrance hall in a flurried rush, almost a logjam, almost a gray mass—could it be a sheepfold full of forty fellows? If that wasn't the exact number, we are definitely close, and so the following question becomes apt: would all these penned-in people be eating? If so, there wouldn't be enough seats, wherein arose a problem, the need for restricting numbers when the time was ripe. Vigilance at the entryway—but how? A red-hot unforeseen . . . alas . . . At fifteen minutes to eleven the groom arrived with his mother and his aunt. The three were dressed in black, they looked like mourners, but you should know that the color black also symbolizes good fortune, especially if adorned with a flower, and here we evoke coquetry: he with a carnation on his lapel, and Doña Telma and Doña Zulema each with a yellow rose on her bodice. So, black elegance—unique, solemn, warranted . . . The real event was the arrival of the bride and the bridesmaids and groomsmen and Renata's sisters with their husbands: a fragrant front, perfumes that swooned when pooled randomly together; an aggregation of nerves, uneven: rising, but then arrived the parish priest draped in green, with his red sextons, and now finally the wedding march began with no music, nor chorus nor anything at all, one had to imagine the sublime sounds of what could have been uplifting, for bringing the music of wind or strings to a parish church, that would have been really expensive. Demetrio didn't care a whit if he walked to the altar holding his mother's arm without even one strum of a guitar; he cared more about grabbing for good the green-eyed gal than about the rise and fall of any harmony whatsoever.

45

Even so, the march—ascendant, rhythmic, pompous, a bit dramatic or however you wish to interpret it. Let's consider the altar as the symbol of limpid purity, full of glory—right? or something like it? Let's imagine, therefore, a tremendous sacred heart, which was opening, in other words, let's imagine something of the sort, even if it's not true, ergo: the crystallization of love. Or rather: reaching the bosom of the bosom, but first Renata had to walk holding the arm of one of the groomsmen, a really ugly old guy. She was taking supernervous steps, much more so than Demetrio, who was barely watching where he stepped, instead turning often to look at his mother, whose face was full of hope, more than ever before, her eyebrows pitched as if wanting to form an arrow . . . What was she thinking about? We can venture to guess a logical longing: her daughters; the ones who lived in the United States; the ones who didn't come; the ones who had to get to Parras and then travel to Sacramento: a real drag, not for them but for their gringo husbands, but, well, let's say that for now we must turn our attention to the affected stride of those walking. And finally the bride and groom's encounter at the most important moment of the prayer; the rest of the parading people found places along the two front benches, each one—such precision!—had their very own prie-dieu, as did the bride and groom.

We're going to dispense with the various stages of the Mass and

the agreeable duties performed by the bridesmaids and groomsmen so we can focus (a bit) on the sermon given by the four-eyed
priest, who wished to show off his elucidation of a definitive
union's imponderables in a shrill voice. He mentioned the many
children, if possible the founding of a battalion, or if we must point
out without naming the fever the four-eyed man was alluding to,
then let's at least clarify the allusion, as follows: each holy lying-
together should bring about a treasured issue. Yes, yes, he didn't
say it so crassly, but in a roundabout way, that's what could be
understood . . . He also spoke about comprehension, the sweet
communication between the spouses, that at all times God would
be taking notes, in other words—no shouting whatsoever! If you
like, pure treacles of tenderness for all eternity. And you can guess
the subsequent eulogies: a rosary of good things, apt and honeyed
advice, if we can call it that.

When the meaningful Mass was over, the newlyweds were
showered with a surfeit of dry rice. In the atrium: dual purity, purity in the sense that not even now wedded did they exchange even
the tiniest of kisses, not anywhere. Renata didn't want to; he did,
for he felt happy and spontaneous. However—no! Understood!
Understand, once and for all, the absolute freedom of privacy. Far
from all the decorum, from the filthy familiar . . .

Not long now.

The honeymoon.

The escape.

The release.

May it be a long kiss without any applause.

In the face of Renata's refusal, Demetrio—not a chance!—
passed his right hand over his typical impeccably groomed groom's
hair, that is, all the hair combed back.

Patience—a toast!, more patience.

46

The food posed no problem. No reason it should when all was said and done. In the end people flowed naturally to the feast that would be offered, as announced, in the courtyard. One bridesmaid and one groomsman were in charge of letting everyone in: a steamy responsibility requiring supine tolerance—why them? Could be they were the first to have responded, yes, with a (timid) raising of an arm in response to the question—who? let's see, two index fingers, as we must consider the fact that Renata's sisters, their husbands, Doña Luisa, and Demetrio's mother and second mother deserved a respite; the chores passed to others, in their entirety, after the main event (such a thorny achievement); the crucial part over, and the chairs, oh, we must say that the most important chairs and tables were for, yes—huh? we've already named them, and, well, the rest of the guests—how can we put it?: may the melee begin; those who arrived first and got a seat, and the rest left standing. Or rather: who told the last ones to arrive so late? In the end there were about fifty people without seats for the banquet. How unfortunate, such dining distress! once and for all let's say it; the distress of watching and watching and waiting for one, two, maybe more speeches, the groom, one of the groomsmen, some of the mothers. But there was none of that, damn it. Just a large measure of noise (a continuous stream of trivialities) throughout the peaceable meal: the rustle of cutlery and dishes: sustained. And, taking advantage of the lapse while the chewing lasted, let's mention that the marrying chaplain was not invited, perhaps the fact that he charged a fee for the Mass justified the slight. A hefty sum that actually did cause sorrow.

Apart from that we must say in all honesty that a lamb and a pig had been slaughtered the previous day. Even the blood of both was used to make the broth for the soup, that is (ahem), with the incomparable additions of onion and cilantro and *guapillas* and oregano. Numerous soup bowls, and so, soup spoons sui generis and pounds of the aforementioned garnishes. Dessert: *dulce de leche* candies, which were ordered a few days before. Here we will be more specific: they were *dulce de leche* cones (a bit messy . . . and there were even some left over), and it could be said that they were the most popular traditional sweets in Sacramento.

If we could look through a lens that would magnify this whole radius of people, we would train our sights with mordant delight on the changing expressions of the newlyweds, for the most part frowning, then a bit happier, also hesitant, all quite a sight. It seemed like the groom wanted to leave already and the bride, on the sly, told him to wait—how to attenuate such words, few and sharp? So he brought himself up short, quickly recovering his rigid equanimity. Worth mentioning that those waiting on the tables were an ad hoc combination of kin in the first and second degree, because the closer ones didn't: not the sisters, their husbands, the two widows, nor the aunt, who'd been awarded the role of second mother; of course: those already mentioned: unscathed the whole banquet through. Monarchs for a few hours. And as far as the others went: their duty was to quickly find things: glasses, plates, cutlery, those necessities that run out one at a time.

Finally, and thanks to God, the party was coming to an end and the worst part began: the swath of precious embraces, the most annoying being the personal comments, for those offering congratulations felt they had the right to also offer advice to the man and the woman, both inexperienced in affective matters, which nobody ever knows anything about; tolerate, with a half smile, the outpourings, in themselves full of (almost spiraling) exaggerations expressed in poorly constructed sentences. Let's add, as a final touch, that the few who remained in the courtyard—by that time the banquet was already waning—were the uncles who, in the company of the aunts, were waiting to see what . . . It was said, after jousting with several ideas, that the next day the nuptial cortege would leave for Piedras Negras. It was obvious that the blue truck, driven by Demetrio, would lead the way, with the still-virgin bride by Demetrio's side. Behind would follow seven trucks: sentimental and important relatives, including Doña Luisa, who, naturally, would be the one to shed the most tears due to the departure, ah, of her last daughter. Surely the other relatives would shed a tear or two, but it was yet to be seen how many. Picture it: pickups, driving along, lasting aggravation all the way to Piedras Negras. An excessively long way with paved bits in 1949, especially near towns, but the most difficult stretches were miles of dirt road, not graded as they should be. Or rather: clouds of dust, let's imagine them (an arousing oddity), which made the convoy quite conspicuous. Anyway, it must be said that they all agreed to leave Doña Luisa's house very early the next morning so as to arrive in Piedras Negras before the sun went down. Correct, highly correct—yes? and now for the worst: Renata and Demetrio would not sleep together: the eventual breaking of the bond (now for the last and vague almost-never). A quick good-bye. This last-minute disappointing delay. A few hours. Time's most lonely ones. In fact, the moment came to watch the scene when the newlyweds had to separate without wanting to: they did so slowly: an unlocking of hands, oh. And tomorrow the solution: tomorrow, yes!

47

Suitcases in the bed of the blue pickup: only Renata's and Demetrio's, because the relatives would return to Sacramento as soon as they said good-bye to the green-eyed gal at the hotel in Piedras Negras. Clearly each truck would carry its own extra can of gasoline (as usual), and the simple task of filling eight such cylinders took time. More than two hours, to be precise. Let's also add that there was a skinny man whose hair stood on end by the name of Manuel Soto Pizarro, who sold fuel informally and had a tank on the outskirts of Sacramento, one that was almost always full of the precious liquid because he almost always had very few sales, but when this ensemble journey came about: oh, my: what a windfall, for he got sold out. And this, then, is what followed: the caravan moving with proper slowness toward the border. A caravan led by Demetrio's truck: impetuous modernity. A caravan seen off by a crowd of people of all ages, a true swarm staged in the main plaza, among which Doña Zulema and Doña Telma were seen, showing up momentarily and bidding an effusive good-bye. Squashed bodies: theirs, who at the last minute declined to make the trip . . . So futile, as well as an unforgettable hassle, for sure. Was that whole melodramatic course of events even worth it— no! too much lavish groaning. Better to think of Demetrio being happy with that rural lass, who was, among other things, skilled at culinary concoctions, and on to other issues, an omission that was also fortunate, no (grim, grown-up) guesswork there. Immediately crass would be the seven hours there and seven hours back, at the very least. The worst would be traveling (back) at night, onerous and, of course, sheer exhaustion would evoke bad thoughts. Hmm, just to think about those considerate relatives making the sacrifice for no reason—well! What Doña Telma did instead was say goodbye to Doña Zulema with a heartfelt hug. Both knew they might never see each other again. Returning alone to Parras: the mother, by train, yes, now for the imminent tedium, also the uncertainty of her intuition that whatever would befall her would not be so horrible. The good part is that Doña Telma would soon see if everything there was in order; she would have to pray the whole way for it to be so. In fact, when she left Sacramento she knew that a new chapter in her life had begun. Something reductive and red. The seed of a precursory idea, yet to see how it would germinate . . .

48

Seesawing, constant shiftings, wishes cut short, a sudden braking and a sudden brutal acceleration. Thus the pace. Let's call them "capitular jumps," which made the trip one of constant renewal (so to speak) from one surprise to the next.

Renata, feeling like a very tender wife, wanted to cling to Demetrio's arm. We could say that he drove with one hand, the skillful devil, believe it or not. He freed himself from her grip only to change gears: *One moment,* many *one moment*s, and she allowed him the moment.

There were lapses in their conversation, which, if they could be drawn, would be shaped like protuberances, something that rose oblong, and oblong descended, the peak being two or three vigorous sentences, then a waning, for the emotions seemed to have a high degree of ephemeral intensity and . . . the silence lasted . . . and new waves, new protuberances and . . . Out of everything they talked about during the trip, we will highlight the following:

"Listen, my love," Demetrio began, "I need to tell you something."

"What? Dearest. Tell me," said his beloved.

"When we move to Parras, we'll have our own room in my mother's house."

"We are going to live with your mother?"

"For a little while. I figure about two months."

"What about our privacy?"

"Our room is very private, and my mother is very discreet, more than you can ever imagine. In addition, I am making so much money at the pool hall that we will soon have an enormous house on the outskirts of Parras. I can even promise you that."

"I will go wherever you take me. But I want privacy. A lot of privacy."

"Really?"

"Yes, yes. Don't forget that."

Demetrio turned and planted a solid kiss on her cheek. Explosive surprise. She wiped off the bit of saliva left by the furtive smear: her fingers were trembling.

"Don't do that again. Wait till we get to the hotel in Piedras Negras."

Wait, wait, wait, wait. Penitence. Repressive feints. Desire on the verge. Insidious respect, still. How much longer till . . . ? Pain below. Pain above. Pain—where?

"You can't wait, can you?"

"To tell the truth, no . . . I want, I want . . ."

"Me too, but you must understand . . ."

49

Glorious, exuberant, incredible arrival. The trucks were parked along the width of the country hotel, strategically placed. An event that was—inimitable? The cream-colored building in question was two stories high, though fairly imposing. An outstretched building. Modernity in the countryside, for Piedras Negras was still about two miles away. That is, the circulating air mussed the hair. Well— why did Demetrio choose this place? Had he been here before? According to what the newlyweds discussed on the way, they were going somewhere far away from any city thicket. Supposedly they would find something somewhat like paradise, and they found it and very evident it was . . . Demetrio's lucky star, et cetera . . . Now let's watch the crucial scene: the big guy got out of the truck, tucked in his shirt, and went in to request a room for himself and his wife. This action was watched by the accompanying kin, who were no longer sitting and waiting but rather had placed their feet on the ground (heads like pennants), including Doña Luisa, who began to cry a little.

Renata was the only one who remained seated. She didn't want to get out. Instead, she cracked her knuckles, so anxious was she for her husband to get a room. Meanwhile she thought: *Will it hurt when he sticks it in, or the opposite?* A few minutes later she thought: *This very day I will lose my virginity.* And a little later: *My mother never told me anything about the sexual act.*

Everything will be new for me. Finally, about fifteen minutes later, Demetrio sauntered out and made a gesture with his hands—what did he want? Yes, they should unload the suitcases, there was a room, a beautiful one overlooking the road and the tilled fields beyond. And Renata got out and offered to help. She raised her hand to say good-bye to her gawking kin, who nevertheless didn't leave, who watched as she entered the building behind Demetrio, who was carrying everything. Outside, the remnants of stoicism. So many gentlemen, so many ladies, all with long faces. Some with more tears than others. A frenetic gathering. It's just that Renata was on the verge of losing . . . that's already been said—and what would it be like? What kind of wild dumping inside—a lot? Not to even think about the cruelest of the cruel. Perhaps first there would be a more sentimental wave good-bye. In fact, the cry spread; cries in the open air; many, of many. A few of those outside were just smoking and staring. Others, farther away, were smoothing out the shapeless dirt. Otherwise: motel, depravity, the dusk that colors and discolors, here and there . . . Then: if you like, imagine the naked heat: minutes, attrition, more and more. Though first Renata had something to do. Imagine the nature of the wait. Then it happened. After they'd settled into the room, Renata said to Demetrio: *Wait a minute.* She walked over to the window and opened the curtains wide. In front of her was the array of trucks and the relatives posted next to them. It was getting late. Renata lifted her hand and began to move it from side to side; those below, watching, mimicked her. A total, grandiose good-bye. You should have seen the people crying as they moved their arms. More and more movement over here and over there, until the trucks started to depart. A reluctant row—perhaps?—: slow going, and once everybody had left, Renata kept waving good-bye: indefatigable oscillation of her arm that Demetrio observed from a chair. When supposedly nobody was left to say good-bye to, this deduced from the distance of the motors, the anxious wife closed the curtain and now finally . . .

In the semidarkness they approached each other: thoroughly cautious and with no bluff possible. Finally, Renata and Demetrio: profiles on the prowl. First came the proximity of their mouths, close, closer, bonding. With God's blessing the sin was diminished; oh-so-vigilant God: his tall staff prevailed—yes or no?: and see and feel the soft approach. And when the kiss came: what fine and discreet movements!: lips sliding along lips: a long, agreeable affair. From there the holding of hands and, without ungluing above, the arms, such mischief, agile caresses over here and over there, until there came the pressing of one to the other. To hell, finally, with all that ancient suffering!, though . . . They had difficulty getting settled standing up because Demetrio was very tall and she wasn't. So they sat on the edge of the bed—careful!—without ungluing their lips. It seemed like a necessary bond, the salivation they were giving each other intentionally, so mature. A question of silent loving. That first kiss, after such a long sacrifice, tasted to them like pure sublime lust: endlessly slippery, almost. It was like climbing the tallest mountain in the world. Sin—contorted sin! The sensation of pleasure that can never fully console, so just as they were (so dependent on the long kiss that just kept going) they began to get undressed. A juggling act, somewhat deficient, and no, they couldn't. They had to stop kissing in order to fully undress. Garment by garment: a spectacle. Once they were totally naked they threw themselves on the bed: yes, more comfortable—right? And they were getting to know their naked selves, as well they should. The green-eyed gal's breasts—this is just one example—were two erect expressive oranges. And so both their detailed inspections went and, in fact, so many years dreaming about the nakedness and now the shape of things: the operative, as well as that bush thereabouts. Will we neglect the most delicious part? Demetrio would seek the inaugural screw: engine-sex, anxiety-sex. The delectable goal they both longed for. Renata made her debut and without saying a word opened her legs: offered, won. The truth is, neither spoke, though they did think: he moved slowly until finally there was an (adequate) encounter between the hole and the member: the final juncture: the sex that begins, that spreads, that expands. However, the difficulty of the insertion. The battle: the ripping penetration. She began to shout like a woman half mad, but still she begged for more flesh to wound her. Blood, in consequence. Increasing passion. Pleasure that soon finds amplitude. And the discreet movements were mutual, achieving a better rhythm, and:

In.

Out.

In.

Out.

In.

Out.

In.

Out.

In.

Out.

Sex that bewitches, nourishes, lasts. Committed sex. Sex: a routine thing. Sex: convention.

In.

Out.

In.

Out.

In.

Out.

In.

Out.

In.

Out.

Ecstasy-sex. Sinking-in-sex. Sex that shapes. Sex that sparkles.

In.

Out.

In.

Out.

In.

Out.

In.

Out.

In.

Out.

Truth-sex. Bouquet-sex of radiant flowers. Behavior-sex. Vaccine-sex. Sex that knocks down all obstacles. Though: each time they did it would they have to wait for their issue to arrive? Or what was that all about?

In.

Out.

In.

Out.

In.

Out.

In.

Out.

In.

Out.

Perhaps some kind of affective penitence would come about. May all the problems that had to be pushed away end up breaking apart. No! No! No! Fear. Horror. Invasion-sex. Skillful-sex. Delirium-sex. Mania-sex. Formal sex. Sex that prostrates, crushes, cleanses, alters, conquers.

In.

Out.

In.

Out.

In.

Out.

In.
Out.
In.
Out.
Sheer relief.

Daniel Sada was born in Mexicali, Mexico, in 1953, and died on November 18, 2011, in Mexico City. Considered by many as the boldest and most innovative writer in Spanish of his generation, he has published eight volumes of short stories, nine novels, and three volumes of poetry. His works have been translated into English, German, French, Dutch, Finnish, Bulgarian, and Portuguese. He has been awarded numerous prizes, including the Herralde Prize for his novel *Almost Never*. Just hours before he died, he was awarded Mexico's most prestigious literary award, the National Prize for Arts and Sciences for Literature.

Katherine Silver is an award-winning translator of Spanish and Latin American literature. Some of her most recent translations include works by Horacio Castellanos Moya and César Aira. She is the codirector of the Banff International Literary Translation Centre in Canada and lives in Berkeley, California.

The text of *Almost Never* is set in ITC Century. Book design by Connie Kuhnz. Composition by BookMobile Design and Publishing Services, Minneapolis, Minnesota. Manufactured by Versa on acid-free 30 percent postconsumer wastepaper.